RAVI'S GUIDE TO BEING A COOL INDIAN

D1613986

A novel

Riani Saunhil

L,

I hope you enjoy the book. Stay Cool!

Riani

To learn more about me, listen to the Buzzthief songs mentioned in the novel, or offer me millions of dollars to adapt this novel into a movie, go to www.buzzthief.com or scan this QR code:

Love this book? Great! Recommend it to your friends and review it on Amazon.

Hate this book? Great! Recommend it to your frenemies and review it on Barnes and Noble.

Table of Contents

Part II – November 2007 – The Reckoning

Excerpt from Ravi's Guide– Food
<u>Chapter 10 – Thanksgivings and Misgivings</u> - <u>Vineeta</u>
Ann Arbor, MI

Excerpt from Ravi's Guide – Partying
<u>Chapter 11 – Vinod's Reunion</u> - *Ravi*
Ann Arbor, MI

Excerpt from Ravi's Guide– Mistakes
<u>Chapter 12 – Lakhi's secret</u> - *Ravi*
Manhattan, New York

Excerpt from Ravi's Guide – Adventure
<u>Chapter 13 – Jag in a Jaguar</u> - *Vineeta*
Manhattan, New York

Excerpt from Ravi's Guide– Sports
<u>Chapter 14 – Catharsis</u> - *Pankaj*
Manhattan, New York

Excerpt from Ravi's Guide– Literature
<u>Chapter 15 – Buddhist Retreat</u> – *Vineeta/Ravi*
Catskills, New York

Excerpt from Ravi's Guide – Religion
<u>Chapter 16 – Ravi's apartment</u> – *Pankaj/Ravi*
Manhattan, New York

Part III – May 2008 – Just Desserts

Excerpt from Ravi's Guide– Final Thoughts
<u>Chapter 17 - The Premiere</u> - *Ravi*
Manhattan, New York

The Review of Ravi's Guide II
<u>Chapter 18 – Just Desserts</u> - *Ravi*
Manhattan, New York

For S, S, E, S, V & M

Though the characters and events in this novel are obviously fictional, the one element taken from my own reality is the depth of familial love that the characters ultimately realize binds them together.

Part I
September 2007
The Wedding

Excerpt from
Ravi's Guide to Being a Cool Indian

Lying

Indians make it obvious they are lying by repeating the same excuses for why they have to suddenly cancel a get-together. That's because they don't care whether you know they are lying because they assume you will lie back to them and it will all even out. *Principle #1: lying is fine as long as it is done in moderation and in a spirit of fairness.*

Principle #2: Indians have so many cultural expectations that the only way to actually satisfy all of them is to lie. My sister Vineeta has been dating an Austrian architecture student named Hans who she met while attending Columbia for a Masters in International Affairs. Hans keeps a beige man-purse slung over his shoulder and sports trapezoidal glasses with purple side-rims. He mostly talks in some robotic algorithm about architecture. All facts, no fiction. Vineeta correctly suspects that Mum won't approve, even though the question of whether Indians should date non-Indians has been settled now that Indians have variously bagged Liz Hurley, Gwen Stefani and Derek Jeter. So she keeps hiding the fact that they've been dating for the past year.

Unfortunately, this leads to *Principle #3: Lying about where you were the day before might not catch up to you, but lying about where you were the whole prior year just might.* Mum called Vineeta about meeting an Indian doctor who was doing his residency at Johns Hopkins. Vineeta tried to avoid the set-up by complaining about the distance. But in hiding her relationship with Hans, she had claimed to be doing weekend trips with friends to Philly and DC, which are no farther than Baltimore.

Vineeta called me for advice on avoiding the set-up, though I had no advice for the dishonest but obedient child when my success in parrying parental interference was premised on being the honest and disobedient child. She asked me what I thought of Hans. I maturely avoided the question because of *Principle #4: Maturity means knowing when to lie, when to tell the truth and when to say nothing at all (wisdom means knowing when others are lying).*

So off she went to Baltimore for an afternoon date with the doctor in the hope that "his parents are forcing him into this, too." Or because she thinks that Hans is not a long term partner. If she broke up with Hans, she would definitely find someone else. Some of my friends tell me that Vineeta's attractive, but I can't evaluate that any more than I could distinguish a squirrel from a chipmunk.

She told Mum she didn't connect with the doctor, but that just means Mum will keep setting her up. So maybe the main take away is *Principle #5: if you're going to lie, make sure you're the type of person who is okay dealing with the consequences.*

Chapter 1
Foibles and Secrets
London, England

Vineeta

Vineeta needed this *puja*. She would appeal to the Hindu Gods to quickly bless her cousin Shushruth in advance of his wedding and then move on to more important issues, like her impending confrontation with her brother Ravi.

The bare-chested priest set up the religious accoutrements—a fire pit, coconut, orange petals and an hourglass-shaped copper jug of holy water—on a blanket in the middle of the living room. It seemed far-fetched that this man was a representative of the Gods, but it was possible he was a switchboard operator who could get their attention when the ceremony began.

Vineeta maneuvered around arriving guests, over the cheap mustard-colored carpet and past an oversized sofa that had been pushed to the perimeter. Though her own apartment in Manhattan had tasteful modern furnishings and scent sticks, she felt cozier in Shushruth's Ealing home, where she had spent many hours before her family had moved to America when she was six years old. In fact, she had grown up down the street in one of the uniform row houses—two stories, a chimney, and a large sloped dormer window.

She arrived at the galley kitchen to help Shushruth and her other cousin Pankaj with food preparation. They were biological brothers born to her mom's youngest sister. But the middle sister had been infertile, so Pankaj's mom had fulfilled her duty as the youngest sister to give Shushruth to the middle sister to raise as her own. They had both grown up in this suburb of London about twenty minutes apart and still lived with their parents.

Pankaj's bald dome reflected light like lacquer under the overhead lights, blossoms of hair puffing out of the V of his Polo shirt. He was the crown jewel of the family. The banker whose Saudi prince level demonstrations of wealth made his parents beam with pride—gaudy gold chain necklace, oversized watch, name brand clothing that didn't necessarily match. He was bright and analytical, but she had never really connected with him.

Whereas with Shushruth—shorter than her and dressed in a knock-off Polo shirt and corduroy pants that didn't necessarily match—she felt some emotional connection which didn't require sophisticated conversation to make the relationship satisfying. He was smart, a doctor, but always made the predictable observation—the weather was cold, stocks were up, vacation was nice, food was tasty.

Pankaj was pouring cups of water, so Vineeta assisted Shusruth with transferring the cooked food into serving dishes, careful not to accidentally stain her glittery orange blouse. She was dressed in a traditional salwar kameez, with a tasteful gold necklace and group of bangles. A voice interrupted her serenity.

"The gang is back together again!"

Vineeta turned to witness Ravi's outstretched arms and beaming face, somehow appropriately dressed in an oversized linen shirt with string necklaces that made him appear both like a rock-star and a Hindu disciple.

"A feast for the man of the week, our beloved cousin, the youngest of the bunch who has decided to get married first. Good to see you again," Ravi said.

He walked in to give each cousin a bro-hug before turning to Vineeta.

"Long time no see."

"I was wondering when you would show," Vineeta said. "For you this is almost like showing up early."

"IST, Indian standard time."

"I'm so glad you made it. It's so nice to be all together," Shushruth said.

"Yeah, it's almost worth getting married for, isn't it?" Ravi asked. "Where's the bride?"

"I think she's still getting ready upstairs," Shushruth said.

The four of them formed a tight circle near the stove in the cramped galley. They spoke briefly about wedding prep, flights and jet lag before Shushruth and Pankaj were summoned to meet arriving guests.

"Our little excursion to Blackpool will give us a chance to properly catch up," Ravi noted as they departed.

Vineeta was curious what type of bachelor weekend Ravi had planned. Would he push the bounds of decorum or stick within the cultural mores that Shushruth followed?

"So. How's Mum and Dad?" he asked.

"They're good. You didn't see them outside?" she asked.

She needed to confront him, but his presence also comforted her. The physical being she had spent more time with than anyone else in her life, even her parents.

"I did, but there's their version and your version."

"No major fights, if that's what you mean. Your absence has been duly noted, however. Nifty trick booking a hotel," she said.

He had conveniently avoided staying with the rest of the family by claiming he was on assignment for the t.v. show he worked for. So while he luxuriated at a hotel in downtown London, she was stuck with her parents at her cousin Pankaj's house.

"It wasn't a trick. It made the scheduling easier. No going back and forth to London or having to explain why I need to be somewhere," Ravi said.

Vineeta began re-arranging refrigerator magnets—a picture of Sathya Sai Babu, the phone number to George's Pizza, a realtor's calendar and a "Greetings from Switzerland!" postcard. She felt cold perspiration drip from her armpit to her blouse. She hated confrontation, but certain things needed to be said, with or without celestial help.

"Or having to talk about your book."

"What's wrong with the book?" Ravi asked, helping himself to a fried pakoda from a pyramid on the stovetop.

Ravi's Guide to Being a Cool Indian had been published a few weeks before. Amongst the various humiliating revelations about her life, Ravi had detailed her secret relationship with her Austrian boyfriend Hans. While her mom had skimmed it with minimal comprehension, her professor dad had read it. Fortunately, he was withholding the information from her mom in the hopes that Hans would eventually go away. Vineeta had to tell Hans that she had lent the *Guide* to a friend so Hans couldn't ask to read it.

She hadn't seen Ravi since the *Guide* had been published and had avoided confronting him over the phone because he was her portal into the secret privileges of New York—the candle-lit lounges with belly dancers, celebrities and free drinks. Not to mention that she feared he was right.

When she had first met Hans, the cultural differences made him seem interesting— the sexy Austrian accent, tales of skiing in the Alps, jokes which seemed original the first time he told them. But he did talk about architecture in some "robotic algorithm". Was he really just too stoic? Or like Ravi wrote, all facts, no fiction?

"Maybe you should have previewed it with everyone before letting the world see our family's foibles," Vineeta said.

"Foibles? Who uses that word?" Ravi asked.

Vineeta's therapist, Dr. Doris Jenks, used "foibles" every few sentences in lieu of problems, mistakes, dysfunction, abuse, deprecation, degradation. But the doctor's assertion that it was important to know all her foibles had become expensive, even if the doctor's notepad made Vineeta feel important. No one else had ever recorded her thoughts.

"I don't know, I use 'foibles', who cares? You didn't exactly paint Mum in the best light. Or me. Or Hans."

She tried to look him in the eye, but he was searching for a kitchen towel to wipe his hands.

"I just think you should tell Mum and Dad you have a boyfriend. What's the big deal?" Ravi asked.

"It's complicated."

"People usually say things are complex when they're incredibly simple but they don't have the courage to deal with them."

"That's easy for you to say because Mum puts up with whatever you do. With me it will lead to Armageddon."

When she had first told Hans about Shushruth's wedding in London, he had reacted with such enthusiasm that she had realized he had thought he would be joining, even suggesting a side trip to Vienna. She had tried to emphasize how bored he would be because she would be busy catching up with old relatives, but he had said he didn't mind quietly observing. She finally had to tell him that she hadn't mentioned him to her parents because her mom expected her to marry an Indian. Vineeta had expected Hans to get angry, which would have been good because it would have forced a decision. Instead he had accepted her explanation that she would talk to her parents about him right after the wedding when she could prep them properly and when they weren't mainly focused on her cousin's wedding.

Hans had still sulked for days, making sarcastic references to his irrelevance, and this morning had called to ask whether she had met any nice Indian men. She wondered whether he knew that she had gone on a number of brief set-ups with Indian men over the last year to stop her mom from getting suspicious. She could have managed all these issues in due time but for the *Guide*. Her brother's desperate attempt to stay in the spotlight as his musical career waned.

Ravi turned to face her.

"She's always pissed anyway. They moved out of India, they need to get used to the idea that we're not going to be Indian. You can't keep living your life to please them."

"I haven't been. I didn't become a doctor, and I'm dating a non-Indian," she said.

"Fine, you can't keep spending your life resenting them for wanting your life to be different."

"Meaning them wanting it to be different or me wanting it to be different?"

"Either."

"Who said I want my life to be different?"

She did, but she hadn't actually told anyone. She began twisting strands of her blow-dried dunes of hair into a tight rope.

"Whatever, that's for you to decide."

"You're changing the subject. Your *Guide* made us all seem like ignorant dolts."

"I was just trying to be funny. You got that it was just a joke?" Ravi asked while chewing on a bulge of pakodas in his mouth.

"There's a difference between a joke and mocking the core of someone's identity. And not just someone. People who have loved and supported you."

There. She had gotten to her core point. He wiped his hands again, creased his eyebrows and started nodding.

"Okay, maybe I should have checked with you first. But it's because I love you and Mum and everyone else, I figured everyone knew it came from a good place."

He was so smooth. He could deliver apologies with a nonchalant sincerity that made it hard to stay mad at him.

"That's why I haven't brought it up. But you did hurt my feelings a little. And Mum's feelings weren't hurt only because she wasn't patient enough to try and understand what you wrote."

Despite the tense relationship she often had with her mum, Vineeta didn't like to see her publicly ridiculed. When Vineeta had visited home, their mum had sat in the living room flipping through the *Guide* as if she was cross-referencing horse races in an off-track-betting pamphlet, slowly picking out random words.

"What this means? He's ming-ling?"

"It just means he made a lot of friends while he was traveling."

Vineeta tried to remember that her mother had grown up in Jobner, a town of ten thousand people. She had attended middle school in the same white blouse and pullover blue dress every day, with braided pigtails coated in coconut oil and tied with violet ribbons (as displayed in the only picture they had of her as a child). Her father had bought and sold large canisters of heating oil to support the family and save enough for his three daughters' dowry. At age 15, her beauty facilitated an arranged marriage to Jeevan, a middle-class city-dweller. She moved in with her in-laws and acclimated to the sprawling chaos and noise of Bombay, only to be shifted at 21 to London. There she tried to recall English lessons from her youth to navigate stores, manage the household and raise Ravi and Vineeta. The arrival of her sisters restored her sense of community until Jeevan decided to move to America, where she was stranded in a large house in the suburbs.

While their dad derived self-esteem from his job and stimulation from his colleagues, their mum sacrificed both in cooking incessantly, taking Ravi and Vineeta to swimming lessons and clipping coupons to help finance Ravi's Star Wars toys and Vineeta's board games. She never had choices, so when she instructed or argued with Ravi and Vineeta, it was because she wanted some say. Her most prized possession after a gold necklace that belonged to her great-grandmother was a doll collection she had started in London. Vineeta occasionally saw her adjusting a doll's clothing or hair and advising it how life worked.

Reflecting on her mom's life, the intensity of Vineeta's morning finally overwhelmed her. She turned around to open the fridge and stealthily swipe away her tears with the back of her hand. She took out a can of Coke and turned back around. The snap and fizz calmed her down. She took a sip to pretend she had actually wanted the soda when a second surge of tears betrayed her. She didn't know she had so much pent up frustration as the tears snowballed into sobs and more intense crying.

"Jeez, I'm sorry," Ravi said.

He leaned in and hugged her. She wanted to resist, but appreciated his secure hug, a primal connection to the brother who had held her from the time she was a baby. They could argue and disagree, but in the end, she knew he was always there with a hug. She had always looked up to him, from the time she was photographed as a baby laughing at his silly dances and made-up songs, right to his stardom. In some ways, he was the perfect older brother. Someone with whom she could share secrets without fear of having them leaked to her parents. The rebel who made all her choices seem mature when their parents compared them. In other ways, he was still the same adolescent who would swing open the bathroom door on her once he discovered the lock could be released with a hairpin. She disliked fighting with him because she always suffered a tense melancholy until they patched things up. It didn't take much for her to forgive him. As she calmed down and he released her, she felt like she should say something positive about the *Guide* to soften her criticism.

"It had a lot of good ideas, too, your book. At times I thought you were making the point that Indians had lost a sense of their own identity in trying to assimilate. And that your own identity was shaped by the way people treated you. Though it's strange, I don't recall ever being called racist names."

She wiped her eyes with her sleeves.

"That's because the same people who were insulting me were secretly hoping to sleep with you."

"That's gross."

"Anyway, I'm sorry. No one's reading the book, anyway."

Ravi yawned and brushed his hands down his face. The moons under Ravi's eyes suggested a lack of sleep. She was about to ask for Ravi's input about the situation with Hans when he pre-empted her.

"Speaking of which, there was actually something I wanted to ask you. A little thing I could use your help on," he said.

"Okay."

He started talking, moving his gaze back and forth between her eyes and the stovetop.

"So, the book's not doing well, and my gig hosting *Cool Kids* might be coming to an end, and so that's about to present me with a bit of a cash flow issue. Usually we can turn to Dad for a short term loan, but I don't want to tell Dad I'm losing my job because I don't want him to be worried. And I know sometimes he helps you out, so I was hoping maybe you could say you need money for your school and lend me the money until I get my next gig."

She looked through him for a moment. That was the thing she forgot when assessing him a moment before. His ability to spoil a perfectly good emotional moment.

"You okay?" he asked.

"Yeah, sorry. Your show is ending? I'm sorry to hear that," she answered impassively.

"Might be ending. Might not. But it's a stupid show, let's be honest."

"I know, but it's a job. You're doing okay?"

He looked down, his hair cascaded over his face, and nodded.

"Yeah, I'm used to it."

Was it possible to get used to rejection? Didn't it get harder with age? Ravi's universe had its own logic. It was his ability to ignore odds that allowed him to make it this far, though maybe the odds were just catching up to him. She hated to admit it, but she felt some schadenfreude at his comeuppance.

"Well, of course I want to support you however I can, but I'm surprised you don't have any money saved up. Especially with the publication of the *Guide*. If you were going to sell the family out, I would have hoped it was at least for a meaningful amount."

"It's going to make some money, it's too early. I just need to promote it more."

"So you didn't get an advance?"

"What little there was has been spent."

Her head swirled from the convergence of these four issues. The *Guide*. Hans. Her parents. Loans. Actually, five issues. The awful droning of the priest from the next room requesting God's blessings for Shushruth's wedding, which was distracting God from helping her deal with her expanding list of problems.

Should she help him out? Maybe he needed to face the consequences of his choices to learn his lesson. If things got bad enough, he could get their Dad to bail him out.

"I'd like some time to think about it. If I ask for money, then he's going to wonder if I'm mismanaging my money," Vineeta said.

She adjusted the skirt half of her salwar kameez to avoid looking him in the eye, though she could tell he was slowly pulling on an eyebrow in reflection.

"Good point."

"How much do you need?" she asked.

She peeked up to see him with knitted eyebrows and glazed eyes staring at a spice rack.

"More than chump change. New York City is expensive."

He snapped out of his reverie and swung his head to look at her with narrowed eyes.

"Don't worry about it. Just trying to plan ahead. Were you planning on going in to watch the puja?" he asked.

"I thought I would pretend to be doing something in here for as long as I could. Except right now, I need to go to the bathroom," she said.

She left the kitchen as a steady tambourine jangle set the beat for the puja's final ceremony. Each guest approached the front to bow and accept a streak of red paste and rice on their forehead from the priest. Vineeta saw a picture of Ganesh behind the priest and snuck in a silent request for assistance before tiptoeing to the upstairs bathroom. She didn't want the whooshes and tinkles of her visit to be heard by the audience. She also hoped to find a painkiller in the medicine cabinet from a developing headache.

After washing her hands, she desperately checked the medicine cabinet for anything that would ease the pressure in her brain. Orajel. Pepto Bismol. Preparation H. Why couldn't Indians suffer from depression or migraines or opioid addition like Americans? Instead everything related to eating, digesting and shitting out spicy food. She found tablets in a sheet of foil sealed pockets, but it wasn't labeled. Should she gamble that the tablets might cure her throbbing headache instead of giving her a case of violent diarrhea? She splashed some water on her face. She put the toilet cover seat down, sat down and placed her arms out in a Sukhasana pose, her fingers shaped to suggest everything was okay. She breathed deeply and tried to clear her mind. She imagined herself in the same pose on an empty beach, the wet sand on her thighs, inhaling salty air while the breeze brushed her hair across her face. In two minutes she had successfully cleared her brain and stood back up. She was ready to socialize again. She needed to get back down quickly so that people didn't think she was having an interminable bowel movement.

Ravi was looking at pictures on the refrigerator. She began ladling lamb, potatoes and eggplant floating in orange oil into a compartmentalized foam plate, adding a couple of puris and handing the plate to Ravi.

"What's this for? I'm not hungry."

"It's not for you. Just put it on the counter there for people to take when the puja finishes."

Ravi began rolling up a puri like a cigar and stuffing it in his mouth.

"I thought you weren't hungry?"

"I wasn't, but now that I'm looking at it, I might as well have a couple of puris to soak up the vodka from last night," he said.

A new thought occurred to her. If her parents somehow accepted Hans, they would immediately pressure her to get married. What if she had been using her parents as an excuse to avoid making a decision about him? Her head started throbbing again. She extracted vegetarian gummi bears from her purse, a pacifier in times of stress. Maybe today was a test of her Buddhism. Suffering was a condition of life to be embraced. If she could embrace Han's fidelity, Ravi's fallibility, her parent's meddling and her own public humiliation she would be one step closer to nirvana.

The puja suddenly quieted to silence before building back into chatter and rustling clothes. Shushruth and his mom entered the galley as Ravi excused himself, probably to go outside for a smoke.

"Oh, you already served everything? You warmed it? No, don't eat yet. I haven't even added *kothmeer*," her aunt said, scrambling to heat plates in the microwave and chop the cilantro as a garnishment while instructing Shushruth and Vineeta to fill up water cups in anticipation of the first wave of male diners.

Shushruth would have been a great brother, always calm, always de-escalating conflict. Ravi and Pankaj used to make fun of Shusruth behind his back, but he was the most balanced of the three. Vineeta never really bonded with Pankaj's sister, so she spent more time playing board games with Shusruth than playing with the others.

"Did you have a lot of *pujas* in Michigan?" Shushruth asked Vineeta while ladling out food.

"No, never. We'd sometimes go to other people's *pujas*. Not that we didn't believe, we still went to temple."

"I thought Ravi had written in his book you're Buddhist."

"I forgot he mentioned that. I mean, I'm still Hindu, but I also like Buddhist philosophy, so maybe I'm Buddhist Hindu?"

As a Buddhist Hindu, when her choices went well, she expounded philosophies she thought sounded Buddhist and promoted her vision of a Utopian love field in which people did what they wanted. When her choices went badly, she turned to Krishna or Ganesh or Shiva to interfere on her behalf. Which God should she pray to today?

The puja was dedicated to Krishna as the God of compassion and love, but he kept sprinkling Cupid dust on all the wrong people. Ganesh was the remover of obstacles, but it's not like he could extricate her from her family. Vishnu was the protector, but it seems like he had fallen down on the job a long time ago. If anything, it was like Shiva was running the joint. The God of Destruction.

"There are lots of ways to reach the same destination. I think it's great," Shushruth said.

She wasn't sure what her destination was. Buddhism taught that to conquer the suffering of existence, she needed to have the right views, resolve, speech, action, livelihood, effort, mindfulness and concentration. The list was both insightful and so long as to be useless.

"Do you know why people pray to Shiva? I mean, given that he destroys things?" she asked.

"He uses his power to destroy the illusions and imperfections of the world in order to re-create it and make it better."

Is that what was happening? Shiva was destroying the illusions of her life? A boyfriend she liked but didn't really love, a lifestyle that only pleased her parents and a brother who she loved but lived in another universe? Maybe Shiva was forcing her to make some decisions so she could get back to some beautiful parallel life she was living in another dimension where everything made sense and she was satisfied.

Excerpt from

Ravi's Guide to Being a Cool Indian

Money

All people value money, but Indian immigrants convert every decision into a monetary one. Am I thirsty? Only if the water is free. Do I need a haircut? Only if it's been six weeks since the last one. Mum buys milk at one grocery store and bread at another to save a few pennies after she's factored in petrol. Dad's failure to deploy a coupon leads to nights of recrimination and vitriol. Friends allocate restaurant bills by the dish and to the penny. Some Indians never learn the value of time, experience or goodwill, while wondering why no one invites them out to eat anymore.

Principle #1: don't save pennies while wasting dollars in the currency of life.

Of course, Americans are often eating out while their house is in foreclosure. The Bhagavad Gita says don't borrow money. Or at least it probably does. Who's right, the borrowers or the savers?

Accountants like Dad say that leverage can fuel innovation and productivity by allocating financial capital to its best use. His theory would explain why the GDP of India lags the GDP of America, Indians are too cheap to lend or too pious to borrow. In my experience, borrowing can lead to life-changing experiences. Principle #2: borrow enough to maximize today without screwing up tomorrow. Depending on the lender and the enterprise you're investing in, this may be easier said than done....

Chapter 2
Dalinc's Proposition
London, England

Ravi

Ravi had begged off the first of the pre-wedding dinners so that he could sneak in drinks with members of a band that had opened for his band on tour. Both bands were now defunct, but while his friends were stuck working as store managers and mobile phone salesmen, he had a gig hosting *Cool Kids* on MTV. He regaled the group at the oak wood counter of a pub in Soho with stories about teenagers who performed various tasks in order to have him designate them as "cool". They laughed even though he could tell that his timing of the punchlines was off. The stories not only bored him, but triggered a nagging sense that his life had become meaningless.

At the end of the evening, he posed for selfies with his friends and the pub staff and magnanimously threw his credit card on the bill before realizing he had failed to convert each pound to two dollars. In for some pounds, in for thousands of pennies. He owed so much money it no longer made a difference.

His dad's quarterly loans had tided him over fairly well until he had recently gotten carried away at a private table playing blackjack with some other celebrities while visiting London a few months earlier. The guy from Nickeljack kept raising him. It was humiliating enough that Nickeljack was scoring hits while his band was defunct, so he kept matching the raises until he was thirty-five thousand dollars in debt to the Croatian who had organized the whole thing. He couldn't exactly tell his Dad or Vineeta in his requests for a loan that he needed to squander a large chunk of his parent's retirement savings because his ego had surpassed both his accomplishments and his bank account.

When did the road fork? Ravi's songwriting had led to a Grammy nomination for Buzzthief's debut album only five years ago. His songs had moved people, at one point an entire stadium waving their cellphones in appreciation. The band was making good money touring. The Killers and The Strokes had even emulated their sound, with melodic vocals, guitar riffs and synth backgrounds. But then Ravi had written two albums of Radiohead- inspired muezzin wailing set to electro beats and guitar shrieks. The pop fans had abandoned them, and the music critics had laughed at them. The label might have given one more chance, but Ravi had finished Buzzthief off in a single interview:

"Thing you like best about your label mates Coldway?"

"Their success."

"Thing you like least?"

"Their music."

Still, his agent found him a financial lifeline with the MTV gig. Even that had initially been an artistic challenge, finding the right vocal tone, facial expression and interviewing rhythm to be entertaining.

If he was going to pinpoint when he had lost his emotional connection to what he was doing, when he had started seeking solace in superficial things like gambling, it would have been right after he had broken up with Pilar eighteen months before. Or she had broken up with him, depending on how one looked at it.

After leaving the pub, he decided to walk back to his hotel to breathe the city back into his veins—the Victorian buildings, the red double-decker buses, the null signs at the bus stops. It allowed him a respite from all this self-reflection and self-loathing. He lucked onto Regent's Street and kicked a plastic bottle cap with his Converse high-tops. A hint of a tree or flower, something moist and unpolluted, suggested itself through the car exhaust and stale radiance of street detritus. He headed toward the Ionic columns of All Souls Cathedral at the far end earmarking his residence, the St. Georges Hotel on RIDING HOUSE STREET W1. The black and red Univers font of Westminster's placard street signs were not only classier than the green street signs of Ravi's native New York City, but also evoked memories of his early childhood, when his extended family had taken summertime excursions from the suburb of Ealing to see Big Ben, Westminster Abbey and other attractions. It evoked a period of his life when he had felt supreme and life had felt secure, when he had spent every weekend lording over Shushruth and Pankaj at his house or one of theirs, before his family had relocated to America.

Was America the problem? Did it foster some individualistic ethos that caused Ravi to live beyond his means? Had he assimilated too much? The funny part was that Ravi had written the "Money" chapter to his *Guide* long before the gambling incident, not realizing that he had been flippantly predicting his own future.

This week his parents and sister were staying at Pankaj's house in Ealing in advance of Shushruth's wedding, though he had justified staying at the hotel by claiming he was on assignment for *Cool Kids*, thus avoiding having to listen to his aunt and mum discuss his moral failings. Not to mention having to invent an alibi for when he appeared in court for a pub fight the year before.

He had told MTV he needed to research potential cool kids in London for a special international episode in order to expense the hotel. If he ever wrote a sequel to his *Guide* (not that many people had read the first one), he would observe that consistent lies were better than inconsistent truths.

He took the elevator up to his room and managed to brush his teeth and disrobe before rolling under the covers. He was twisted in the sheets face-down, dreaming about driving away from an assailant when his Porsche suddenly became a jittery '78 Chevy, bouncing and rolling left and right.

He awoke to his body being pushed back and forth by a man with big ears and a dark crew cut. He jumped up into a seated karate pose. Light from the floor-to-ceiling window haloed the man's head like an apostle.

"My friend," Dalinc said.

Ravi relaxed and put his arms down. He untangled himself from the sheets and picked up the phone in a daze. 11 a.m. How had so many hours passed by? He had expected to wake up without an alarm, but hadn't calibrated the hangover/jet lag coefficient correctly.

"What the hell, man? Can't you just call?" Ravi asked.

His heart started beating fast as his body realized the implications of Dalinc's appearance.

"You never leave your phone on. I don't like to write. You don't like to read. Doesn't leave many options."

"Jesus."

Ravi kept his cell phone in airplane mode except when he wanted to make a call. All the ringing, flashing, vibrating—just so people could ask him where he would be or when he would show up. He liked to joke with friends that he showed up where and when the time was right, which didn't always sync to a place or a number.

"How'd you find me here?"

"We are international business. I have my ways."

Ravi pawed at a few thin hairs on the desert landscape of his chest when he blearily saw a metallic flash wave through the air. A revolver?

This was an unexpected escalation. Movies made guns seem like a casual threat or a bluff to be negotiated. None captured his fear at that moment, at a bullet intentionally or accidentally ending his life because some guy who wasn't diligent enough to graduate high school casually waved a gun at him. He didn't deserve to die in his underwear with a ski-slope level case of bedhead. Would that guy from Nickeljack have gotten the same treatment?

He peered more closely at Dalinc's hand. A metallic credit card.

"Please," Dalinc reprimanded, lifting the cross pendant from around his neck, releasing it and waving his index finger left and right. "You owe me money. Today you're going to pay it. I don't care the fuck you take the money from, even your dying grandmother. You will give me thirty-five thousand dollars today, or it will not be pretty."

What would not be pretty? The damage to Ravi's body or Dalinc's unorthodox diction? Dalinc often used the f-word for emphasis, which Ravi attributed to an inferiority complex stemming from their dueling accents, London English vs immigrant Croatian, the educated vs. the blue collar. They had always been friendly on the phone, comparing musical tastes, joking about sour Polish food and laughing when Ravi noted that he could pay the loan off in six months with some economizing. They both knew that if Ravi had the discipline to economize, he wouldn't have racked up this gambling debt in the first place.

Ravi closed his eyes and put both hands on his head as he tried to simultaneously figure out how to get the money and how Dalinc had found him. Ravi hadn't answered Dalinc's calls for the past month on the premise that Dalinc wouldn't fly from London to New York just to recover thirty-five thousand dollars. Dalinc's organization must have hacked into Ravi's email account and discovered that Ravi would be visiting London.

"I can get the money," Ravi said, opening his eyes.

"From where?"

A good question, to which he knew only one answer.

"My dad. Maybe not all of it today, but some of it."

Dalinc picked up the hotel phone and handed it to Ravi, a cloud of Dalinc's musk cologne inciting a sneeze.

"So, get the money."

"Now?"

Dalinc nodded. Maybe Ravi could talk his way out of this. Flattery and evasion had saved him from accountability many times.

"How did you get into the room?" Ravi asked.

"Visa. It takes everywhere you want to be."

Dalinc mimed swiping the credit card through the side of a door to release the lock.

"Aren't you cold? You didn't wear a jacket?" Ravi asked.

"When I was child, my father take me for walk by the Sava River in Zagreb with no jacket in the middle of winter. That's cold. I don't need a jacket in this, this is like summer. My father teach me to be tough. He was man, real Croatian man, with strong hairy forearms, working on building ships."

Dalinc also had big hairy forearms. Would he knot Ravi's limbs into a rolling hitch or a butterfly loop? A trickle of perspiration tickled across Ravi's scalp.

"How's he doing?"

"He's dead. He had heart attack last year."

"I'm sorry."

"You're sorry? I'm sorry. But sorry's not going to pay the bills, As my son reminds every day."

"Meaning, your son tells you sorry? Or you tell him you're sorry? Or you're sorry you had your son?"

"The last one. I mean I love him, especially when he goes like this," Dalinc said, clenching and unclenching his fists, "but if I had put the thing on, my wife could have kept working as a hairdresser, I could have returned to school to become an electrician and make lot of money. My father always said, the difference between stupid people and regular people is who learn from their mistakes. The difference between regular people and smart people is who learn from other people's mistakes."

"So, you're the regular person?" Ravi asked.

"Of course, what you think? I'm stupid person?"

"No, the smart person."

Dalinc's quick wit belied his lack of education and lulled Ravi into believing that his prior accounts of injuring people might have been fabricated. But that was before he showed up uninvited. Maybe he would only break something peripheral as a warning, like a toe. Ravi nervously sniffed at his imagined joke. He could offer up his small toe. He had broken it before and could still move around.

"Yuh. Maybe if my mother's visa comes through, she can babysit and my wife can start working again. Or maybe I start driving taxi, although all you Indian people, you're like mosquitoes everywhere in your taxis. Someday my son is going to go to college, get better job. But not whatever college you go to."

"Why? It was a good college."

"They didn't teach you anything. Enough talking. You don't want to find how I can make you do things, especially if you want to keep playing guitar. Make the phone call."

How was he going to explain the situation to his Dad? Maybe he would just come clean. It would be a relief confessing that his life was a mess. If he showed enough remorse, maybe his father wouldn't berate him too badly. Ravi could even offer to move back to Ann Arbor to go back to school. His mom was always begging him to get a corporate job, something she could relate to. Would it be that bad leaving his entertainment career behind? Leaving behind the constant angst of judging his self-worth on the art he produced?

"They might not be awake," Ravi said while dialing on his cell phone.

"Not on cell phone, I want to listen on other phone."

Dalinc went to the suite's living room. Ravi peered at his reflection in the mirrored picture frame above the headboard and adjusted his hair before dialing from the desk phone. His accounting professor father was probably at his aunt's house riffling through sheafs of paper summarizing "capital structure efficiency" or some other academic concept Ravi only loosely grasped.

"Hello?"

"Dad, it's me."

"Everything's alright? There's no problem?"

His father usually assumed a call from Ravi before noon indicated a problem. A loan from a loan shark would certainly qualify as a problem, "unless it qualifies for a tax write-off", Ravi thought, filling in his dad's favorite saying.

"Yeah, all good. Headed to Blackpool tonight for Shushruth's bachelor party. So I know it's a little early and a bit of an odd request, but I could use a favor. I've started recording a solo album, and there's an incredible producer here who I'd like to record with and just freed up, but he requires cash, and with the bachelor party, which I've got to cover 'cause I'm like the elder cousin-brother, I'm a little short at the moment. Could you float me a few dollars?"

Ravi called Shushruth "cousin-brother" because he knew it would pull on his father's sentimental Indian roots, where all cousins were considered "brothers" and "sisters".

"How much do you need?"

"Maybe thirt…um, maybe like, ten thousand dollars?"

"Ten thousand dollars?!"

"It's actually more expensive, but that would get me started. It would give me chance to lay down some tracks before I head back."

Not bad for an impromptu excuse. That was the thing Ravi had overlooked just moments before—his ability to talk his way into things, out of things and around things as necessary. His career was floundering, but he was only just finishing the second act. Every story needed three acts. He had one more to go.

He bounced out of his bed in black briefs and stretched the telephone cord taut to reach the door between the bedroom and the living room to gauge Dalinc's reaction, but he didn't give one.

"And you have nothing in the bank?" his dad asked.

"I do, but this fellow is a little more expensive than my spending money at the moment."

"So then why did you stay at the hotel instead of with us?"

"I'm not paying for the hotel, remember? It's on MTV's tab."

"I don't understand what you do with all your money. Your rent is what, four thousand dollars a month? Maybe your other expenses are four thousand a month. This is only ninety-six thousand per annum, which requires one hundred and twenty-five thousand before taxes. You're making more than this, no?"

The money from hosting *Cool Kids* was generous, but so were his spending habits. A luxury one-bedroom apartment in the West Village. Clothing. Drinks for himself and his friends. Donations for breast cancer research at star-studded charity events.

Why hadn't he reduced his spending after hearing that the show was about to be canceled? Maybe deep down he wanted the second act to be over. To stop interviewing high schoolers for a living when he used to be the one being interviewed, and to create a crisis big enough that he needed to take some action.

Dalinc covered the receiver and shout-whispered from the other room, "Tell him, you don't live like big man, no one think you are big man."

Ravi nodded.

"You're not factoring in my lifestyle, Dad. If I don't live like I'm important, no one will think I'm important, and then no one will want to hire me."

"What are you doing with your paychecks? You're doing drugs?" his father asked.

At least if he was doing drugs, the highs would last for a little bit longer. The irony of his dad's interrogation was that he had introduced Ravi to gambling when he had invited the teenage Ravi to substitute for an absent professor in his dad's monthly poker group. The game had been held in a frigid wood-paneled basement of a bearded colleague with glasses of scotch and beer. His dad's three colleagues had puffed cigars, reminisced about the Reagan era, speculated whether the Lions would make the playoffs and chuckled as he and his dad had lost money. Two of them gave dismissive glances to one another whenever his dad had offered an opinion. When Ravi had gotten back home, he had asked his dad if he liked playing. He'd said it didn't matter, that sometimes you had to do things to fit in.

Ravi looked at Dalinc, who offered, "Good drugs more expensive than ten thousand."

"I can't tell him I know how much drugs cost," Ravi whispered back while covering the receiver. "New York is expensive, Dad. I just cover my costs. The album is an investment."

"Ravi—stocks are an investment. Marriage is an investment. A new album, this is…"

His dad showered Ravi with words in the earnest belief that his latest polemic, probably inspired by the thesis of some paper that intelligently applied equity capital (in this case represented by Ravi's ability to work) trumped debt capital (represented by Ravi's ability to mooch off of his dad) for generating outsized returns, would finally be the one that delivered a knock-out blow to Ravi's bi-annual requests for money. Ravi knew that he just needed to hang in the ring long enough for his Dad to relent—usually. Usually he wasn't asking for ten thousand dollars.

Dalinc rubbed his thumb and index finger back and forth while gyrating his hand to direct Ravi to speed up the conversation. Would Dalinc really use his thick, hairy forearms to injure him?

"Now that you've had some success, shouldn't someone else pay for the recording?" his dad asked.

"Exactly. They should and they will. Just not up front. They'll want to hear the new material."

"I thought you had said you wouldn't need more money once they paid you for the book you wrote. *Ravi's Guide to Being a Cool Indian*," his dad said in a mocking theatrical tone.

Dalinc gave Ravi a puzzled look that suggested he didn't think Ravi knew how to read or write.

"Well, they have to see how the book does first. It's started a little slow, but it should pick up once it gets some buzz going," Ravi said.

"What does this mean, 'buzz'?" his dad asked. "I gave Vineeta money to get a useless degree at Columbia, and now she is buzzing me to give her more because her job doesn't pay her enough. I've given you money in the past, you have buzzed through it so that you are buzzing me for money. Is that what this 'buzz' means?"

His dad paused for effect. Ravi's parents lumped Ravi together with Vineeta, choosing the worst of their respective behaviors to criticize both of them. Ravi had endured countless monologues about Vineeta's failure to find a spouse or become a doctor, while she endured speeches about his shameless womanizing and mediocre grades.

Ravi's ear began throbbing from the inadvertent pressure of the receiver. He looked at Dalinc for an idea, but Dalinc was just nodding in agreement with his father.

His father continued, "You know, sometimes I wonder if it would have been better if we had stayed in India. We tried to teach you good values, but with the television, newspapers, music and other people here, what could we do? You had a free education from a good school, and this is where you are at. But then I think, I'm a professor, I should have been able to teach you something."

Ravi could tell his dad would relent as a paradoxical penitence for not having raised the kids in a manner in which they could support themselves. He had never used the words "I love you", but that was one thing he was able to clearly communicate without any words.

"I can give you five thousand. This can get you started, then you can find some other ways to get the rest."

Ravi peered into the other room. Dalinc formed his hand into a gun and waved it toward Ravi, as if it was the gun controlling Dalinc and not the other way around, mouthing, "Pow pow".

"Let me see what the producer says…" Ravi told his father, before softly pleading with Dalinc, "Come on, five is pretty good."

"Ten is better. Five today, five next week," Dalinc countered.

Ravi made the suggestion to his father.

"How many songs can you record for ten thousand?" his dad asked.

"Four, maybe five?"

"So pick your best two and a half songs, and record them for five thousand. If the label doesn't like those, then they won't like the other two and a half."

Ravi looked at Dalinc.

"He's smart," Dalinc said softly, shrugging his shoulders in resigned approval.

"Okay, Dad, that's a fair offer. It will be worth it. I've already got some good songs. How's Mum?"

Once Ravi concluded the call, he snapped his fingers in satisfaction and breathed out. One crisis averted. He could get breakfast after Dalinc left, go to a record store to bolster his vinyl collection and in the afternoon head to Blackpool with his cousins for Shushruth's bachelor party.

Dalinc walked into the room nodding in appreciation of Ravi's performance.

"That's not enough."

Ravi recoiled his head.

"Come on man, you just said it was okay!"

"No, I was just agreeing with your father. You don't know what you're doing."

"You ap-pp-pear out of nowhere and expect me to produce thirty-five thousand dollars on the spot?" he stuttered.

"You already one month late. Which is good if you want baby, bad if you owe me money."

"So one more week isn't going to make the difference, is it? Let me get you the five as a first installment."

"When will I see the cash?"

"Let's say he withdraws it by tomorrow, then Friday?"

"Boss will want something today."

"How am I supposed to get it today?"

"Have him wire you the money."

"I don't want to look desperate. He'll think I'm a drug addict."

"That's not my problem."

Ravi had a vague recollection that his backpack might hold another solution.

"What if I paid some of it now? That's worth a discount, right?"

"Discount? I'm not Walmart," Dalinc scoffed.

"And I'm not good with money."

Ravi began scavenging the pockets of his backpack. Whatever happened to the royalty check from the hit rap song that had sampled his hit "Glitter in the Road"? He probably hadn't been responsible enough to deposit it.

In the very last pocket, he felt something papery stuck in the crease, but not the right texture or size. A photo booth picture strip of him and his ex-girlfriend Pilar, a series of silly faces culminating in a kiss. A true moment. How many of those had he had since their break-up? If he had proposed to her eighteen months earlier, would his life be the mess it was? He would trade places with that Ravi if he could.

He noticed a promotional toy guitar in a side pocket. He removed it and tossed it to Dalinc.

"A gift for your son."

At least he was headed to Blackpool, where there were multiple venues to fix the problem in a few hours with a little luck.

"Good, he appreciate. But not worth thirty-five thousand."

"I had gotten a royalty check for one of my songs. Maybe I put it in my wallet."

Dalinc saw Ravi's jeans on the floor by the bed, walked over and removed Ravi's wallet. He extracted a check and two hundred Pounds before replacing the wallet and tossing the jeans to Ravi. Ravi looked at Dalinc expectantly.

"Nine thousand, not bad. Must have been good song. You know 'O Marijana'?"

Dalinc boomed out the chorus of a Croatian song. Ravi shook his head. Was Dalinc letting him go?

"You should listen to Croatian music, it give you some ideas."

Ravi started to respond, but stopped himself. Everyone had an opinion about music despite not understanding the process, knowledge or effort it took to write songs. Some people thought great songs came as a flash of genius, but Buzzthief recorded six versions of "Glitter in the Road" before they had a version that made girls flick open their cell phones at concerts. Ravi could have written ten songs a day, but he didn't want to make art that was common or eccentric. Genius was making the uncommon seem common, and that took work, not inspiration. He waited for a snippet of music that sounded true. He spent days adding a bridge and chorus to build to something bigger with the help of a producer who tweaked chord structures, tempo and instrumentation to interpret the song in a way that more people would relate to. If he didn't succeed within a few weeks, he hated listening to the song so much that he settled for something decent, even though it might have been great. When the song did turn out great, there was no cooler feeling in the world, regardless of whether it was a hit. The only problem was that he needed hits to pay the bills.

"Put these on. I can't look at…this anymore," Dalinc said, indicating Ravi's mostly naked body. "You know, you should listen to my father's advice."

"About the difference between the stupid person and regular person? Am I the stupid person?" Ravi asked as he stumbled into his jeans.

"Exactly. Here, sign it. You still owe the difference, but…I'm tired of these stupid visits. Stop gambling. You're no good at it."

Dalinc started walking toward the door and glanced at his watch. Ravi relaxed.

"Ah, shit! I have to call my wife. She gonna be pissed if I don't wish my boy good night. I got to go. Three days, you need to get me the rest of the money."

"Three days? I just gave you more than what you were expecting!"

"I don't agree with nothing. Boss wants his money. London, New York, wherever you are, I will find you. Three days. Understand?" Dalinc asked.

Ravi understood. He needed to be the rare person who made money at a casino.

As Dalinc closed the door behind him. Ravi realized he was still holding the picture of Pilar. He looked at it closely, took out his wallet and put it in the transparent window over his driver's license.

Excerpt from

Ravi's Guide to Being a Cool Indian

Nature or Nurture?

When people meet me, they remark on my cool accent. Fortunately, even half a British accent can score you a VJ slot at MTV, not to mention three of my top five hook-ups prior to my rock and television stardom. If you're reading this and thinking, "I have an Indian accent, this is just as good," you need to study this guide more closely than the Gita. If Indians had imbued their accent with the same sense of superiority as the English, they would have colonized the world instead of bootlicking the English. Principle #1: While you can't help India reclaim its jewels from its colonial oppressors, you can help it reclaim its pride by moving your accent from the horn section to the strings.

Just as important as your accent is your name. Hopefully your parents named you something like "Jay", "Ravi","Lina" or "Nisha", names that Westerners can easily pronounce. Principle #2: If you've been saddled with "Bushit", "Anaal" or "Fakhra", adopt a new name before others do it for you.

Did my accent and name send me down a pre-determined path to success? Is my coolness—the hair, the girls, the swagger—a style that can be learned or a quirk of birth? Let's take a trip back to the 1970s for a little informative interlude.

When I was seven, we lived in a suburb of London called Ealing, where I simulated fights from Hindi movies with my cousins Pankaj and Shushruth, who lived close by. I invoked my name to claim the role of Amitabh Bachchan because Amitabh had played a character named "Ravi" in four movies. Amitabh was famous for his "angry young man" characters in movies like Sholay and Deewar, fighting for justice with the intensity of James Dean, the voice and charisma of Elvis, comic timing of Charlie Chaplin, suavity of Cary Grant and fighting skills of Bruce Lee. As I pushed Pankaj onto the bed and wrestled Shushruth to the floor, our play fights often became real fights, which led to complaints from the neighbors through the second floor wall:

"Wot's that? Keep the camel jockeying down!"

The difference between a good London abode and a bad one was whether you had a neighbor who shouted through the paper-thin walls. Shushruth's family lived in a bad row house one block down from us in Ealing, while Pankaj's lived twenty minutes away in a peaceful detached house with a small back garden in Chiswick. We had neither. We had that one in a million, AB negative, six sigma travesty in which one neighbor cursed at us through the wall and the neighbor on the other side cursed back.

"Stop your fuckin' curry pollution, you damn towelheads."

"Don't make me call the dothead police!"

"Shut up, you Pakis!" (Londoners paid little heed to the geographical distinction between India, Pakistan and Bangladesh, despite London's role in separating them in the first place.)

I ignored our neighbors' admonitions in straddling Shushruth, who was two years younger than me and Pankaj and weighed only sixty pounds.

"Tum Amitabh nahi bhansakte. Tum Shatrughan Sinha bhanjao." You can't be Amitabh. You'll be Shatrughan Sinha.

Of Amitabh's various sidekicks, Vinod Khanna was the coolest, sporting a mischievous grin, white tank top and gold chain. Shashi Kapoor was the most complementary, balancing Amitabh's brooding with optimistic charm. Shatrughan Sinha was the dorkiest, with curly hair, a bushy mustache and a safari suit.

Shushruth struggled beneath me on our shag carpet, his cheeks red and his breath strained as he projected a spray of saliva. I feigned a blow to his head, "Dish-oom!", and discovered the joy of a timely pun, "You're Shushruth-aghan Sinha!"

Had Pankaj known at the time that Shushruth was his biological brother, he might have helped him get out from under my weight. Mum had mentioned this fact while shouting to be heard on a fuzzy overseas phone line to one of her cousins in India. Fortunately for adolescent eavesdroppers, the delayed voice transmission made her repeat herself as both sides tried to anticipate moments of silence. The same voice delay benefited me whenever my parents forced me to talk my grandparents in India:

"How are you?" they would ask.

"How are you?" I would ask.

"How are you?"

"I'm fine."

"Fine."

"Fine."

Anyway, I'd discovered Shushruth's mum (the middle sister) had been infertile, so Pankaj's mum (the youngest sister) had fulfilled her duty to give her second biological son (Shushruth) to the middle sister to raise as her own. Shushruth and Pankaj only learned the truth when they were much older.

As I straddled Shushruth, he began laughing with tears in his eyes. The door suddenly opened, and I worried that the world's greatest drama queen and tattle-tale, my sister Vineeta, might enter the room at any moment. Then my bum would have met the steady snare drum strike of my father's palm while I distracted myself searching for a face or animal in the psychedelic eggplant swirls of his polyester shirt. Instead, Pankaj's mum entered.

"What is this? Come on, 'shame shame'," she said.

I released Shushruth and stood up. "Shame shame" was her designated punishment whenever we misbehaved, and consisted of making us cross our arms, pull our own ears and squat up and down as she gestured tears down her face saying "Shame, shame. Shame, shame." I started bouncing up and down while Pankaj looked at me with his arms crossed, silently counting my squats with a satisfied faith in Indian grade school discipline until I began making farting sounds and laughing. Pankaj's mum pretended she didn't notice and left.

Pankaj saw his opportunity to reason his way to the title of Amitabh.

"You can't always be Amitabh."

I lowered my voice.

"Chup! Saaaaala, kuthe." Shut up! You no good dog. "Name one movie where his name was Pankaj."

"It doesn't matter, it's more about how well you imitate him."

Pankaj was a strange combination of determination and cowardice, his pout inversely arced to the smile of his belly, the rolls of fat exhibiting his family's prosperity relative to ours on the strength of a chain of Indian grocery stores they owned. We weren't in the same classes at school, but I knew that boys like him were called names like Paki, Haji, Gandhi, sand-nigger, towel-head, and had the blue shorts of their uniform yanked down if they weren't paying attention. He probably tried to ignore the taunts as a crowd gathered to join in, or took his Dad's advice to say something like, "Thank you, Gandhi was a great man" instead of offering to fight or retorting, "No one thinks you're cool for being able to kick my ass, just like no one thinks I'm cool for being way smarter than you."

"You think you look like Amitabh?" I asked.

As you know, Amitabh is tall and lanky, closer to my proportions. I even wore a turtleneck and plaid slacks like he sported in a number of movies throughout winter.

"No, but I can actually speak Hindi."

"I know Hindi. Bakwas bandh karo, aur ek goli maardunga." Stop the nonsense, or I'll shoot you.

"You only know Bollywood Hindi."

He had me on this point. My Hindi skills should have been decent after all the Bollywood movies I watched, but was mostly limited to:

Mein tumhare bachche ki maa bannewali hoo. I'm going to be the mother of your child.

Uski jaan, uske pariwar, uska sare khandan ke tukde (dramatic pause)...tukde kar dunga. I will tear up his life, his family, everything he owns, piece by piece.

Still, I wasn't going to easily concede my rightful Amitabh-hood.

"Well, you can be Amitabh if you let me have your James Bond car, right."

Pankaj and Shushruth always had the latest gadgets or sports equipment. I spent much of my time at their place wearing out the battery of their remote control cars or *making them chase errant soccer kicks. Shushruth actually looked more like me than Pankaj with his large, black-marble eyes and big grin (his flashed with naïve innocence and mine flashed with calculated mischief), so people often assumed we were brothers. Shushruth's mum would sometimes scold Shusruth for not sharing after he complained about me using his stuff even though I was the one who wasn't sharing his things with him. She was afraid to confront Mum about my behavior. Pankaj's mum wasn't shy about setting rules for all of us, even though she's the youngest sister.*

After Pankaj finally took his turn as Amitabh, wafts of fried onions had begun to reach us on the second floor. I could hear Mum and my aunts gossiping in the kitchen below us to the clinks of dishware as they prepared dinner. The three sisters talked every day, but never ran out of things to say. Gujaratis like us were usually vegetarian, though Dad and my uncles started eating meat to assimilate. Mum and my aunts learned recipes for lamb kheema and curry chicken from their Punjabi friends, even though they didn't eat it themselves. They called us down for dinner, where Pankaj's mum mentioned that Pankaj had won some mathematics honor. Mum countered with Vineeta's grades and debate successes, a sacrifice of the queen before Pankaj's mum's checkmate inquiry about how I was doing academically.

Later, Pankaj and Shusruth squished into the lower bunk bed which Vineeta vacated to sleep in my parent's room. I threatened to pee in my bed if either one snored. We drifted to sleep while arguing the merits of a Porsche (me, because it was sporty), Jaguar (Pankaj, because it was sophisticated), and Mazda 929 (Shushruth, because of the gas mileage).

Now some of you will read this anecdote and miss the whole point. You'll think, "Ravi Anjani is a jackass." You'll believe that justice, facts, logic, and mathematics honors will determine your lot in life. But look closely and you'll see that only one of us played Amitabh and walked away with a James Bond car. Pankaj and Shushruth are smarter than me. More considerate than me. More responsible than me. But cooler and successful?

Principle #3: It's not the smartest who succeed, but the savviest, the cool people with the fancy accent, cool name and willingness to re-define truth and take what they want. Fortunately, you can nurture yourself to coolness. You're in the right place for guidance. Pankaj, hope you're taking notes instead of joining some terrorist organization wiring bombs. If you want the James Bond car back, give me a call.

Chapter 3
Chump Change
Blackpool, England

Pankaj

On the car ride to Blackpool for Shushruth's bachelor party, Pankaj reminisced with Shushruth and Ravi about when their parents packed their three families into two cars every summer to go to Blackpool. They recounted strolling past the millions of light bulbs on the Golden Mile with an ice cream in hand, riding roller coasters on Pleasure Beach, competing for stuffed animals in the game parlors and taking donkey rides near the ocean shore. They joked about songs from Hindi movies they used to sing and pictures of them with tight shorts and bad haircuts. Though he didn't see them often—in fact, the three of them hadn't been together at the same time for years—they were his closest friends.

As they walked to their hotel, they marveled at Blackpool's renaissance, with a renovated Tower and main strip and host of new rides and upscale restaurants. They checked in before Pankaj ushered them to a classy pub called Covent Garden, with the scent of whiskey and sound of jazz instead of the yeasty beer taps and rock and roll of yesteryear. They decamped in a dark wood booth with a vintage monochrome poster, in which a woman in a striped hat and ballooned stockings sat on a unicycle drinking from a bottle of Coca Cola.

"Punk-Man, a bit formal for a night on the town, no?" Ravi asked while sliding into the bench next to Shushruth.

Punk-Man, Punk the Funk, Punky Brewster, Dr. Phunkenstein. Appellations which were an acknowledgment that Ravi thought he was cool, which mattered because Pankaj admired Ravi's ability to infiltrate Western society and even conquer it. His ability to avoid getting bullied, to make non-Indian friends and girlfriends, to wear an earring without looking ridiculous—to become a rock star. A rock star who had mastered the genius of Indian dishonesty, delivering every brazen lie with a sincerity that made Pankaj want to believe the particular lie even though he knew Ravi had just deceived him the sentence before, like his entertaining stories of hanging out with Madonna or being asked to play on the Rolling Stones album. Their relationship was the classic Indian combination of fraternity and mistrust, with the added spin that Ravi had genuinely achieved something and taken Pankaj along for the ride.

"Well, it's just for starters. I mean, we could go somewhere else afterwards," Pankaj said, contrite over having let Ravi down, but also excited about the possibility that Ravi would take them on a new adventure. "I thought we should keep it clean, you know we just had the puja."

"I forgot, you believe in that religious stuff. You still sleep in the room with your Mum's mandhir for Sathya Sai Babu?" Ravi asked.

"Yeah, why?"

"You might want to sleep bum side down just in case Sai Babu really is an incarnation of God and his floating spirit gets tired of little boys."

Pankaj didn't necessarily follow all the prophets or tenets of Hinduism, but Ravi's attitude toward religion would certainly explain why, despite his success and status, his life was a mess. Pankaj had heard from his mum that Ravi needed loans from his dad to stay afloat.

"C'mon, I'm joking, man. Just trying to get a smile out of you. I'm sure you've read the articles about his ashram, though. But whatever. Our little cousin is getting married. We've got to celebrate properly," Ravi said.

The waiter delivered two pints of Guinness and a glass of their finest scotch. Ravi gave a toast to Shushruth. In the shadows of their booth, Pankaj noticed that Ravi looked exactly like a less responsible version of Shushruth. Which was strange, because Shushruth looked nothing like Pankaj, his biological brother.

"You know, if you got the same haircut and clothing, the two of you might look alike," Pankaj said.

"And I'd save a lot of money on haircuts and clothing," Ravi said, looking at Shushruth.

Shushruth was sporting the only shirt in the Western hemisphere that managed to clash with a pair of jeans, some motley denim-plaid-corduroy quilt. Pankaj had counseled him to look at clothes that weren't on the clearance rack, but Shushruth couldn't overcome his upbringing.

"Not that you don't look perfectly nice. So, how'd you meet, ummm….your fiancée?" Ravi asked.

"My parents found out about her family through their friends and introduced us. We spoke a few times over Skype, we liked each other, so we said, 'Yes, let's get married!' I keep telling Pankaj he should do the same thing, then we can have kids at the same time," Shushruth said.

Shusruth was smart, so Pankaj never understood why he had agreed to an arranged marriage. His fiancée was mildly cute with her sparkling eyes, but also plump and simple. At their first meeting, Pankaj had asked whether she had any siblings, to which she replied, "No, silly! We're not even married yet."

Not to mention impetuous. While cooking with Shushruth's mum a week prior, she was briefly left alone with the Telugu-speaking housekeeper. She instructed the housekeeper in Hindi to cut the okra fingers. The housekeeper misinterpreted her gesticulations and began frying them, causing her to banish the housekeeper to the backyard porch in the rain until Shushruth's mum returned. The housekeeper quit, causing Shushruth to beg for her forgiveness by touching his head to her feet.

No nutter simpleton from India was going to drive Pankaj to touch his head to some housekeeper's feet. Perhaps Shushruth's medical training enabled him to view other's agitation with detachment, but Pankaj could never remain so blithe while the world made him its fool.

"It's not my thing. She's a nice girl, you guys are a good match, but I think about things differently," Pankaj said.

"Yeah, that's the problem, you think too much. I could understand if you were getting some. At least this way you'd be guaranteed some action. You prefer wanking while reading the Wall Street Journal. 'Oh, mortgage bonds, mortgage bonds!'" Ravi said.

"It's foreign currencies."

"Ah! Much more stimulating. 'The ruble! The ruble! The rupee!!! The ru..'"

Ravi stopped mid-sentence.

"Are you any good at trading?" he asked.

Pankaj slowly sucked the scotch between his teeth and rolled it on his tongue before swallowing, nourishing his taste buds with an affirmation of control. Was he a good trader? Was he drinking one of the best Scotches in the world? Was Blackpool the bachelor party capital of the UK? He shook the ice cubes, the slick transparencies melting down to their opaque core.

"Yeah, I'm pretty good."

"So if I gave you money to trade, you could make a bunch of money?"

Ah, that was Ravi's angle.

"It's not that easy. Sometimes you lose and even lose big, but over the course of the year, if you're any good, you make more than you lose. Anyway, I don't do any trading that presents a conflict of interest with trading for the bank."

Ravi nodded as if he was taking Pankaj' commentary seriously for once.

"That's too bad. Ah well. Anyway, you should consider getting married. I saw a picture of Shushruth's wife, she's a pretty girl," Ravi said.

"No thanks."

Pankaj stiffened his neck, swept saliva from the back of his mouth by jutting his jaw forward and swallowed it back down hard, a tic that triggered whenever he felt embarrassed. The fact that Pankaj had masturbated to the thought of Shushruth's fiancée was not an approval of what Shushruth was doing, but a necessity borne of the fact that she was the only young female he had spoken to in two months. There were no women working on the trading floor, and other women seemed to instinctively avoid him.

He watched Ravi peeling a layer off his coaster and tearing it into pieces. Why did women go for guys like Ravi over sensible, sincere men like himself? Not that Pankaj wanted the type of girl who would sleep with someone after a few dates. His parents had arranged a number of introductions with girls, but so far they had all seemed disinterested in finance and all that he had accomplished. It was just a matter of patience. Ideally she would be studying or working and could discuss the latest world events with him. She didn't have to cook—he was used to ordering in every night—though it would be a bonus if she did.

"This is good. I missed you guys. I don't know if you read my book, but we're like the three musketeers, you're my team, we have to stay in touch better," Ravi said.

Growing up, it did feel like they were the three musketeers—playing cricket in the yard, racing matchbox cars, watching movies together, kicking each other under the dinner table. Even after Ravi moved away, his summer visits made it feel like he had never left. They grew apart a little during university, but once Ravi's band started touring, Ravi invited Pankaj for an occasional bender that made it seem like they were at least the two musketeers, when Shushruth was busy with his residency.

Pankaj couldn't pinpoint when things had changed. The last few years, Ravi still invited him along, but spent more time talking to others than Pankaj. Which wouldn't have been a big deal, except for the *Guide*. It might as well have been titled *Ravi's Guide to Not Being Pankaj*.

Not that Pankaj cared. He had constructed a life where he was respected, graduating from London City College and working his way from a support position to a foreign currency trader for National United Bank. He was a Director earning 600,000 pounds a year, within striking distance of the big quid. This was the year he was up for promotion to Managing Director, a coronation that would finally allow him to eclipse Ravi's career. He grabbed beers at the pub with the other traders every Friday and sipped espresso at the corner cafe on Saturday morning while reading the paper through his black rectangular glasses, nodding at the other regulars.

"Yeah, the book. I don't recall that exact sentiment, but…whatever, this is about celebrating Shushruth's wedding and having a nice evening out," Pankaj said.

"With that in mind, we could sit here all night staring at each other, or we could take advantage of the fact that we are a few buildings away from some casinos."

"I don't know anything about gambling," Shushruth said.

"I'll teach you. I have been banned in some casinos, but in Blackpool they won't necessarily recognize me right away."

"You've been banned? For what? Inebriation?" Pankaj asked.

"Counting cards. I'm in the database."

"Bullshit, man. You can't add two and two."

"No, it's true. They usually try to mess me up by having the dealer talk to me to break my concentration or restricting me to flat bets. But we can get around all that with the two of you and the right casino."

"This should be good," Pankaj said.

"We've got two things in our favor. One, I know how to count cards, and two, I used to have a goatee, so they won't recognize me. Actually, three things. If we partner up, they won't realize I'm counting. I assume you know blackjack?"

"Of course," Pankaj said.

"So I'll start playing at the table. You play at the adjacent slot machine slowly losing a few nickels. When I scratch my head, that means the odds of the deck spitting out a ten is higher than normal, which means the dealer is more likely to go over 21 and you're more likely to win. So join the table and bet big on every decent hand. When I scratch my chin, you cash out, and then I'll meet you out front and we'll go somewhere else."

"How are you going to know what the odds of a ten are?"

"Don't worry about that. It's the Wong system of counting cards."

"Which is what?"

"Too complicated to explain."

Ravi had a habit of describing his ideas as "complicated" when he really just meant "illogical", like when he criticized his record label for dropping his band for dwindling sales.

"I'm smart enough to understand."

Pankaj had studied gambling strategies, which had similarities to currencies trading. If anything, it was Ravi who could never understand what it was like to trade currencies—all the inputs in the financial model, the gut feel on a large trade, the frenetic days holding one phone to each ear and using one hand to gesture yet a third message to someone standing in front of him, the stress of holding an unhedged position overnight, the fights with stupid brokers who didn't process an order correctly.

"Well you see, every dealer has a "tell", so you have to know how to read their look. You also have to look at the way they shuffle the cards," Ravi said.

"They usually use automatic shufflers."

"I'm just saying that's one element, it doesn't mean it's the only element."

"What does any of this have to do with counting cards?"

Pankaj pressed him on how he counted cards, and after five more minutes of nonsense, he finally admitted it was the standard Hi-Lo method, where cards were assigned a value: 2-6 = +1, 7-9 = 0, and 10-Ace = -1. The player kept a running tally of every card played. A high positive number with a low number of remaining decks meant there were more tens in the deck than non-tens and the player had a betting advantage.

"The main risk is that they assume a link between the brown fellows. Or they think you're a terrorist," Ravi said.

"Why do you keep saying I look like a terrorist?"

"When else did I say it?"
"In your book."

"Well, you have to admit, that beard scruffy thing you're doing looks suspicious. Not to mention this whole tacky purple button-down thing, though it could work out well for tonight. It'll make you look like a big bettor."

The whole situation was ridiculous, but Pankaj was curious how much money Ravi could manage to lose pretending to count cards. It would finally him a perfect story to make fun of Ravi for years to come instead of the other way around.

"*Bhaio*, I'm tired. I think let's just go the hotel, go to bed early and drive home in the morning," Shushruth said.

"First of all, we're booked for two nights. Second of all, we won't be out long. You can't come to Blackpool and not gamble. Grosvenor Casino isn't that far from here. We play for like an hour, then we'll leave," Ravi said.

"You heard the man, we should head home," Pankaj said.

"I promise, one hour and done," Ravi said.

Ravi covered the bill and led them to the single-story building near the shorefront. They walked through a small parking lot as the ocean swells whooshed peacefully behind the casino.

"So Pankaj, I heard your sister's pregnant. The new generation finally coming out. It's like the anticipation before those Star Wars sequels. Though I guess those were prequels. And they weren't so good. I don't know. Maybe more like…most sequels suck, don't they? Not that this kid will suck. Except literally, I guess he will, but we don't want to think about that." Ravi said.

They arrived at the front of the casino to the buzzing of go-kart engines on the adjacent track.

"The two of you go in through the entrance that way and get a bucket of quarters. I'll go in through the main door. Find the slot machines closest to the $100 Blackjack table and start playing until I scratch my chin," Ravi said.

"I thought you said scratch your head?" Shushruth asked.

"Head, chin, crotch, whatever. I'll scratch something. If the deck is in our favor, I'll scratch, let's go with my chin. Then you come to the table like I said before and bet big."

"And you expect us to finance the chips?" Pankaj asked.

"I'll get you back," Ravi said.

"I'm not interested in playing with my money."

"Well if you use my credit card, they'll know we're connected, and it defeats the purpose of my plan."

"So be it."

"Okay, I'll buy the chips. After ten minutes, one of you meet me in the bathroom closest to the entrance to get them."

Pankaj and Shushruth navigated the gambling floor and situated at machines with fruit scrolls. Pankaj went to the bathroom and waited. Ravi arrived a few minutes later to fund him with half his chips, twenty five hundred dollars' worth, and a bucket of quarters. Ravi departed to sit at the Blackjack table run overseen by a Filipino croupier with a gelled crewcut. Pankaj re-joined Shushruth and ordered drinks.

"It's like he thinks he's some secret agent," Pankaj said.

"Do you think he knows what he's doing?" Shushruth asked.

"Are you kidding me? He couldn't win a game of Go-Fish. He'd be better off putting the money in a savings account."

"Once he sees his friends settling down and having fun with their kids, he'll calm down, find joy in smaller things. He's good at heart," Shushruth said, depositing a coin and pulling the lever.

"You sound like our parents."

"What's wrong with that? It got us here."

"You go in for that traditional Indian stuff. Doesn't make sense to me."

"I like being Indian. It's made me a better person," Shushruth said.

"In what way?"

"Well, like…getting a good job, getting married, hopefully having children."

"Everybody does that. That's not Indian or non-Indian."

"But the families facilitate it. Mum and Dad always taught me to derive my happiness from the happiness of others. So there's that. It's not just about yourself or getting fancy things."

But it was about getting fancy things. Most of Pankaj's Indian colleagues were driving Mercedes and BMWs. What did being Indian mean to Pankaj exactly? People had to grow up as something—Indian, black, Chinese, Lithuanian—with the attendant cultural complications. Each person had to take what suited him—diet, music, values, living arrangements—to form an identity he could live with. Cultural background certainly played a part, but at what point did gleaning "cultural traits" in a *Guide* become racism? Was Indians' financial success a positive result of being industrious or being cheap? Were Indians morally conservative or backwards religious zealots?

Yet the liberal establishment would probably embrace *Ravi's Guide*, showing their fundamental contradiction—a desire to embrace cultural differences while pretending they didn't exist. If they really wanted to know what it felt like to be Indian, they only needed to know about one trait—the immense sense of self-loathing, at not being good enough at anything.

He pulled the lever of the machine for the third time, already bored by the mind-numbing repetition of this Pavlovian rat experiment.

"Maybe you should write a guide," Pankaj said.

"I actually thought his *Guide* was pretty good. I wouldn't have guessed he'd have so many insights about human behavior. Not that he always applies them in his own life."

"I heard some Indian kids on the Tube making fun of it. It's already outdated. They had tattoos on their arms and chains around their neck."

As they accepted their drinks from the waitress, Pankaj spotted the pit boss, a six foot five behemoth in a sports jacket and white turtle neck, at the far side of the room eyeing them. Did they stick out because Indians didn't usually gamble in Blackpool?

"Well, they were probably missing the point. I thought he was kind of indirectly making the case to be more Indian," Shushruth said.

"I didn't get that."

"Regardless, you have to admire the creativity."

"It was more like mythology. He makes more shit up than Tony Blair did."

"There's an art to that."

Pankaj hadn't planned on reading the book, but Shushruth had said that he should check it out if he didn't want to be blindsided by friends or family. Pankaj preferred reading *The Economist* or *The Financial Times* on the Tube to work, but had sacrificed them for a week to see the extent of the distortions. Of course Ravi had portrayed himself as some James Bond hero, defending the pathetically porcine Pankaj at a cricket match, sleeping with women around the world and mastering card games. All while mocking Pankaj's romantic vacuum, suggesting he was a terrorist and making his family's grocery store business sound like the product of greed instead of determination.

At first, Pankaj had stewed over every page, making notes in the margins which he turned into a letter as a response to Ravi's various assertions which he kept on his nightstand, notating it with additional arguments and examples that prevented him from falling asleep. Had Ravi played golf at Ballybunion in Ireland? Could he identify a '95 Chateau Cheval Blanc Bordeaux? Had he read *When Genius Failed: The Rise and Fall of Long Term Capital*?

But as the days passed, he had calmed down and ultimately stuck the ten page screed in a drawer instead of giving Ravi the satisfaction of knowing that he had gotten to Pankaj by mailing it. What was the point of joining this exhibitionist culture where no one had a right of privacy from embarrassing videos on the internet or tell-all blogs or guides on being cool? To sell out friends and relatives as meek cheap chumps in exchange for a few laughs and a few quid.

For forty-five minutes they pulled the slot machine lever, a mindless endeavor which Shushruth seemed to enjoy.

"You won!" Shushruth exclaimed as ten dollars' worth of coins clanged down.

"You do realize on average we're losing?"

"Of course. If you're going to lose the money, you might as well as enjoy it when you make a little back. You have to admit, this is kind of fun."

"It's like an elliptical machine without the exercise."

Pankaj did secretly enjoy the novelty of the evening. The charade was ridiculous, but strangely exciting, too. Ravi couldn't count cards, but if Ravi won money, even by pure chance, it would give the evening a mythical quality. The pit boss wasn't eyeing them anymore, so there was no reason to be paranoid. Maybe Pankaj was being too sensitive about Ravi. Every time they hung out, Pankaj had a good time.

"No one thinks less of you for saying it," Shushruth said.

"Okay, it's an okay time."

Ravi finally signaled for Pankaj to join his table with a conspicuous stare as he scratched his head instead of his chin and nearly tumbled off his stool. Pankaj stood up and realized that having fun with Ravi wasn't the problem. It was the inevitable hangover the next day when he would reflect on being treated like Ravi's lackey.

"Okay, see you later," Pankaj told Shushruth. "This should be a laugh."

As Pankaj sat down at the blackjack table pretending not to notice Ravi, Ravi excused himself to the bathroom, sweeping up what remained of his chips. Pankaj nodded at the other players and tapped the table to show he was in. He wasn't sure why Ravi thought they would win much money—Pankaj couldn't bet more than double on a given hand, and given that the casino was using four decks, even if Ravi was correct that the player's odds were higher, the difference would be negligible. The dealer dealt him a jack and eight vs. the dealer's eight. Good start. Double, stand, collect chips. The dealer distributed a seven and four vs. the dealer's King. Pankaj sensed someone standing behind him watching from behind. Double, hit, another win. More chips.

The man behind him tapped him on the shoulder.

"Excuse me sir, I'm sorry to interrupt. I work with the casino and just need to talk to you for a few minutes."

The pit boss. A sinking feeling in his stomach. He knew it related to Ravi. What had Ravi done? He could see Shushruth watching him, starting to get up. He shook his head, better if Shushruth stayed out of this. He collected his chips, stuffed his pockets and started walking with the pit boss to a hallway at the back of the room.

"Is there a problem?"

"We'd like to ask you a few questions, and then you'll be free".

Which of course wasn't true. The pit boss led him to a closed door at the end of the hallway and knocked. A man in an oversized suit opened it to reveal a tiny windowless room with eerie neon lights and a wall of mini televisions. The pit boss excused himself while the man in the suit closed the door and asked Pankaj to sit down at a small circular table. He produced a deck of cards and spread it out on the desk in front of Pankaj.

"Notice anything unusual?"

Strong Liverpudlian accent, like the man was one of the Beatles.

"No, should it?"

"Your friend made a few alterations while playing."

"What friend?"

The man stood up and fiddled with a computer and replayed some video footage showing Ravi leaving the table. Pankaj didn't know whether they had detained Ravi in another room.

"That friend."

"Don't know him."

"Okay, so now you're going to play dumb. Do we look stupid? Do you know how serious an offense it is to cheat at a casino?"

The man spoke with a strange indifference that belied the content of his words.

"If I had cheated, I'd worry about it. But I didn't."

The man picked up a King from the cards on the table and pointed out a notch on the side.

"Look at this. Your friend just happened to notch his fingernail on the upper right edge of every card worth 10, and lower right edge of every Ace."

So that was the issue. Ravi had actually attempted to mark the cards.

"My only friend was the guy I was playing with at the slot machines."

"Who has conveniently left the building."

"He's probably wondering where I am."

"Funny that he didn't think to wait around."

"Why aren't you questioning the man in the video?"

"What makes you think we aren't? You know, we get a lot of people in from London. They think they're smarter than us, with their posh accents and fancy watches.

But you'd be surprised how smart people often say things that don't make sense, particularly when one person says one thing and the other person says another."

The only time someone was finally noticing Pankaj's Breguet watch was in an interrogation. He unconsciously pushed the watch down his wrist.

There was no way Ravi escaped. Someone else was probably grilling him in another room at the moment. Maybe Ravi would leave Pankaj and Shushruth out of his confession. Even if he didn't, Pankaj wasn't the one marking the cards. So Pankaj was better off sticking to his lie and trying to escape the simple way.

"Look, it's late, I'll be happy to leave."

"I bet you would."

"In fact, I think I just will."

Pankaj stood up.

"Well, if you want to get your money back for your chips, you might want to hang on a bit longer."

If Pankaj sacrificed Ravi's money, it would look suspicious. But if the man asked how Pankaj had paid for the chips, he was also in trouble. At least the latter was a future problem. Pankaj sat back down.

"How long is this going to take?"

"Well, there's one more person I'd like you to meet."

The man called someone on a phone and disappeared. Pankaj fidgeted in his seat looking at his fingernails. When he realized he was intentionally being made to wait, he touched his pocket and realized he had forgotten his phone in the hotel room. After an hour, he stood up to leave but realized he had been locked into the room. He banged on the door for a few minutes without a response. He thought about using the desk phone, but the only numbers he knew by memory were of people who were asleep in Ealing. He accepted his fate and lay down on the floor to nap.

The door creaked open some indefinite time later—twenty minutes, an hour, two hours? Pankaj's eyes blinkered open to a buff man in a checkered peak cap. A limo driver? No, a copper. Pankaj stumbled up, stroked his head and wiped his eyes.

"Have a seat. You come here often?" the cop asked.

Pankaj staggered back into the chair.

"No."

"Ever before?"

"No."

"Gamble often?"

"Not really."

"So you were having drinks with your friends and you decided to go to the casino for the night?"

"I came with my friend. He's getting married. Thought we should do something out of the ordinary."

"Go on."

"That's it. We played the slot machines. A couple of hands of Blackjack."

"A couple. You mean a lot."

"No. Literally two."

The cop looked puzzled.

"Two?"

Pankaj nodded.

"Hold on."

The cop left the room to confer with the suit, who was standing outside. Pankaj saw the time: 4:48 am. He had been asleep for a couple of hours. They moved out of sight, but Pankaj could hear them debating something. The suit returned.

"So, today's your lucky day. If you'll leave us with your fingerprints, a headshot and an autograph, you will be a permanent celebrity at our casino. And we'll be happy to cash out your chips in exchange."

"This is wrong."

Pankaj paused, looking down at his hands.

"But it's late, so I'll do it."

The man shuffled through his drawers to retrieve an inkpad, a pen and the necessary papers. He guided Pankaj's fingers on the inkpad and the relevant papers and even gave him a wipe to clean his hands.

"How many chips do you have?"

Pankaj extracted them from his pocket and dumped them in the man's hands.

"So, how'd you pay?"

"I...had the chips from a visit last year."

Shit. He had contradicted himself, though only with the answer he had told the bobbie.

"Oh, you've been here before?"

The man in the suit stared at him.

"Is that odd?" Pankaj asked.

"No, just interesting. I'll be back."

Pankaj looked at the video screens for signs of Ravi or Shushruth. Nothing. The door was cracked open. Another forty five minutes before he heard his interrogator chatting with someone outside the office. Did the cop hang around and flag Pankaj's lie? Pankaj could overhear his interrogator say that the other two had somehow escaped the building. How was that possible? Why had they waited so long to apprehend Ravi? Or was the man saying that to see if Pankaj asked about Ravi and Shushruth to trap Pankaj into a confession? The interrogator came back in.

"So, it's interesting, your friend left the building at the same time the other person you say isn't your friend left the building. We pulled the video while you were sleeping."

Pankaj shrugged his shoulders and shook his head to demonstrate the irrelevance.

"I'm betting they had a chat."

"You've taken my fingerprints and contact information. You can always call me if you have more questions. Right now I'm tired. I've done what you've asked and just want my money and a good night's sleep."

The interrogator stared at Pankaj. Pankaj stared back. He could tell the interrogator was weighing whether to continue his power play or allow Pankaj to get away with his lie.

"Here's what I'm going to do. I'm going to hold onto your money. If everything comes back clean on you, we'll mail you a check this week."

"What bearing does my background have on the money? If I did something wrong, the courts can take care of it."

"For now, I don't care to deal with courts. I just want to make sure you and your friends weren't up to anything else. So consider this a security deposit until I find out."

Did Pankaj really care? It was Ravi's money. Let Ravi try to get it back.

Pankaj stood up to leave.

"Whatever. You have my address. I'll expect the check this week."

"Don't want to see you here again, understood?"

"You won't."

Pankaj dragged his feet out of the building. He was exhausted. Unsurprisingly, there was no sign of his cousins.

Blood rushed to his face in shame and anger. How could Ravi set him up like that and then just disappear? The words he had written in the letter he had never sent to Ravi flooded his brain. Ravi could apologize, shower him with gifts, praise him, save his life, but it wouldn't change the fact that Ravi made him feel small, insignificant, a cipher. Ravi was fatally flawed with ego, arrogance and dishonesty. If this was what a best friend did to another, they were better off not being friends.

Pankaj assumed Shushruth and Ravi had returned to the hotel. He reached the motorway and tried to flag a cab while preparing a diatribe for the ages.

The Review of
Ravi's Guide to Being a Cool Indian

"Cool to Be Cruel"
<u>Music Scene</u> – August 12, 2007
By James Ewert

I admit to being occasionally entertained by musician Ravi Anjani's tongue-in-cheek commentary about the dynamics of Indian society in his <u>Guide to Being a Cool Indian</u>, such as his observation that "you achieve vocational nirvana as an Indian by ascending the generational ladder from motel owner to engineer to Ivy League MD or MBA." However, the supposed memoir ultimately fails to deliver a detailed template for "being cool", a sophisticated take on the merits of assimilation by Indians into Western societies or any insight on Anjani himself. He hides behind absurd megalomaniacal dissimulations, such as his claim that his gambling has "drafted [him] into the casinos' card counter database."

In fact, no one has made so much out of such a trifling musical career since Vanilla Ice. Anjani repeatedly invokes his two minor hit songs as evidence of stardom (Vanilla Ice at least hit #1), but his vanity can't gloss over the fact that no record label is interested in his band Buzzthief post their horrific noise concoctions <u>Eclectic Bloom</u> from 2002 and <u>Sonic Wave</u> from 2004.

Having failed to invest time providing any real insight about being Indian or about his own life, Anjani tries to pre-empt an evaluation of his work: "I try not to read reviews anymore. Journalists have no training in the subject matter about which they're writing…" Perhaps that's true with regard to music, but with respect to <u>Ravi's Guide</u>, journalists of course have been trained to write. It doesn't take much training to conclude that Anjani should stick to his field of expertise, interviewing teenagers on the preeminent intellectual program <u>Cool Kids</u>.

Anjani's swipe at Indian literature for its focus on pathos also identifies his failure to understand what his <u>Guide</u> could really use—a description of even one relationship Ravi has with someone who loves him and whom he loves back. At the risk of being assaulted in a pub, I predict that Anjani may have a future in the late night circuit, but as an ostensible "guide", Ravi Anjani isn't Siddhartha, Deepak Chopra or even Ann Landers.

Chapter 4
Falafels
Blackpool, England

Ravi

Ravi snuck through a row of slot machines and ran into Shushruth walking briskly on the blue carpet through a perpendicular intersection.

"Some guy went up to Pankaj and…" Shushruth began.

"I know, come with me."

Ravi scurried towards the side exit. His leather jacket swung in and out with each step. Was this the time he had gone too far? He had done many immature things in his life and said many ridiculous things in his life, but he was the one to bear the consequences. If he went back in to take the blame, Pankaj and Shusruth might be able to drive home without disrupting any wedding festivities. On the other hand, if they didn't all give the same account to the bored Bobbies of Blackpool, it might also triple the chances of spending a night in jail and violating the sentencing terms of Ravi's probation.

A year prior, Ravi had drunkenly pushed a music journalist in a pub for giving the band negative reviews and comparing Ravi's songs to a "blenderful of pens", which unfortunately caused the journalist to fall, sprain his wrist and press charges. It was cruel for the journalist to dismiss the years Ravi had spent perfecting his song craft in exchange for a cheap laugh. Though was that what Ravi had done to some of his family members in the *Guide*?

Two days ago, Ravi had convinced the magistrate that the push was accidental and escaped with a day of street cleaning in London, subject to a probationary period.

"What about Pankaj, shouldn't we help him?" Shushruth whispered.

"Nah, he didn't do anything, they'll let him go."

Could they really have detected the marked deck? The gambler on YouTube made it seem like it was nearly impossible to catch.

Ravi broke into a run after exiting the doorway, but a coughing fit allowed Shushruth to pull ahead of him. They crossed the motorway to a side street full of two-story lodgings, a blend of residences and bed and breakfasts. They gasped for air while walking briskly.

"You sure we shouldn't go back in?" Shushruth asked.

There were many things Ravi wasn't sure about. They had cleaned the mafia out of most the US casinos, but he wasn't sure if they were involved in the UK ones. And if they were involved, he wasn't sure if they were somehow connected to Dalinc's organization. And if they were connected to Dalinc's organization, he wasn't sure if they would pull a gun on Pankaj. At the same time, Pankaj really hadn't done anything.

"Look, if you get arrested and miss your wedding, it will raise more problems than if only Pankaj doesn't show up. Beyond which, he can handle himself. I bet he's out of there soon," Ravi asked.

"So, then what?"

"Let's grab some food. Then we come back to see if he's come out."

"Why don't we try calling him?"

"Then they'll see who's calling."

"Maybe I should go back in. They don't know who I am," Shushruth said.

"If you go in, then they'll try to get you to contradict whatever he said, even though no one did anything. Pankaj didn't do anything, they'll let him go."

"How do you know they'll let him go?"

"What are they going to get him for? Putting coins in a slot machine and playing two hands of Blackjack? Look, we can eat here and check back in a little while."

After twisting through a couple of streets, they stood on Station Road in front of an establishment called "Kebab Kasbah", surrounded in smaller letters by "French fries", "falafels" and other nutritional hazards. They entered and approached the counter, where Ravi ordered a falafel and Shushruth ordered a grilled cheese from a Middle Eastern man with a beard. They sat at a small table against the wall.

"So what just happened?" Shushruth asked.

"Not really sure. After I left the table, I accidentally went into the women's bathroom. Some woman gave me a dirty look, so I left and saw someone in a suit with an earpiece standing outside the men's bathroom. When I got back to the floor and saw the pit boss talking to Pankaj, I figured it was time to leave."

"So they were looking for you."

"Maybe. I didn't care to find out."

"Except that Pankaj is left picking up the pieces."

If he mentioned his probation, it would get back to his aunts, which would get back to his parents and set off a different firestorm. He needed to maintain his charade a bit longer.

"If they detained me, we might have been there the rest of the night. At least he'll be out in a little while."

The logic made sense, though Ravi knew it looked like an act of cowardice. Ravi saw Shushruth silently pondering the evening while scratching designs into his placemat with his fork. The back cook delivered their food and a coffee for Ravi.

"We'll go back in a little while," Ravi offered. "One of us can go back in."

Shushruth nodded.

"Why do you enjoy the gambling?" Shushruth asked.

"You can win big."

"You can also lose big."

"Some people think like that, some people think like rock stars."

"I've heard that you lose more than 50% of the time. The casino is the one making all the money," Shushruth said.

"Unless you bet big on good hands and small on bad hands. When the odds aren't in your favor, you just have to play more often. Eventually, the royal court will tap your shoulder."

"I guess that's another way to look at it."

"It's the only way to look at it. It's what got me here. Vineeta says I need counseling, but what exactly have any of these therapists done with their lives? I've actually lived. I wanted to be a rock star and I am. How many people have written one platinum album and two top forty songs? I wanted fame, and they almost dedicate a column to me in the *Daily Mail*. The only thing missing is a little hacienda in the islands with Pilar, recording music and hanging with you guys. I mean, I'd miss playing Wembley or appearing in *NME*, *Melody Maker*, *Q* and *Uncut* at the same time, but I don't need it. I just need some money."

"Money for what?"

Ravi stared at the tahini leaking onto his finger from his sandwich. He should have picked up a napkin to stop it, but it felt more natural than the speech he had just given. The words were a reflex, a tic of showmanship that was completely at odds with the fact that he had gotten his cousin detained at a casino, was in debt to a loan shark and was about to have his show get canceled. He could take them back, confess to Shushruth that he knew he was putting on a show. He felt the urge to open up, but couldn't show his vulnerability to the younger cousin who had always looked up to him.

"Nothing, an album I'm recording."

He could theoretically confess his sins to Ian the next day. On the one hand, Ravi's best friend and lead singer of Buzzthief. On the other, someone who had required ten phone calls to be convinced to come to London to testify in court so Ravi could avoid jail time for the bar fight, and in fact hadn't returned Ravi's phone calls since Ian had started dating his latest girlfriend. Ravi had written in the *Guide* that his best "friendships [were] grounded in loyalty to a person, but…some friendships only exist within a context." While the band was together, Ravi had been so busy with gigs, studio sessions, parties and travel that he had never reflected on the fact that maybe for Ian, their friendship only existed within the context of the band, even though they had been roommates in college. So maybe the right person to talk to was not Ian, especially after this failed casino outing. Ravi needed to convince Ian to re-form the band in time for the lucrative corporate Christmas parties, which he couldn't do effectively while also venting about his life.

After he finished his falafel and pulled out his wallet out to leave a tip for the cook/cashier/busboy, he realized that karma was pointing him in a different direction: on top of his driver's license was the picture with Pilar. She was the last person other than Ian whom Ravi had trusted with his authentic self. She always had good advice. Maybe she could offer him a pathway out of his mess. If he could get her contact info, maybe she would give him a second chance.

***

Pilar had introduced herself to Ravi with an ice cube down the back of Ravi's shirt at a post-concert party in Madrid. A series of rhythmic flamenco dance songs played on the stereo at the Café Central. It was a large room with a grand piano in the middle and an elegant bar fronting a fancy coffee machine and an arrangement of alcohol bottles. The organizer had booked it for the private gathering after its typical jazz show had ended.

"Whoa!"

"You looked hot. I thought you could use some air conditioning," she said.

Ravi turned around from the small group discussing something meaningless and laughed.

"Is that how they do it here?"

She smiled suggestively.

"That was a good show tonight. I really like the way you play the classical guitar on 'Somewhere Slowly', it's really beautiful."

Pilar beamed proudly at the fact that she was indeed Pilar. Her curly brown tresses flowered down from a headband, framing an exaggerated Mediterranean visage—thick eyelashes, a slightly round nose, full lips. A picture of Pilar made her appear cute, when in person she was enchanting. She had a small diamond pierced into her nose and a dark green vine tattoo ringing her upper left arm. She wore jeans and a tank top with a picture of Che Guevara. Ravi was surprised to find that she has been invited to the party as his guest, an acquaintance of Pankaj.

"Come, this is a good song, let's dance."

Her Spanish accent peaked in unusual places and made him focus to understand her. She grabbed his hand and pulled him to an area that had been cleared of its tables and chairs and could be interpreted as a dance floor. She moved her hands above her head like a flamenco dancer and shimmied around him. Courtship on tour didn't follow standard rules. No dinner dates in a week.

Pretty soon they were intertwined in a kissing dance and then wrestling in his tour bus bed before she called off the finale as premature. As she was leaving, he noticed a pocket book copy of the US Constitution in her purse. He asked her why she had it, and she said she liked to study it and think about why America became the dominant super-power of the world on the back of a single document. He immediately knew she was smarter, deeper, more insightful and curious than him, which gave him more of a sexual thrill than he had ever felt before. He invited her to join them in Paris. He still had their picture in front of the Eiffel Tower, her in a blue manga t-shirt borrowed from Ian and him in a Buzzthief t-shirt, both with an affected sneer and a dangling cigarette.

Over a bottle of wine that first evening, Pilar asked him what he thought the next album would sound like. He said he wasn't sure. She said that he should experiment more with tracks like the slow tempo closer "Without You" instead of trying to rewrite their two hits. Ravi had written that song on a keyboard. The synthesized strings conveyed some emotional truth about himself which he wasn't able to convey with words.

His ex-girlfriends were always interested in his true feelings and capacity for empathy. Were feelings ever true? Real men didn't coddle feelings, they controlled them. He liked living in the moment. Yet before meeting Pilar, his mind had begun struggling with a dark labyrinth of jealousy, insecurity and pride—about inferior bands with greater popularity, Indians who had made more money, people who had never heard of him, women who preferred other men.

They were on a ferry boat to one of the Greek isles a few days later, a day off in between performances. He leaned on the railing entranced by the waves in the moonlight, undulating like the heartbeat of the planet.

"Sometimes this all seems kind of meaningless," he said.

"What do you mean?"

"Music, performing. Like people act like you're a big deal one day, but they move on to some other artist the next. So it's not you that matters. You're just playing a role. If it wasn't you, it would have been someone else."

"But it was you. And it wouldn't have been someone else in the same way. Like the Beatles. If it wasn't the Beatles, who would it have been?"

"Yeah, but that's the Beatles. I'm not Paul McCartney."

"To some fans, you are. Maybe not as many as Paul McCartney, but if anything, he's the one who is just playing a role. Now he has to be 'Paul McCartney' wherever he goes, he can't just be some guy Paul who enjoys normal things, but you, you can just be Ravi the rock star when you feel like it, and Ravi the regular person whenever you feel like it."

Pilar had a special talent for repeating his thoughts back to him in a way that made it sound like there was a purpose to the whole thing. She had a special talent for telling the truth without making it sound bad.

Within a week they had become more intimate, and she had encouraged experimentation in the public parks, janitor's closets, movie theaters. She electrified the setting, making anything seem possible or better than it was. While Ravi needed alcohol to unlock his personality, her vivacity didn't require such fuel or mask deep emotional scars. She updated her parents, corporate lawyers in Barcelona, on her whereabouts every morning. His bandmates Ed and Steve called Pilar his wife, annoyed that he had broken an implicit pact to go out every night and give high fives in the morning, like picking up girls was a team-building activity he refused to show up for.

Pilar was a stabilizing force. Life on tour was more work than it seemed. In the morning, the band had to make sure no one needed to be bailed out from jail. They visited the venue to see how their equipment would be set up. They rehearsed to work out kinks. In the afternoon they did interviews with the local papers and then spent an hour on social media promoting the band. At night they performed regardless of a headache or a cold or diarrhea. In the late night, they tried to seem appreciative of fans who knew their opinions and habits better than they did (to the extent the stage speakers hadn't made them deaf). In the morning they took a cramped tour bus with stained velvet seats to a new city. They argued with each other over who was spending, drinking or copulating too much, and with their manager about why he wasn't promoting them properly or why he claimed they were running out of money.

Ravi remembered the call with Pilar after he had returned to New York. She had been about to start work at a law firm in Barcelona. She asked him what he wanted. He could have invited her to find a job or get a Masters of Law degree in New York and live with him, but he worried that the relationship would have less allure stationed in one place. He was fine giving up other women, but giving up the lifestyle and status he had worked so hard to achieve? It would have meant the end of hanging out with Ian and his friends, of going out for late night poker games, of retreating to a recording studio whenever he felt like it, of waking up whenever he wanted. And if it hadn't worked out, he might have found it difficult to break up with her after having dragged her across the Atlantic. He had needed to be sure she was the one first, so he had suggested they go on a vacation together on her next break, but she had said she wasn't interested in a part-time commitment. They had spent enough time together on tour for him to make a decision. He had clearly made the wrong decision, which seemed to spawn many more afterwards.

He had kept calling her, but at some point she had mentioned going on dates and eventually stopped answering. And now, after eighteen months of silence, he had found that her phone number had been changed and her "aol.com" email address was no longer active.

***

"Why don't you take a job, find a good wife and settle down?" Shushruth asked while finishing the last of his grilled cheese.

"Well, it's funny you should mention settling down. There was a girl I used to date on tour, Spanish. I fell out of touch with her, but she's friends with one of Pankaj's friends. I was hoping to ask Pankaj to ask his friend for her latest contact info," Ravi said.

If Pilar was still single, he would invite her to New York and try to bring some order to his life. "Marriage" lurked as a term in his sub-conscious.

"You can ask Pankaj for her contact info when we get him back," Shushruth said.

"Funny irony, trying to advance my romantic life through the most desperately celibate man in Europe. He might not be in a talking mood. Anyway, she's probably married or something."

"Don't worry, we can get the number. I'll make sure he gives it to you."

"He seemed upset with the book, too. It seems it's rubbed a few people the wrong way."

"Were you writing because you thought it was funny, or because you thought others would think it's funny?" Shushruth asked.

Ravi had thought publication of his *Guide* would fuel a third act to complement the band's reunion. MTV had polled its employees for ideas about drawing more young Asian viewers because they had high discretionary incomes. Ravi pointed out that their incomes were higher because they were more studious, so MTV should be selling them books instead of video. Something literate and hip, like *Leo's Guide to Shagging Supermodels*, *Tom's Guide to Becoming a Midget Superstar*, *Oprah's Guide to Starting a Cult*, *Kim's Guide to Being a Well-Rounded Exhibitionist*.

A senior executive asked him to attempt writing a book, which he declined until ideas blossomed as he showered, ate and slept. He started a notebook of advice and reminiscence which an editor shaped into a narrative she labeled a "self-help memoir". He felt confident about the book's potential as an impulse buy at the cash register until the *Music Scene* journalist did his hatchet job to look witty. Ravi was tired of opinions from journalists who had never worked through pacing, style, emotional resonance, continuity, credibility and point of view. These charlatans who equated whether they liked something to whether it was good or not. Ravi hated Bob Dylan, but knew he was talented. He loved one of Take That's singles, but knew it was terrible. Didn't journalists have more important things to do, like figure out if the president was lying, than analyze his book like serious literature?

"I usually assume that's the same thing."

"I don't think that's the best assumption. You probably need to swallow your pride and say sorry," Shushruth said.

Ravi saw a cockroach scurry across the floor.

"I thought I did apologize. I told him I screwed up, right?"

"I don't think you did. And acknowledging a screw-up isn't the same as preventing a future one."

"Obviously I'm not going to do the same thing."

"That's true. Tonight you did something different," Shushruth said. "Anyway, it's not about assigning blame. If the two of you talk, you can work everything out."

Shusruth delivered advice with the placid disposition of a psychiatrist. But even psychiatrists had an ulterior motive. Shushruth was like some strange alien, not only acting sincerely and without resentment but believing that everyone else was capable of the same.

"I know, you're right." Ravi glanced at his watch. "Let's go back."

They began the walk back to the casino. The street was a strange sequence of quaint two story homes and more industrial buildings that housed fast food restaurants, discount stores and small amusement parlors with colorful, decrepit frontage signs. Nothing else was open.

Should he volunteer to go back in? If they detained him and the court discovered he had violated his probation by trying to cheat at a casino, he would miss Shushruth's wedding and humiliate his family. But if he sent Shushruth in instead, he'd be compounding his cowardice. It was rare that he didn't know what decision to make.

"What were you saying about money? I can help you out if you need it," Shushruth said.

"That's generous, but this is a different level of money we're talking about," Ravi said.

What little Shushruth had to offer wasn't worth the risk of having the extended family learn about Ravi's predicament.

They crossed the street as a chilly wind blew off the water. His head spun from the intensity of the deliberation. He felt slightly nauseous, but as he walked past the parking barriers, he decided to continue through the casino doors, telling Shushruth to remain outside. A blank feeling of calm flowed through him. Having accepted the possibility of being detained, he wasn't worried about it happening. He would just claim he had a nervous habit of pressing his fingernails into things.

A different pit boss stood off in the corner looking at his cell phone. Ravi hurried in before he looked up. Checkpoint one cleared. He scanned the tables and slot machines without anyone accosting him. No Pankaj. Checkpoint two cleared. He returned to the scene of the crime. A different blackjack dealer manned the table.

"You can play for only five dollar stakes," she offered.

"Sorry, not here to gamble. I was looking for someone. Did you happen to see another Indian fellow around?"

She shook her head.

"Semi-bald, shirt unbuttoned to here?"

She shook her head again. Checkpoint three cleared. He took another lap around the casino and observed the pit boss from behind a slot machine. The pit boss would probably know what had happened to Pankaj. Ravi started walking in his direction, but at the last moment veered to the exit. No need to press his luck. Pankaj wasn't there.

He exhaled as he left the casino and approached Shushruth, who looked at him with kneaded eyebrows.

"He wasn't there. Did he call you?" Ravi asked.

Shushruth shook his head and tried dialing Pankaj's phone without success.

"He must have returned to the hotel. Let's take a cab there," Ravi said.

They hailed a black taxi out front, entering the back booth in seats facing each other on their way to the Imperial Hotel. Ravi lit a cigarette and cracked open the window. Shushruth brushed his nose twice with the back of his index finger and held back a cough. He had not only blown the money his father had just lent him, but had also managed to get Pankaj detained.

"All in all, a good trip," Ravi said.

"How can you say that? Pankaj isn't with us. He could be anywhere."

"I was being sarcastic. It would have been a good trip for him if he was with us. But now he's got a story to tell. Is the smoke bothering you?"

"No, it's fine."

Ravi tossed his cigarette out the window and rolled it back up. He thought of a way he could make it up to Pankaj.

"I should quit anyway. I heard you been curing cancer, or something like that. What's that about?" Ravi asked while pecking out an email to his agent.

It was already the workday in New York, so she could deal with his request immediately.

"I'm working at a research lab. We're trying to see what effect a certain type of protein has on cellular division, then see if we can block it from happening in cancer cells."

"Impressive stuff. You're saving lives, I'm interviewing high schoolers who's main goal in life is to have me tell them they're cool."

The taxi pulled up to the brick building, a stately manor with over one hundred rooms topped with dormer windows. They climbed the stairs to their room overlooking the sea, but entered their room to find no sign of Pankaj.

"Well, now what?" Ravi asked.

"Should we call the police?"

"And what would we tell them? I mean, he'll probably show up in a little bit, it hasn't been that long."

Ravi spotted a cell phone on the desk.

"He forgot his phone here, so we can't call him."

They kicked off their shoes and lay down on separate beds debating Pankaj's possible whereabouts. Ravi shook himself awake a couple of times, until he finally saw Shushruth asleep on the other bed. He turned the light off, lay back down on the bed and drifted into a peaceful slumber before he realized that the loud knocking he started dreaming about was actually loud knocking in real life.

Shusruth reached the door first, allowing in a crack of light.

"You made it," Shushruth groggily said.

"What the fuck was that?" Pankaj asked, stepping past Shushruth and glaring.

Ravi leaned over to turn on the night lamp. He closed his eyes at the shock of light, before allowing them to gradually adjust to a vision of Pankaj, with red eyes, stubble and a worn face that made him look twenty years older. Ravi wasn't quite ready for a high energy dispute.

"We can get into the details, but are you okay? What did they do to you?" Ravi asked.

"I spent the night in an office answering questions that were meant for you. I could have gotten you thrown in jail," Pankaj said, pointing his finger at Ravi in rage.

"And I'm grateful you didn't. And sorry you got nabbed."

Ravi tried to hold his face still to show that he was sincere, which he was, but as his brain processed the scenario—Pankaj fuming like a maniac in the middle of the night in Blackpool after getting detained in a casino—he also felt his lips twitch with a strange urge to laugh, like when they were kids and something silly had just happened. He jumped out of bed before Pankaj could see it and retrieved his phone. He scanned his emails and saw the one he had asked his agent to arrange for.

"I thought you might still be a little sore, so I did a little something. What do you think about this?" Ravi asked, thrusting his phone forward.

Pankaj looked down without taking it.

"Come on, take a look."

Pankaj relented and began reading.

AP (September 18, 2007)

It has come to my attention that my recent work entitled "Ravi's Guide to Being a Cool Indian" may have offended some of my friends and relatives, and that my behavior has not always met the standards I wish to uphold. I wish to assure everyone that the work was intended primarily in jest, and that it is solely my fault if some of my exaggerations may have cast others in a comical light. I offer my sincerest apologies for the aforementioned and herewith wish to demonstrate my goodwill by offering all future profits on the book to charity.

Sincerely, Ravi Anjani.

"Is it a…press release?" Pankaj asked.

"Had my agent send it out first thing this morning," Ravi said.

As he had drifted off to sleep the night before, he had already conceived of a whole series of press release apologies he could do. 'Rock star apologizes to Japanese girl—I don't remember your name, but we hooked up in that park close to the subway near that big temple in Tokyo. I promised to send you some signed CDs for your autistic brother, but then I left your address in my pants which we sent for cleaning. If you reach out to my management company, I'll make sure we get you a signed copy of our latest CD.' "Rock star apologizes to College Professor: Professor Wilshire, I know you suspected me of cheating on all of our exams, but the fact is, I only cheated on one quiz after a late night gig with the band, which only counted for about 5% of our overall grade and I was likely to have scored at least 60% on anyway, so it didn't make much difference in the end. However, I apologize for betraying your trust.' 'Rock star's Personal Plea to Dalinc—I should have paid you back by now. I will pay you back soon. You've made your point, and you don't need to make any further demonstrations of how serious you are.'"

The press releases would demonstrate his reformation as the new improved Ravi, one capable of self-reflection and remorse.

"It not only hits the high points, it does so publicly. It's like that commission they had in Africa, what was it, that truth commission, where people had to publicly admit they killed someone and express remorse? I mean, anything I did can't be as bad as killing someone, right? So it's almost like I've done more than I should have to do," Ravi said.

"Interesting point," Shushruth said.

"You're an idiot," Pankaj said. "Not just an idiot, a fucking idiot. Not just a fucking idiot, a…a…"

"Fucking fucking idiot?" Ravi asked.

If it had been later in the day, he would have filtered that one out.

"Ah, fuck you," Pankaj said, turning back towards Shushruth.

"I would have thought you liked the efficiency of it," Ravi said.

"I…I…I" Pankaj stuttered. "You realize I almost got arrested because you tried to cheat. At a casino for fuck's sake!"

"I mean, I didn't cheat, right. The system wasn't working, is all," Ravi said.

"Your fuckin' system! It's just the basic Hi-Lo method of counting cards, which you have no ability to actually use, so you tried to mark the fuckin' cards," Pankaj said.

"You know, it's still early, people might hear us," Shushruth noted.

"That wasn't the system. That was the back-up plan."

"So you planned it?" Pankaj asked.

"Well, I saw this book about some blokes who count cards, right. But then I made improvements upon their method of counting cards, which including little reminders I put on certain cards to help with the counting. So in a way it was part of the Wong system which I had fully disclosed before we went to the casino."

Grudges never made sense to Ravi. Fight, argue, move on. He didn't understand why so many people invested in a portfolio of drama when there were adventures and comedies available. Pankaj composed part of his own identity, bridging eras and familial relationships, yet Pankaj portrayed him as malicious and dishonest, when his actions were at worst negligent. He was willing to try harder, though his life wasn't structured like Pankaj's.

Shushruth fanned his palm outward and said, "*Bhai-bhen* (*brothers and sisters*), let's put this behind us and have fun today."

"How would you feel if I stranded you?" Pankaj continued.

"I mean, that wouldn't be so bad, I know Blackpool pretty well. I get your point, but it's not like we didn't come back for you. And remember, things could just as easily have gone the other way. We could have walked out with bags of money, waitresses on our arms and people cheering your name, 'Pankaj! Pankaj!' But I get your point. I shouldn't have left the place. It was a mistake. It was a big mistake. Like the press release says, I apologize," Ravi said.

This was usually the point when most people in Ravi's life would chuckle and let him off the hook for being Ravi. They forgave his Ravi-ness because deep down they knew he loved them and liked the excitement of hanging out with him. Things sometimes got out of hand, but it was Ravi being Ravi. Pankaj understood that deal as well as anyone. Was this time seemed different, or would it just take a little more smooth-talking?

"You're unbelievable," Pankaj said.

"That's what she said."

He noticed Pankaj glaring, jutting his jaw and sweeping saliva from the back of his mouth before swallowing to suppress the tic. Maybe he should have previewed his press release with Shushruth. Though maybe this was just the intermediate step before Pankaj forgave him. If he showed he cared about Pankaj, this whole thing would blow over. He grabbed each ear with the opposite side hand and began squatting.

"Come on. 'Shame, shame. Shame, shame.'"

Pankaj shook his head in disgust.

"Oh, fuck off. Everything for you's a joke. Some of us have real lives and don't care to explain ourselves to a copper. You're an idiot. Bona fide idiot." Pankaj said. "Stop talking to me."

Ravi sat back down on the bed. His grogginess started wearing off, making him feel like himself again. His verbal tricks weren't going to get him out of this one. He became aware of his socks and jeans, a costume that couldn't hide the fact that he was a charlatan in clothes. For months now, he had been given little reminders that he wasn't the transcendent star he had thought he was.

He had imagined this wedding trip restoring his confidence. At least with his cousins, he had always been the acknowledged leader. He thought back to the days he and Pankaj had spent as kids playing cricket, play-acting spy movies or roaming Harrods. Now his reign as the king of his cousins had come to an end. Pankaj was moving to a different kingdom. With the convergence of his professional and social status, he felt like what he really was, just another person.

He looked up.

"Look, I know I'm not always the easiest guy, I like to follow life where it takes me, and you like to make life do what you want, so sometimes there's a mismatch in outcomes, etcetera etcetera. But the main thing is, we've had a life together, and so we're part of each other whether you like it or not. And see, if you want to know the one thing that's cool about being Indian, it's that. Americans get annoyed with their family and ditch them. Indians get annoyed with their family and double down. Maybe it's some guilt complex, but we're wired to keep coming back, because we know that no one else is really going to care what happens to us when we get older. I care about you, and despite all the things that have happened, I think somewhere deep down you care about me. Which is all to say, I'm sorry about all… the stuff."

He looked at Pankaj for a reaction. It was hard to express his true emotions without a smirk or other gesture that indicated that he didn't take his emotions seriously.

Shushruth walked over to Pankaj, who was shuffling through items in his suitcase.

"He's apologizing. Let's get past this," Shushruth said.

"I don't want to think about it right now," Pankaj said without turning around.

"I mean, the best part about the last few years was just hanging out with you and Ian and the others. I loved the rest, too, but what did it all mean?" Ravi asked.

He didn't like to reveal his vulnerability and true thoughts to other people— his success in the West had been premised on never allowing himself self-pity. But lately he had been feeling that he had been chasing a mirage, that the entire premise of his career was to earn acceptance from Westerners. Maybe he needed to show Pankaj that they weren't all that different in order to earn his forgiveness.

"Meaning?" Pankaj said.

"What's the whole point? We work, we play, it's fun, but so what?"

"Everyone wonders what for. I've been wondering that since I was five," Pankaj said.

"Yeah, that's true, you did. I always thought you thought too much. But now I'm thinking too much. I guess if I don't stop, I'll end up like you," Ravi said.

Pankaj recoiled his head.

"What's wrong with ending up like me?" Pankaj asked.

"Nothing's wrong. It's just…at some point, you lost your sense of humor."

"That's because at some point your humor just became making fun of me."

Ravi looked at the ceiling with his lips twisted to one side and his eyebrows knitted in thought. He looked askance before flickering his eyes between Pankaj and the floor.

"Well, I thought…I didn't realize…you know, then my apology is meant to cover that, too," Ravi said.

Pankaj looked around the room as if he was weighing the need for Ravi's friendship.

"Maybe I've lost some of my sense of humor. The world tells you what part of your personality it's willing to pay for, so you double down on that. Pretty soon it's all you're left with, and you can't get back what you already lost because you've changed too much," Pankaj said.

"You're right. See, it's like I went one way, and you went the other, but we both just got lost in different ways, and now we're trying to get heading in the direction we had started out for in the first place," Ravi said, pausing.

He braced his chin with his hand and reminisced about his years with the band. It wasn't all meaningless. He had written songs he was proud of. He had formed good friendships. He had met Pilar.

"Not that I would change anything that's happened," he added.

Shushruth sat down next to Ravi. Pankaj pulled up a chair and sat across from Ravi, seemingly engaged by the topic.

"I've thought about that question a lot. If I'm being honest, for years I thought I wouldn't change anything too, but now I've started to realize I was just rationalizing my existence so that I wouldn't feel inferior to you. Because if I would trade my intellect for your experience, then that would mean you won. And it's tough feeling like Salieri when Mozart is a clown."

"Ravi's not a clown," Shushruth said.

"See, everyone thinks I'm just a clown. That impression always pissed me off a bit. Because it took a lot of hard work to get where I did. Harder than just interviewing for a job and sitting at a desk, no offense. But people think it's some magic wand that I just wave and people do my bidding," Ravi said.

"It's not mutually exclusive. You're a successful clown. My point was just that I used you as my barometer of success even though I didn't want to. I couldn't help myself," Pankaj said.

"You never needed to. My parents always held you up as the standard bearer in the family. At least career-wise. 'Pankaj is a Director.' 'Pankaj is making six figures.'"

Pankaj shifted in his seat and put his hand over his mouth, though Ravi could tell he was hiding a smile.

"Well…"

"But our parents never put any value on the social side, which is where you could have used some help," Ravi continued.

Ravi had invited Pankaj on a few of the band's tour dates and witnessed Pankaj alienating every girl backstage by telling them why their favorite band sucked or their understanding of a political issue was naive. Then he blamed their lack of interest on his being Indian. Even with men, he would insult them behind their back to make himself feel better. It's as if his mum's constant lectures made him insecure even though they gave him everything else. He was always so arrogant that Ravi never tried to advise him on how to improve, though maybe Ravi could help rectify that as penance.

Pankaj leaned back into his chair.

"That doesn't come naturally to me."

"That's what I'm saying. You could have learned it. Who's born saying, 'What's up, bro?' It's all an act. You just chose to play the straight man."

"That's easy for you to say, because the lines come naturally to you."

"When people are calling you 'Haji' and 'Paki', nothing's natural."

"I didn't know they called you that, too," Pankaj said.

"Because if I had told you, they would have won," Ravi said.

"You don't think you would have been successful if you weren't Indian?" Shushruth asked.

"Sometimes I think I wouldn't have been successful at all if I wasn't Indian."

"Because of the work ethic?" Shushruth asked.

Shushruth always wanted to conclude that Indians succeeded because of their superior work ethic.

"Because I would have less to prove. They could call me Haji, but I achieved their dreams. I could get their girls. I could make them want to be me."

"Isn't that what you wanted?" Pankaj asked.

"Maybe I just wanted to be accepted. And it's a lot harder when you don't look and act like everyone around you."

"I didn't realize you had put that much thought into it," Pankaj said.

"That's because I realized no on in America cares about what we think, so I kept my thoughts to myself."

"You don't think you lived the life you were meant to live?" Pankaj asked.

"I lived the life I had to live. We grew up in the West. Either we adapted or we didn't. I'd rather win at their game than lose at mine. None of us really exist, we're just a reaction to our circumstance," Ravi said.

"I wouldn't have thought you had read Sartre," Pankaj said.

"I haven't. It's just what I think."

"That's the difference between you and me. I'm always aware of my otherness. It never bothered you," Pankaj said.

Ravi scanned Pankaj's clothing

"Well, there are probably a few other differences, but I get your point. You can still change it."

"That's the paradox, I don't know that I want to. The otherness is part of my identity. So as much as I hate being the other, I can't imagine not being it. It's how I view the world, as a permanent outsider. I don't want to play all their games."

"You can be whomever you need to be inside. But how you deal with people on the outside is up to you."

"Easy for you to say. You would have been as social even if your parents had never left India," Pankaj said.

"Yeah, I suppose. I don't know the answer to all these things, but I know we're better off when we deal with them together. I promise I'll try harder. I'll even help you get a date. Deal?"

He held his hand out to shake Pankaj's hand. Pankaj stared at it a moment before extending his hand. Ravi gripped it tightly to show he was serious. One issue partially dealt with.

"I'm tired," Pankaj said.

"We could all probably use more sleep," Shushruth said.

Ravi stood up. It wasn't the best time to discuss money, but he needed to know the depth of his problem.

"You didn't happen to get cashed out of the casino chips, did you?" Ravi asked.

"They're supposed to mail me a check," Pankaj said.

At least Pankaj didn't get angry. Unfortunately, a mailed check wasn't going to reach him in two days. Ravi's debt was back to twenty six thousand. A hundred dollars for every bone in his body. Or was it 206 bones? Either way, a painful number depending on how Dalinc meted out punishment.

"You know, maybe we should just go home," Shushruth suggested.

"Remember when you turned fourteen? I gave you a birthday present," Ravi said, turning around to face Shushruth.

"I remember."

"And I told you it was nothing to be embarrassed about, because your parents weren't going to teach you."

"And to hide it, because my mum would know where it came from if she found it."

"You tried to give it back, but I made you take it. And you have to admit, it taught you something you needed to learn."

Shushruth blushed, but gave an almost imperceptible nod.

"So tonight is the final chapter of that textbook. Whatever happened last night is done. You need to graduate before you get married."

"I don't want…I just want to be with Falguni."

"These clubs aren't like that. I promise you nothing will happen that you don't want to happen."

"Why don't we drive back to London and celebrate there? That way there's no risk the cops stop us again," Shushruth offered.

Shushruth's suggestion made sense. If he was caught violating his probation, he could get thrown in jail. He nodded.

"Okay, good idea. Let's drive back after lunch. I'll have to let Ian know."

They slept for a few more hours before taking turns with the bathroom and packing up their weekend bags. As Ravi added his toiletry bag to his suitcase, he noticed a small box in the side pocket of the suitcase.

"Ah! I forgot to give this to you." He took the box and extended it towards Shushruth. "Your first wedding gift. It's a multi-pack with different styles. I figured you'd be too embarrassed to buy these yourself, but you're too young to be a dad just yet. Too many of these couples just jump into things without thinking about what they want."

Shushruth glanced down, blushing furiously.

"I don't…"

"Trust me on this," Ravi said.

Ravi knew Shushruth would rather be back in his cocoon where he could pretend sex didn't exist. Back to evenings on the couch watching the world news with his father while his fiancée and his mother cooked together in the kitchen. Back to playing The Sims, where he created avatars for himself and his family. He had told Ravi about how his avatar had discovered a vaccine which cured cancer, won the Nobel Prize and played tennis with Roger Federer. He had offered to replicate Ravi and Pankaj during their visit for dinner the night before last, but Pankaj had dismissed his offer by asking, "Still playing kids games, eh?"

Shushruth had surprised Ravi with his response.

"Better to be an adult playing kids' games than a kid pretending to be an adult."

Who knew that the youngest of the three of them would be the wisest?

Excerpt from
Ravi's Guide to Being a Cool Indian

Ignorance

Schadenfreude is such an integral part of Indian culture that it is hard to believe they needed the Germans to invent the word for it (albeit with a language derived from Sanskrit). Germans may enjoy schadenfreude, but Indians survive on it.

Did you hear, Shilpa's son is doing drugs?

I don't think Chandumama bought that house by himself. I think his brother helped him.

If you want to know the truth, Sanchita didn't leave her job, she was fired for talking back.

To be a cool Indian, you must resist the temptation to know everything about your friends and family members in order to satisfy your need for schadenfreude. If you're lucky, they'll resist the temptation to know everything about you. Principle #1: Ignorance is bliss. Sure you need the courage to accept the things you can't change. But isn't it better not knowing about those things in the first place?

Chapter 5
Jeevan's Secret
London, England

Vineeta

Vineeta wasn't sure she had heard her mom correctly.

"What?"

Her mom was tracing her finger slowly over the *Daily Mail*'s headline at her aunt's coffee table just outside the kitchen. A politician had just resigned after sending unwanted texts. There was a blurred photo on the cover.

"What is this… diii..ck…piii..ck?"

"Just…a text to someone…asking for…"

"He trying to get the dirty business?"

"Yeah, basically."

In the morning, Hans had texted a picture of a large orchid plant awaiting Vineeta's return in Manhattan, and she had realized that she had over-reacted the other day to his predictability. Predictable was good. Having a boyfriend who sent pictures of an orchid instead of his dick was good.

"You find nice Indian boy. He don't do this kind of thing," her mom said.

"There are plenty of non-Indian men who don't do this kind of thing."

Here was the moment she had waited for, the one to reveal Hans' existence, when her mom seemed to be in a placid mood. What was the point of a relationship, really? Had anyone in her life really made her feel so stimulated by their presence that she could conclude she needed to be with them permanently? It was unrealistic. She could get fulfillment for specific aspects of her personality from multiple people. Hans at least satisfied her need for reliability and urbanity, which was more than a lot of people could say about their partners.

"I don't want someone eating hamburgers, meat loaf, steak," her mom said.

"You wouldn't be the one living with him."

"Purnima has American daughter-in-law. Don't let her see grandson! Only on holidays."

Her mom was riling herself up.

Here was the strange dissonance of family—in her normal life, Vineeta would never associate with someone like her mom. She would dismiss her judgments as those of a crazy person. But having been raised and unconditionally loved by her, she took her judgments to heart, even when she didn't agree with them. More disconcertingly, she worried that she was genetically pre-disposed to be a crazy person. Just look at Ravi. Maybe Vineeta already was, but just hadn't realized it yet.

"I would never marry someone who wouldn't let you see your grandkids, if we had them."

"What, you don't want children?"

Why did Vineeta let that caveat slip? If there had been a moment to reveal Hans, it was now gone. Her mom now had all the ingredients to complete her recipe for anger. Better to table the whole idea until after Shushruth's wedding.

"I probably want children , but I haven't decided."

"What is point of life?" her mom asked.

So began a twenty minute monologue about everyone having kids, Vineeta being self-absorbed, the amount of effort her mom was wasting trying to get her married, Americans' value system being messed up, her mom's suffering being far greater than her friends, her father being too weak and distant to teach Vineeta and Ravi anything, her father messing up by leaving India. Vineeta endured it without objection before exercising the only sensible response to her mom's diatribe, excusing herself to take a shower.

She approached the front door of the house before pirouetting around the handrail of the stairs to her bedroom. A hot shower would help her clear her mind. Then she could go to the National Gallery and wander around London to escape the mental oppression of living with her parents in someone else's house.

She couldn't wait to start working after graduation so that she'd have something to distract her from men and family, though even that choice would be informed by her father's preference for a job in the private sector to one in the public sector.

As she walked by her aunt's master bedroom, she heard low monotone voices. She paused to listen to the conversation in Gujarati.

"But I want to. I need to. It's my obligation to give this money. If I don't give it to Shushruth when he's getting married, when else can I give it?"

Her father's voice? Pankaj had left for work. Her uncle had gone to the grocery store. Yes, her father's voice.

"He doesn't need this. He's doing fine." Pankaj's mom.

"I am old, let me do this one thing, no one else will know. You just say it's from you," her father said.

"And what will I tell my husband?"

"You say you were saving your money. Everyone knows he was born to you so it will seem normal. They don't know the rest."

"I'm saving from what? The thing happened, okay, but that was long ago. Now it doesn't matter. If you want to give it, you can give it directly."

"How can I give so much directly? Everyone will wonder why."

"Enough. You decide what you want, this isn't my problem."

Movement inside the room caused Vineeta to tiptoe to her bedroom, where she gently turned the knob so that the door wouldn't click shut. Her heart started pounding in her chest. Why would her father want to secretly give a big gift to her cousin Shushruth for his wedding via Pankaj's mom (who was also Shushruth's biological mom)? She could see her mom dreaming up such a convoluted arrangement, but for what reason? Were her parents secretly supporting people in the extended family?

"They don't know the rest….The thing that happened…long ago." It could mean anything. Maybe her father somehow caused Shushruth's family to lose money? Or maybe it wasn't Pankaj's mom who birthed Shushruth and gave him to Shushruth's parents, but her mom? But she would have known. She alighted on an even more far-fetched possibility that didn't involve her mom and had driven her to a therapist in the first place—an affair.

During her senior year in college, Vineeta had witnessed her father kissing another married professor on campus. Maybe that affair wasn't his first. Maybe he had slept with Pankaj's mom. As she imagined them in their current form, the possibility wasn't just unlikely, but gross. She rewound her mental image to pictures from their younger days. Her father was handsome, but why would he have gone for the youngest sister? She was smarter. Not as pretty, but warmer, more engaging.

It all started clicking. Shushruth was their son. Her half-brother. That's why the youngest sister had been okay giving Shushruth to the middle sister to raise. That's why Shushruth looked more like Ravi than Pankaj. That's why her father wanted to give Shushruth a big wedding gift but needed to channel it through Pankaj's mom, so that whoever didn't know about that affair wouldn't learn about it now.

She looked around the room. Maybe this was the bed Shushruth was conceived in, possibly on this very floral bedspread, raggedy with decades of use. She shivered with disgust and walked over to the window to look over the back garden, past the house behind and out into clouds on the horizon. Somewhere out there on another planet, a satellite was just receiving the images of her father's decades old affair.

She re-considered the preposterous notion that Shushruth was her half-brother. A half-brother who looked a lot like Ravi. The half-brother who lived down the street from them in Ealing and spent half his time at their house, while Pankaj and his family moved twenty minutes away to Chiswick.

The possibility threatened to unravel all of the work Dr. Jenks had done. As Dr. Jenks had explained, witnessing her father's kiss that senior year at Michigan may have lowered Vineeta's expectations so that she dated stable but boring men. She might have been avoiding Indian men, but also afraid of committing to non-Indian ones. At the same time, it had subconsciously empowered her to confound her parents' expectation that she apply for medical school at Michigan, because if she had remained in Ann Arbor she would have kept passing Jeevan's paramour on campus. Instead, she had lined up a job in New York.

Discovering this new ancient affair changed her entire understanding of her family. Her mom had not only been cheated on, but by her own sister. Did she know?

Shushruth was really her half-brother. Her emotional connection with him made more sense. She had plenty of fodder to analyse for years to come—little moments when her father had paid extra attention to Shushruth, hand gestures that both Ravi and Shushruth used, nature vs. nurture personality analysis.

And what did the behavior of her boring, predictable father infer about Hans? Maybe beneath Hans' boring and predictable veneer, he was the type of guy who was sending dick pics to half the women in Austria right at that moment. She wouldn't know. At least if she was going to settle for a guy who was boring and predictable, he should undeniably be a man who was faithful. And since there was no way to ensure this was the case, maybe she should aspire for better.

She felt furious. She felt sad. She felt lost. She felt confused. She needed to get out of the house. She changed quickly, eschewing a shower, and skipped down the stairs. She could hear her parents and aunt in the kitchen preparing tea and chatting. She peered in briefly to announce she was leaving to meet Ravi and started leaving. They started asking questions, but she had already moved towards the front door.

"I'll be back before dinner," she shouted.

She closed the door and began walking through the neighborhood, realizing that she wasn't sure how to get to the Tube, or even what Tube line to board. She wondered whether she actually should call Ravi. She had never told him about their father's first affair. The knowledge was like a virus, and she hadn't wanted to infect him with it. But this was different. This changed everything.

But what could Ravi do? He couldn't change the facts. It wouldn't make his life better to know. It wouldn't make anyone's life better to know. It just angered her that her father had been giving hypocritical advice his whole life. It angered her that he had treated her mom with so little respect. Cheating with her mom's sister! Should she confront him? That would be as pleasant as revealing Hans' existence to her mom.

Vineeta wished she could trade her brain in for someone else's brain for the rest of the day. Anyone's. Pamela Anderson. SnoopDogg. Even George W. Bush.

Was it possible her mom had known this whole time? It would explain a lot of her resentment. There was no one she could confide in. If so, maybe Vineeta needed to do with her mom had done for all these years, bury her thoughts away.

She saw a woman approaching her and asked for directions to the Tube. Ten minutes later, she had reached Chiswick Park station, but continued past it into the Gunnersbury Triangle Local Nature Reserve. The wonder of finding a nature reserve with a proper wooded trail and pond in the city briefly distracted her from her thoughts. She should have wandered out from Pankaj's house days earlier.

After finishing the trail loop, she resolved to spend the day on her terms. She would go the National Gallery as planned and possibly check in with Ravi later.

On the outdoor Tube platform, she observed the fashions of London—Doc Martens and high heel boots, slick vinyl and leather jackets, tight jeans and neon skirts. There were business people and frumpy looking people, too, but on the whole, the attitude was…punkier than New York. An advert for a gym on the platform's curved wall showed an overweight man and the caption *It's New Year's somewhere. Time for a Resolution.* The sense of humor here was sharper and less sensitive. Maybe she was living in the wrong city.

She boarded the train and squirreled past people to an open seat. She played the scene she had overheard back in her mind. There were other ways to interpret the words. Did she really need to reach a definitive conclusion that her father had cheated with her aunt? She was probably being hysterical and overly dramatic. Still, even the possibility pulsed a depressing pall through her whole being. She probably wouldn't get rid of that feeling for at least a few days. The more she could distract herself from them by keeping busy, the easier it would be.

After spending a morning of looking at paintings, an early afternoon of eating a salad and roll and a late afternoon of wandering SoHo, she didn't feel like going back to Pankaj's house and seeing her father. She called Ravi and arranged to drop by before he and their cousins left for Shushruth's bachelor party on the eve of his wedding.

The lobby of the hotel was more modest than she had expected, with a small front desk and atrium. She took the elevator up and arrived to Shushruth opening the door.

"Hi, come in!" Shushruth greeted her.

His shirt was buttoned to the top. Pankaj nodded his head from a chair in the corner, while Ravi came out of the bathroom in a long sleeve ringer t-shirt with a steel circle necklace.

"Nice view," she offered, with a sky top view of an expanse of buildings. "They gave you a suite?"

"You don't get what you don't ask for," Ravi said.

"So, did you manage to meet some 'cool kids' this week?" she asked, wobbling her head to parody coolness.

"You act as if coolness isn't cool. What's cooler than cool?" Ravi asked, slapping on some cologne.

She gave him a puzzled look.

"Outkast? 'Hey Ya'?" he said.

"Oh, right."

"Even I knew that," Shushruth said, cradling himself into a love seat.

Now even Shushruth was showing her up.

"You okay?" Ravi asked.

"Yeah, why?"

"You look a little frazzled. "

Did it show on her face? Or was her hair a mess? She hadn't checked it before she left the house.

"I don't know. Probably too much time with the parents. What time were you going to go out?" she asked.

"Right around now. We were going to go for drinks and tapas. You should join," Ravi said.

"I don't want to intrude."

"No, she should come, right?" Ravi said, looking at their cousins.

"Definitely," Shushruth said.

"But…what about later?" she asked.

"You mean the traditional bachelor party stuff?" Ravi asked.

"Are you doing that?"

She didn't really care to see naked women dancing around.

"That's the plan. You don't have to stay for that if you don't want. Not that we would do anything exploitative, if that's a word."

"It's not exploiting them as long as they're controlling their bodies on their own terms."

"So…you want to go?"

It was strange being invited to a strip club by her brother, but it was also very…Ravi. He had an uncanny way of making you alternately feeling secure and insecure.

"That doesn't mean I want to see you…you know."

"It will be well-behaved. Reasonably well-behaved."

Maybe she should go. Maybe she should do something that no one expected her to do to forget about her father and to shake her doldrums. Maybe if she followed Ravi's guidance, her life might get better. It couldn't be any worse than Shiva had done for her.

"Look, Shushruth is getting married. You have the right to help him celebrate as much as anyone else. And Ian will be there," Ravi said with a relish that suggested he knew about what had happened the year before.

"Ian's in town?"

"Lucky coincidence."

An awkward coincidence. For the past year, she had avoided talking to Ian whenever Ravi convened a broader group.

***

In college, Ian occasionally joined Ravi for dinner at the family home. He was calm and curious, a contrast to Ravi's ostentation and superficiality. He listened while Ravi talked. Vineeta felt comfortable around him. And yet he also had an edge, experimenting over the years with dreadlocks, a short blonde afro and a ramp cut.

But she was too shy to suggest they go out, and he justifiably didn't seem to notice her in her baggy jeans and cringe-worthy tops. Once the band took off, she assumed she couldn't compete with his other choices. It was only after the band had broken up a year earlier that she had summoned the courage to make her interest clear.

Ian had been chatting with someone near a white radiator at a Christmas party in a Brooklyn brownstone. He had matched a tight conservative haircut with a pencil-thin mustache. Vineeta had just arrived and felt confident in her contact lenses, bronze highlights, and taut blouse.

"Haven't seen you in a while," she interjected, causing the other person to leave.

"If I had seen you, I wouldn't have recognized you," he observed.

"Oh, the Santa hat? You'd confuse me with an overweight bearded white man?"

"No, quite the opposite. I would have thought you were modeling in the Macy's parade. If I'm allowed to say that," Ian said.

"Why wouldn't you be?"

"Just, Ravi, sister, you know."

"I do have a life independent of him."

"I know, I didn't mean it that way."

"Well, let's just pretend I'm an adoring fan who you've met after the concert. Should I ask for your autograph?"

"That'd be a bit weird."

"Come on, go with it," she said.

"Are you asking? Do you have a pen?"

"I thought you'd be ready with one."

"I intentionally don't keep one so I have a built in excuse."

She dug through her purse to find one.

"On your arm?" he asked.

"I don't have any paper."

"Alright. Won't be the oddest place."

"Really? Where else."

"I'm sure you can imagine," he said.

"Okay. That gives me an idea."

She wasn't sure what her plan was, but summoned him to the host's bedroom, where she had added her coat to the others on the bed a moment ago. He looked at her in puzzlement.

"Okay, I can't match whatever happened on your tour. But how about you sign around my belly button?"

"Seriously?"

His hesitation and tone made her realize that she had made a huge error. He wasn't interested in her.

"Sorry, this is awkward, forget it," she said.

After a quick pause, he said, "No, it's fine."

He approached her and knelt down. She lifted her blouse slightly, resisting the urge to tousle his afro, and looked up at the ceiling. The nib of the pen tickled. Just as he began to stand up, an attractive woman entered the room.

"Hey. I was looking for you."

Vineeta felt herself blushing. She hadn't known that he had been dating someone. Ian introduced her as Ravi's sister, and like that she was returned to the same junior status she had always felt around Ravi and his friends. She had begun dating Hans shortly thereafter.

***

She glanced out the window at the endless grid of buildings. She wasn't ready to go back to Pankaj's house. She didn't want to wander the streets of London by herself anymore. She eventually had to face Ian again. This could be the first of a series of decisions getting herself on the right track.

"I like Ian. That makes it even better."

"Okay. The only rule is that whatever happens tonight is never mentioned again."

Did she really want to see what happened tonight? Would she want to see Shushruth ogling or perhaps even groping a stripper, if that was what seemingly respectable men did at a strip club and it was allowed? Did she want to see Ian again in circumstances that would undoubtedly remind them both of their awkward experience a year earlier? Did she want to lose all respect for men so that she would never want to date another man, ever?

"Fine."

If Shiva was going to destroy her illusions, she might as well do the dirty work herself. Maybe it was her first truly feminist act.

Excerpt from
Ravi's Guide to Being a Cool Indian

Career

You achieve vocational nirvana as an Indian by ascending the generational ladder from motel owner to engineer to Ivy League MD or MBA. Your parents inculcate this need for ascension by enviously remarking upon your classmate Sandeep Khosla's admission to Harvard Medical School or their friend's daughter Anita Devakurni's perfect SAT score. They push you to become a well-rounded sportsman, artist and philanthropist to gain admission to Harvard, only to find out that there's a maximum quota for Asians. So you attend another top school which funnels you to Goldman Sachs in order to stop being well-rounded. You work all hours on some boring niche that makes you wealthy so you can donate money to your alma mater and make sure your child is guaranteed admission in the future. Nirvana turns out to mean wasting your life in front of a computer to give your child the opportunity to do the same.

Principle #1: don't buy into some checklist of life achievements when there is another Nirvana and another way. The Ravi way.

The Ravi way means finding your passion, like playing the guitar. Playing guitar as a hobby is cool. Playing it for a living is euphoric (give us the dirt, Ravi, give us the dirt). The initial press coverage was enthusiastic, calling our sound "fresh" and "sophisticated". "Glitter in the Road" charted at #24 and was licensed by Muzac. "Lovely Girl" hit #37. "Blow Out the Moon" hit #103. Crowds in London, New York, Berlin, Paris, Tokyo, Sydney, moshed in the pit, chanting our chorus. Prince even congratulated us at the Grammys.

This could be you. Now I'd rather be lead singer, shaking my rump, never lugging around gear, posing for the cover of TeenBeat, having the girls shout my name. But I can't sing and don't begrudge Ian the spotlight (as long as the royalties keep coming my way). He shakes his rump better than I do and is, according to one fan blog, "a sexy bloke with sensitive eyes". His voice is not only a mellifluous wave of beauty, but stick him in front of a microphone in a leather jacket and he makes you believe the words.

Principle #2: make sure you actually have the skill to follow your passion.

Mum was happy about our notoriety, but still reminded me about "brilliant" CEOs who were making more than I was. It's hard to refute assertions of brilliance. You can say "I could have done that," and the other person will always say, "But you didn't, did you?", which to my mind only proves the limits of the other person's imagination. Maybe you were bright enough but too lazy, distracted with a better social life, playing guitar, or maybe you didn't want to get to the top of the heap by stepping on a few people and missing out on the view. Mum would trade my years with Buzzthief for a Harvard degree, but I'm sure Sandeep Khosla would trade his degree to have been a member of Buzzthief. At least if he really has the genius Mum thinks his degree demonstrates.

Principle #3: Don't listen to the naysayers, or you'll spend your life sitting at a desk married to someone who sits at a desk waiting to have children who spend their lives sitting at a desk.

Need proof? Google "Anita Devakurni" and "Sandeep Khosla": Research approval director for a bio-tech company and management consultant, respectively. Ravi's still in the lead.

Chapter 6
Diamonds
London, England

Ravi

The taxi driver left them a few streets away due to an adjacent walled off construction site with a massive crane. Ravi led the other three to where Ian was standing beneath the flashing neon sign for Diamonds dressed in an untucked plaid button-down.

"Muchacho, long time," Ravi said ironically, pulling Ian in for a shoulder bump.

It was only ten years earlier that Ravi had approached Ian during their sophomore year in Ann Arbor as Ian struggled with an acoustic guitar on the steps of one of the Michigan dorms. Ravi had motioned for the guitar and picked out "Day Tripper". Ian had started singing along. Ravi enhanced their origin story by claiming that he had heard Ian singing to his fictional dog, because "what girl could resist a singer in a leather jacket with a dog named Shyness?" Within a few years, Ravi's unflappable visions of success had mostly came true—hitting number one, playing Letterman, renting hacienda style mansions.

"Yeah. How was the community service?" Ian asked.

"Not too bad. A bit sore from all the sweeping."

"Better than jail."

Ian gave Vineeta a quizzical look before they did the kissy-cheek thing. He nodded at Pankaj and Shushruth. Ravi motioned to his Vineeta and his cousins.

"So I told Vineeta to come tonight. She's been cooped up with our parents and could use a night out with old friends. You remember Pankaj? And this is my cousin Shushruth."

He had invited Vineeta along because she seemed to be floundering in her love life, career and relationship with their parents. She needed the security of his orbit, no matter how tenuous the bonds of gravity holding him in it. But now he considered the possibility that she might help nudge Ian to re-form the band.

Ian responded better to women, almost too much so. In college, there had been a series of damsels in distress who had managed to move in with Ian within weeks of meeting him. Ian would sleep in Ravi's room to avoid whoever was staying in his until they eventually roomed together their junior year.

If Vineeta suggested they get the band back together, he might actually agree.

"Pankaj, dude, long time. Good to see you again. Shush.." Ian said.

"Shushruth."

"Shushroot, nice to meet you. Getting married, congrats," Ian offered.

"Thanks, I'm excited," Shushruth said.

"Maybe we should go in, it's cold," Pankaj observed.

The muscled bouncer checked their IDs, and the host escorted them to an extended booth with its own pole. An unhappy waiter appeared, gruffly reminding them of the two drink minimum. He pointed to each one to elicit an immediate order, which he punched into an electronic keypad.

"Any preferences?" the waiter asked.

"You just took our preferences," Ravi said.

Ravi found strip clubs demeaning to both sides, but adapting to the West meant embracing the commodification of all things beautiful—sex, art, music, nature. And while it had been a perfectly fun ride, he wondered if he would have been happier growing up somewhere else.

The waiter shook his head.

"Black, white, Asian, you know. There's a one girl minimum for every two guys, er…," the waiter said, puzzled by Vineeta's presence.

"Two's fine, she's just here for a school project," Ravi said.

The waiter left, and Ravi glanced at Ian.

"I should have seen if they had a girl from the Southern Hemisphere for you."

Ian seemed to glance at Vineeta in embarrassment.

"Well, she was …This isn't, we're not dating the girl. It doesn't matter, whomever they bring," Ian stammered.

"You have a thing for darker girls?" Vineeta asked, tilting her head and propping it on her fist.

"Well, it depends. It's not…I don't think of it that way."

"How do you think of it?"

"Well, I'm obviously black, or really half-black. So I don't really focus on skin color."

"Why? When people see you, or me for that matter, that's exactly what they're doing."

"I know, but it would be depressing to live your life in such a reductive way. I'd rather just judge people on who they are."

Ravi started clapping.

"Bravo, bravo. You're ready for an Oprah interview. You know the only reason we're friends? I wanted to look more 'street'," Ravi deadpanned.

Shushruth and Pankaj sat further down the row. A tall black girl with straightened hair in a red corset and short blonde in a black skirt and white halter top appeared, escorted by a bouncer that reminded the boys to keep their hands to the side.

"How are all of you tonight?" the blonde asked.

"Quite nice, thank you," Ian said.

"You guys look like you're ready for a business conference. Relax, this is going to be a good time," the tall girl said. "I'm Crystal, this is Raven."

"Girls, it's a pleasure. Our good man over here is getting married in a couple of days, but he's a strip club virgin, so we appreciate all efforts to provide him a proper education," Ravi said.

"You're at the right place," Crystal said.

The girls began their routine, caressing the pole, caressing each other, hip-thrusting to the music, disrobing each other to reveal outfits that like matroyshka dolls were even more implausibly tiny than the previous one. Ravi saw Vineeta curiously observing them

"So, did you end up doing the book reading?" Ian asked Ravi.

"The book reading was fine. Good reception, there were twenty…maybe it was fifty people. You can tell, the real fans are excited about seeing us together again. What'd you think of it?"

"Yeah, funny, just like I expected," Ian said.

Ravi could tell he hadn't read it, but he wasn't offended. Ian had probably heard most of the jokes and anecdotes over the years.

Ravi swayed in time with the music.

"What about you, things are good with Jessica?" Ravi asked.

"Well, she's pretty settled, working for her dad's insurance company. It's good, it's nice to have something stable."

"Yeah, weekends in the Hamptons, workouts with private trainers, tickets to shows. Everything you always wanted," Ravi taunted.

"I thought that's what you always wanted?"

"If I meant half the things I said, I'd be a real asshole. Not that you're an asshole. I'm just saying you're meant to be making music."

The undulating triangle before Ravi made it difficult to concentrate. Not to mention his sister was sitting a few feet from him observing the whole thing. He politely nodded at the woman as a sign of acknowledgement without approval.

"Boys, if you don't want to be here, I'll save my energy for someone who wants to tip," Crystal said.

"Yeah, sorry," Ian said, tucking a five Pound note in the string around her hips.

Ravi added another five, reminding him that he needed a plan to get some money. His father's $5000 dollar loan was now represented by a $2500 IOU from the Blackpool casino and $2500 worth of chips that would require him to go cash them in. And he would still be $21,000 short. Outside of confessing his dire situation and triggering a family crisis, he wasn't sure how to persuade anyone in his immediate orbit to lend him cash. Ravi would have asked Ian to front a loan from his girlfriend, whose father owned an insurance company, except that said father had broached hiring Ian. A loan would raise questions about Ian's character. Not to mention that Ian's girlfriend didn't like Ravi. He had admittedly not made a great first impression when he had drunkenly described her hairstyle as "one of them smurf thingies, the hats they wore."

Which left him with two possibilities: convince Ian to re-form Buzzthief in time for the lucrative Christmas corporate party circuit and in turn convince Dalinc that he only needed a few months for solvency, or reach the airport after Shushruth's wedding before Dalinc showed up. The former option at least would at least demonstrate his sincere desire to pay back the loan and reduce the odds of an unexpected accident. He had already formulated the pitch—show Dalinc a clip of their performance on *Letterman*, give a short acoustic performance with Ian (on the pretense that Dalinc was an A&R rep), and invite Dalinc to watch them perform on the corporate party circuit (while mentioning the standard $10,000 appearance fee for a band of their stature).

"Oh God," Shushruth intoned as Crystal's breasts cycled like propellers directly before his eyes. Whether in excitement, disgust or embarrassment, it was unclear.

"Would your friend like a private room?" Crystal asked.

"I'm getting married. That wouldn't be…" Shushruth started.

"It's impossible to cheat on a woman you've only known for two weeks. Let me ask you a question. When you watch t.v., do you watch one channel or flip between all of them?" Ravi asked.

"I change channels."

"Okay. So, I'm helping you change the channel. You can change it back tomorrow. But tonight it's okay to watch HBO instead of BBC. This isn't even the Playboy channel. You don't have to do anything, just sit back and enjoy. Crystal, how about this—don't do anything that would make me feel guilty every time I saw his mum," Ravi said, handing her a hundred pound note.

"My friend will be gentle," Crystal said.

Crystal led Shushruth away by the hand as he looked back at Vineeta as if he was the one who had recently been convicted.

"You don't have to…" Vineeta began.

"Look—the man's a doctor but the only naked woman he's seen in real life is a cadaver. It's okay," Ravi interrupted. "Alright, Raven, sorry about all the distractions. Ian and I have seen enough without paying for it, but we couldn't let my little bro get married without some point of comparison. Are you honestly checking the markets right now?" Ravi asked, espying Pankaj on his phone.

Pankaj seemed to ignore Ravi's comment until he noticed everyone looking at him.

"The US markets are open. I have to make sure nothing's blowing up."

"Your…"

Ravi held back finishing with, "innovations in wankerdom never cease to amaze."

"Put it down and come over here," he offered.

Pankaj reluctantly slid down the vinyl bench to join Ian and Ravi.

"Wouldn't it have been better if he had never found out what he was missing?" Pankaj asked.

"Yeah, that's a good point. Oh well, too late now," Ravi said. "Anyway, the band."

"Well, I don't know if you've been in touch, with, you know, the guys, but they've joined other bands," Ian said.

"Do you like working here?" Vineeta asked Raven as she gyrated.

"Honey, I like money," Raven said before Pankaj's face with her hair. "And I bet he has some that he feels like contributing for a good cause."

Pankaj fumbled for his wallet. Vineeta stood up and moved to sit on the far side of Ian.

"Look, they're good chums, but if they don't want back in, you and me, we're the band. You're the voice, I'm the songs. They left us," Ravi said.

"They didn't leave us. They went to earn a living when our thing fell apart."

"Well, this is all semantics. They're gone, we're here. We can recruit a new bassist and drummer, hit the corporate Christmas party circuit, bring in some easy money. Vineeta, tell him it's time to get the band back together."

Ian looked left at Vineeta, and Ravi could tell it was going to work. Ian couldn't resist a pretty face and some tenderness.

"You…should do whatever feels right for you. I've spent my life doing what other people wanted, and I can tell you, it doesn't make you any happier," Vineeta said.

What was she doing? He was the one who had encouraged her to assert her independence. Now she was sabotaging his efforts.

"See? She's right. Don't let others stop you from re-joining the band. It's what you're meant to be doing," Ravi said.

"That's for him to decide," Vineeta responded.

Crystal interrupted them by returning with Shushruth, who sat down next to Ian, to the far side of the strippers.

"I'm done for the night boys. I think your friend is a new man. Should I send in a replacement?" she asked.

Ravi looked at her blankly before turning back to glare at Vineeta for a moment and then looking back at her again.

"I think we're done for the night."

The strippers left and the bill arrived, which Ravi whisked from the table.

"On me."

Ravi looked at the bill. Drinks at 20 pounds each. Stripper fee of 100 pounds an hour per stripper. Service charge of 25%. Nearly five hundred pounds. He bit his nails as he placed his credit card in the folder.

"You sure you're good?" Vineeta asked.

"I think I've had enough of your help for the evening."

"What's that supposed to mean?"

The waiter returned with the receipt folder for Ravi's signature.

"You never know when these things are going to run out," Ravi said, waving his credit card. "All right. Where to?"

"We should probably go to sleep, we should stay on schedule so we're rested for the weekend," Shushruth said.

"There's plenty of time to get bossed around by your wife. Let the women do their thing, you enjoy your last couple of nights as a free man," Ravi said. "Karaoke?"

"Fine by me," Ian said.

Ravi had managed to extend the evening. If Vineeta wasn't going to persuade Ian, Ravi would have to dig deeper into his bag of tricks. With the help of the concierge, they boarded a van taxi and started on their way to a karaoke place.

"Was that whole thing normal? Like, you ignore them and just talk the whole time while everyone else pretends to care just to be polite?" Vineeta asked Ian.

"Don't ask me, it's the first time I've ever been to a strip club," Ian said.

Everyone seemed to be looking at Ravi for some insight.

"Depends who you go with. I don't usually pay attention," Ravi said.

"Then why did you force Shushruth to come?" Vineeta asked.

"Had we stayed in London, I could have made sure he got a proper education like an older sibling should. But given the time crunch, I had to resort to a crash course education."

Within twenty minutes, they were being served beers, peanuts and microphones by an Asian hostess in a private room with a red cushioned sofa and a coffee table. Ravi, Vineeta and Pankaj browsed the song books, one sorted by artist and one by title, and began punching some numbers into a remote control.

"Shushruth, you're up. 'Like a Virgin,'" Ravi said.

"Not anymore, right?" Pankaj said.

Three alcoholic drinks seemed to have finally loosened Pankaj up.

"Nothing happened," Shushruth said, blushing.

"I'm just kidding."

The t.v. screen flashed from a Songbook logo to a man and a woman lounging on a tropical beach with the song information in the corner.

"Eminem? Wouldn't have pegged you for it," Ravi said to Pankaj.

Pankaj took the microphone. He bounced his knees and thrust his hands forward to rap like a gangster, though neither the motions nor his stuttered rapping matched the rhythm of the music. He kept falling behind on the words, getting halfway through boasts about being the real Slim Shady and insults about others' deviant sexual behaviors.

"'This is hard!"

"Keep going," Ravi said.

The spooling chorus at the end finally forced him to give up.

"Okay, Ian. Guess the song," Ravi said as he entered the next numerical code.

Their biggest hit, "Glitter in the Road". Maybe this would stir Ian's emotions. Ian looked at the screen.

"I knew you were going to do that."

"Sing it like you've never sung it before."

"I see the glitter. In the. Road. The glitter. Floats. Like stars. Above."

"No, come on man, sing it."

"Like I never sang it before. That's what you said."

Ian perfunctorily ran through the verse before they all joined him for the chorus.

It was a beautiful day it was a beautiful place

It was a dream that I had just like a lie

It was a play in my head and all the words that I said

Within the role that I cast were just a lie

I will seek something deeper

Ian took the song back from the verse and revved up his vocals into a proper performance. He handed the mic to Ravi when he finished.

"That was good, but you know where the chorus is supposed to go up and you take the note down—that's something you used to do in concert, but it subtracts from the emotional resonance of the song a bit," Ravi said.

"You can sing it from now on then," Ian said.

"Any song requests?" Ravi asked.

"I put one in. It's for Shushruth. I remember how you always wanted to listen to Michael Jackson *Thriller* album," Vineeta said.

"But I can't sing Michael Jackson," Shushruth said.

"No one can sing Michael Jackson. That's why it's entertaining," Ravi said. "Just do it one octave down, in your speaking voice. So, Ian, when are we getting the band back together? I've got some bills to pay."

The band wouldn't immediately bring money in hand, but it was a credible pathway to solvency. Dalinc was someone who could appreciate that.

Ian stopped flipping through the song list and said, "I...I don't think I want to. Look, I know you put together Buzzthief and kept it going, but that phase is done. Jessica wants to get married."

Ravi realized that at some sub-conscious level he had already known what was coming, but hearing it stated made his stomach drop.

"You're getting married?" Vineeta asked. "That's great!"

She turned to Ravi. "Did you know?"

He could tell she had put on her insincere voice.

"Not exactly. I mean, they've gone out a while," he said, turning back to Ian. "Look, I know your girl never liked me, but I don't care. Meaning, it's not that I want her to dislike me, but I don't mind if she doesn't, it doesn't change our friendship. I don't blame you."

"She's never said she doesn't like you. She thinks you're fine. And she's never really gotten a chance to know you."

Were only two of those contradictory, or all three?

Shushruth brayed about beating it in the background.

"Come on, grab your crotch. Well, congratulations. That explains why you didn't return some of my calls," Ravi said.

He hadn't planned on revealing his vulnerability by confronting Ian about the one thing that had hurt him most. Ravi had made plenty of mistakes in his life—verbal gaffes, tardy appearances, petty loans and the like. But he had always been loyal. He was always the one checking in on Ian. On Pankaj. On Vineeta. On Shushruth. How often did they call or text him out of the blue? How often did they suggest a cool new event to check out?

Money problems he could probably solve. His circumstances were scary, but at least they were clear-cut. A best friend pretending to still be his best friend was a lot harder to deal with.

"I was busy moving and stuff. I mean, I'm sorry. I should have been better about it," Ian said.

Shushruth shuffled from one leg to the other and back and waved the microphone back forth like he was conducting a waltz during the instrumental. Vineeta was staring at the wall in a daze.

"I should learn this guitar solo. A classic. It wasn't like that before," Ravi said, glancing at Ian.

Ian didn't respond.

"So what are you going to do? Write a book about trying a different Ray's Pizza every day?" Ravi asked.

"Well, the label suggested I record a solo album."

Ravi couldn't fake his smile anymore. He stared at his drink. Insult to injury. He had made Ian's career, and now Ian was ditching him, just like the lyrics from that Human League song.

"Right then. So…you're going to write the songs? Or they're bringing in the hired guns?"

"The whole model's changing. We've talked about it. Everyone's using professional songwriters."

"So I'm not professional enough."

Ravi looked at Shushruth.

"Michael Jackson, did you notice Britney Spears showed up tonight? Britney is going to record a solo album with her professional songwriters."

"I'm sure you can submit some songs, too," Ian said. "I mean, it will probably be more R&B Dance, but…"

"Right. I can go from being your bandmate to your employee. Doesn't matter, I don't do that Britney Spears shit. It's all good. Are they going to give you dance lessons?"

Ravi stood up and started doing robotic dance moves.

"Look, it's early. We haven't defined what it is, I'm sure it's not…that kind of stuff. And you wouldn't be working for me, we'd both be working for the label."

"Well, tonight is supposed to be about Shushruth, so sorry I brought it up. Are you coming to his wedding?"

Ravi towered over Ian. He was aware that disco lights kept shooting from behind him silhouetting his figure onto the wall. He wasn't going to let Ian off the hook so easily.

"I'm not invited, not that I expected to be."

Ravi looked over at Shushruth.

"Michael Jackson, tell Ian he needs to show up to your wedding, right?"

"You should definitely come," Shushruth said, unsteadily using the mic for the first and last words of the sentence.

"See, Michael Jackson is inviting you to his wedding. And you don't have to let him see your willy."

"I'm sure the invite list is already set."

"There's no such thing at an Indian wedding."

"Okay, well…I just need to figure out my schedule."

"You have to figure it out? Or Jessica has to figure it out? Or she has figured it out, but you haven't figured out whether you want to tell me what she's figured out?"

"It's a family event. I don't want to intrude."

"You should come," Vineeta said, looking up. "You've been part of our family for a long time now."

"Okay. I'll be there," Ian said.

Shushruth finished the song and looked at everyone for a reaction.

"Excellent. Your turn to sing," Pankaj said to Ravi, handing him a mic.

"Oh, you chose this? Alright, but everyone joins in on the chorus."

Ravi began singing in an exaggerated British accent about whether his friend would walk out on him for singing out of tune. When the chorus arrived, he waved one arm to conduct the others, so that they could all agree that they with a little help from friends, they would be able to get by.

When the song ended, Ian told them he was leaving. Ravi kept perusing the songbook without looking up. Ian looked at the other three.

"I'll catch you at the wedding. It's tomorrow night?"

"Yeah, I'll send you the details," Vineeta said.

"Sounds good."

"Get home safely," Ravi said without looking up.

He had no money. He had no band. And now he no longer had a best friend.

Excerpt from
Ravi's Guide to Being a Cool Indian

Family

Mum likes to say that Indians always put family first, though she attributes it to some inherent nobility in the race instead of the fact that in India, no one can afford to buy their own place and move out from the ancestral home, so everybody has to get along. Which they don't always do a great job of doing, because they're always fighting over something like who forgot to yell down from the fifth floor terrace to the servant on the street to buy a loaf of bread. Eventually someone yells instructions and complains that he or she is always the one who has to yell down. Meanwhile the servant runs up five flights of stairs to get money, back down the stairs and three streets away to buy the bread, and back up five flights to deliver it, all with a smile on his face.

Who's right, Mum or me? Do Indians have a superior sense of family duty, or are they just as selfish as any other race? Let's do a case study, starting with my first visit to Bombay with my family in 1982.

My father's younger brother waited for two hours outside the airport at 3 am pressed up with a throng of people against a glass wall just to wave at us. When we got outside, he gave me and Vineeta 5 Star and Cadbury chocolates before chauffeuring us in a bulbous vinyl-lined Ambassador to the apartment his family shared with the youngest brother's family. By Indian custom, my father had inherited the apartment, but had allowed his brothers to use it without charging rent.

Mum/Family 1, Ravi/Selfishness 0.

The thousand square foot apartment itself was depressing, with a brown-tiled floor, open grilled windows, a rickety fan that threatened to decapitate us, neon lights and occasional cockroach. Still, the eight of them were constantly laughing with, shouting at, accusing or cajoling each other, which made it feel like a long slumber party. My cousins praised my cricket skills and British accent, gushed over the receipt of gifts of London's superior cheese, electronics and clothing and inquired about London schooling. My older uncle obtained tickets to the premiere of Namak Halaal and said that I looked like Amitabh Bachchan. He let me join in on rounds of theenpati, a card game he and his friends played to stay awake in observance of Lord Krishna's birthday. My cousin showed me how to brush my teeth on their balcony so that we could spit toothpaste on the people walking below.

Mum/Family 2, Ravi/Selfishness 0.

The apartment had two equally terrible chamber pots, with wet green-black concrete floors and porcelain holes in the ground under dangling lightbulbs and water tanks with flush chains. I held my breath in gulps to avoid the stench of decades of defecation and removed my shirt to bear the heat, sweat rolling down my chest as my quads trembled from squatting. There was no toilet paper, only an ankle level faucet and plastic cup for cleansing. After I complained on one of our visits, my youngest uncle saved the day by installing a Western toilet.

Mum/Family 3, Ravi/Selfishness 0.

Mum wins, right? Except on my return trip in 2000, after my father had gifted the apartment to his brothers, things had changed. At the airport, my younger uncle sent a driver with a sign to pick me up instead of coming in person.

Mum/Family 3, Ravi/Selfishness 1.

My older uncle had moved out to the suburbs after starting a successful catering business. He no longer spoke with my younger uncle because they had fought over how much money he should get for relinquishing his half of the apartment.

Mum/Family 3, Ravi/Selfishness 2.

When my father requested that my older uncle take me on a trip to Goa for fun, he said he was too busy with other commitments.

Mum/Family 3, Ravi/Selfishness 3.

Sudden death, who was going to win?

My cousin took me to a club with a twenty dollar cover, or the equivalent of a month's pay for most locals. The neon blue warehouse was packed with girls and boys in Western clothing drinking martinis and vodkas and dancing to techno just like in London or New York. My cousin recognized a girl in a tight blouse and skirt sitting on a stool at the island bar, and tapped her on the shoulder.

"Aren't we distantly related?"

She looked over her shoulder.

"Are we?"

"I think you're cousins with one of my cousins on the other side. I met you at one of her parties, but didn't get a chance to talk to you much."

"Well, I think they say ignorance is bliss," she said as she turned back to her friend.

Mum/Family 3, Ravi/Selfishness 4.

Familial duty is contextual. All the attention I had received on our first visit stemmed from my relatives humoring a nine year old and following a manual of obligations, not my charm or Western-ness or Mum's Indian family values. After they had gained ownership of the family home and become more prosperous, they began editing the manual, like everyone else does.

Principle #1: If you expect your family to put up with you, figure out how you're going to put up with them.

Chapter 7
Wayward Children
London, England

Jeevan

Four days at his sister-in-law's house was starting to wear down Jeevan's stoic ability to deal with just about anything. Their refusal to turn on the heat at night. Their refusal to turn off the television during the day. The clogged bathtub that required him to stand in filthy water as he showered. The spicy food that was prickling the walls of his rear end.

He combed his hair facing a dresser mirror with arabesque borders, listening for a floorboard creak that might suggest someone was eavesdropping outside while Bharti demonstrated her uncanny ability to recite verbatim a list of complaints about Ravi and Vineeta, i.e. the thing he needed to deal with at this moment.

She summoned him into the adjoining bathroom to hook together the back of her purple blouse as they dressed for one of the four pre-wedding dinners. They sometimes spoke in Gujarati, but when Bharti really wanted to make her point, she insisted on English.

"I not have opportunities like them. Ravi, he do something, but where's the money? Vineeta. Straight-A student. Could have been genius, but throw it away. Bhavna's son was same year in school. He start internet thing, sell it for 20 million dollars. 20 million! He was genius. So many Indians now big-shots—geniuses! Like this Pepsi woman, but our children can't even hold job. I'm not sad for me, only them, I only care about their happiness."

Bharti had never attended high school, but that didn't stop her from being a four foot six dynamo who summarized difficult issues with the nuance of a hand grenade. Jeevan had tried to tutor her, but she had ignored him, asserting common sense, street smarts, intuition, a sixth sense, powers which cumulatively made her more insightful than someone who relied on reason. Jeevan could have pointed out that there wasn't a direct correlation between money and genius, but that would only make Bharti retort that his statement was proof that Jeevan wasn't a genius, because having intelligence without money was like being a king without a kingdom. Or he could have pointed out that their children seemed perfectly happy while she was perpetually unhappy, but that would have made her retort that she was only unhappy because Jeevan wasn't man enough to deal with their children.

"You need to tell them, you stop this rock star box star business, no more Columbia Balumbia, get job! Everything in US, me me me, I want this, I won't do this. Not even ABCDs," she said, referring to the acronym for American-Born Confused Desis, the kids of Indian immigrants who struggled with their identity as half-Indian half-Americans, "just straight, boom, let's be American. It was my fault for letting you take us from India. You could have been accountant there. Children could have gone to IIT, Harvard of India, even Ravi, because in India you can make things happen right way, with *baksheesh*." A bribe.

Jeevan had heard Bharti's satisfying loop of dissatisfaction multiple times—anger at her children's selfishness, followed by scapegoat martyrdom over how she had failed as a parent, followed by resignation and detachment, followed by re-ignition of anger. How could his wife relax and enjoy her life while these Big Issues remained unresolved? Their children didn't understand what it meant to be a parent. Every one of their hurts (even if they didn't know they had them) was her hurt.

Was it better than if they had stayed in India? The question was ironic proof that Indo-phile Bharti had been infected by the Western concept of everything being a competition. In Jeevan's view, there were so many elements to experience that one shouldn't rank one versus the other. They just were. One had to extract the joy out of whatever situation presented itself. Bharti had been guilty of the homogeneous immigrant expectation that their children would study hard, attend Ivy League colleges, become doctors or engineers, get married, live close by and have children. She had expected to exploit America's opportunity while instilling Indian values, but she was no match for television, music and school friends.

Of course, Jeevan's illegitimate son Shushruth, raised by Bharti's college educated sister, checked every box of Bharti's wish list, which begged the question of whether the problem wasn't the children or Western influences, but Bharti and Jeevan. Bharti had been a child raising children. If his wife could only read at an eight grade level, how could she teach the kids to appreciate literature? If she lived according to her whims, how could she expect the kids to do otherwise?

Jeevan had been too busy avoiding Bharti's emotional rampages to be wholly present. He had used the Socratic method to instill some sense of logic when Ravi or Vineeta did something wrong and helped out on math homework as needed, but otherwise secluded himself in his study to grade papers and make the occasional secret compromise necessary to make their lives work, like his loans to the children.

He sat down on the bed waiting for Bharti to finish getting ready when there was a knock on the door. Vineeta announced herself and came in, wearing a t-shirt and an Indian skirt. She looked at him with a frozen glare. Jeevan never understood why women got so stressed over getting ready for a party.

"Is Mom here?"

Jeevan pointed to the bathroom.

"Mom, you had said you wanted me to wear specific jewelry, but I need to see it to make sure it matches my outfit."

Bharti poked her head outside.

"You wear Ma's diamond necklace," Bharti said, referring to Vineeta's deceased paternal grandmother.

Bharti motioned to Jeevan to extract the necklace from the luggage.

"Show her computer thing, too," Bharti said.

"I can only do one thing at a time," Jeevan said.

He handed the necklace to Bharti, who began clasping it around Vineeta's neck, and picked up a laptop from the corner desk. For years, Bharti had been setting up Vineeta on blind dates with Indian men, explaining that they were sons of family friends. In reality, Bharti had been sourcing the men by advertising Vineeta's "bio-data" in the newspaper India Abroad. In a frisson over mastering the internet a few weeks earlier, however, she wanted to show Vineeta the profile she had posted to the Indian Abroad dating site. Jeevan loaded the website and put the laptop on the mattress. Bharti finished with Vineeta, sat on the bed and looked at the profile proudly before inviting Vineeta over to look.

"Hindu family seeks alliance for daughter with tall, attractive, well-educated male from good family in finance, medicine or law.

Heritage: Gujarati

Weight: 110 lbs

Height: 5'5''

Occupation: Student

Religion: Hindu

Eye color: Brown

Skin complexion: Medium brown

Caste: Kshatriya

Age: 28

Food: Vegetarian

Education: B.A."

"What is this?" Vineeta asked sharply.

"I wrote it. Now everyone can see on internet, even with picture, and you can choose best man. Cheaper than newspaper!" Bharti said, beaming.

Vineeta hunched over to examine the profile before glaring at Bharti with her lips quivering.

"How could you do this to me?" she shrieked.

"Do what? I did good job," Bharti said, looking at Jeevan for support.

"Your mom thought if we put up your bio-data, you would get to meet men who are better matched to you. You can see their picture, too. It doesn't mean you have to do anything," Jeevan conciliated.

"Everyone can see this! I don't want to be on the internet! This is so humiliating," Vineeta shouted.

She began to cry and looked up at the ceiling.

"Ssshhh, they can hear you downstairs," Jeevan said.

"You think you're the Queen of Sheba, people will line up to marry you? You're not getting younger," Bharti whispered ferociously.

"This is my life! You're so selfish," Vineeta said.

"I'm selfish? *Salli!*" *Wretch.* "You think this is normal? Everyone's children getting married and having children. Why God give us such ungrateful children? How you're going to meet a nice boy?"

Jeevan prepared to get involved as Vineeta's eyes raged in defiance. In Bharti's administration, he was Chief Officer of Smoothing Things Over.

"My definition of a nice boy is different than your definition," Vineeta said.

"So, what is this definition, beti?" Jeevan interjected with his soothing voice.

She glared at him and he could tell she was considering whether to do what he hoped she would do, finally reveal the Austrian boyfriend Ravi had mentioned in his *Guide*. Better to get everything out on the table and dealt with. Would he have preferred if Vineeta agreed to an arranged marriage? Sure, from a utility maximizing perspective, arranged marriages were just an extension of what royalty had been doing for centuries across all cultures. His marriage to Bharti had been arranged when he was twenty one and she was fifteen, and after she joined him in Bombay at age eighteen, he had used her dowry to move them to London and earn his PhD in Accounting.

But he was fine the other way, too.

"Dad, I'm not going to answer this…these questions. Especially from you. Just leave me alone," Vineeta said, leaving the room and closing the door a bit more forcefully than was polite while staying in someone else's house.

Bharti began ranting against Vineeta as she applied makeup in the bathroom, while Jeevan sat back on the mirrored Rajasthani bedspread to ponder what Vineeta had meant. Especially from him? What had he done? He was the reasonable parent that his children always appealed to for support, and he had provided it as best he could while sustaining his marriage. It seemed an American pastime to observe one's parents, analyze them, write about them, talk about them, dissect them, re-assemble them, and still end up in the same place while missing the bigger picture.

It's not like Vineeta knew about his side escapades that made his arranged marriage workable. There had only been two of them.

He had started seeing Julie Zignewski, another professor, while the children were in college because she was smart and had opinions about the world. She didn't compare in beauty to Bharti, but actually provided access to her body. Jeevan was careful not to call Julie while Bharti was around and only met Julie at restaurants and hotels in Ypsilanti—but Bharti's powers of ulterior motive and conspiracy speculation also made her right on occasion.

"You're sleeping with this woman?" she had asked him one afternoon while dropping off Jeevan's lunch at his campus office as Julie was leaving his office.

He jerked his head back.

"What kind of thing is this?" he asked in the dumbed-down English he used with Bharti. "What you're saying?"

"I see how she looking at you. You think I'm stupid?"

"You're being silly."

"I'm not silly. You don't answer."

"Of course not."

He had read articles about the stereotypical signs of lying and was aware that he had probably looked sideways to think for a split second, retorted in a slightly higher pitch and fidgeted in his chair. From then on, Bharti began accusing him of cheating with different Indian acquaintances whenever she was losing an argument about whether he had misplaced her glasses or forgotten to pay a bill, and his frequent concessions were a tacit admission that something had once happened. And to add insult to injury, he faced these recriminations even after Julie had called off the affair.

His first affair had been less calculated. Back when he and his family lived in London, his brother-in-law had asked him to help Bharti's sister Lalita with the accounting for their Indian grocery store. He and Lalita spent a few evenings a week in the backroom under a dim, crooked incandescent bulb. Jeevan set up T accounts in the ledger and pointed to numbers as he heard her breath and felt her warmth. She wasn't a scholar, but demonstrated curiosity and an aptitude for learning that Bharti lacked. He began to think about her at night, suspecting that she liked him as well. His brother-in-law was short and bald with a pocked complexion, whereas Jeevan was always told he looked like *fillum* star Dev Anand, right down to the shiny black hair slicked to the side like the grooves of a vinyl record. His brother-in-law was more apt to talk about store inventory during lovemaking than Lalita's melon breasts, while Jeevan knew how to acknowledge a woman's clothing or hairstyle. His brother-in-law was street savvy and could run a store, but Jeevan sounded authoritative with his erudite vocabulary.

When he looked at Lalita one evening instead of the numbers he was explaining, their breaths fast and hearts pulsing, the kiss was less a decision than a closure. Jeevan told his brother-in-law that he would help Lalita close the store, since there was no point for all three of them to be there. The affair continued for a few months until Bharti finally asked with a specific stare whether Lalita was planning on getting a Masters in accounting, as well. Jeevan and Lalita decided not to risk ruining both their marriages. When Lalita gave birth to Shushruth and gave him to her infertile sister Sujata to raise as her own son, it both eased Jeevan's conscience and allowed him to observe and help raise his son, though Bharti's constant observations that Shushruth looked like Ravi, walked like Ravi and followed Ravi around like a little brother gave him an additional reason to move the family to America.

Despite his two infidelities (which were not the moral failings of a chronic philanderer, but momentary lapses which actually bolstered his ability to stay married and hold the family together by making him feel desirable), Jeevan loved Bharti. She made sure Jeevan was properly fed at every meal. She organized their social calendar. She was a doting mother. Their shared history bound them, regardless of Bharti's limited education. If he had felt comfortable advising his children about romance, he would have explained that love was simple—stick around someone or something long enough, and you grow to long for her or it no matter how unpleasant, like a stray dog or the smell of spoiled fruit, both of which he encountered with pleasure whenever he returned to his family's apartment in India.

Liking was much more difficult. His children wanted to like the person they married, and he feared that their expectations would leave them intolerant and unhappy in the long run. Jeevan didn't like (or dislike) Bharti. He didn't like (or dislike) accounting. He didn't like (or dislike) Ealing or Ann Arbor. They just were. When people did what they liked, they usually got in trouble, like with Jeevan and his illegitimate child. Or Ravi with his music.

Still, a part of Jeevan secretly envied Ravi. Ravi didn't recognize that he had inherited Jeevan's wanderlust because Jeevan masked it under a stoicism acquired from his own upbringing—a schedule of cold showers at 5 a.m., temple at 6.a.m., school at 6:30 a.m., playtime from 3p.m. until 4p.m., prayers with his grandparents at 4 p.m., studying from 5 to 7 p.m., then dinner. Ravi was getting to be the person Jeevan might have been under different circumstances.

Bharti finished her rant as she admired herself in the mirror.

"Maybe there will be nice boy at wedding."

"Good thing you're already married to me, he can't take you away. You look beautiful," Jeevan said, seeing his opportunity to change the subject.

Bharti's smile suggested that she knew that she was beautiful already, but was glad he was acknowledging it.

"Shall we go down? It's almost 2," he said.

His secret son was about to get married. He had seen Shushruth grow up by bringing the family to London every summer. His son looked like him—same body type, same head shape and hair line, same coloring, though a mix of facial features. He wished there would come a day he could share the truth and hug him as a father. At least Ravi and Vineeta shared a sibling-like relationship with him. On the one issue that mattered, Bharti had managed to take a stoic approach, never asking Jeevan about what she knew inside without ever being told and never treating Shushruth any differently. As long as they never acknowledged Shushruth's provenance, things would be fine. He just needed to suppress any overt emotion for the week.

He had three children who were taking different paths, though in the end, he was confident their lives would eventually be the same. Work, get married, have children, screw some things up or complain about other people screwing some things up. He had taken the family out of India to give his children the opportunity to screw things up in a more interesting way and to give Bharti the opportunity to complain about it, since she never had the chance to screw things up for herself. And along the way, he had snuck in a few screw-ups of his own. Given a choice, he was glad to have screwed up instead of spending his life complaining about other people's screw-ups, even if he had to pay the price by stoically listening to Bharti complaining for the rest of his days.

Excerpt from
Ravi's Guide to Being a Cool Indian

Dating/Marriage

My travails with Buzzthief have allowed me to mingle, shall we say, with a broad range of cultures. Western courtship is not, to my mum's disappointment, a Bollywood movie where you both start singing, magically transport to the Matterhorn with gazes of affection, change costumes a bunch of times and fall in love. It's not just enough to smile at each other. You have to make a move.

Guys and gals who don't learn to make a move end up getting arranged marriages to gals and guys from India. I'm not saying arranged marriages won't work out, in fact, knowing that you don't have the guts to kiss someone you weren't set up with probably will keep you from getting divorced. Nor am I defending non-Indians who are puzzled by arranged marriage but have a 50% rate of divorce. Principle #1: You don't learn what sex and romantic fulfillment mean unless you practice a bit, and the older generation, for all their emphasis on education, doesn't seem to understand this fact.

While the infinite amount of internet porn may make staying single seem like a palatable outcome, successful dating only requires a good hairstyle and an ability to feign interest in art/dancing or sports. Just don't assume your desirability as a potential mate correlates to the number of inebriated persons who have attempted to sleep with you.

Principle #2: As you try to find the perfect mate, categorize potential romantic interests:

Indian or non-Indian who prefers to marry an Indian

Indian or non-Indian who will marry any race

Self-loathing Indian or non-Indian who will never marry an Indian

Non-Indian who will date an Indian but only marry a non-Indian

Make things easy and date Categories 1 and 2. Don't be insecure like Pankaj and deem every potential mate as Category 3 or 4. And most importantly, don't end up as a self-loathing Indian who wastes their prime years with a Category 4, or you'll reach your mid-thirties with a receded hairline, limited fertility and the need to tell your parents you're ready for that arranged marriage.

Chapter 8
Shushruth's Wedding
London, England

Vineeta

The wedding and reception was taking place at the finest primary school gym in Ealing. Vineeta, Ravi and her parents followed the handwritten signs on the cinder block walls in the school hallways. They arrived at a cavernous gym, where a balance beam, gymnastics horse and parallel bars had been pushed against the wall in the far left corner. She had vague recollections of the one year she had attended the school— all the kids in blue and white uniforms but socially clustered with their respective races.

In the far right corner, Shushruth and his bride Falguni sat on thrones on a canopied mandap platform while a priest sat on the floor in front of them chanting wedding prayers in Sanskrit that no one understood. Shushruth wore a red Rajasthani style turban and ivory Jodhpuri suit, while Falguni wore a red and gold sari draped over her head with various gold accessories, heavy eyeliner and red lipstick.

It was not only customary to arrive late given the three hour length of the ceremony, but also for everyone to socialize while it was going on. Her parents situated near a portable bar at the front of the gym and began introducing her and Ravi to distant relatives. She nodded politely while observing younger girls wearing modern sari wraps and lehenga skirts with sharp blues and silvery embroidery. Her clothing still had the motley colors and mirror adornments of yesteryear. They looked like princesses, with bared mid-riffs and shadowed eyelids, while she looked like…her age. Her outfit was more authentic, but if modern Indian clothing copied Disney at this point, what did authentic even mean?

She could impress the girls by telling them she was dating an Austrian. But she hadn't even managed to tell her parents even after they had boasted about auctioning her like chattel online. It had been the prime moment in her life story when she was supposed to have demonstrated her character development by asserting her independence. Except that instead of giving an eloquent speech about how they needed to modernize their expectations, how she was dating someone and how she was going to live the life she wanted to lead, she had simply slammed the bedroom door.

She was sure she had the courage to confront them it, but deep down she knew Hans wasn't worth it. If given a choice between hanging out with Ravi and his friends or Hans, she knew which one she preferred. So her life story would be the boring life story where nothing interesting happened. It would be the life story where she dated a boring architect until they both got bored and she would find some other boring person to date who wouldn't be worth boring her parents about.

Ravi excused himself to get a drink. He brought back something for Vineeta with an orange red color, but as he began to speak, Pankaj's mom came by and grabbed him by the arm. Without saying anything to anyone, she pulled him away as if he was a five year old about to get scolded.

So Vineeta was left to endure the greeting ritual by herself. She wondered how Hans would fit into a crowd like this. She had never appreciated what "marrying into a family meant", but this ceremony highlighted the stark difference in the various lives she led. It would certainly be nice if there was a charming Indian hunk who came to this ceremony dressed in a custom-tailored suit and wooed her, thus sweeping away all her dilemmas at once.

She felt a tap on her shoulder.

"Hey."

Ian, dressed in a sport jacket, slacks and a button down. They gave each other a hug.

"You like nice."

"Thanks. And you look handsome."

She began nervously sipping from her drink from a narrow mixer straw. What could she say to avoid bringing up the prior night's awkwardness, from the strippers to Ian's engagement to his argument with Ravi? Not that she regretted going to the bachelor party. It had taken her mind off her father's infidelity. And while this morning's hullabaloo with her parents brought back dark emotions, she felt the convergence of all these conflicts was forcing her to make some necessary decisions.

"I think those are just for mixing the drink, by the way, not drinking," he said.

"Really? I've been drinking from them for years. It's a good way to pace myself."

"Makes sense. Where's Ravi?" Ian asked, scanning the crowd.

The question triggered a different alarm in her mind.

"One of our aunts pulled him away. By the way, please don't mention, you know, the other person…"

She grabbed Ian by the arm and pulled him away from her parents, who seemed engaged in a deeper conversation with a man who may or may not have been a relative.

"Sorry. My mom doesn't know about Hans," she said conspiratorially.

If she was going to break up with Hans, better to avoid having her mom know she had ever dated him in the first place. Though she couldn't tell Ian about it before she had told Hans.

"Seriously? You've been dating, like, a year."

"Seriously," she confirmed.

"What's the issue?"

"She wants me to marry an Indian guy."

"It's not like Ravi has dated an Indian girl."

"Ravi is his own category. I think I'm supposed to make up for all the things he's not doing. She thinks I can set an example for him."

"Didn't Ravi mention him in, you know, the book?"

"Well, Dad read it and knows, but Mom kind of skimmed it and didn't understand anything. She asked me to interpret it, and I left that part out."

"And Hans isn't curious about your family?"

"He's met Ravi."

"Well, it's kind of like, you probably have to deal with it at some point."

"I suppose."

She stared at the black sneakers of a middle-aged man in a suit. All her conversations kept coming back to the same thing.

"I mean, if you think it's worth it," Ian said.

"Yeah, I don't know. Why don't you tell me about your fiancée. How did you propose?" she said.

"Well, I kind of didn't."

"But you said you were getting married."

Ian shuffled his feet and digitally stroked his mustache.

"How do I explain it? I've never proposed to her. At some point she started calling me her fiancée as a joke, and when I never objected, it just kind of became assumed."

"Which you're happy about or…not?"

"Look, she's an amazing woman. On tour we met some messed up people. So she's probably good for me."

"'Probably' isn't the best standard for marriage."

He puckered his face and appeared to be choosing his words carefully.

"I know. But put it in context. She organizes our workouts, our weekends, our meals. She's a bit like you—confident, ambitious, opinionated. And maybe that's better in the long run."

Did that mean he was still available? On the other hand, if Vineeta was just like his fiancée, did that mean she had no chance anyway?

"But the long run is really long. Do you find her interesting?"

"How to put this. We watch sophisticated movies. Read acclaimed books. Go to popular restaurants. And I would love to talk about the plot, filmography, acting, novelty, presentation and credibility of these things in some detail instead of assessing everything as "good" or "terrible". But then I wonder, why is that so important? Can I expect to find that trait in the same person who's great in every other way?"

She wanted to exclaim, "Yes! Exactly," but it seemed strange to try to bond over the way they were equally disillusioned with their partners.

"So you're planning on proposing?" she asked.

"No, it's more complicated. Her father always asks me what I plan on doing next. He's offered me the chance to join the insurance company he runs. But that's not my thing. So I'm fairly certain he wouldn't be unhappy if we broke up. I'm not sure what I'm going to do. She tells me to ignore it, but there's always a nagging sense that I don't belong in her world. Everything's a five star buffet, and I'm just a guy who belongs in a diner."

"I would think you could fit in anywhere."

"Yes and no. I can dress the part, but inside I know I'd rather be somewhere else."

"Because you prefer it or because people make you feel out of place?"

"You're referring to me being black?"

She shrugged her shoulders in assent.

"I don't know. You love talking about race."

"You avoid talking about it."

"Because it never makes anything better. People get defensive and act like you have a persecution complex. It was actually Ravi that made me approach things differently. He was the first person I met who could start a debate about which racist epithet each of us had been called was funnier. He never lets the possibility of being judged by his skin color stop him from engaging with people."

"I never thought people took life lessons from Ravi."

"Maybe you're missing out."

Had she been too quick to dismiss Ravi's input? As much as she loved him, she also resented his glib and blunt assessments and his older sibling's pretense of being wise. Especially when his life had as many challenges as hers did.

"Is that why your fiancée didn't come to London? We're the folks in the diner?" she asked.

"Not at all. She's busy with work. And she kind of thinks I'm hanging out with my uncle."

"Why?"

"I was visiting him because his health is declining. But I didn't want to tell her who else I was hanging out with or what we'd be doing."

"So we are the folks in the diner. It's not a good sign that you're hiding things from the woman you're going to marry."

"But it is a good sign of how good an influence she is that I'm ashamed to mention them," he chuckled. "I'm joking."

"Should I be offended?"

"It's obviously not about you."

"Ravi."

"Ravi's great, he's my best friend. But you have to admit, he is an acquired taste."

"I've always thought of him as a harmless clown," Vineeta said.

"Except when he's making fun of you."

"I know it more than anyone else does."

She rubbed her eyes. Her contact lenses had been drying up all morning, so that the elementary school recycling posters on the wall appeared like blurry modern art paintings above the mingling crowd.

"Really. Did he say he thinks of you every time he pees because you look like an asparagus stalk?" Ian asked.

"Did he post a YouTube video of you fighting with your mum for the world to see?"

"Did he tell you to start smoking so that you stop sounding like Alvin and the Chipmunks?"

"Did he say he can't tell if you look more like a squirrel or a chipmunk?"

"Alright, it's a draw."

"Hardly. I have a lifetime of insults," Vineeta said.

"You're probably right. I love Ravi, but I don't think he understands that life moves on."

"If moving on means this is where we end up, can you blame him? You had some good years together," Vineeta said.

"We did. I just can't seem to convince Jessica that Ravi isn't so much a person you judge based on normal human courtesies, but more a force of nature who makes things happen."

A waiter interrupted to offer them chaat puri, a fried wheat disk topped with potatoes, onions, yoghurt, tamarind chutney and spices. Vineeta took one, eyed it and placed it in her mouth whole, covering her mouth with a napkin to hide the process of eating it. Ian consumed one in a bite and took a second, while observing her chewing with a smirk.

"Don't look at me while I'm eating!" she said.

"Why not? You look cute. And I love these things," Ian said.

She felt herself blushing. She paused to finish, dabbing at the corners of her mouth with a napkin.

"They're awesome, just messy. Anyway, if Hans didn't like my friends, I think I'd dump him before I dumped them."

"Doesn't say much about your relationship."

"Or it says something about my loyalty."

"Fair enough. I'm an asshole."

"That's for you to decide. Maybe Ravi's the asshole. I don't know what's happened between you two."

"We've had a lot of good times. But it wasn't real, was it? It…do you want to go for a walk outside for a moment? I don't know if it was those hor d'oeuvres, but I feel suddenly feel really hot and dizzy," Ian said.

"Yeah, sure."

They weaved through a crowd of mostly Indian men in suits and Indian women in colorful traditional garb before reaching a hallway with short lockers and speckled concrete leading into a playground. The moon was just starting to show in the distance behind a jungle gym. They started walk a lap around the perimeter of the playground. Vineeta's skirt dragged on the ground.

"What were we talking about?" Ian asked.

"You were saying the time with the band wasn't real. But nothing's real. Reality is whatever set of memories you have. And he's better at creating them than most people."

"Do you think we should get back together?"

"Are you sick of the band?"

"Let's be honest, he is the band. He wrote the songs, booked the gigs. The rest of us were just tagging along. I don't know. People don't really listen to bands anymore. It's all pop stars and DJs. Like Jessica says, I'm the recognizable voice. Our third album bombed. What's the point of repeating that?" Ian asked.

"Makes sense. It's your right to do what makes sense for you."

"Right. But I wouldn't exist without him. And he probably would have existed without me."

"Maybe. But that doesn't mean you always have to do what he wants."

"So instead I just end up doing what the label or Jessica or her father wants."

"That's a choice," Vineeta said.

"I know. I've never been good about pushing back."

"It's a skill. You can learn it. Especially if you have a sibling like Ravi."

"Fair enough. Anyway, enough about me. I think you graduated, right? What's next?"

"I was supposed to start a job with GE working in compliance in their finance arm when I got back. But then a few weeks ago a job opened up at the UN drafting resolutions relating to human rights abuses. They called me in, and I think the interview went well. Dad wants me to stick to the GE job because it pays more, but it feels like I'm going against my principles."

"What's wrong with working for GE?"

"I don't know, it's trying to make money off people without worrying if they're actually helping people?"

"Isn't it for the people to decide if they're being helped?"

"I guess. I don't know, it just feels off. Hans says I should take it."

"He knows you pretty well. So it's probably good advice."

"You say things, you do things, and sometimes you feel like two perfectly good people leading parallel lives."

"So you don't think he knows you?"

Vineeta began playing with the gems on her necklace.

"I don't know, I guess he does, but sometimes I think Mom is right. Maybe the only people who can really know you are those that have been through what you've been through. But then, as a woman, your clock is ticking, so you're also weighing whether it makes sense to gamble when you see how badly it's turning out for your friends."

"You'd have no trouble finding someone else."

She locked eyes with him.

"You have to say that."

"No. It's true. Lots of people are attracted to chipmunks," Ian said.

"You think I look like a chipmunk?" she asked, bewildered.

"I was referring to what you said earlier …chipmunks are better looking than squirrels. And if you look like a chipmunk, Halle Barry looks like a squirrel."

"That is the strangest compliment I've ever received," she said, warmed by the possibility that he did find her attractive .

"Strange is better than boring."

"Well, thanks. Should we go back in? They'll wonder where we went."

They returned through the corridor. She dragged a finger nail across the lockers to create a rhythmic click-click-tuk-tuk-tuk before leading them to the vicinity of the gym they had left.

"How much longer are you in London?" Vineeta asked.

"Sunday. I thought I'd be hanging out with Ravi, but I'm not sure he'll want that now."

"He does want you here. He just doesn't know what he wants to say to you yet."

"He's never short for words."

"That's not true. There are some words that don't come as easy to him."

"Yeah, I guess. When do you head back?"

"Tuesday."

"Do you have more wedding events to go to?"

"Fortunately not, I could use a day to unwind a bit. We're staying at Pankaj's place, but I'll probably excuse myself to go to the museum or something."

"I've always been meaning to go. You're going to the Gallery? Or the Tate?"

"The British Museum. You're welcome to join."

"For as many times as I've been here, I've never made it to any of them. But you'd probably want a day to yourself."

"You'd be okay company."

"What time are you thinking?"

She noticed Ravi returning with Pankaj. Awful timing. Ravi placed his arm around Ian's shoulder. They looked at each other sheepishly, clasped hands and pulled each other in for a prolonged chest hug. Once they released each other, Ian acknowledged Pankaj with a head nod.

Ravi explained that he was helping Pankaj meet a girl. When the DJ started playing music, a girl invited Ravi to the dance floor, and Ian invited Vineeta.

He had rhythm, but his moves were robotic and repetitive. She had taken enough dance classes to swing her hips and torso with graceful confidence. Rainbow lights shone from revolving lamps next to the DJ. She wished the rest of the night was just dancing, but after twenty minutes, the DJ announced dinner. Unfortunately, Ian's scribbled place card had him seated with a group of teenagers, while Vineeta, Ravi and Pankaj were seated with the bride and groom and their respective parents. She couldn't invite him to their crowded family table. The bride and groom came by, and each member started to give their blessings.

Pankaj

When the wedding began, Pankaj joined his parents in the front row squirming in the plastic seats. He was simultaneously annoyed he had to sit there for three hours, and annoyed at the group of people his age chatting in a circle to the side instead of suffering like he was. To make things worse, an attractive girl wearing a silver and bronze salvar kameez and tiered-diamond earrings smiled at someone's comment with mischief and sincerity. Pankaj waited for a viewing angle of her butt, which he hoped would be big so that he wouldn't have to feel the shame of not having the confidence to approach her. Unfortunately, her butt was perfect, and Pankaj immediately felt the harsh pang of infatuation. While he hated discussing his love life with his parents, his mum probably knew who she was and could introduce him.

Pankaj still remembered having his pants yanked down while hanging from the parallel bars in this gym. The gym teacher had told him to laugh it off and get even. In winters, the dark gray skies had cast a pall through the large grid windows, while gym class had cast a pall inside. Primary school had been a series of humiliations—kids making pig noises at him, Steve Gadberry chewing up cookies and spitting the goo into his hair, Pete Morrissey stealing his fancy new mechanical pencil which re-loaded simply by shaking the lead out—punctuated by racial epithets. Once Ravi had moved to Ann Arbor, Pankaj had lost his occasional defender and friend and had gone from being just bullied to being bullied and ignored. He had weathered secondary school by joining a similar set of outcasts in the chess club and science club. Grades had been his salvation, his path to showing all of these chavs he was better than them. Now, as he felt his Porsche's key fob pressing through the wool of his custom tailored Savile Row suit, he knew that he had. In a few months, he would make Managing Director and take it one step further, donating enough money to get the school re-named after him. Though maybe that was expensive? He could donate the thousand quid it would take to get the gym named after him.

When the ceremony finally ended, people dispersed for cocktails from a bar near the front of the gym. Pankaj got a scotch before asking his mum about the girl he had seen. She lit up with excitement, identifying her as the daughter of a cousin of a friend from Bombay. Pankaj felt heartened by this information, thinking she would be impressed by his accent and English upbringing. His mum didn't know the family, but she would find out more. In the meantime, she suggested that Pankaj take Ravi with him to meet her. Pankaj demurred, but his mum sought Ravi out and dragged him over to Pankaj.

"Your mum asked me to help you get married," Ravi said.

Pankaj hadn't decided whether he had completely forgiven Ravi or not. He had been cordial at the strip club because he had wanted Shushruth to have a good time. He looked at his mum. If Pankaj didn't go with Ravi, his mum would ferret out the real reason he didn't want Ravi's help. Then their fight would become a whole family saga, eating up weeks of Pankaj's time as elders called him to force him to reconcile. Not to mention his mum would probably say that Pankaj was partially to blame. Even if an earthquake hit she would somehow find a reason he had caused it to happen.

"Don't say anything stupid," Pankaj whispered.

"Then I'll have nothing to say, and we'll be left with whatever stupid thing you plan on saying," Ravi said.

Pankaj was envious of Ravi's wit. Ravi liked to attack a conversation, ready for a good joust, while Pankaj could only sit back and observe the other side's moves before parrying. Could Pankaj really conclude he was smarter than Ravi? Maybe he was just more educated.

Ravi continued, "When we get there, play it cool, like it's a fun game we're having and we could have approached anyone, and if the girl doesn't show any interest, just act like it doesn't matter because we're having such a good time and she's the one missing out."

Pankaj tried to mentally record the advice verbatim. He had no idea how to approach a girl. He always felt judged, which felt unfair. Why should a girl have the right to judge him anymore than he judged her? He was already judged enough by his parents, so he usually avoided meeting anyone.

Ravi walked right up to the girl her as she chatted with her mum or aunt or some older lady.

"Sorry to interrupt, but my aunt says she thinks you're visiting from India. My other aunt says you live here somewhere. I said, 'Well, why don't you ask them?' and they looked at each other like I was crazy. So, which is it?" Ravi said.

"You mean me?" the younger girl asked.

"Aren't the two of you related?"

Ravi guided the conversation through the women's relationship to each other (aunt and niece), their country of origin (India) and their association with Falguni before introducing Pankaj and effusively praising his success in banking. Pankaj said a few short words before Ravi told the ladies to save both him and Pankaj a dance. He began leading Pankaj toward Vineeta.

"Alright, what do you think? We even?" Ravi asked.

"I could have met her on my own."

"You could have, you should have, etcetera etcetera, but now you have. I'm really sorry about the other night, it didn't go according to plan, but life only moves in one direction, so let's go forward together."

Ravi held his hand out for a fist bump. If Pankaj actually got a date with this woman, this week's events would have been worth it. He pressed his fist against Ravi's.

When they returned to the crowd, Pankaj followed Ravi as returned to where Vineeta was and greeted his friend Ian with a bro-hug. After fifteen minutes of small talk, the DJ started playing an upbeat Bollywood song. Shushruth and Falguni made a grand entrance in a Western suit and dress and danced below a basketball hoop before the DJ invited everyone to join.

Pankaj got another scotch and felt himself sweating as he tried to work up the courage to ask the girl they had met to dance with him. He replayed Ravi's advice: play it cool, talk to her just like she was anyone else and that it didn't matter if she didn't like him. He noticed her approach him. He turned, pleased with how much easier this was going to be than he thought.

"Hey, do you like…dancing?" he said, shimmying his hips to be playful.

She gave him a shy smile and said, "You know, you read my mind," but continued walking to Ravi. "Can I have that dance now?"

Blood rushed to Pankaj's face. His mind briefly blanked out. He felt his heart thumping. How could he have been so stupid? Just when he thought he had overcome Ravi's ability to deceive him, he had been deceived again. Ravi had included himself in the invitation to dance so that he could get the girl.

He tried to calm himself down. He could play this game. It was like chess, for every move there was an effective counter. Ravi had the initial allure of being in a rock band, but Pankaj was a trader, which was also sexy, not to mention more stable. He would get his chance.

The group dispersed as Ian asked Vineeta to dance. Pankaj spotted the girl's aunt. That was it. Indian society was run by the elders, especially the elder women. The girl's aunt would help the girl recognize that Pankaj was the real catch, the man to give her a stable, prosperous life. He invited her to dance. She looked a little puzzled, but he shuffled in front of her while mentioning his title at the firm, the fancy district of London in which he lived and the Porsche he drove. She excused herself after one song, after which Pankaj hovered at the edge of the dance floor hoping the girl would leave Ravi and ask him for a turn. No luck, but hopefully her aunt would argue in his favor.

The DJ stopped the music for dinner, but said there would be more dancing afterwards. Pankaj got another refill of scotch, searched out his dining table by the recessed bleachers and pretended to play with Yagna's baby so that no one could ascertain his state of mind. He also sat where Ravi wouldn't be able to sit next to him. Eventually his parents, Ravi's parents and Ravi and Vineeta sat down. Shushruth and Falguni stopped by to receive blessings from the elders by bowing down as they were tapped on the crown of their heads.

"Maybe Pankaj and Ravi will get inspired now," Shushruth said.

"So Pankaj, when are you getting married?" Ravi's mum asked.

Pankaj assumed she was striking first, before her own children were mentioned.

"Maybe tonight his luck will change, he likes this one girl. We introduce him to so many nice girls, he just keeps saying he's not interested. A good looking boy with a good job, why does he have so much trouble?" his mum asked.

"Mum, I don't have any trouble! They're not my style," Pankaj said.

"Why not? This girl tonight is your style?" his mum asked.

Did she have to announce it to the table?

"There's no girl tonight, I've met a bunch of people. Anyway, these Indian girls are all traditional, and I'm not traditional."

"What does that mean?" his mum asked.

"Do we have to have this conversation now?"

"I'm just curious what kind of girl you'd like."

He couldn't volunteer the one drunken girl in college who had pulled him into a room and started kissing him before passing out while he ejaculated in his pants. The internet provided him with a more efficient outlet for his physical urges, anyway.

"I want someone who can discuss world events."

"What, like whether they like Princess Diana?" Ravi's mum asked.

"She's been dead for ten years and didn't have any role in anything, but something like that," Pankaj said.

He pressed down on a bhajia to remove some oil and avoid their stares.

"Falguni has a nice cousin. You should meet her," his mum offered.

"Yeah, she's going to visit here next year. You could Skype with her now," Falguni said.

"I'm sure she's nice, but I'm fine."

"Just one call, nah? What will it hurt you?" Falguni asked.

"Let him think about it, don't put him on the spot," Shushruth said. "I was asking Pankaj if he knew how to reach this girl Ravi wanted to meet again."

Years before, Pankaj had lined up passes to one of Ravi's concerts for a college friend, who in turn had brought a girl named Pilar. Pankaj wasn't in attendance, and though he had subsequently met Pilar, couldn't distinguish her in his memory from some of the other girls Ravi had dated. Pankaj wasn't interested in contacting his college friend for Pilar's number because in retrospect, the term "college friend" was a generous description for someone who only contacted Pankaj when he wanted something.

Not to mention that Ravi seemed to be stealing the girl Pankaj was interested in this evening.

"Ravi has a girl he likes?" Ravi's mum asked.

"Pilar, wasn't it?" Shushruth asked.

"Peelar?" Ravi's mum asked.

Pankaj had no intention of helping Ravi, but at least they weren't talking about him anymore. Ravi sat up in his chair, shaken from his lethargy.

"Not the best place for this, right," Ravi said.

"I just want to get you her number," Shushruth said.

"What kind of Indian name is this?" Ravi's mum asked.

"It's not Indian. It's Spanish," Ravi said.

"I don't want a Spanish daughter-in-law. *Su fish-bish khais badu deevas?" You'll eat fish-bish every day?*

"Your input is duly noted," Ravi said.

"It's okay if she's not Indian, this is a modern age. If Ravi picks one girl and settles down, that's a big step," Shushruth said. "Pankaj, you can get her number?"

"Probably not, I'm not in touch with that person anymore," Pankaj said.

"So, you get her number, then maybe we'll have two more weddings next year," his mum said.

"I just said I don't think I can."

"Come on, it can't be that hard. You young people have your internet and the Facebook and the Google," his father added.

"So now I'm supposed to help Ravi? This girl's better off being left alone, anyway," Pankaj said.

"What kind of statement is that?" his mum snapped.

"Ravi's your cousin," his dad said.

"She's Indian girl from Spain?" Ravi's mum asked.

Pankaj wiped his hands on a napkin, looking past Shushruth and Falguni and through the large window on the back wall into the black void of the back alleyway. He had spent numerous hours in this alley as a child, but now the neighborhood and the dinner all felt foreign to him. He pushed on the table to shift his chair back, accidentally knocking a fork to the floor, which he kicked under the table in annoyance.

"I don't get this family. Ravi makes a fool of all of us. Which he's been doing for years, but this time he does it in print so that everyone we know can read, and for some reason we're acting like he's a poor child to be pitied and helped. Why exactly?

Because we have some genetic commonality? So fucking what? I'm sorry, I didn't mean to curse. But strangers treat me better than he does."

"You're embarrassing all of us," his dad said.

"No, no, it's okay. Let him get it out of his system. I've apologized, now he vents, then we can move on, this is a good step," Ravi said.

"Your press release to everyone in the world, that's an apology?" Pankaj asked.

"What press release?" his mum asked.

"It's just a phone number, you give it to him, then you do what you want," his dad said.

"Oh, come on. You're going to do this to me?"

"*Chal, chal.* I'll give you extra *kulfi* after dinner," his mum said. *Come, come, I'll give you more pistachio ice cream after dinner.*

He hated being manipulated, the whole… Indian thing. He had earned his independence but kept getting dragged into matters that weren't his concern. He wanted to kill his relationship with Ravi, and his family kept arriving like an EMT team to resuscitate it. His colleagues hardly even spoke to their parents, let alone live at home at their insistence or man their stores on weekends when an employee was sick (he imagined the *Evening Standard*'s headline of "Million Dollar Banker Moonlights at Convenience Store for 5 Pounds an Hour").

"I don't even have the number," Pankaj said.

"But your friend has it, right?" Shushruth asked.

Pankaj looked around at everyone looking at him.

"Fine, I'll give Shushruth my friend's number. Then I'm out of it."

"*Bahoth dayo,*" his mum said while a waiter added two more bhajias to Pankaj's plate under his objecting wave. *Very obedient boy.*

"Thanks man. I owe you one," Ravi said.

Pankaj waited until the DJ announced that it was time for wedding speeches. As Shushruth's father ascended the stage, Pankaj walked over to Ravi. He leaned in and whispered into his ear, "Don't think I'm doing this for you. It's only because they pressured me into it. Once this wedding is done, so are we," before sitting back down.

Ravi

Ravi hadn't expected the girl to approach him for a dance. He had tried to get her to dance with Pankaj, but she had said there were plenty of men like Pankaj she could meet in India, only better-looking. He hadn't been able to turn her invitation down since he had been the one who had suggested a dance in the first place. So now he was back to square one with Pankaj.

The alcohol was making him feel maudlin and sentimental. In case Dalinc maimed him in the morning, he should probably clear up all these resentments now. As Shushruth's dad finished his wedding speech, he instinctively stood up, ascended the podium and took the microphone as Shushruth's father hugged the bride and groom. He stared out at the two hundred attendees, inspired to give a speech no one had requested.

"I know all of you are a little nervous about me giving a speech at Shusruth's wedding, but here's a fact—we're brothers, me, him and Pankaj. We grew up together in Ealing. We played together every weekend. And that means we have a connection that goes beyond words. I can tell you which superhero underwear Shushruth wore each year of his life, from Spiderman to Iron Man. So when he's lucky enough to marry a beautiful girl like Falguni and start a new chapter in his life, I have no choice but to embarrass him a little and let him know how proud I am of him and the fact that I'm lucky enough to have him in my life.

See, of the three of us, Shushruth was always the one who never overreacted to anything. You could punch him in the face, and he would apologize and just keep enough distance so that it didn't happen again. You could blame him for breaking a window, and he would take the punishment because he figured you were all in it together. I suppose that you could say we prepared him for marriage, apologizing for shi…things he didn't do.

Even now, Shushruth is the glue that keeps Pankaj and us together when life is pulling all of us in different directions. We make a good team in a way—a banker who causes the problems, a musician who distracts you from them and a doctor who fixes them," Ravi said, gesturing towards his cousins to a few chuckles in the crowd.

"When Shusruth told me he was getting married, at first I thought he was a bit young to settle down, but then I realized it's his chance to finally spend time with a woman. It's the only subject in school in which I studied more than him."

Dead silence. Ravi jumped down from the podium and paused in front of Falguni, who was now wearing a pink outfit with silver jewels. She looked at him through a mask of makeup, while her family gave him nervous, expectant looks.

"So Falguni, now is when I'd like to some nice words about you, but really, I don't know much about you. For that matter, neither does Shushruth, but hell, if he can put up with me, he can certainly put up with you. Shushruth, he understands what it means to be family. No matter how many mistakes you make, he's there, because he's your family. Hell, you're marrying into a family that includes me, which most would consider a big mistake, but…" Ravi waved to her family members, "…your family is right there. So Shushruth will fit right in. If I had one piece of advice, it would be this…"

Ravi noticed Vineeta on the edge of her seat biting her bottom lip. He paused to look around as some sixth sense tried to alert him to something. He paused, but felt like he couldn't keep the crowd hanging.

"…if you happen to get a pole in the mail and you're wondering what it's for, it's not for tetherball. And it comes with a bonus instruction manual, inspired appropriately enough, by the *Kamasutra*, which, for those of you who have read it, was …"

Shushruth was walking over with a frown, and Ravi realized his sixth sense had been trying to alert him to the possibility that ensuring Shushruth's future sexual well-being in front of this crowd was not the best choice. Shushruth took the microphone from Ravi's hand.

"Sorry, '*thodi si jo pili hai, chori tho nahi ki hai,*'" Shushruth said to the crowd, reciting a line from a famous Amitabh movie song to describe Ravi's state. *He may have drank a little, but at least he didn't steal anything.*

The crowd chuckled, and Ravi felt the blood burning his face after being dismissed by the one person who had always stood by him. His younger cousin, the one who had always looked up to him, was now clearly just embarrassed by him and had made him the punchline to get out of an awkward moment. Shushruth put his hand on Ravi's back and pushed him toward his seat without thanking him for his speech.

He sat back down. Everyone avoided his eyes except Vineeta. The sharp freeze of her eyes confirmed what the crowd had already let him know. An uncomfortable sweat made his collar feel itchy. He hadn't bombed in front of a crowd by himself for a long time.

He tried to rationalize what had just happened as someone else began another speech. He was trying to be funny. Sometimes jokes didn't sound as funny spoken as they did in his head. If it was him, he wouldn't have minded the attempt. His American friends would have been in hysterics, like it had been a scene out of *American Pie*.

He took a big gulp of his vodka.

Of course, it wasn't him, it was Shushruth, but he was always the one pushing Shushruth out of his comfort zone and helping him adapt. Then again, Shushruth was older now, getting married in front of his family and friends. Was Shushruth upset with him? He had chosen an Amitabh song, which meant that Ravi was Amitabh in this situation, which maybe meant that Shushruth still perceived Ravi as the hero. Except that sometimes Amitabh was the immature alcoholic who needed to grow up, get his life together and do something heroic to win over a girl.

Ravi could blame the stripper pole reference on the alcohol. But in the context of the prior week, Shushruth's act felt emblematic of something bigger. His friends and relatives were all distancing themselves from him.

Was it something specific about him? Ravi used to give them the agendas they were too confused or insecure or passive to choose on their own. Had he lost his charm or had they changed? He had embraced being Western from an early age because it was easier than trying to please everyone, like Vineeta, and ending up confused. It was more effective than mostly following the Indian rules, like Pankaj, and being a social misfit. It was more fun than completely following the Indian rules like Shushruth. And he had shared his success by giving all of them an entrée into Western society, but now it seemed that as they had gotten jobs and romantic partners and figured out their own identities, their needs had changed.

Though it was more than that. Apparently they had just been putting up with "his charm" as the price of admission, which was a cost they no longer needed to bear. Their words were hiding there in plain sight.

"Everything for you's a joke. Some of us have real lives…Even strangers treat me better than [you do]."

"Better to be an adult playing kids' games than a kid pretending to be an adult."

"There's a difference between a joke and mocking the core of someone's identity. And not just someone. People who have loved and supported you."

"I know you put together Buzzthief and kept it going, but that phase is done. Jessica wants to get married."

Was it just his words or also the way he acted? Pankaj's anger was justified over the casino. His family's anger was justified over some passages in the *Guide*. What exactly had Ravi done wrong with Ian? He wasn't entirely sure, but he just wanted to move on. He considered asking for the microphone one more time so that he could apologize. To confess that he went overboard at times, but that going overboard had gotten him to where he was. To explain that each of the cousins had taken a different path to get to where they were, and each of them had achieved exactly what they had wanted, so not everything had gone badly. Somehow their parents' messages of working hard and succeeding had gotten through. That friends and family shouldn't judge each other on the things each other said or did. What did the Talking Heads say about the matter? Something about words not exactly doing what you needed them to? Or was it "facts"? Either way, his point was that friends and family should know what was in each other's heart and forgive the rest.

But it was Shushruth's wedding, not the place to make himself the center of attention. He would have to just sit there, playing with the folds of the white polyester table cover, trying to convince himself that his speech wasn't that bad.

The remaining speeches went by in a blur. When it was their turn to go to the buffet line, Ravi asked Ian to join them, hoping to get some emotional support, but Vineeta engaged Ian in a conversation about cooking Indian food. Ravi felt a pang of loneliness as he doled out heaps of rice, chickpeas, spinach and chicken curry on to his plate and accidentally onto the tablecloth. Ian not only seemed to prefer his fiancée to Ravi, but also Vineeta. How had their friendship had deteriorated so badly?

As they returned to their table with their plates, Vineeta invited Ian to eat with them. The two of them continued an intense conversation, while Ravi assessed his dinner plate. A mound of greasy gravies that would help absorb the alcohol in Ravi's system. The only problem was the new alcohol that replaced it.

After dessert, Ravi followed Vineeta and Ian to the dance floor and joined a circle which was dancing to a recent popular Hindi song. The Indian girl who had approached him earlier maneuvered Ravi out of the group dance into the corner with some clever foot moves.

"Bold wedding speech," she said, slanting her eyes at him with mischievous accusation.

He shrugged. He didn't want to betray Pankaj, but her interest in him briefly restored his confidence—not everyone thought he was a buffoon—until she peppered him with questions about his music career. She was more interested in his fame. Like Nala, the model who had constantly evaluated whether she and Ravi looked good together in the mirror, or Sheila, who had texted friends whenever they met another celebrity. Women who were haughty and needy because they were raised to believe they were princesses, or were insecure and needy because they weren't so raised. Love seemed simple until you saw the number of ways people could screw themselves up.

His answers felt disjointed. Was it because it was too loud or because he didn't make any sense? But she started rambling after each of his answers and he realized his answers didn't really matter. They danced to a couple of songs before he tried again to convince her to dance with Pankaj. This time he offered to introduce her to the celebrity of her choice if she would dance with Pankaj and pretended that he knew Orlando Bloom to close the deal. He directed her to the dining table where Pankaj was sitting by himself, scrolling through his phone. He saw her tap Pankaj on the shoulder, who nearly dropped his phone in excitement. Ravi retreated to the bar and struck up a conversation about Muai-Thai training with the bartender. Then he retreated to an empty dinner table to observe people chatting in the crowd by the door.

Ravi saw the flat-top of the man's head first, towering over the others. The crowd seemed to part as if the man was Moses at the Red Sea, except that instead of a robe and staff he wore jeans and a t-shirt with the crest of a soccer club called Hajduk Split.

"Good party," Dalinc said.

"What the fuuu…I didn't know you had been invited," Ravi said.

It must have been his phone. Somehow Dalinc had put a tracker on his phone.

"Well, I think these people have lots of money. I'm sure if I explain the problem you are having, they will gladly help out. You already have the speeches? I can give speech."

"Do we have to do this here?"

"Where else? You prefer the bathroom?" Dalinc asked, lifting his hands.

"No, this is good. You said three days. It's only been two."

"This is the problem when you don't go to college. Where you go again?"

"Michigan."

"Yes, they probably teach you to count, so then you can play cards with money you don't have. Me, I don't count so good, so not a problem. Two days, three days, who can tell? I also worry that maybe you won't be here tomorrow."

"Here's the problem. In my efforts to pay you back quickly, I may have used my dad's funds in a way…"

"You gambled."

"Look. You clearly seem to know everything I do. But it's not as bad as that. I'll be getting the money back, because I didn't lose it, but the casino I went to refused to give it back right away and…"

"I don't have time for stupid story. Here is what we can do…"

Ravi's mom suddenly appeared to Dalinc's left dressed in a red and gold sari. She motioned her head toward Dalinc.

"Who this?"

"A friend. He, um, used to be a roadie for the band."

He wasn't sure where this was headed.

"What your name?" she asked, peering up like David to Goliath.

"Dalinc."

"You like the food?" she asked.

"I don't eat."

"You have to eat. You can't come and not eat."

"I'm not hungry."

She looked at his belly.

"You always hungry. Come, I show you."

She grabbed Dalinc's hand and began pulling him toward the buffet, which was in the process of being cleared. He reluctantly followed while looking back at Ravi, who trailed them. She grabbed a plate, instructed various workers not to clear the remaining trays of food until she was done and began filling it up. She handed the plate to Dalinc and walked over to an empty table.

"Sit here. You're still hungry?" she asked Ravi.

"No, I'm good."

She motioned her hand up and down towards Ravi's body.

"You're too thin. Have another plate."

"No, I'm really full."

"Have dessert."

"I'm good, mom."

For the first time in years, he was touched by her dietary harassment. This specific moment made him appreciate the shield of love his parents had always surrounded him with, even if it their approach was occasionally aggravating.

She turned back to Dalinc.

"This is good," he said, nodding his head in surprised satisfaction.

"You like Indian food?" she asked.

"First time I eat."

"First time! You come over to my house in America, I make you good Indian food."

He sucked in his teeth.

"It's very spicy."

She looked over at a passing waiter.

"Ayy! You get him water."

She looked back at Dalinc.

"I'm glad you like. I'm going to go to my sister, but if you want more, you just ask them, they will give you, you just have to push them a little."

She walked away.

"She would be good in my job," Dalinc said.

"That's true," Ravi affirmed.

He felt like he was riding a roller coaster in the dark. Dalinc wiped his mouth with a napkin and stood up. He bobbed his head in thought while sucking in his cheeks with a reverse whistle.

"Your parents, they care for you."

"Yeah, probably more than they should."

"Okay. Okay. Here's what we do. I give you three months more to pay, but you got to pay ten percent more. I will tell Boss you are getting the money. But if you don't pay then, I will break your arms. I will take all your things. And I will make sure your mom and your dad know what is happening."

Ravi felt an overwhelming release of chemicals that made him feel like he was about to cry.

"Thanks."

He kept it short so that he could hold his tears in.

"I got to go. Good food. Maybe I eat it again some day," Daline said, turning to head back to the exit.

Ravi had been saved by his mum. She wasn't the smartest, she wasn't the politest, she wasn't the most sensitive, but in many ways, she was the most reliable. He should have felt relieved, but his prior state of abjection still lingered. So much had happened that his brain and emotional center had given up trying to make sense of it.

He felt himself being pulled backwards by the shoulder and nearly lost his balance. He recovered to face a beaming Pankaj.

"She asked me to dance. You always think it's going to be you, but some girls can see through you."

"You're right. You're a better man than me."

"Here's the number of the girl you had asked about," Pankaj said, holding up his phone to show off a text.

Ravi fumbled with his phone to take a picture just as the girl approached them from behind.

"It's a picture? Let me see," she said.

"No, just the number of a girl he likes," Pankaj said.

If Pankaj knew anything about women, he would have realized that his comment would only make her more interested in Ravi.

"Oh, you're getting around the party, is it?" she asked.

"No, he's just making things up," Ravi said.

"Then why did he flash you a phone number?"

"I told him to do it to make you jealous. But really, despite his inability to dance, he's a much more interesting person than I am. Ask him about how he almost got arrested at a casino. I'm sorry, I have to leave for a moment," Ravi said.

If Pankaj couldn't parlay the casino experience into the girl's phone number, then there was nothing more that Ravi could do to help him tonight. He walked away, out of the disco strobe lights, under a basketball hoop, into the hallway and past a series of lockers until he reached a classroom. He let himself in. The walls were papered with students' colored artwork and essays, large sunflowers and a poster of pastel balloons with an inspirational quote:

"You're off to Great Places! Today is your day! Your mountain is waiting, So… get on your way!"

He looked at Pilar's number. It looked legitimate, starting with a 34, the country code in Spain. It took three attempts at memorizing it in order to change to the phone keypad and dial. He had made a mess of things, but for some reason, karma was giving him another chance. If he won back his girl, he could figure out what other heroic acts he needed to do in order to get his life back the way it used to be.

Excerpt from
Ravi's Guide to Being a Cool Indian

Friends

People say you discover your true friends when you're in trouble, but I think you discover them when they're in trouble. Principle #1: Most friends who are drowning aren't reaching out their hand to escape, but to pull you in. At first, you try yank them out with sound advice about how to dump their condescending romantic partner, stop shooting coke, stop spending money they don't have, or study harder (not that I would know anything about these things). After months of hours-long advisory sessions, you realize sharing their misery is their hobby.

I'm not saying you can't give a small loan or an afternoon moving a mattress. In fact, you have to hand it to the older Indian generation. If someone contracts a cold, everyone in the community rallies to deliver meals. Our generation just posts a get well soon wish on Facebook. But beware of chronic dissatisfaction.

What is friendship? Is it the childhood friend who's loyal and understands you but has become a Scientologist? Is it the boring neighbor who's there for you when you need help moving a mattress? Is it the engaging socialite you love to hang out with but only tells you whether they can make your party the day it's happening?

It's all of the above. Let's face it, the odds of finding one person who is interesting, kind, sensitive, reliable and funny and thinks the same about you are the same as the odds I can make you cool with one book (give me another book or two, and let's see where we get). Principle #2: find different friends for different needs. A lot of older Indians think a friend needs to be the whole deal, which is why they're often not talking to one another. Expectations are the thief of happiness.

Having a group of friends also makes it easier to ignore them when you start dating someone, because they will notice it less. But make sure you maintain at least a couple of friendships. Romantic relationships embolden people into thinking that their annoying observations are insightful because one person keeps putting up with them. Only someone who has no interest in seeing you naked can tell you what they really think. Principle #3: A true friend is one who tells you what you need to hear instead of what you want to hear...

Chapter 9
Pilar's Secret
Madrid, Spain

Ravi

Ravi had claimed in his brief conversation with Pilar that he would be in Madrid the next day for a promotional event. She had reluctantly accepted his invitation for coffee, stumbling over her words because she was the type of person who couldn't conjure up an excuse on the spot. The perfect yin to Ravi's yang. He had his London hotel concierge book him on a cheap EasyJet flight in the morning, and by late afternoon, he was debating whether to buy her flowers outside the northern entrance to Buen Retiro Park. He decided not to make things awkward by acting out of character.

As most of Madrid frolicked in shorts and t-shirts, he wore his jeans and leather jacket, unprepared for the warm weather. He made his way to the famous Colonnade with the monument to Alfonso XII and tried to determine whether a pretty girl with cat-eyed sunglasses, a wavy penumbra hat, cork sandals and a floral summer dress was Pilar.

"Ravi!"

"I almost didn't recognize you."

She removed her glasses. A flipbook of memories cascaded through his mind—taking a picture of her on a ferry on the Danube, staring at her asleep on a hotel armchair, watching her gaze up in the glow of billboard lights at Picadilly Circus. He embraced her with a kiss to the cheek and held her arms to examine her.

"You cut your hair. It's a bit lighter. And you're looking…"

"Yeah, I know, a little thin. My friends call me '*la flaca*'. '*Pides la flaca. Dices a la flaca.*' Which is kind of a joke, because it means skinny, but also beautiful , and also it's a popular nickname for female gang leaders."

"Well, you're still beautiful, so it's no joke."

She put her hand to her face.

"You make me…what is the word? *Sonrojo*."

"Blush."

She looked handsome without the round cheeks, though her sweat channeled through a few wrinkles around her eyes. He felt a surge of physical desire while touching her and wished they could just hold hands and walk without talking. Her face trembled just enough to betray nervousness and the possibility that she still found him arousing.

They began walking down a wide tree-lined path past families with strollers and chatty students.

"It was tricky tracking you down. I think your number and email changed."

"I'm sorry, when I send my change of contact email, I didn't think…" she said, blushing.

"It makes sense, you don't have to explain."

"But I don't know why your cousin would know my number."

"Not my cousin, his friend who is also your friend. Remember, you showed up backstage to our concert because your friend was a friend of Pankaj?"

"That sounds familiar. I'm trying to remember who that was. I can't believe I forgot."

"It doesn't matter."

"You know, I heard one of your songs on the radio recently and was thinking about you," she said, touching his arm. "It was your big hit, but I always preferred the other songs. What was that one you played on the classical guitar that I loved? I think it was called "Somewhere Slowly". I would always sing along in concert."

"Which was funny, because it was about a jilted man who's angry at his lying lover."

"Yes, but the song is beautiful. Are you still recording and playing?" she asked with a twinkle in her eye.

"On and off. Right now I'm focused on promoting a book I wrote."

He said that he was visiting Madrid as part of a book tour, hoping that it would make him sound more mature and intelligent than if he mentioned *Cool Kids*.

"You wrote a book?" she asked.

"Yeah."

"You…wrote a book?" she asked, biting her thumbnail to hold her grin down.

"What, you don't think I know how to read or write?"

He had trapped himself. When she asked what the book was about, it would be further affirmation of his frivolous life. A guide to being cool. Had his history been fiction? The feelings of pride and joy which were now a core part of his being were developed on the basis of having admiration and respect. But maybe having fans wasn't the same as having admiration and respect, and once the fans had gone away, his pride and joy should have joined them.

"No, no. It's very, um..*impresionante*. Impresionative? Impressive? You are so busy, to have time for this is very good. So the band is no more?"

"It's more like we've been taking a break. I still want to record, the other guys said they needed some time to do other things. I'll get Ian into the studio at some point."

"Yes, I like Ian. He was very nice."

Ravi wasn't going to risk the reconciliation by detailing his problems. He pulled out a cigarette pack from his jacket pocket, but put it back after catching her look. He remembered on tour when she had complained that the smoke was bad for her complexion. She would start and end the day with a series of lotions— clarifying toner, anti-aging moisturizer, tightening eye cream and plumping lip balm.

"I know, I promised you I would cut down. You know, this time, I will."

He took out the pack and found the closest trash can.

"You don't have to do it for me."

Was that her way of saying she wasn't interested in a reunion? Or just a marker for her own pride in case he hadn't come to suggest one? Or maybe just words that meant nothing at all?

"I know, but anything I do for you, I'm indirectly doing for myself."

He stared into her brown eyes, and she seemed to be taking him in.

"You now, all these memories are coming back. Our trip together!"

Again, she touched him on the arm. Was that a sign or a natural gesture? Did she used to do that when meeting people when they were dating?

"You jumped into that fountain in Rome while we were waiting for a taxi. Or when we went out for falafels and orange juice in Tel Aviv and we met that musician, Lenny something."

She turned with a hop and started walking.

"Kravitz."

"Yes. Everything was so much fun. Sorry, I'm just enjoying the memories. Rodrigo! That's the friend who knows your cousin Pankaj. He gave me the backstage pass to your concert."

"He's the man who opened the door to happiness that I accidentally closed."

There, he put it out there. She stopped walking to squint at him ponderously. She was the only woman he had ever met who had the perfect blend of mystery, intelligence, self-awareness, sincerity, humor, sexiness and confidence.

***

They had been in Rome when he had thought that she might be the one. She was leading him on a sightseeing tour, bombarding him with facts and stories about Romulus and Remus, Caesar, the gladiators. They had exited the Colosseum and started towards the Forum. She wore a large backpack, which she refused to let him carry. Her hair was tied up in a ponytail and she was wearing a tank top.

"Are you paying attention?" she asked.

"Every other sentence or so. Romulus killed Remus, they named Rome after him."

"That was ten minutes ago. I'm not going to waste my breath if you don't care."

"I care. Keep going."

"No. You can stay ignorant."

They walked along the cobblestones of the Via Sacra, bordered by iron gates, past various statues and ruins before reaching the grand pillars of the Forum.

"So what's this all about?" he asked.

"This? You are so…ahhh," she said in frustration, sweeping her hand around at the grounds.

"It's called the Forum, I got that. They sold stuff, had speeches, hung out here. Got that."

"You want to know?"

"Yes."

As she described some of the history, he focused enough to prove he was paying attention in case she tested him. They arrived at the New Rostrum.

"So this is where Marc Antony gave his famous speech after Caesar died. People only know the version by Shakespeare. I can read it to you," she offered.

"Only if you act it out."

And she did, waving her arms out wide, putting on an exaggerated Italian accent, which sounded different than an American doing an exaggerated Italian accent.

"Friends, Romans, countrymen, lend me your ears. I come to bury Caesar, not praise him."

He chuckled and knelt before her.

"Caesar, give me your blessings."

"Marc Antony, not Caesar!"

"I knew that, I just…my brain and mouth got crossed up."

"You should join Caesar in his grave."

She mimed cutting off his head before they cheerfully walked away from the rostrum swinging their hands back and forth on the way to a gelateria.

This was a woman who could educate him, entertain him and challenge him all at once. When they had met two months earlier, she had just finished a two-year internship after five years in law school. She was supposed to be studying for the civil exam to get qualified as a lawyer, but had instead followed the band around and listened to Ravi's philosophical digressions about life and art. Starting in Rome, she had begun to assert her personality more. She stayed in the hotel room to study while the band rehearsed. She visited churches, ruins, markets, libraries. In the ensuing cities, she stopped going to every Buzzthief performance, but made up for it by giving Ravi little mementos from her day—a sketch of schoolgirl, a kitschy souvenir of the Pope, a suggestive picture of herself with bare shoulders, a copy of a book called *The Club Dumas,* which had been adapted into a movie with Johnny Depp, who Ravi reminded her of.

In August, as they approached their second month together, she had left the tour to take her law exam. He said he would fly to Madrid for a couple of days before he went back to New York, but his bandmates arranged for her to surprise him at the final tour date in Berlin, cheering from the front row. The instinctual thrill of seeing her there without expecting her there made him play the opener—"6:35 Tonight"—with a thunderous energy, strumming the chords with a taut groove.

They decided to stay in the Berlin for the week instead of going to Madrid for their last hurrah. Over the course of the week, they touched on how the relationship could work long distance. It was clear that both had wondered whether it was just an infatuation, a short term adventure whose magic would dissipate if they settled down in one place, with him spending days and possibly nights at the studio and her doing the same at a law firm. They both agreed that they didn't want her to be the girlfriend who followed him around. She had her own career goals, and he was attracted to her because she was substantive. They agreed they didn't have to make a decision right away, it was the 21st century, they could video chat and email and call.

He flew back to New York to recuperate from the tour, settle up bills that were past the due date and catch up with people he hadn't seen in months. She started work at the law firm. At first, their video calls were fun and flirty, but after a few weeks, she became weighed down by her anxiety over all the work she had to do. He encouraged her to see friends and go to the parks, but she went into work on weekends so that she wasn't behind on Mondays. He also couldn't call her on a whim. She became insecure over the fact that he was still going out at night, and any mention of another female led to an interrogation. She was self-conscious that she didn't have much to talk about other than work. Soon all the differences which had made them complementary in person—her discipline- his whimsy, her serious interest in history and books- his lighthearted take on them, her professional career-his musical career – prevented them from finding enough common ground over video chats to energize a conversation.

Within two months, it became clear that they needed to make some sort of decision, because unless they lived together, they would never be forced to make it work. He dismissed the idea of moving Madrid—"Everyone will think I'm an idiot, because I look like I could be Spanish, but can't speak a word of it. Beyond which, the band is in New York, it would make it hard to record." She suggested she might be able to get a job or an LLM in New York, and in her phrasing made it clear that she had been pretending to be indifferent in Berlin, that she had expected him to invite her to New York then.

He was anxious about asking her to live with him. He liked his lifestyle-staying out late, recording when he felt like it, hanging with the boys. He vaguely worried his mum might disown him for living with someone before marriage. Unlike a casual relationship, it was a fact that couldn't be denied or ignored. And the uneven video chats called into question whether the relationship would work longer term.

She called him on a weekend, right before he was leaving to meet Ian for a drink. He could tell from her nervous greeting and tense facial expression that she was ready for a serious conversation, which he tried to pre-empt.

"Let's plan a vacation together. I'll fly over, we can go somewhere in Spain, maybe down south to the beach," he said.

"I don't think so. That's just pushing back a decision."

"I thought it would help make a decision."

"You aren't going to learn more about me than you already know on a vacation. I think…you need to decide what you want. Because if we're not going to be together, then I will start dating again," she said.

He knew it was a gambit to force his hand, but it worked in making him feel hurt.

"The thing I worry about is, what if you come over here, and we're living together, and it doesn't work out? You'll have moved your career here. But at least if at first you're on your own in your own place, then you'll have your life and we won't have the pressure and feeling like we have to make it work," he said.

It was a rare moment where he was direct and truthful.

"I'm not coming because I want to be in New York. If I come, it's to be with you."

"Well, my mum would have a heart attack if I was living with someone and we weren't engaged."

He said it expecting it would lighten the moment, implying how ridiculous his mother was, but it immediately backfired.

"Your mother doesn't know about me? I'm just a someone?"

"My mum doesn't know about anything in my life. We're both happier that way. She doesn't have to get angry over the details she can't control."

"So what is wrong about me?"

"Nothing. If she met you, she'd love you. But she has preconceived notions about anyone who isn't Indian, and about people who live together before marriage."

"So then why are you with me? My parents have been asking to meet you."

"I would work it all out, but my mum…takes a special approach."

"I was calling because I thought you would want me to move there, but...I...I don't...I don't think you want me there."

"I do, but, it's a lot of pressure."

"Pressure? Only you have pressure? You're not the one offering to move."

"I'm sorry, you're right. Come stay with me."

"I don't want to come as a compromise. You need to figure out what you want, and what your parents want, and how it would all work."

In subsequent conversations, he tried to make the invitation sound more sincere, but as she grilled him about when she might come, the cultural expectations of his parents, whether his apartment was big enough and other details, she concluded he still had doubts.

She was right. At some basic level, he hadn't been ready to conform to a routine, to sacrifice some of his goals to help her achieve hers, to lose part of his identity, to deal with his parents. Had he been scared?

Shortly thereafter, she had stopped returning his phone calls, and he had landed the *Cool Kids* gig, which had kept him too busy to mope.

***

She tilted her head and stopped squinting.

"If we had stayed together, it wouldn't have worked out," Pilar said.

"Why do you say that? I never cheated on you."

Was she playing coy? Did she want him to argue for why it would have worked out so that she knew he was sincere?

"It's not that."

Pilar removed a bag of hard candy from her purse and offered Ravi one before unwrapping one for herself.

She gestured towards her body.

"Maybe you can guess from looking that...there is some trouble. I take treatment for breast cancer. I found out about four months ago."

He had just spent all this time talking about himself when she was the one with the biggest news. She looked down at the ground.

"My God, I'm sorry."

He tried to process a convergence of thought and emotion—the possibility she might not be around, his ability and desire to help her with the diagnosis, the impact on the likelihood of their getting back together, the way he should be reacting to show his concern.

"No, no, I'm okay, I go to the best doctor, he took out most of the bad…tish, tissue? I go next week to make sure there's nothing left inside, otherwise they'll…What are you thinking?"

He realized his face had tensed up as the acrobatic reach of his mind had unconsciously narrowed into singular focus on her well-being. He hugged her, and she returned the embrace before releasing him.

"I'm sorry. I don't even know what to say. If I can help in any way, I will," Ravi said.

"I'm getting a lot of support from my family, from my friends, from…Sebastian."

"Who's Sebastian?"

He already knew and felt himself get dizzy, his mind detaching from the moment before he could get the chance to feel like the jilted lover. He gamely smiled through the details.

"We're engaged. You would like him. He plays the guitar. Not like you, more classical, but you would enjoy talking to him about music. He's very funny, very nice. He's working at a bank."

She explained that he was a lawyer like herself, with a dry wit and a terrier. They were living together and started each day with a run, at least before her diagnosis, and a quick breakfast. Their schedules didn't always align, but they tried to have dinner together at least three times every week. One year into their relationship, as she had cried at her diagnosis and Sebastian had hugged her, she had told him that it was okay for him to find someone else, but he had said she was being silly, that whatever happened, he would be there, but nothing was going to happen because they had caught it early.

They reached the other side of pond in front of the colonnade watching blue paddleboats drift about while walking under trees on a path spotted with crushed berries and leaves.

"Ah. That's good. Really good. You deserve someone like that," Ravi said.

He briefly wondered whether he should quickly suggest a coffee and get the meeting over with, but knew that if he loved her, being there meant bearing through this meeting no matter his own discomfort and disappointment. And given that he had flown all this way, maybe he would just tell her why he came.

"Yeah. He knows about you. He couldn't believe I went off with you and the band. I told him it was the one crazy thing I've done."

"That's funny, because you were the least crazy thing I've done," he said.

He paused and looked at his feet before looking back at her.

"Is that why you think it wouldn't have worked out? It was just a crazy thing?" he asked.

"Well…once I found out I have cancer, I'm not sure you would have been able to help me handle it."

"Really? I definitely would have."

How could she, of all people, not understand his heart? His willingness to step up when necessary?

"Like you did in telling your parents about me," she said.

"Wow."

"I'm sorry, we shouldn't talk about these things. It's all in the past."

She turned away and started walking again.

"How can we not talk about it? You're telling me that…I'm not trustworthy."

Is this how Pankaj, Ian, Shusruth and Vineeta also viewed him? The unreliable friend? If they needed a shoulder to cry on, he would fly around the world to provide it. If a car was headed towards any of them, he would definitely push them out of the way, even at his own peril. Not that he ever got the chance to make these grand gestures. Instead, he was being judged by his occasional screw-up. Maybe he had one big screw-up per year. Everybody deserved a screw-up a year. He wasn't even sure which screw-ups they cared about. Well, other than Pilar, because that one was obvious.

Sure, Ravi hadn't joined Ian's visits to the children hospital wards, but Ravi wasn't particularly good with children. Ian (or more specifically, his fiancée) didn't account for the time Ravi baby-sat their dog for a few hours. Ravi didn't even like dogs. Sure, Ravi said stuff about Vineeta's love life and career he couldn't remember but was incredibly funny, possibly accurate and probably misinterpreted. Vineeta didn't account for all the years of teaching her how to manipulate their parents. Sure, Ravi defaulted to Pankaj for his punch lines and had nearly gotten his cousin arrested. Pankaj didn't account for their summer adventures when Ravi visited England, or the tour parties.

Maybe there were more than a few screw-ups a year. He deserved a screw-up per person, per year. Calendar year or rolling basis?

Okay, maybe he was proving her point. He hadn't been paying close attention to his friends and families' goals and aspirations recently. Maybe relationships were like his songs. It wasn't enough to have a good starting point, he needed to spend the time to craft the details around it to make it great. He should have noticed his friends and family weren't laughing along when he needled them. He was just so used to laughing along with everyone who had mocked his own aspirations that he thought that was how it went.

Pilar turned around as he caught up, took off her sunglasses and softened her expression.

"You're a loving person. You're a fun person. You're many things, but you have a lot of things to work out, no? With your family, with your career, with yourself. It's only when you know who you are that you can give yourself to others. It's fun to be a rock star on stage, but off the stage, there has to be a real person, too."

Had his private persona morphed into his public one? He had thought that Pilar was one of the few who understood his core. She had told him that she had overheard "In the Morning Sometimes" on a friend's stereo and identified with his existential angst—*Sometimes I seek, sometimes I hide, sometimes I feel like there's no one inside, In the morning sometimes, I lie awake with no one, nothing, yeah I need a lover, but not now, the way I need the silence in my soul.* When she had heard "Defenseless"— *I'm leaving myself defenseless, so you can destroy me if you like, I'm a fool for your intentions, tell me if I'm only wasting time, wasting time*—she was hooked by his bleak romanticism, more interested in the Cyrano (or at least Neil Diamond) behind the words than the voice who sang them.

"Yes, but that's not the same. I mean, you're talking about cancer," he said.

"So you would have…you know, you're right, I'm bringing up things that aren't related, and anyway, it doesn't matter now. Why don't you tell me about your book? I want to hear about what you wrote."

She could change the subject, but his gut and his heart and mind were still struggling with the emotional blow of her words.

"I wrote about growing up Indian," he said absently.

"Ahh, interesting. That might explain a lot about you."

"Like you said, it doesn't matter anymore."

"Now I'm actually curious. What did you conclude?"

He reluctantly described the book's structure and some of the advice. She genuinely laughed at the concept and recollections, needling him over some of his idiosyncrasies. He returned the ribbing, and for a moment it felt like they were dating again.

"I will definitely read it."

He felt slightly better than before, and kicked at an acorn.

"So, is there someone you're dating?" she asked.

Ravi smiled.

"I haven't dated anyone since you."

"No, come on, you always have someone in the picture," she said.

His last fling had been months ago, on a business trip in LA with a colleague. In some ways, it may have started him on his quest to re-unite with Pilar. He had realized that if he was going to compare all girls to Pilar, he might as well try to get back the real thing. A boyfriend would have been surmountable, but he hadn't expected a fiancé.

He followed her towards a fountain, three fourths of the way on the square path back to the colonnade.

"I haven't been on a date in months. Too much going on. Anyway, I want to hear more about Sebastian and your job and anything else you want to talk about. Do you want to grab a coffee or something?" he asked.

She looked at her oversized watch dial.

"I have to be back by five, so I think there's time. There's a nice café close to here."

They exited the park by the Puerta de Alcala, a massive concrete gate with two arches. As they crossed the street, a tour group blocked his way, so that she reached the other side first and scanned desk sculptures at a sidewalk stall until he caught up. He had always appreciated her interest in small things that seemed trivial to him. It complemented his tendency to live on a grand scale. She lifted a copper replica of the Sagrada Familia Cathedral in Barcelona into the sunlight before putting it back down, at ease with looking at a touristic bauble and at ease with complimenting the proprietor without purchasing it.

When they reached Grande Café Gijon, the waitress assigned them a table with steel black chairs inside a glass arcade along the sidewalk in front of a concrete sculpture of a woman with a domed hairdo and Bundt shaped skirt.

"We'll probably need to order more than just coffee here. Are you allowed to have wine?" Ravi asked.

"I'm not dead. Right now everything is good."

He ordered a 75 euro bottle and a plate of chicken skewers.

"You haven't changed," she said.

"Well, in what way?"

"The most important way. You always have joie de vivre."

"I try, but things seem to get more complicated with time, like I'm getting spun in a web of obligations and expectations."

"Like what?"

He looked away at the trees that lined the sidewalk on the next block, a still subject behind a blur of buses, taxis and other cars, and felt a complete lack of desire to say anything, to float in the moment.

"What are you thinking?" she asked.

"Nothing. You think you know where you're trying to go, but then one day you look around and wonder where you are and where everybody went."

"I'm not sure I know what you mean," Pilar said.

Now that the chance of reconciliation was over, he could open up.

"To be honest, the band hasn't really been together a while. And when I started to take stock of things, some of the people…well, I have plenty of friends, but some of the close friends, have distanced themselves a bit, and I've just been thinking about whether I did something wrong."

"Your friends love you for who you are and forgive you for who you are, too, no? Or they're not really friends," she laughed. "It's not the same as dating someone."

"That's what I thought."

"Give them some time. Everything, it comes and goes, like a…a cycle. You're so used to living day by day, maybe you don't realize the bigger things that are happening, some good, some bad. So this week or month or year you notice the bad, and maybe a few things change a little, and you change a little, and next week or month or whatever you'll notice the good again."

"If I knew what to change."

"It's not usually the knowledge that is lacking, but the will."

"But you think I should be changing?"

"Everyone is always changing. Life is change. Today you know a little more than yesterday. Today you will develop some habit you didn't have before. Your cells are one day closer to death. So the only variable is whether you make it a positive change or not. Do you read a book? Or write a book. Or re-connect with your heritage. Or think about others more."

He thought about others plenty. His whole *Guide* was about his family, yet it had angered them that he was encouraging them to adapt—for Pankaj to overcome his self-loathing over being Indian to form a social life, for Vineeta to stop blaming their parents for her cultural confusion, for his parents to stop premising their happiness on Vineeta and Ravi meeting their outdated expectations. When he had tried to show them how it was done, like with Pankaj at the wedding, it seemed to backfire.

Pilar said it wasn't the knowledge that was lacking, but the will. What did he need to change? Plenty, given his financial situation.

Suddenly he made a connection that had been hiding in plain sight. It hadn't been sufficient to try and guide his family because his own life was a mess. His debts and exploits had so badly impacted them—his loans from his father, the casino debacle, even the advance he got for writing the *Guide*—that they didn't realize his guidance might actually have value.

Adaptation was the core principle of his *Guide*, in fact, the core principle of evolution. He needed to adapt to by changing his lifestyle and sacrificing some parts of himself to make his family function as a whole. And he needed to show them how to adapt without ticking them off again.

He gazed at her.

"This is why I love talking to you. You always make things seem better. Probably wasn't ready for our relationship at the time. I shouldn't have let you go."

"Oh, is that what you think? You let me go?"

He hadn't been ready for stability, predictability and a family. To admit how much he cared about Pilar by revealing her to his parents. He hadn't realized how giving her up would send him on a fruitless search for meaning through gambling, alcohol and nights out.

The waiter approached with the first taste of wine, which she approved.

"Well…however it happened, you let me go, we let each other go, the ocean got between us. I wish I had…" he said. "Well, you know. To staying in touch."

She had an inscrutable expression. Did she doubt his sincerity? Did she feel sorry for what he had become? Did she regret a moment that couldn't be recaptured? Was she open to a reconciliation even though she was engaged to Sebastian?

They clinked their glasses.

"So, Pilar, Pilar, my fabulous Spanish star. Do you still like to eat French fries with yoghurt?"

He listened intently while she updated him on the details of her life—how the past few months felt like a collapsing room from a thriller film controlled by the villain Cancer. How work helped her keep her mind off of things, though she realized that life can be short so she should follow her dreams. How she wanted to resume piano classes and have time to listen to a Sinatra album with a glass of wine. How she had thought about starting a tax advisory firm or teaching at a law school.

"You're talented enough. Smart enough. Caring enough. There would be no one better."

"You are so smooth when you want to be."

"That doesn't mean I'm not being honest."

She said that she was re-considering life—the point of it, approach to it, evaluation of it. For the year before she had gotten cancer, she had been seeing things through a pragmatist's eyes. Ravi reminded her that she had once been a dreamer—immortal, carefree, romantic, vulnerable, full of highs and lows.

While she spoke, Ravi both listened and mentally guessed songs on the restaurant stereo by the bassline. The red elixir had slowly restored his control—the ability to follow reality and imagination at the same time. He felt sexy, charming, interesting, capable of solving everything. He wanted to do everything he loved at that moment all at once. As she talked about a movie she had recently seen, he imagined walking with her out of Madrid, into a field of olive trees with the whistle of crickets shining in a yellow moon glow against a royal blue sky, making love in a single sleeping bag next to a small fire. When he erupted into a carnival of colors and space, he would float over the world and absorb every sound, movement, line and scent, then send it back to the world via the greatest song ever written.

A near accident between two taxis culminated in a tire screech and extended honk, which shook him out of his partial reverie as he glanced at a man walking three dogs on the sidewalk. When he looked back, she held his gaze, and he could tell from the sparkle in her eyes, the unguarded affection, the appreciation for his *joie de vivre*, that at least a part of her still loved him.

When she placed her hand on the table, Ravi reached out to hold it. She not only didn't remove it, but traced her index finger over the crest of his fingernails.

He knew he could still win her back. They sat like that for a while without saying anything, just examining the details of their palms, the pattern of hair on their forearms, the moods of their eyes.

When she realized she was an hour late, she immediately called Sebastian. Ravi covered the bill. She walked him back to The Principal, the five star hotel where he had claimed he was staying. He would book a room at if she agreed to accompany him, though he'd have to claim the hotel staff had forgotten to bring his luggage up.

With dozens of people walking by on the wide avenue, he grasped her upper arm. He leaned forward to kiss her on the lips, and she stared at him as he came closer. He paused to look into her soul, and in her expression he was reminded of a scene from some Julia Roberts movie, just a girl in love with a boy—open, vulnerable and trusting. He knew he would honor that trust forever, and leaned forward to seal the pact.

She tilted her head to accept his kiss on her cheek. He pulled back, uncertain what that meant. She seemed to be gathering her thoughts before looking up.

"I'm sorry, I can't…You know, you really hurt me. And I thought I was going to meet you and show you how you avoided my sickness, but also how I have someone who loves me so that you would feel bad. But now I see that was stupid, because it only proves that still somewhere in me I love you."

"So then give me a second chance."

"No, I can't go backwards. I've built something good, and it does mean something when someone is there for you."

"I'm sure Sebastian is a nice chap, but like you said, life it too short to settle. I'll be there for you. I just wasn't ready before. Come to New York."

She looked at him in a way that made him think she was considering it.

"I think…you're in a tough moment in your life. And maybe you love me, but maybe you are searching for answers. And I'm happy with where my life is now. Maybe our two months traveling were more special than the beginning of with me and Sebastian, but that doesn't mean our relationship would be any better, because having a companion is more than just going out for fun. So, I'm sorry. You will find other answers to your problems."

A lyric ran through his head about finding multiple answers to tough questions. Indigo Girls, "Closer to Fine".

"I'm not asking you because I need answers to any questions. I'm asking you because I love you," Ravi said.

"I believe you. But it doesn't matter anymore."

It doesn't matter anymore. What song was that? Something by Sinead O'Connor? He didn't need these lyrical brain twisters in the middle of an emotional twister.

She continued, "You're a good person. And if I can get through cancer, you can get through whatever you're going through. Just speak from the heart, act from the heart, and things will get better. I'm sorry, I'm late and have to get back."

They looked at each other for a moment before she leaned in to kiss him on the cheek and started walking away, her skirt flouncing in the wind. She looked back with a yearning expression, but continued. The end felt sudden, incomplete, wrong, like a nightmare Ravi should wake from to find out it wasn't true. He struggled to process her words. She had chosen prudence over instinct, which was why Ravi had loved her in the first place, because she was everything he wasn't.

He stood staring in her direction, as she disappeared into pedestrians emerging from the angular horizon walking towards him. Would they stay in touch? Or were the last few hours a rainbow on the ocean, a sprayed collision of waves which projected magic colors before moving in different directions?

He considered going into The Principal to drink away the soft nausea in his gut and give a final f-you to his credit card limits, but started aimlessly walking. He realized he was mouthing the chorus to "Defenseless'—*I sift through cards that tell me that you care for me, I wish I could convince you that our love is once and for all, once and for all.* His body slowly began making peace with Pilar's judgment. At least he had tried and found out for sure.

He passed a group of children enthusiastically laughing at a clown who had theatrically fallen down after being pushed. Those smiles went straight to his heart, a bittersweet shot of joy which inspired a strange optimism.

He still had his family. Unlike a girlfriend, they would still be there for him. Just like the clown, who didn't need to re-invent mime to elicit smiles, but only needed to do the same pratfalls that had worked for centuries. Ravi didn't need to make grand gestures of apology to win back his loved ones. He just needed to go back to the person he used to be, without the frills. If he was willing to change for Pilar, he could do the same for all the others. If he acted from the heart and helped them find their own path without detouring them onto his, he could make everyone smile again.

Part II
November 2007
The Reckoning

Excerpt from
Ravi's Guide to Being a Cool Indian

Food

Indians have fortunately seeded restaurants in every major city on the planet. I dragged Ian and the boys to every one of them, because if food doesn't jump with chilies and coriander, it's simply sustenance. *Principle #1: A good meal draws light perspiration on the brow, tingles gently on the tongue and leaves room for a little alcohol at the end.*

Of course, Indian restaurants only give you half the portion of a Chinese restaurant for the twice the price, but who else is going to cook the meal? You're not going to come home from work to chop vegetables, roll and flame-puff five rotis, fry and season two sabjis and one dal and boil a pot of rice. No wonder Mum and her friends are always trying to give us guilt trips over their years of labor while ironically trying to convince the next generation of women they should be cooking more.

As it is, you shouldn't eat Indian too often. The turmeric will yellow your fingernails. The fried bhajias will cause you pimples. The spices will seep through your pores, evade your deodorant, overpower your cologne and cause your cousin Pankaj to face daily childhood chants of "Curryboy".

Fortunately, the proliferation of international cuisines and restaurants give you many choices. Mojitos and shrimp at Ocho Cinco with palm trees, a citrus scent and waitresses with nice chumchums augur an evening of levity and energy. Sushi at Shabu Shabu conjured up by paper-hatted mutes elicit a mood of meditation and sensory appreciation. Foam salad and infused polenta at Maze served by aspiring actors give you the vicarious thrill of a character in an HBO sitcom.

Still, eating out all the time can be hard on your wallet and your digestive system. Fortunately, nothing beats a home cooked meal from Mum, even if you used to secretly throw them out in grade school and buy the cardboard pizza lunches to avoid the ostracism. *Principle #2: A good Indian meal has all the things you look for in a cool person—intensity, variety, color and heritage—even if you need a stick of gum afterwards to camouflage the scent.*

Chapter 10
Thanksgivings & Misgivings
Ann Arbor, MI

Vineeta

Vineeta shivered with her arms wrapped around herself, her stylish black winter coat providing neither warmth nor fashion. She spotted her father pulling up to the airport curb in their decade-old Cadillac. She could see her mom peering into the flip shade mirror to apply a thick streak of red lipstick as the car parked. Normally Ravi would be stealthily stepping out a cigarette at this point, but she sensed that her teeth would chatter if she tried asking him if he had stopped smoking. The trunk popped open as her mom emerged from the car to squeeze Ravi's torso and start crying while Vineeta joined in for a group hug.

"What's wrong, Mum?" Ravi asked.

Her brother didn't understand basic human emotion. Nothing was wrong, their mom was just overwhelmed by a tumescent rush of love, happiness, longing and sadness. It was these moments that justified their entire trip, including all the difficult moments that would follow. Vineeta had experienced enough Thanksgivings to know that while the official weekend agenda consisted of having Thanksgiving dinner at home, shopping on Black Friday and meeting their parent's friends on Saturday, the unspoken weekend agenda consisted of their mom asking Vineeta about when she was going to get married (with the recently added angle of limited fertility, out of concern for Vineeta's happiness), whether Vineeta's new job paid enough to support herself (probably her father's assignment) and how much longer Ravi was going to live like a vagabond while all the good women got married (possibly her mom, possibly her dad).

After their mom released them, her dad hugged Vineeta and ran his hand over Ravi's head, which caused Ravi to stroke his bangs back to the side.

"You look nice, Mom," Vineeta said.

"Yeah, are we going to a party from here?" Ravi said.

The compliment pumped air into their mom's cheeks. They entered the car, which nearly overwhelmed Vineeta with the Revlon perfume her mom had been using for the past forty years. Her dad lowered the volume of NPR so that their mom could proudly describe the retail provenance of her sari, bangles, earrings, necklace and sandals, too distracted to give her normal recriminating speech about how Vineeta and Ravi acted like dignitaries who expected to be pampered for three days after abandoning her post-college.

The Anjanis were a family again. If only they could keep it that way for four days.

As they neared the house, her mom directed her dad to a 7/11 convenience store.

"Pull over, lottery is 100 million."

"This is just a tax on stupid people," her dad replied, obeying her instruction.

"So when I buy big house with servants and parties, you stay in your house, kids will come to stay with me. And I buy Mercedes like Smita and Jaya. You keep Cadillac, freezing because it gives no heat."

Vineeta wasn't sure what her parents would talk about if they weren't bickering.

"You have to let the car warm up. It's good to buy American," her dad said.

"Everyone we know already retired or fired from car companies. No one buys American car no more."

"Mercedes are expensive," her dad said.

"At least you're not driving a Ford Lincoln," Ravi added.

Her father went inside and came back with five lottery tickets.

At home, they settled at the dining table for a cup of chai while their mom cooked. Vineeta raised topics to avoid making her and Ravi the topic—weather, best Black Friday sales, politics, status of friends, Ann Arbor specific issues, her father's job—until one took her mom's fancy.

Her mom started a rant about Anupama, her mom's best friend: First of all, Anupama knew that her mom had asked for a ride to Chintu's place (her mom's best friend of six months before) because she didn't like to drive at night, so that when Anupama cancelled at the last minute (denoting the end of their best friendship) her mom had to ask her dad to leave work to give her a ride, second of all, Anupama was just being mean because her mom had declined to make rotis for Anupama's party, but only because she had already committed to make rotis for someone else's party the same weekend, third of all, her mom couldn't vent to anyone because Anupama was responsible for choosing who would organize the New Year's puja and she wanted to be chosen, and fourth of all, Anupama would definitely choose Reema and Abha, even though they were senseless (though possible candidates as new best friends).

Vineeta relaxed through the diatribe as she thought about the reckoning she had been avoiding for years: revealing the existence of her boyfriend to her mom. A non-Indian boyfriend. A boyfriend who happened to be Ravi's best friend. This weekend was the time to follow the advice in *Ravi's Guide* and clear things up.

Vineeta had always liked Ian's introspective nature. He tended to observe people without reacting. He had a calming presence, but could also say something unexpectedly funny. He was also familiar, a person she could trust and who she'd seen just lounging on her parent's couch in shorts and a t-shirt. She could envision him playing basketball with kids in the backyard. He was the crush she had never seriously pursued. And then they had visited the British Museum in London after Shushruth's wedding.

It was carefree, comparing people in the paintings to people they knew and pretending to have high society British accents. It was also an opportunity to vent about everything they disliked about Jessica and Hans. With Hans, there were moments that at times felt clinical and slightly awkward. A lot of conversations about topics, few conversations about feelings. For Ian, it seemed Jessica was too dominant.

"Sounds like we should make one of those suicide-type pacts, but instead of suicide we agree to break up at the same time," Vineeta had suggested.

"I'm in," he had said.

"And then you can ask me out properly."

He had started blushing and looked away.

When she had returned from London and Hans had finally asked what was wrong after three days of intentionally curt or distracted answers (or finally asked her for the fifth time, since the first four times she had to appear to be struggling with the issue by denying there even was one, which was starting to actually drag on her mood), she had said it wasn't working for her. He had accepted her judgment like a business deal, saying he hoped she would reconsider but respected her decision.

The UN job had allowed her to stay in the city and see how things went with Ian. Funnily enough, he was now the one who needed career advice. He wasn't happy with the sessions for his solo album. He had asked her whether a Buzzthief reunion was a good idea given that their last album had bombed. She had pointed out that all bands become obsolete until their fans became nostalgic and wealthy enough to support reunion tours. Buzzthief was at the exact right point of that cycle.

Their relationship had been good so far, casual but meaningful—dinner dates, roller blading and ice skating in Central Park, shopping in SoHo, a couple of off-Broadway shows. They were taking it slowly because if it didn't work out, they didn't want it to affect Ian's friendship with Ravi.

Vineeta was aware that if ever there was one person her parents would accept that wasn't Indian, it would be Ian. He had eaten and slept at their house multiple times, because despite her mom's stated views about different races, Vineeta knew she didn't have any issues with Ian or black people in reality. Perhaps the strongest evidence in favor of the relationship was that she had stopped seeing Dr. Jenks. The fact that Ian's father had died when he was young after falling down the stairs made her concerns about her father seem petty. Better to have a philandering dad than a dead one.

As everyone finished their chai, Vineeta decided she should wait to reveal her relationship with Ian until the next day, after her mom had exhausted her pent-up tribulations. She spent the afternoon skimming a stack of old *Time* magazines, practicing the phrasing of her revelation and biting her fingernails in anxiety.

Thanksgiving morning, she sat at the dining table tapping out emails. Her mom began cooking while strains of Ravi's acoustic guitar resonated from upstairs. Her dad was completing student recommendations in his study. As long as no one interacted, the chance that her mom exploded in a rage before Vineeta's revelation was low. Vineeta just had to pick the right moment.

Around noon, her mom instructed her to set the table in the kitchen extension and instructed her dad to summon Ravi for a meal her mom had been preparing since Monday—lamb, chicken, cauliflower, okra, cucumber raita and tadka dal. Her mom removed a lid from a pot and set it down behind another pot. After filling a third pot with water, she looked left and right before shouting, "Jeevan, where you put the lid?"

Her mom had perfected the art of the leading question, so that in case her father had the courage to snap back at prefaces of "why didn't you" or "aren't you going to", her mom could ask what was wrong with just asking a question. The questions usually implied her father's devious role in enforcing the physics of existence, where objects remained where she had placed them rather than where she had expected them.

Her dad looked up from the dining table as Ravi entered the kitchen.

"Right in front of you."

"Need my help, Mum," Ravi asked without moving to actually help.

"No, you rest," her mom said, while directing Vineeta to courier the food. "You know, I was talking to someone last week, Kanta Khandelwal, dead."

"Really? How?" Vineeta asked.

The Khandelwals had been her parents' best friends when Vineeta was in high school. They had met right after her family had moved to Ann Arbor in 1984.

"They say cancer, but *khai cancer-bancer nathi. Old age saath marighai,*" Bharti said.

She didn't have any cancer-bancer. She died of old age. Her mom often postulated how the medical community was constantly conspiring to discover new reasons for death, when it was just God's will.

Vineeta had always regretted that her parent's friendship with the Khandelwals had fallen apart. Her mom chatted and cooked with Kanta. Her father had beamed whenever Vinod Khandelwal had invited him to play golf or attend the Rotary Club. The Khandelwals had treated Ravi and Vineeta like the kids they had never had, organizing trips to an amusement park or a swimming pool. Unfortunately when Vineeta was in college, her father had suggested Vinod invest in a rental property right before Vinod fell victim to Ford's corporate strategy of perpetually eliminating workers to pay for the CEO's raise. Her father had offered to buy the property, but had haggled with Vinod over the purchase price, insisting that $3000 worth of renovations were standard maintenance costs and not capital improvements. After an intense argument in the kitchen which Vineeta listened to while perched on her knees at the top of the stairs, they never socialized with the Khandelwals again. Her father had spent his life on solutions—research papers on whether to characterize something as an asset or liability, improvements in Sarbanes-Oxley—but didn't realize that being generous was often a better solution than logic.

"Maybe we should send Vinod a card or something," her dad said.

"You can send. They stopped talking to us," her mom said.

Her mom could harbor a grudge into the afterlife. Vineeta looked at Ravi as she finished bringing all the food to the table.

"You know, you can start serving."

Vineeta had given up challenging her mom's world view that a woman's place was in the kitchen and that the first born male son should be served his meal first, but couldn't resist a shot of sibling rivalry.

"Why you telling him? Let him rest," her mom said.

"It's okay, Mum. Happy to make my contribution," Ravi said as he ladled out the okra to the plates before sitting back down to let Vineeta serve the rest.

After Vineeta finished serving the food, her mom told her to sit down to eat. Her mom puffed rotis on the stove, flattened them back into soft disks with a circular stroke of clarified butter and delivered them one by one as everyone else began eating. Every ten seconds her mom offered to bring a different condiment—sweet mango pickle, garlic chutney, chopped onions—with no takers.

Okay, now was a good moment.

"There's something…" Vineeta began.

"You know, Shushruth got back from his honeymoon. He not go right after the wedding," her mom said. "Sujata said he had good time."

"That's great. Where did he go?" Ravi asked.

"They go I bazaar. It has beach. Sujata says it's famous place."

"Ibiza?"

"Yes, I bazaar."

"I'm happy for him," Vineeta said.

Maybe she could tie her romance in with Shushruth's marriage.

"Speaking of…" she began.

"Did you ever call Pankaj?" Jeevan asked.

"Left him a voicemail, texted him, never called me back," Ravi said.

"Lalita says he don't know anyone in New York. He not make Managing Director, so they send him there. You call him again. Maybe he busy with moving and new job," her mom said.

"You heard him at the wedding. I'm not sure that's what he wants," Ravi said.

"Maybe you should call," her mom said to Vineeta, bringing a plate of rotis to the table and settling in across from her.

"It's not like we have the closest relationship," Vineeta said. "He's a bit…awkward."

She started biting her fingernails. She would need to let the family conversation play out.

"Why don't you call him?" Ravi asked their mom.

"Youngsters have to talk to youngsters. Let past be past. *Gadbar hogiya hai, tho su?* Move on, what else."

"Fine, I'll call him again when I get back," Ravi said.

After her mom had accumulated a stack of rotis, she came to sit down at the dining table. Finally. This was probably a better moment than before, when her mom wasn't stressed about trying to feed everyone.

"I…" she began.

"So, how is your roommate?" her dad asked, pre-empting her.

"She's fine, I don't see her that much," she said, though she could tell her dad wasn't really listening to the answer and had already turned to look at Ravi.

"Ravi, how is the job going?"

"It was going well. Really well. And then it kept going, and now…it's gone."

"What? You don't have a job anymore?" he dad asked, putting his spoon down.

"When did that happen?" Vineeta asked.

Well, that was big enough news that she couldn't compete. Leave it to Ravi to mess things up.

How could she have missed such a big thing as him losing his job? She hadn't been meeting up with Ravi lately because she and Ian were keeping things secret in order to see if they would last long enough to make it worthwhile to tell her family, but Ravi could have told her about his job when they spoke on the phone. He was usually an open book. Was he embarrassed or was it that nothing fazed him? He always managed to spin negative things into something positive.

Her mom started humming a Hindi tune.

"I'm trying to remember this song. I don't know who sang it," her mom said, eating a bowl of rice with yoghurt.

"Officially, I suppose about a week ago. Unofficially, about a month ago. It was good while it lasted, but now I finally have a chance to figure out what I want to do next."

"How are you going to pay the bills?" her dad asked.

Vineeta looked at her dad to see if it was a serious question, or an insensitive attempt at a joke. Everyone had stopped eating except for her mom, who was lost in thought.

"There's unemployment insurance. And one-off things my agent lines up, like session recording for other artists."

"That won't be enough."

"That's why I'm writing new songs. And my agent is talking to MTV about a new show. In the entertainment business, you have to be ready for the time in between the jobs."

"What about your job?" her mom asked.

"Ravi lost it," Vineeta said.

"You lost your job? When?" her mom asked, suddenly stricken with a look of distress.

"Last week. Don't worry, I'll have another job soon, I'm already talking to the station about something."

"You can come and live here. Jeevan get you job at university."

"It's not that easy. But you can always go back to school, get an MBA," Jeevan said.

"It's only been a few weeks, right? Give me a chance to work it out."

Her father resumed eating, clearly pre-occupied with this new issue.

"You could have at least told us," her mom said.

"I didn't want to stress you out. Look, it's not like this is the first time, and it won't be the last. I appreciate you helping me through these patches, but it will be fine in a few months."

Ravi took a large bite of chicken, as if to indicate the topic was closed.

They finished the meal in silence, and Vineeta stood up to clear the table. So much for revealing Ian. Ravi jumped up to help out, presumably to avoid being interrogated by their father, who moved to the couch to ostensibly read the paper.

"Why didn't you tell me you lost your job?" she said as they both cleared the dirty dishes. "You had told me they ended up picking it up again."

She saw an honest look of concern in Ravi's eyes.

"That was just because I didn't want you to feel pressured to borrow money on my behalf after, you know…I would have told you after it happened, but you've been too busy to hang out lately. And it seemed weird to just do it over the phone," Ravi said.

"I'm your sister. It's not weird."

"Make sure you put the *dahi* back in this container," Bharti said holding up a Tupperware for the yoghurt from behind the counter separating the dining table from the cooking area.

"Sorry. I just figured everyone has their own problems. Not that this is a problem," Ravi said. "But now that it's out there, maybe this is the weekend you tell them about Hans. It will seem less of a big deal in comparison."

Except that it wasn't Hans, it was Ian. Should she tell Ravi first, and then tell her parents? But given that the band was on hiatus, maybe it would make Ravi insecure that his best friend was dating his sister. On the other hand, maybe it would actually lift everyone's mood because she was dating someone everyone liked. She wasn't sure, so she finished clearing the table and deferred the decision to the evening.

After Ravi filled the dishwasher, he joined Jeevan on the couch, where their father unexpectedly rubbed Ravi's head in a gesture of sympathy. Their father would undoubtedly raise his unemployment again before the weekend was out, though Ravi would bounce back like he always did.

"Last week we had dinner at Abha's. Her daughter just engaged," Bharti announced from the sink as she rinsed a dish they had missed. "Abha telling me of a boy who went to Brown, he works in New York. Abha says this is Ivy school, this is true?"

"It's an Ivy league school," Vineeta said.

"She want you to meet him, but I tell her, 'My children don't want get married. They like be with themselves too much.'"

"That's not true. I don't like being by myself. I just want to be with someone I love."

"So good, then you meet him, maybe you fall in love."

"I'm dating someone already."

The moment had snuck up on her. Her confession had slipped out naturally, like a runner who false started at the track after waiting too long for the starter's pistol. That morning, she had been confident they would be happy with the relationship, but now she worried that she had invited the wrath of Indra by diving into a pool while lightning approached. Ravi and her father both looked at her.

"Oh? Who you're going out with?" Bharti with a hopeful expression. "Gujarati boy?"

"No."

"Punjabi boy?"

"No."

"Not South Indian, eat this smelly-belly fish-bish."

Vineeta looked at Ravi.

"Ian."

"Fuck me. What?" Ravi asked, leaning forward on the couch.

"This is Ravi's friend?" Bharti asked.

"Yes."

"You serious? What happened to *die wienerschnitzel*?" Ravi asked.

"It's *der wienerschnitzel*, and his name is Hans."

"Okay, Hans, then."

"Hans? Who's Hans?" her mom asked.

"We broke up," Vineeta said.

"So who's keeping secrets from whom?" Ravi asked.

"We wanted to see if it was going somewhere before telling anyone."

"Well, I didn't see that coming."

He bit his lip in contemplation, but then seemed to nod to himself after some internal deliberation.

"I guess if you're happy about it, I'm happy about it," Ravi said.

"Of course you're happy about it, you told me to leave Hans in your book," she said, slightly annoyed that he was now acting indifferently when she had taken an action that should have made him happy.

"I've always wanted what's best for you. But, you and Ian…You're not putting me on?" Ravi asked.

"We started talking at the wedding. It's just been kind of building up."

"You're dating Ravi's band friend?" her dad asked socratically, always double-checking his facts before making a pronouncement.

"Yes. I decided it's time I stop pretending so you stop bothering me to live the life you want me to lead."

"Ian. He's black friend?" Bharti asked, her head accusatorily bobbing with each question.

It was more aggressive than Vineeta had expected.

"Ian's half-black," Ravi said.

Good, he was going to help her through this. Vineeta felt guilty that Ravi was catering to her mum's superficial prejudices, but maybe it was more necessary than she had anticipated.

"Oh, what is other half?"

"His mom is white. She grew up here," Vineeta said.

"Doesn't matter, he looks like black," Bharti said.

"I can't believe you're saying this. He's been over to the house, like, a hundred times. He's smart. He's nice. I don't know if we'll end up together, but he's everything you should want in a son-in-law."

She felt her cheeks warming.

"Blacks, all are talking funny, having the crime," Bharti said.

Her mind blanked. What the hell was her mom saying? Her dad interjected, just like he always did, an interpreter who converted all of her mom's offensive remarks into something that almost seemed reasonable.

"There are good blacks, we know that. It is more…we always thought, and maybe it wasn't right, but that we would become close friends with his parents, we could drink our Indian chai together, discuss Indian politics, maybe go to India together. Of course, blacks are just like other people, but to the Indian community it's not yet what people have seen. They are starting to get used to the white girls and boys, but still the black ones…"

"Are what? Going to mug them while they sleep?" she said sharply.

She realized she was resting her hands on the dining room table, leaning forward as if she was only being held back by the table from attacking her father.

"No, these are your words, I know Ian is a very good boy."

Her dad could get as shifty as her mom when necessary. He didn't want to admit that it was the Indian caste system all over again. Why had she expected a better response? She knew her mom talked about gays and blacks as if their existence was still somehow gossip-worthy, but she also saw that in reality, when she actually dealt with them, she liked them. Somehow the ones she met were viewed as the exception to some perceived rule. But apparently there was an exception to the exception, and Vineeta shouldn't be dating someone who was black, even if he met all the other criteria of a good son-in-law.

"Also, the band has been very good, but the number one problem between all couples is money. So how will he support you with no job? Or will you have to support him?" her father asked.

"And you don't wonder about that for Ravi?"

She was mildly grateful that they had moved from race to economics, but their layers of hypocrisy kept the venom flowing. It was a stupid gambit throwing Ravi under the bus, but she had just said the first thing that came to mind. Vineeta had long accepted her parent's double standard, whether it was money, dating or grades. Her mom bothered Vineeta about her ticking fertility clock, but always made peace with Ravi's romantic exploits. She had even asked Vineeta if Ravi might be gay, cataloguing various celebrities—Ellen DeGeneres, Ricky Martin, Rock Hudson—to validate the choice.

Vineeta saw Ravi glancing at her curiously, before looking back into the kitchen at their mom.

"Mum, did you know there's an Indian girl working on the show?" Ravi asked.

He had let her off the hook by not taking the bait and cleverly re-directed the conversation completely. Would it stick?

"You don't date anybody, just playing around, spoiling girls. Shameful," Bharti said, shaking her head in anguish. "What did I do wrong? My daughter can't even date a nice Indian boy."

"So, everyone is going to ignore this?" Vineeta asked.

"If you want to date black man, you…you…" her mom said, starting to cry.

"And your marriage is so perfect?" Vineeta asked.

There, the clincher to her closing argument. She knew she should be handling things more strategically like Ravi, but some emotional rush kept compelling her to retort with twice whatever she was getting.

"What you mean?" her mom snapped.

Her mom's eyes transformed from a water delivery system into an aiming system, blazed and bulging, providing the sight line for her mom's open mouth to fire back a response to whatever Vineeta said.

"Don't go there," Ravi said.

Was Ravi on their side? How could they not appreciate the clincher? It was the irrefutable fact that no one could rebut. But Vineeta didn't want to stay in the target line of her mom's mouth.

"Ask Dad," Vineeta said.

"What I ask?" her mom asked.

"About all the things you've been ignoring over the years."

Her mom looked at her dad.

"What you told her?"

"I didn't tell her anything," her dad said.

It was only when Vineeta saw Ravi's wild-eyed expression did she appreciate that he had been attempting to stop her from setting off a bomb that would blow up the weekend, with atomic ripples that would last for years. Her mom sat down at other end of the dining table, crying and wiping her tears with the corner of her sari before speaking.

"Go home. Jeevan will buy you a plane ticket, I don't want to be with any of you."

"Mum," Ravi said.

Ravi stood up with a look of distress Vineeta had never seen before, as if he was about to cry. He reached their mom and tried to put her arm around her, but after a few seconds of accepting his comfort, she pushed him away.

"Look, if it makes it all better, I'll get married. Tonight. Just give me about three hours to line someone up," Ravi said.

Her dad remained seated, while Ravi went to a display case on the living room and retrieved a porcelain figurine of a Spanish woman with a flowing gown and a lily in her hair.

"Mum, where did you get this, what's it called, figurine?"

A moment before Vineeta was ready to get out all her frustrations and settle up years of resentments, but as her rationality came back into focus, she started hoping that Ravi could steer things back to the way they were. He was capable of great feats— could he go back in time and remove Vineeta's words from the ether? Trying to litigate her parent's entire world view was futile and unnecessary. Pointing out their faults was not going to persuade them that she was right. Her parents couldn't force her to marry anyone and would eventually make peace with whatever choices she made. That's why Ravi had been trying to perform his magic act of misdirection. This whole battle had been unnecessary. If only she had shut up long enough to let him handle things instead of humiliating their mom by alluding to her dad's infidelity.

Ravi placed the figurine in her mom's lap to look at. The three of them looked at her to see if she would accept the gift of remorse on Vineeta's behalf.

Her mom peered into its eyes sadly, stroking the hair as if it was real. The porcelain dolls somehow represented promise, purity, perfection, the life her mom could have had in a different time and place. A doll was never an object, but a gamine or ingénue with its own story. A fancy sari wasn't just cloth, but a regal elevation in class. Her mom stared at it for a minute, then threw it with two bounces toward the kitchen, where the arm broke off. Her dad belatedly stood up.

"Vineeta's sorry. She didn't mean anything, she just isn't ready for marriage," her dad said. "Vineeta, say you're sorry."

Vineeta clenched her jaw.

"*Beti*," her dad said. *Daughter*.

She didn't want to concede the moral high ground. They were wrong. But she also didn't want to destroy her family.

"I'm not sorry about dating Ian, but I'm sorry about everything else," she whispered.

Why had she taken the bait? There were no good responses to her mom's criticisms, only bad and worse. She had wanted her mom to feel as much pain as her mom had caused her, but as she recalled a lifetime of her mom's tantrums and accusations, it became clear that her mom had always known about her father's affairs. Her mom was just a girl from Jobner who had been forced into an arranged marriage, a move to another country and a philandering husband. But then why was her mom pushing her to get married to an Indian?

"You heard that? She said sorry," her dad said.

Her mom stopped crying and silently picked the fingernails of one hand with the fingernails of the other.

"Come, Vineeta and I will clean the table and the dishes. You should rest in the room," her dad said.

Her father guided her up from the chair and into the bedroom upstairs, where Vineeta could hear her sobbing. The conversation had not gone the way she had expected. Shiva was winning the day again. Once he had shattered all of the Anjani's illusions, would there be anything left to give meaning to the word "family"?

Excerpt from
Ravi's Guide to Being a Cool Indian

Partying

What is the point of learning how to be cool unless you have a forum to show it off? Your parents interpret "party" as a polite chat with your friends about politics or Indian movies. Principle #1: a party is a place where you can pursue a self-realized state of quintessential coolness via drunken boasts and come-ons. You pick out the velvet blazer or tight skirt, spray on a scent, toss down a vodka, drag a cigarette and trawl the late night circuit to share the privilege of being around you. Free of intellectual thought, you enjoy the heightened sense of touch, sight, taste, smell and sound. The pounding music permanently de-decibelizes your hearing, but the collective energy and pheromones make you feel an important part of something where anything can happen. And why shouldn't something happen? You have confidence, which stems from self-esteem, which stems from being cool, which you've learned from this Guide.

Some of my finest memories stem from late night activities. Alessandra of Athens. Dominating a pool table in Dublin. Makiko of Osaka. Jumping into a fountain in Rome in forty five degree weather in my underwear. Ausanat of Bangkok.

Principle #2: If you want to become a skilled partier, you need to choose a position, just like a sport—organizer, participant, observer or life-of-the-party. You already know which of these you are, but if you aspire to become the "life of the party", know that it comes in two species, the copycat and the natural. The copycat dirty-dances on the bar counter or tells tales about a friend who got drunk and woke up in a tub with a kidney missing. The natural is rarer, invigorating the party without contrivance. I've only known one natural, and he proved his skills in the most challenging of formats, the Indian community gathering. Take notes.

I was in high school, forced to attend a luncheon honoring the retiring community association president. The speeches had ended and everyone stood up to leave. Then Vinod Khandelwal moved to the center of the room in his baggy button-down and pleated pants. He rapped the closest table with the palm of his left hand and knuckles of his right.

"Dhu-oong a chaka, dhu-oong a chaka, dhu-oong a chaka," he said in emulation of a dhol drum, the one that's looped around your neck and played on both sides.

People started looking at him, and he fluttered his eyebrows and shoulders to indicate they should join him.

"A hey, a hey, a hey…" another friend syncopated, moving in next to him.

"Do ladki ka kama hai toh meri anjana hai," one of the women sang, floating over their percussion in a nasally tone.

The room of thirty five gathered around Vinod. Four wives rotated in a circle, dipping their bodies inwards with cupped right hands, then drifting their hands back towards their heads like floating petals. Their midriffs jiggled in the gap between their blouse and their sari.

Vinod pulled Mum out to dance, twirling her by her arm and circling around her as she tried to pick out the rhythm by snapping her fingers. She shook her torso while looking at the audience to see if she was doing okay. Vinod bent his knees, lifted his arms above his head and snapped his fingers with his eyes closed, as if the singing was the most divine melody he had ever heard.

"Chalo!" Let's go!

Dad observed with a smile. Mum occasionally accused him of an affair if her attempts to start an argument over how he left the car seat too far back or something similar failed, but seeing the purported mistresses jiggle their flabby bellies highlighted the absurdity of her paranoia.

Everyone in the crowd began clapping. A few people joined the dance. Dark circles of perspiration soaked through Vinod's shirt. He stutter-stepped one way, shoulder-bowed another, and circled around various observers with such joy that everyone was smiling and cheering. At the end, some of the men lifted him on their shoulders and chanted his name. Before we left the restaurant, Vinod uncle asked for a glass of water from a waitress, a cute blonde with Cancun beach-blue eyes who I had been eyeing the whole evening despite her belligerent body language.

"The kitchen's closing down, I can't serve you anything more," she said in passing, piercing my heart with her obvious disdain for the dancing, the food and everyone there.

Including me, just for being Indian. Then Vinod uncle gave me the ultimate lesson in being cool. He walked back up to her.

"In 1982, there was a song. "Let's Be Serious". It's fine if the kitchen closes down, I just need you to fill a glass of water."

She huffed off with a flash of her eyes, and came back a minute later with a wet glass which she slid onto the table without looking at Vinod. He picked up the glass, eyed it for saliva, shrugged his shoulders and gulped.

"I will take antibiotics when I go home."

Principle #3: The natural life-of-the-party celebrates existence in the face of malice and doesn't need accoutrements for a party. He makes everyone feel more interesting, sexier and more alive. If you don't have the adrenalin or psyche to be the life-of-the-party, you can instead settle for communion by boasting about alcohol consumption, wearing stylish clothing and feigning nonchalance over outrageous drink prices.

Chapter 11
Vinod's Reunion
Ann Arbor, MI

Ravi

Ravi woke up from a dream in which an elderly man in a Bollywood movie was telling another character, "You don't tell someone who's upset not to cry, you just listen and give them something sweet." As he laid in his childhood twin bed looking at INXS and Smiths concert posters his parents had never taken down, he quickly realized which old man could give his mum the candy she would need to move on, which would allow their family to move on, which would allow Vineeta to move on.

He verified Vinod Khandelwal was at home by calling his phone, asking if it was him, and hanging up on him. He snuck out of his parent's home before breakfast, driving out to the address he had found in a handwritten address book his parents still kept by their phone. The neighborhood consisted of modest 1950s colonial style houses with snow-covered lawns. He pulled into the driveway of a house he hadn't seen in years—a small green one with an integrated garage and stairs leading from the gravel driveway to the entry door. As he waited for Vinod to answer the doorbell, he jogged in place to stay warm and blew clouds as if he was smoking a cigarette.

Vineeta had mucked things up at home even worse than Ravi could. It was one thing for her to expect forgiveness for the lies her life was based on. It was another to expect forgiveness for calling out the lies their parents' lives were based on. Ravi had been tossing and turning in bed the previous evening when he had applied this logic to his own life. Ian, Vineeta and Pankaj had always forgiven him for the lies his life was based on. If anything, his lies had made him who he was. But it was when he started pointing out the lies their lives were based on – for Ian, his relationship with Jessica, for Vineeta, her relationship with Hans, for Pankaj, his relationship with… kind of everything and everyone– that things had headed the wrong way.

The door unsealed like the vacuum release of a refrigerator. Ravi expected the old Vinod, but instead saw a degraded copy of the original—physically shrunk, a few wild white strands of remaining hair, and wire-framed glasses which magnified one eye to the size of a gumball. He was dressed in cotton drawstring pants and a baggy white long sleeve shirt. Ravi wouldn't have recognized him if he had passed him on the street.

"Vinod uncle. It's Ravi. Ravi Anjani."

Ravi had been taught to refer to older Indians as uncle or auntie. It was both a way to show respect, and hide the fact that he had usually forgotten their name. At what age would he become the uncle whose name no one remembered?

"Ravi?"

Ravi could see Vinod scrambling to assemble the file on Ravi, evolving him from a young teen into the stubbled man with the drooping shoulders standing in front of him.

"Ravi! How can I…"

"It's a long story if you have the time."

"Of course! Come in, come in. The house is messy, but…"

Ravi was already past Vinod. He waited in the foyer as Vinod closed the door with shaking hands. Vinod directed him to a sofa in the side living room. Stacks of bills sat next to the telephone on the side table. Stacks of newspapers obscured the coffee room table. Stacks of magazines sat next to a recliner, where Vinod plopped himself down to showcase the chapped white soles of his feet.

"This is quite a surprise. You're still in Ann Arbor? How is Vineeta?"

"Yeah, she's good. Living in New York. Like me. My parents are still here, though."

"Yes, I had heard that."

"I heard about Kanta auntie," Ravi said.

"Yes, *beta*. She passed away six months ago." *Son.*

Vinod's eyes betrayed fragility, fear, emptiness, yearning. Where was the energy, the humor? Ravi saw him gazing outside at a bird with dark stripes on its chest that landed on the windowsill.

Death was curiously irrational. Ravi could mourn the death of a character in a movie, really feel it, like Amitabh's classic expiry in his mother's arms at the end of *Deewar*, and yet the news of Kanta's death, whom he had actually known, didn't affect him directly. He felt sad for Vinod uncle, but that's largely what mourning was—feeling sad for other people. If Ravi died, who cared other than his parents and sister? For all the time establishing his own importance, his friends would always have other friends, in fact, they would probably bond further over stories involving him.

"I'm sorry, uncle. I was really sad to hear. Someone is here, and then they're not. And so all that's left is everyone's memories, people feeling sad about the person who's not there, and then people feeling sad for the people who are feeling sad. But that's not what the person who died would want, unless they were the type of person who would, in which case probably no one would have been sad in the first place."

"Well, I don't understand, but I know Kanta loved you, so I know she will hear your good thoughts."

Ravi smelled something familiar.

"You like incense?" Ravi asked.

"You know, I pray every morning, I have my mandhir upstairs. Kanta liked to burn it, so now I do it because I think it's like her spirit is going through the house."

"Yeah, I can feel it. She's definitely…here with us," Ravi said, respectfully playing along with Vinod's sentimental fictions.

They looked at each other silently.

"So, what are you doing these days?" Vinod asked.

"I work, worked, I don't know, for a t.v. channel called MTV, I don't know if you've heard of it. I go around interviewing people. And I've been in a band for the past few years, we had some success."

Ravi was rushing out details which he could have spent hours talking about, and yet he abruptly felt like there wasn't much to say. He pushed his hands into his pockets. The wood paneling of the room and yellow and green furnishings made him feel slightly uncomfortable, like he had been transported back to the 1970s without the disco and free love.

"Yes, that's very good. You want something to drink?" Vinod asked.

"No, I'm fine."

Vinod coughed and blew his nose in his handkerchief.

"Do you still play ping pong?" Ravi asked.

Ravi recalled sessions in the basement. Vinod had always looked awkward playing, but managed to get every ball back. He had followed every miss with an "Oh, sill-ee!" and every winner with some zany comment like, "See? You bring me good luck, why don't you move here, we'll adopt you and let you watch movies all the time" or "You have to let the old man win once in a while, otherwise I'll get depressed and eat too much and become too fat to get off the couch, then you and your father will have to come lift me off."

"No, no. That was a long time ago. I haven't played in years. I don't even know if we still have the table. Did we sell it?"

Vinod seemed to ponder his own question. Was he in the early stages of dementia?

"Anyway, that was a long time ago. The only I thing I like to play now is with is my brother's grandchildren."

He stood up to retrieve a studio picture of his brother's family from a bookshelf and hand it to Ravi, naming each of the children.

"Rakesh likes to drive the car. I put him on my lap and let him steer the wheel. Ajanti sits with me and sings *bhajans*. They all like the tricks." *Religious songs.*

Vinod demonstrated the removable thumb and the tongue controlled by the pull of his ears and looked at Ravi as if he should believe in the magic.

"Good stuff. Cute kids, yeah. Looks like…well, looks like things are going okay. So, are you…still working?" Ravi asked.

"Nooo, no. I retired five years back. Everything's too fast now. Email, shmemail, cell phone, bell phone. Now I just relax. I volunteer at the temple. You want something to drink? Tea, coffee?"

"Am I interrupting your morning?"

"What is there to interrupt? Only God can interrupt, but he's usually busy."

Ravi had envisioned a rollicking reunion, sharing Jack Daniels while Vinod made quirky reminiscences with stentorian guffaws, perhaps dancing or suggesting a game of ping pong or bowling, but instead Vinod led him to the kitchen. Vinod filled a red tea kettle with water and turned on the stove while Ravi sat down at the dining table. Ravi recounted the first time they had met.

His family had just relocated from London to Ann Arbor in 1984. They had been roaming the local mall when Ravi had seen a man with a halo of oily salt and pepper hair perusing the clearance bin at Waldenbooks. Despite Vinod's square plastic eyeglasses, which made his right eye appear twice the size of the left and possibly implied retardation, serial killing or supernatural deviancy, Ravi had run back to his parents as fast as he could shouting, "Dad, Indian! Indian!" Jeevan had introduced himself and confirmed that Vinod was Indian before connecting that Jeevan's friend Abhijit Modi was from Vinod's home neighborhood of Walkeshwar in Bombay. Vinod had said he believed the Modi's were friends with his friend Naresh Ranbhir, and Jeevan had confirmed that Naresh went to school with Jeevan's cousin Nigesh, and Vinod had said that Nigesh's brother-in-law had done dental work for Vinod's brother back home.

Kanta had sidled up to Vinod during the conversation. They were Marwaris, not Gujarati like the Anjanis, but they had still hit it off when Vinod had invited them for pizza and ordered slices with pineapple to Ravi and Vineeta's amusement. When he had moonwalked across the floor singing, "Beat it! Beat it! Come on now it's time to eat it," he had won them over for life.

Vinod said he couldn't remember, and Ravi felt hurt, like an important part of his life had been erased. If the people he loved couldn't remember their collective past, what was the meaning of it? A unique past when you could make a friend by approaching them in the mall. Now when Ravi looked at other Indians to acknowledge their heritage with a head nod, most just ignored him.

Ravi explained the concept of *Cool Kids*, and said that Vinod might have made a good interview subject as the first Cool Kid he had ever known. Ravi scanned the family room—a plastic beaded runner over the carpet, tube t.v. in the corner with rabbit ears, a musty yellow knit blanket draped over the couch, a side chair covered with translucent plastic.

"Though if we filmed you, we'd have to do something about this," Ravi said, pointing to the room. "It like you're trying to be the Elvis of newspaper archives in the hope that the AARP decides to turn your home into Graceland."

Vinod laughed.

"Okay, now I'm starting to remember your jokes. Anyway, your kids don't want to watch an old man. Things are good the way they are."

"How's it like without Kanta auntie around?"

Vinod joined Ravi at the table and slowly stirred his tea.

"Kanta was my oxygen. Quietly it's there, letting you do what you need to because you share a world with this person that is more important than anything else you can face. So without her, life goes on, but sometimes it feels like you can't breathe. People say I should meet someone new, but it's not so easy. The mind is very complicated."

Vinod had perfectly described how Ravi had felt about Pilar. She let him do what he needed to do by filling the voids. He had mentally re-visited his trip to Madrid multiple times, wondering if he could have said or done something differently to win her back.

Vinod's eyes misted over as he continued.

"We met when she saw me playing badminton when I was at Elphinston College. Her brother mentioned me to their parents, and in three months we were engaged at my parents' flat. Then we moved here after...I don't know, maybe five years? She took care of everything. I just needed to give her perfume and flowers once in a while, and she would always forgive anything. She gave so much support, like when Ford let me go. Then I was a consultant for a long time."

Ravi had never forgotten Vinod's diatribe against Ford when he was laid off years ago: "These bastards lay off the people who are making the products, while all the managers sit around changing the name of this division and that division and act like they've done some big thing! I worked for them for twenty one years, but it doesn't matter. These white *chuthiyas*."

White fuckers. A rare darkness had invaded Ravi's understanding of the world, of his Dad, of Vinod uncle. It was one thing for Ravi to be called racist names by schoolmates, but it was another witnessing the happiest man he had ever known have his livelihood threatened by classism to the point that he said racist things. Was life so dangerous that you could have trouble surviving despite trying your best? If Vinod had trouble finding joy in life, then life was a formidable opponent. Now Ravi better understood his frustration, though maybe life was a nested sequence of understandings, where you infinitely learned more without getting any closer to truth.

Ravi sipped tea from the mug, while Vinod dribbled tea from his mug onto his coaster plate to cool down so he could slurp it before continuing.

"I was so used to her buying my clothes and the groceries, I didn't know what to do when she...expired. The first time I went to the mall, I actually cried in the dressing room because I couldn't decide whether to buy a sweater. But then I told myself, she would not want me to be that way. So I took it to the cashier and said, 'I am meant for this sweater. I will buy it, then give it to you to give back to me as a gift.' That made her laugh just like Kanta would. The best part was when Kanta would laugh at me and call me a *gandyo*." A fool.

Vinod shook his head in disbelief, looking at the floor before recovering his composure. Ravi could use someone to share his life. Vinod could barely remember details of his everyday life, but recalled every detail about Kanta. Ravi needed to move on from his memory of Pilar and find someone new.

"Anyway, you have someone, a wife or girlfriend?" Vinod asked.

"Not right now. It's tough with the touring and all, though when all your friends start pairing up, it almost forces you to think about settling down."

"There are many nice Indian girls."

"That's what my parents say. Not my style."

Vinod tilted his tea cup in the coaster and slurped his tea.

"I thought I would go before Kanta. I'm eight years older. I used to smoke when we were in India. Now I'm just old."

"You look young."

"No one ever noticed me for my looks."

What if Ravi's Mum or Dad died? Had Ravi and Vineeta shown them enough appreciation? Vineeta was acting like her life was a mess just because their Mum wanted her to get married and their Dad had had an affair, but they had given them food, shelter and unconditional love. His success in music and Vineeta's career forays were only possible because of the secure cocoon in which they were raised. Watching episodes of *The Saint* while their Mum rubbed coconut oil into their hair, getting guitars and book sets as gifts, getting a tuition-free education at Michigan. Not to mention the ongoing loans, though Ravi couldn't ask for another one to pay off Dalinc after Vineeta's bombshell. Ravi had hoped Dalinc had forgotten, but had received a short text from him a few days before: "*12/1/07*".

"You know, I always liked talking to you. You never gave us advice, Vineeta and me. You asked us what we thought, so when you did offer up some insight, I figured it must be true," Ravi said.

"I'm starting to remember now. I knew you would do something special. Parents can be worried about this grade or that test, that's their job. But Kanta and I, we could see you had a spark. When you're good to people, trust in God, you will always get back more than you give."

"I imagine God believes in forgiveness?"

"Of course, everyone should learn to forgive. Is there someone you need to forgive?" Vinod asked.

"Well, it's really the opposite way around. I know you had some falling out with my parents, and honestly I don't know all the details, but you used to be best friends, so whatever the issue was, maybe you can forgive them. My parents would love to talk to you. Because, let's be honest again, time is kind of running out. I could have called, but I thought it might be fun to surprise you. If you have the time, you could all meet up."

"At this age, all I have is time."

"Is now a good time?"

"Now?"

"Well, I know it's Black Friday and all, but it looks like you haven't bought anything in like thirty years, so that's probably not a big concern."

"Let me think."

Vinod looked at Ravi.

"The traffic will be heavy this time of day," he said. "Maybe we should plan something properly."

"I promise you, this will be more fun than anything you have planned for the day. You have to come. I'll drive you both ways."

"Hmm. Okay. I just need to change. You're sure this is okay?"

Ravi considered the fraught situation at home.

"I would actually say it's necessary."

Vinod added a cardigan to his outfit and followed Ravi to the car. This maneuver would relieve the tension at home by medicating the boil. Or was he popping it, like with the wedding speech? No, he sensed his parents' latent regret over messing up their friendship. They would at least be civil with Vinod, if not moved. Vinod spoke the emotional language that resonated with his mum. If he could activate his mum's sense of forgiveness and years wasted in resentment, maybe it would spill over to her view of Vineeta.

Ravi drove them to his parent's house, cranking the heat to an uncomfortable level to make Vinod comfortable.

Vineeta answered the doorbell with dark moons under her eyes.

"We were wondering where you went. Not like you to be up so early," she said.

"Where is she?"

"In the bedroom," Vineeta said. "She said she's moving to London to live with her sisters."

At least she was speaking. That meant that his Mum had reached the second stage of recovery in the Bharti Anger Management Program. Stage one was crying, stage two was threats, stage three was diatribes about the kids being shameful, stage four was cooking as a form of meditation and conciliation and stage five was forgiveness, though there was always the danger of immediate relapse. Ravi had obtained a PhD in Bhartiology, capable of diagnosing her issues and issuing prescriptions for recovery. But he was facing the greatest challenge of his medical career, to rescue this weekend from the destructive mess Vineeta and her belief in Shiva had left behind. Because he suspected that Vineeta wasn't thrilled about embracing their mum's future vitriol with the equanimity of a Buddhist.

"Well, I have a VIP that she's going to want to meet."

Ravi pushed the door wider to reveal an elderly man.

"You remember Vinod uncle."

"Oh my God! Vinod uncle."

His sister gave Vinod uncle a hug, and Ravi noticed he was wearing some ancient barbershop scent, not quite musk, not quite Pine Sol.

"I can't believe you're here."

"I can't believe I'm here either. I think it's the neem tea, it makes you live a long time."

"I know you have a lot to catch up on, but I thought maybe we get Dad first, then surprise Mum in the bedroom," Ravi said.

Ravi jogged inside to Jeevan's study where his father was on his love seat reading *Time*. Ravi ushered him out of the office before he could put down the magazine or his reading glasses.

"What is so urgent?"

Ravi waved his arm towards Vinod.

"What do you always tell us, greet your guests, make them feel at home. You remember Vinod uncle."

"Vinod!"

Jeevan and Vinod assessed each other for some emotional sign.

"The house looks the same," Vinod offered. "And I can always smell Bharti's good cooking. I don't know how you stay so slim."

"You. You, too. You look good. I'm sorry about Kanta, we heard what happened."

"Yes, it was hard, but God has his plans."

"Very good to see you, come in, sit down, we'll make some tea."

Jeevan put his hand on Vinod's shoulder and ushered him in to the living room sofa. They immediately began discussing the weather—that day's weather, the season-to-date, the weekly forecast, the effect of climate change, the heating bills. Ravi observed briefly before turning to Vineeta.

"Why don't we surprise Mum in the bedroom," he whispered.

"She'll be pissed, she's still in her nightgown," Vineeta said.

"True. But we can't exactly tell her to dress up to surprise her. Let's just all go." He addressed the others, "Sorry uncle, my Mum's upstairs, if you come up with us, we can surprise her."

Vinod took a prolonged moment just to stand up and reach the stairs. Ravi led the way, instructing Vineeta to follow at the rear in order to catch Vinod in case he stumbled backwards from his ginger ascent. Ravi knocked on the bedroom door and cracked it open.

"Mum, guess who's come to see you?" Ravi asked.

A curious and collected voice asked, "Who?"

Ravi widened the radius of the door and ushered them all in. Bharti was sitting in a sofa chair in the corner reading. He announced their guest, but it required Bharti to remove her glasses and look at Vinod to comprehend what was happening. Her face lost all its tension and her eyes widened in surprise.

"Vinod! I wish I know you coming, then I get ready properly. You should have called me," she scolded Ravi.

She stood up, pulled her hair back and looked at herself in a mirror behind her.

"You look good. Like the flowers of Lonavla," Vinod said.

"What…how?"

Bharti looked at Ravi for an explanation.

"I made a little visit. You know, life's too short to waste it talking about people when you could be talking with people."

Bharti stepped forward. Ravi looked for signs of rapprochement with Vineeta, but his Mum didn't look at her.

"Do you want something to eat?" Bharti asked Vinod.

"Do you still make the best dhokla in America?" Vinod asked. "You should have a, what is it, an internet thing, like a cooking show."

"Come down, I'll make something."

Everyone descended except Bharti, who took a few minutes to change and put on make-up. Jeevan, Vinod and Ravi situated at the dining table while Vineeta began assembling a peace offering in the form of the ingredients for dhokla—cream of wheat, gram flour, ginger, jalapeno, salt and a variety of spices.

Bharti arrived and gently asked where the cream of wheat was (right in front of her), suggesting she had jumped straight to stage 4 of recovery. For thirty minutes, his Mum healed herself with cooking and gossip. She and Vinod recounted the key events of the preceding years, their current state of being and the current state of relatives the other had known.

"Vikram has three children. They are the best. I see them every month. One likes baseball, one likes to dance and one likes Spiderman."

"We don't get grandkids and even my sisters don't get," Bharti said.

"But you have two smart and beautiful children. Looking at Ravi I thought I was looking at Jeevan, the way he talks, very confident. He's a man now. I remember the kids, when we took them to that amusement park, and Vineeta wouldn't let go of the railing until you bought her cotton candy, Ravi only wanted to go on the rollercoasters that went this way and that way, upside down, backwards, into space. Now he's a big success, a tall handsome man, it's so good to see him."

"Yes, you know he's big music person. Songs are on the radio," Bharti said proudly.

"He was telling me."

Ravi hoped she would make a positive comment about Vineeta, but she stopped there.

"We've missed having you around. No one can make us laugh like you used to. And Kanta would always play the harmonium when we were together so we could all sing bhajans," Jeevan said.

"Just yesterday, I was making tindoora. This your favorite vegetable, I remember," Bharti said.

Vinod started laughing, which evolved into a paroxysm of tears and heavy breathing.

"I'm sorry, *bhai bhen*, I'm sorry," he kept repeating. *I'm sorry, brother sister, I'm sorry.*

"We are the ones who are sorry, *bhai*," Jeevan said. "Sometimes in life we make mistakes."

Vinod wiped his eyes on his shoulder and said calmly, "We were too young to hold on to the good things."

Bharti entered the lachrymose competition, squeezing tears from her eyes and saying, "What has happened has happened. God has his plan, we are just following it."

She crossed the room, sidled up to Vineeta and placed her arm around Vineeta. Ravi could see them squeezing each other. Saved by an orgy of forgiveness and tears.

"Oh! The dhokla!"

Bharti released Vineeta and removed the dhokla pan from the steamer. She loosened the savory cake from its pan onto a cutting board, coated it with fried mustard seeds, cut it into squares and instructed Vineeta to serve it to everyone with coriander chutney and achar masala, in case the jalapenos in the ingredients were not spicy enough. Ravi stood up to get some plates and sat back down. Vineeta circled the table serving pieces of dhokla. Vinod took a bite, smacked his lips and sprouted his fingers away from his mouth.

"Ahaaa! So good. I've missed your food."

Bharti beamed with pleasure and started making tea.

"So, what has God planned for you? You're working, you're married? I know lots of men who will line up all the way to Russia to marry you. When I last saw you, you were a nice girl, now look! Miss India," Vinod said to Vineeta.

Ravi should have seen it coming. Just as quickly as the reunion had fixed things, it was now about to mess them up.

"Yeah, I just started a new job at the UN," she said, sitting down at the dining table.

"Neither one getting married. And now she starting to date American boy. Black," Bharti said from the kitchen.

"So, what's wrong? American, Indian, black, white, as long as she's happy. Blacks are like the new Indians. We have Gandhi, they have this King," Vinod observed.

Ravi looked over at Vinod. It was an odd outdated reference, but then he saw his mum nodding.

"We have Kishore Kumar, they have Stevie Wonder," Ravi added.

Vinod looked back at him.

"We have Sachin Tendulkar, they have this Jordan."

"The British enslaved us, the Americans enslaved them."

Ravi smirked at Vinod. They were in the zone. Vinod looked back at Bharti.

"See? It's like this boy is an Indian. And if we move here, we can't expect the kids to marry someone from there. He's a nice boy? What does he do?" Vinod asked.

"He's a singer. Ravi's friend," Bharti offered.

She was standing in front of the dining table.

"Oh, a singer! Very good. When he visits, you get a free music performance."

"I have friend, her son marry American. Wife don't let her see the grandkids," Bharti said.

"I would never marry someone who wouldn't let you see your grandkids," Vineeta said.

Ravi chimed in.

"Mum, Ian is like an honorary Indian. He and his brother have been taking care of their mum ever since their dad died. He's more Indian at heart than most Indians."

"You know, you have raised two smart children. You have to trust them to do what's right for them, and that will include what's right for you. Just remember, you've lived here longer than you lived in India, so now you're American, too," Vinod said.

"I don't think of it like this. You know, there is one good looking black man. What his name?" Bharti asked, looking at Jeevan.

"Denzel Washington?" Vineeta offered.

"Is that him?" Bharti asked, looking at Jeevan.

"I don't know who you're thinking of. He's good looking," Jeevan said.

"Yes, he's good looking," Bharti said.

"Ian doesn't look like him, but he is good looking," Vineeta said.

"Yes, you're right. Ravi's friend has a nice smile. He's big and strong," Bharti said. "I like him. Are you thinking of getting married?"

"No Mom, we just started going out two months ago. But I wanted you to know that I might end up with a non-Indian."

Bharti nodded in satisfaction. Ravi and Vinod had provided some rationale that seemed to appeal to Bharti. Now if only Vineeta sealed it with some emotional glue. Ravi nodded in Vineeta's direction, and Vineeta stood back up to face their Mum.

"Mom, I'm sorry for what I said yesterday, I was just hurt because I want to find someone to marry just as much as you want me to, and I may not want the type of guy you try to set me up with, but it makes me feel like a loser when you always mention it," she said, releasing a heavier torrent of pearl-like tears, a talent that was just as useful as Ravi's ability to make things up on the spot.

"I love you. I never do nothing to hurt you. You're my baby. I only want the best for you," Bharti said, squeezing Vineeta tight.

"I know," Vineeta said, squeezing back and wiping the tears from her face with the back of her hand.

"My daughter is best daughter," Bharti said. "Ravi good too. You know, I look up things about Spanish. Penny-lope Cruise is Spanish. She almost looking Indian. Peelar looks like this?"

"You talking to me? Not quite," Ravi said, interrupted from rolling stray mustard seeds around on his plate.

"I also learn some Spanish. 'Ho-la, may laa-mo Bharti.'"

"Well, you'll be happy to learn that Pilar is already engaged, so you don't need to take the advanced Spanish course just yet."

"Oh. She's engaged to whom?"

"How would I know? Some guy she met. Anyway, it's already been a couple of months since I spoke to her."

"You're okay?" she asked.

"It's fine Mum, it was just a whim. I have other prospects."

After finishing the dhokla, they moved to the living room and reminisced with Vinod for two more hours before promising to meet again soon. Ravi drove Vinod back home.

The salutary effect of Vinod's appearance allowed them to finish the dinner without further drama. Ravi sustained the weekend's mood into the evening as they sat down on the couch to watch *Murder She Wrote*.

"Check this out, Mum."

Ravi leaned over to hand Bharti a napkin with blurry writing which Ravi deciphered as, "To Bharti, thanks for watching my movies, Deepika"

"Met her at a party. Thought you'd like it."

"This is really Deepika Padukone's signature?" she asked.

Ravi knew that after winning the lottery, building a big house, having a famous or rich child, having a handsome son-in-law or pretty daughter-in-law and having grand-children, hobnobbing with Bollywood stars was the quickest path to community respectability.

"Well, I wouldn't have known she was anybody, but this Indian girl I work with pointed her out, so I introduced myself. Invited her to be on the show, but never heard back."

Ravi sat on the adjacent sofa next to Vineeta as Bharti flossed her teeth with the corner of a postcard while dialing a friend. She had long exhausted Ravi's fame to offset her perception that others pitied her because her children weren't settled. The napkin would refresh Ravi's importance.

"What she looked like? Wait...Huh, Chintu? Bharti. *Ravi aur Vineeta agaya hai, aur...*" She explained her children's arrival for Thanksgiving and the existence of the napkin before turning back to Ravi. "Chintu asking, who else was there? Deepika's seeing a cricket player, Yuvraj something, he was there?"

Ravi shrugged his shoulders.

"Ravi doesn't know. He probably wasn't there, or Ravi would have seen. I bet she's telling him, 'No more, I'm big star now.'"

As their dad watched the tv, they watched their Mum transforming insignificant facts into ulterior motives, formulating urgent conspiracies and distinguishing truth from lies (which usually correlated to what she agreed with and what she didn't, which sub-correlated to how she felt rather than actual facts). They had both seen it so many times that it was a part of their own identity, an identity they were finally starting to understand.

Excerpt from
Ravi's Guide to Being a Cool Indian

Mistakes

Let me yield the stage to my Dad for Principle #1: all your mistakes in life will be because you make bad assumptions or don't communicate well. Ironic advice from my Dad given that his generation of Indians was always shouting at our generation about the ways in which we should be acting in a society they didn't grow up in.

He does have a point, though. There have been many times I didn't communicate well by telling the truth when I should have lied and lying when I should have told the truth, because lying effectively requires you to understand whether someone wants to be lied to. And when I decided someone did but they really didn't, I was also making a bad assumption.

But is it really worth putting in the effort to avoid bad assumptions? Will you net-net be happier? You can get by for years making mistakes, while the consequences of a mistake only lasts a few days, maybe weeks. Not to mention Principle #2: The entire joy of being an Indian is making bad assumptions in order to formulate solutions to problems that don't exist. Mum laments the fact that Vineeta never cooks on the assumption that an Indian woman must know how to cook. So she keeps emailing her recipes and air-mailing packets of lentils in the hopes of spurring her culinary curiosity.

Principle #3: If you're going to make bad assumptions and communicate poorly, at least do it with someone who can't help forgiving you.

Chapter 12
Lakhi's Secret
Manhattan, New York

Ravi

The phone vibrated, desecrated a Chopin nocturne, and finally accomplished its goal of waking Ravi up. He leaned over and picked up the phone. A reminder, loan repayment day. He dropped back into his pillow, simultaneously depressed and impressed that he had remembered to input a reminder. He had returned to Manhattan from Ann Arbor a week before trying to line up studio session work—hourly wages, but at least something—and to concoct a story that would buy him additional time when Dalinc showed up, but he didn't really have anything credible. The phone rang, this time with a vapid techno beat.

A 646 number. It wasn't Dalinc's number, but Dalinc was smart enough to use a different number to get Ravi to pick up. Should he ignore it? Better to deal with Dalinc over the phone than in person.

"Hello?"

He jumped out of bed and paced the perimeter of a Turkish rug he had bought on a whim in Turkey, before he knew how much it would cost to ship it. He noticed his toenails needed clipping.

"Ravi, Sheila. I know this is probably early for you, but I have some good news I thought you'd want to hear."

His agent. He relaxed. He could use some good news.

"So I pitched MTV about making a show based on your *Guide* and they bit. Immigrant stories, cultural zeitgeist, they're a thing right now."

"Sounds promising."

"You don't seem that excited."

"I'm excited, but I'm not sure what it means. At least financially."

"You'll meet with a staff of writers to flesh out a framework. If the studio likes it, they'll pay you probably around twenty thousand dollars I'm guessing to produce a pilot. And if they picked up the show, maybe a few hundred thousand dollars? That's just for using the book. There might be more if you're more involved, like as a producer or maybe even acting."

Twenty thousand would do it. Actually twenty eight thousand six hundred, but this was a story he could sell to Dalinc. His body released some chemicals that loosened his shoulders and made him realize how subconsciously tense he had been. Pilar was right—help others, and karma will go your way.

"You're a genius, perhaps…"

"I know, the greatest agent in the world."

"Have I used that before?"

"Every time we speak."

He looked out the window, appreciating the view of downtown from his apartment while stretching out an arm and waving it like a conductor.

"And what's the timing on that? Two weeks? A month?"

She chuckled.

"You should know by now, it could be a year. It depends on when we can get you in with the writers and after you produce something."

Dalinc was certainly not going to wait a year.

"Well, let's meet today."

"It's the middle of the tv season. We'd be lucky to meet in a month."

So much for being in control. He retreated into the room and fell into his couch with slumped shoulders.

"Any possibility of an advance?"

"It doesn't work that way. People don't get paid for pitch meetings."

He pressed her on the point, but she seemed disappointed that his focus was solely on the money. He thanked her, tossed his phone on a cushion and stumbled to the bathroom to begin his ablutions. It was good news, but not quite good enough. It was like Pilar had been half-right. He had steered his sister and parents off a path of mutual destruction, and voila! his agent was calling him with a pathway to money. If only he could avoid Dalinc for long enough to do something else good that would make the pilot episode happen.

After the shower, he examined the pores of his face in the mirror. He stroked his week-old goatee and decided it was time to get rid of the itchy thing. The razor never quite restored a smooth sheen, but it was nice to see his face again. Maybe it would make him look more sympathetic with Dalinc.

A slap of cologne, a stroke of deodorant and a streak of hair gel prepared him for a day of recording songs on his home computer while waiting for the hammer to drop. If it was the last time he would be able to use his arms, he should at least go out doing the thing he liked best. They were his creation, something unique in a world of homogeneity. The techno beat rang out again. This time it was probably Dalinc. He ran back to the sofa to pick up his phone.

"Hello?" he said, crossing his fingers so tightly they hurt.

"Hey, how are you? It's Lakhi" she asked.

Lakhi, the MTV production assistant he had hooked up with before the show was canceled.

"Oh! Nice to hear from you," he said, breathing out and trying to quickly shift from cool and apprehensive to cool and suave. "Didn't get a chance to say goodbye."

At least this was positive. No Dalinc yet, and an eligible female on the phone. Maybe karma wasn't done with him yet.

"I know, it was a bit rushed. Listen, do you think we could meet up, I have something to ask you, and I'd rather do it in person."

"Ooookay...Sure, ummm...like, maybe this afternoon? Or evening? Around Washington Square Park?"

"Whatever works for you."

"Okay, let's say six at the main gate?"

So much for good news. Was it going to be pregnancy or a transmitted disease (he thought he was clean and had used protection, but he had been drunk and hadn't been tested for a year) or maybe a harassment suit? For years he feared a moment such as this, but never thought it would happen with an Indian girl from a middle class family. Certainly not one that he had assumed was lesbian the first time he had met her when she had started working on the show.

***

For one, there had been her appearance. She had short hair, wore funky t-shirts with lotus prints or political rants and sported a nose-ring and arm tattoo. Not conclusive by any means, particularly given the flirty way she tilted her head to respond to his questions. Quick left-right tilt was yes. Slow left-right tilt with squinty eyes was no, and without squinty eyes maybe.

For two, there had been her caustic sense of humor. He had asked for her opinion about the show, in which a teenager applied to be designated "cool". The show editors spliced footage of Ravi's interviews of applicants and their acquaintances into a classic hero/villain/love triangle storyline before concluding with Ravi's verdict on whether the applicant was cool.

"Anyone who applies for validation that they're cool isn't really. Sorry, I didn't mean to insult your show," she had said.

"No offense taken. You're probably right. Were you a cool kid in high school?"

"I wouldn't say cool, but not uncool, either. I didn't look after the A/V equipment or anything. That's just my adult destiny."

For three, there had been the walk to get masala chai during a break in filming, when they wandered through Times Square past the Naked Cowboy, Army Recruiting Center, a pan-flute rendering of Simon & Garfunkel by a Peruvian band and massive billboards for various Broadway shows. While Ravi had taken off his glasses to wink at people who recognized him, Lakhi had purchased a booklet with *379 New Sexual Positions* for a dollar and noted that it only had a man and a woman in it.

For four, there had been her request to quickly check out a sale at her favorite clothing store on the way back from the masala chai. She had summoned him inside the dressing room to zip up the back of a dress. His blood had quickened, and he had imagined 379 things he could do inside a dressing room. If she had looked at him a certain way, he would have assumed that she had been making a move on him. Usually girls in her looks range were more nervous around him, but she had remained casual. He had thought about asking her whether she had a girlfriend directly, but he hadn't wanted to offend her or get accused of harassment or show he was interested if she wasn't going to show that she was interested.

When she had complained that her job at MTV only consisted of focusing the camera and testing light exposure, making a mockery of her double major in Film Studies and Near Eastern Languages and Civilization from Yale, he had invited her to travel to LA for a special *Cool Kids* episode where she would have more responsibility.

During Ravi's first evening by the pool at the Comfort Inn, Lakhi's lotioned body had made him forget about the possibility she was a lesbian. She had been reading a fashion magazine while Ravi had contemplated whether he could climb to the roof of the building using window ledges and water drains if he was being chased by an assailant, unaware at the time that it might become a realistic possibility.

"So you're a smarty," Ravi had said after floating out of his reverie.

"Why's that?"

"Going to Yale."

"Well, I guess it's okay. I mean, there are lots of smart people."

"There may be lots of smart people at Yale, but I wouldn't say there are a lot of smart people generally."

"What do you base that on?"

"People I know, things I see."

"So you're smarter than everybody else?"

"Exactly the opposite. I'm a regular bloke. I'm not super smart. But I don't see a lot of people that much brighter than me. Which means most of us can't be all that bright."

"But so what? What does it even mean to try to define whether someone's smart or not? Like if they can write a great song or discover penicillin, who cares whether you think they're smart or not?"

She adjusted her sunglasses.

"A very good point. So like I said, you're a smarty. Why film studies?"

"I wanted to chronicle the experience of Northern African refugees trying to adapt to living in Europe."

"What does it mean to chronicle someone? Is that like interviewing the Tuscan Raiders from Star Wars? See if they felt like they were mis-portrayed, find out their true feelings? Cigarette?"

"No thanks, I don't smoke. You know, it was a serious project."

"I'm sorry, I was just trying to be funny."

"Well, I've never seen *Star Wars*."

"Were you living in a bomb shelter?"

"No, just wasn't interested. From what I've read, it was more about special effects. Anyway, I made my documentary to bring attention to how hard it is to assimilate."

"Then why not chronicle Indians?"

"At the time, because that seemed too obvious and I thought people wouldn't take me as seriously, which in retrospect was stupid and actually the opposite of how people view it."

He considered mentioning his *Guide*, but assumed she probably knew about it and wasn't mentioning it for a reason.

"So is it done? Can I see it?" he asked.

"It's done, it's on YouTube. It didn't turn out as well as I hoped. One of the families I chronic…followed around dropped out half way through. Another moved back to Ethiopia. The last one had run of the mill issues. I can send you the link."

"I'll still check it out."

She absent-mindedly flipped some pages in her magazine.

"So whose idea was it to film in LA?" she asked.

"That was me. I figured since there are rumors the show's going to be cancelled, I might as well get them to pay for a vacation. Ralph denied the request, but I went up the chain and promised Phil it would be 'something big', a surprise, something that would take the ratings back up."

"What do you have in mind?"

"Don't know yet."

"Phil just approved it?"

"I think he has a crush on me."

"Who can imagine why?" she asked.

Was she taking a dig at him? Or the opposite? He liked women who challenged him, but couldn't decide at the time whether she was being condescending. At the same time, her skepticism had made him want her approval.

She stood up, dipped a toe in the pool and jumped in with a flail and shriek. She immediately exited up the stairs.

"Why don't you join?" she asked, hovering over him.

Her body looked even better upright—rounded breasts, flat stomach, a perfect hip to chest ratio—not to mention wet.

Was it possible she liked him?

"Not my style, right."

"Didn't they teach you to swim in Michigan?"

Strangely enough, they hadn't. His parents had never suggested it, and Ravi had claimed he wasn't feeling well at the occasional pool party or lake retreat. If he went in now, he risked revelation of the doggy paddle he had developed snorkeling off the coast of Ibiza with Pilar.

Still, after she jumped back in, he found himself following. He was waist deep down the pool's stairs before his vodka-infused brain could protest. She splashed water at him, and he splashed back. She gave him a piercing, sultry look before starting to swim a few laps. So she did like him. She had been fronting with all the sub-textual skepticism in their conversations.

She left the pool, and he followed. They agreed to meet at 5 to venture to the Santa Monica Ferris wheel, where their conversation eased into a comfortable silence, rotating between views of the amusement park and glittering ocean swells layering into foam on the shoreline. When the wheel kept stopping to change passengers, Lakhi got personal.

"What did you mean in your song, I forget the name, but it had the lyric, 'Asked me if I'm happy today, specifically I guess, but generally I can't say,'" Lakhi asked.

"You listened to our album?"

"Maybe I checked out a few songs. Sounded like a hint of angst."

"No, I'm not a fan of angst. That suggests dread, and I prefer embracing. I think it's just the idea that, like right now, we're having a nice ride on this wheel. So I have specific things that are making me happy, but at the same time, I can have good rides and dinners and perform songs and all these specifically happy things don't necessarily add up to making me generally happy."

"There must be some specific things, though, that are making you unhappy."

"I guess. It all wouldn't matter if I had saved some money for a nice hacienda in the islands where I could just hang out with friends."

"Everyone has that fantasy. You'd hate it. You're a city boy."

"You've figured me out, have you?"

"No, but that's pretty obvious. And you can hardly swim."

"But I know how to sit on a beach."

"I don't think you know how to sit still."

"Yeah, maybe you're right," he said as their swinging bench descended on the wheel.

"You never answered my question."

"Which was?"

"What's making you unhappy?"

He squinted at her, unsure if he wanted to open himself up, especially to a co-worker. But she was an Indian who had gone to Yale, so she probably wouldn't gossip with the others. He wouldn't know if she measured up to Pilar unless he took a chance.

"Yeah, okay. I don't know why I'm unhappy, because if I did, I could do something about it, right? The choices are, some friends have been blowing me off. I don't have a record label. I owe someone some money. The show will probably be cancelled. But none of that is all that different than six months ago. So what's different now? I don't know. Is it winter? Is it boredom? Is it old age? You're a smart girl and you can probably add ten more reasons, but in the end, I don't have cancer, I still know how to play guitar, and I just have to figure it out and be a man."

"Oh. I understand."

"You do?" he asked skeptically.

"Well, the friends thing, the career thing, the relationship thing. I don't know, all of it."

"Go on."

She described how she felt stupid for getting a degree in Film Studies and holding a camera for a living when her ex-classmates where getting clerkships with Supreme Court Justices and editorial positions at *Conde Nast*. Her ex-boyfriend had made her more insecure by telling her she was stupid for getting a degree in Film Studies. Her friends had burdened her with more of their problems than she could share back—one had "replied all" with an email complaining about a colleague's laziness, another's father had suffered a heart attack, and a third was infatuated with a boy who treated her like crap while she was treating a boy who was infatuated with her like crap.

Ravi suggested a drink and hor d'ouevres at a bar. They disembarked from the Ferris wheel and walked along the shoreline until they chose a clam shack. Over a few hours, they knocked back a few drinks until Lakhi nearly stumbled off her stool and into his lap. They flagged a taxi back to the hotel. In the elevator, they began making out before she came into his room.

He loved the moment during the sway when he looked into a woman's eyes and felt existence, vulnerability, everything she had ever experienced. It was important that he actually liked the women he had slept with, which was more noble than it sounded given how many women on tour were willing to hike their skirts before even saying their name. Ravi loved love—being loved, expressing love, spreading love, feeling loved. Perhaps it drew him back to his origin, to the comfort in his mother's arms.

After two bouts of abstract impressionism, they passed out. In the morning, Ravi woke up to an empty bed and a silent room. Ravi considered whether Lakhi could be the next Pilar, the only woman who managed to sustain the purity, humanity and spiritual coalescence of their first night together. Lakhi was smart. She was cute. She was authentic. She was assured. Hell, she was even Indian and came from a good family. Given her brother's residency at Chicago Medical School and her mum's likely use of tenses and conjunctions, the problem might have been that it was too good. If her parents were like Ravi's, they would blanche at Lakhi dating a man who hadn't gone to an Ivy league school and whose mother could barely read.

When the phone began ringing, he thought about comforting statements he could make so she wouldn't feel awkward about their night together.

"Hey, how's it going?" she asked.

He heard honks and engines in the background and assumed she was walking around the hotel.

"Yeah, alright, you?"

"Yeah, good. So, this is kind of embarrassing, but I believe in being direct. I don't know that it's a good idea for us to be together like that since, you know, we're working together. You're a really great guy, and last night was fine, we were hanging out in LA, I just broke up with someone…and, anyway, I could use some space. Maybe you're thinking the same thing, I don't know, I just didn't want to have any misunderstandings."

"Yeah, yeah, that's cool. You're right, it all happened kind of fast. It's not a big deal for me if it's not for you."

"No, it's fine," she affirmed.

Which of course it hadn't been. They had shared two awkward days of filming on the beach, avoiding each other at night and on the plane ride home. Let alone the awful disjointed footage of beach kids which the editor had described as "something big—a big pile of shit".

The night after their hook-up, he had called Ian, who had said that Lakhi knew what she was getting into, which was true. But he had still felt like he had let her down in some way.

***

As he awaited their evening meeting in Washington Square Park, he spent the day recording and grabbing take-out from the Chinese place around the corner. Every hallway noise made him think that Dalinc had arrived. His mood dragged with the gray skies and the knowledge that none of the song ideas were good enough to be a hit pop song. He was glad he had somewhere to go and actually left early enough to be on time.

It was night already at 5:35, but the sky was lit up from the reflection of the city lights off the clouds. There were no taxis in front of his building. There were never any available when it was cold or rainy, though the threat of rain may also have explained why Dalinc hadn't shown up. Ravi lit up a cigarette to distract himself from the chill as he walked on Jane Street along the cobble-stones past the red brick townhouses. He needed to buy another set of knit cap and gloves. They always fell out of his pockets. At Greenwich Avenue, he spotted a taxi, but it was going the wrong way, and he was already half way to the park.

He reached the front of the giant archway, which looked like the Arc De Triomphe. Maybe it was a replica? The trees were barren, the fountain dry, and the park was empty. In summer, the park was the best place in the world, brimming with students and musicians and chess players and tourists. In this weather, he would rather have been in LA.

She surprised him from behind, unrecognizable in a brimmed hat and thick scarf.

"Thanks for coming," she said.

"It's all good. I should have suggested a bar or coffee shop or something."

"We can go to one. There are a bunch up the street."

She didn't appear to be pregnant, but who could tell with all the layers of clothing. He asked whether she knew anything about the archway to distract from the fact that he had been staring at her belly, but she didn't. They began walking, recounting the whereabouts of other staff members from *Cool Kids*.

He wiped his nose with the back of his hand, hoping she didn't notice. Lakhi slowed down as they approached Union Square. What were the chances she had a communicable disease? If he had made it this far without one, she should have, too.

"So, I know we talked about this, but remember, well of course you remember, but the one night we hooked up...we kind of agreed to forget about it, and..."

He played it cool, inhaling enough nicotine in one breath to spell out a poem in smoke, a haiku or dirty limerick if he could remember one, but he was a bit nervous. He remembered that he had promised Pilar he would quit smoking and stepped the cigarette out on the sidewalk. Lakhi wrapped her arms tight around her torso and scraped her right shoe back and forth on the sidewalk before looking at the people walking by and lowering her voice slightly.

"Maybe it wasn't the worst thing to happen, meaning, maybe we could have given it more of a chance."

He crinkled his eyebrows and tilted his head.

"You're...really?"

She liked him? If he had bet money on who liked him and who didn't, he'd be in far more debt than twenty nine grand. He felt a pimple on his chin. Lakhi's eyes tracked his face for a preview of his response.

"I'm flattered, but...your boyfriend, wasn't that kind of on and off?"

"Officially off."

"It's kind of cold, should we go inside somewhere?"

"Yeah, good idea."

This was turning out to be a suspensefully good day. There he was worrying about Dalinc, and instead he was getting a sitcom and a romance. He had really enjoyed Lakhi's company before things had gotten awkward. It would be nice for some intimacy. He hadn't been with anyone since his tryst with Lakhi. They continued to the Coffee Shop and took a booth. Lakhi ordered a tea and Ravi ordered a scotch to warm up and French fries to keep the scotch company. He rubbed his hands together and sat on them. She kept her cap and scarf on.

Pilar's advice was bearing all types of fruit. But what if this fruit was Adam's apple, not a reward, but a test?

"When I first moved to New York, somebody took me here and said this was where the models hung out. But it was really a place where a bunch of guys expecting models to show up hung out," Ravi said.

"It all worked out for you in the end."

"I suppose it looks that way. For a while it did."

"What do you mean? You had the show, your band, the *Guide*."

"'Had' is the key word."

His whole conception of himself had been as some great musical messenger. The music was just a means for people to feel bigger than they were, to connect with others who shared their emotions and thoughts. But if people weren't supposed to shoot the messenger, they probably shouldn't have been idolizing him either. He had been lucky enough to be the messenger for a while, but now he was just another guy trying to figure out where he belonged and what he should do with his life. So it hadn't all worked out in the end, because his life was still in the middle.

"There'll be something else."

He began playing with his cutlery. He wanted to pursue her, both because he liked her and because he hadn't met anyone else in a while, but knew he shouldn't involve her with loan sharks, his unemployment, his failed social life and his raving mom. Not to mention that Pilar had said that until he knew himself, he couldn't commit to someone else. Could he honestly say that he knew himself?

He could do right by her. He didn't have to mess up first and then clean it up. Maybe this was his path to twenty nine thousand.

"Look, I'm flattered by what you said out there, but…the timing's not ideal right now," he said.

It was mature of him to worry about timing, to plan his life instead of shooting around like an untied balloon. Of course, the consumption of three more scotches might make later that evening seem like ideal timing. In which case he could rest his conscience on the disclaimer he had just made.

"Oh. Okay."

"You're a really nice girl, and I'm not, well, not a nice boy, right? So you're better off steering clear anyway."

"Why do you say that?"

"Which part?"

"That you're not a nice boy."

"I don't want what most people want, and that can complicate things."

"What do you want?"

He smiled and returned her stare without speaking. He didn't want to ramble inarticulately in hopes of figuring it out on the spot.

"You know, when I met you I thought you were a joker," Lakhi offered. "Like, when you said charities should give more to cancer research instead of AIDS research, since AIDS had a fifty cent cure called a condom, I thought that was pretty cruel and ignorant. And so when that thing happened, you know, out in LA, I was kind of unhappy with myself. But then I was browsing a book store and started paging through your *Guide*, and I thought, 'This is pretty good.' I didn't expect so much clarity and coherence. And I realized you make interesting points but in a funny way, though a big part of it is an act."

"And your tattoos and earrings aren't an act?"

"Yeah, maybe. I mean we're all pretending to a degree. But I wondered how you decide when to be real and when to pretend."

"It isn't really a choice, is it? If you're brown and you want to succeed in entertainment, you'd better learn to pretend pretty much all the time."

He had invented his life, so the pretend was the real, at least for him, because he had made it into what he had wanted. When people had alluded to him losing sight of what's real, he had felt they had lost sight of what was possible. They weren't able to fake it until they made it, and blamed him for pointing out they needed to adapt if they wanted to achieve their goals. But he was starting to think that Pilar was right. In pretending all the time, maybe he had lost sight of whether he was even achieving what he had set out to achieve.

"That's loaded. I don't think you pretend all the time. I saw you on set. You say some shit, but you treat everyone well," Lakhi said.

Ravi thought about his interactions with the gaffer and the interns and the others. He was never condescending.

"Anyway, you don't want to go out and that's fine, I get it, just thought I'd see," Lakhi said.

The waiter delivered their order.

"I'll pay for the tea, I can get going," she said, reaching into her purse.

"It's cold outside, the tea will warm you up. And I shouldn't eat all these French fries by myself. Didn't you tell me you like to write?" Ravi asked. "Is that where all the psycho-analysis comes from?"

He needed this conversation, even if he wasn't going to pursue something romantic. He tapped out ketchup onto the plate as she looked back at him.

"I guess I like to think about what motivates people."

"What have you written?"

She described the plot of her unfinished novel, about an Indian shipping magnate's daughter who tries to sail around the world but capsizes in Madagascar. As she interacts with the locals, she is haunted by dreams of a friend who committed suicide, but finds new purpose after her two pet fish Twisty and Whippoorwill begin advising her on key decisions. Lakhi explained that the magnate was based on her first boyfriend's father and the description of Madagascar was based on her own visits to relatives who lived there. The protagonist was inspired by the first woman to sail around the world solo, and the fish on her real-life pets, one of which swam predictably while the other swam whimsically.

"And what about the friend who commits suicide?" Ravi asked.

Her eyes angled away for a moment.

"My roommate at Yale. Hung herself."

"That's heavy," Ravi said.

Now she seemed to be in a trance, her eyes locked into a mental movie.

"I still dream about her...She's usually a statue watching me, like when I'm floating in a hot air balloon over Mars with prince charming, or cutting through rice fields with a toothbrush in Vietnam on a charity mission, or cooking giant pakodas the size of a house with my mom."

She snapped out of her reverie and looked back at Ravi.

"It's strange, you know stuff like this happens, and you know you should care, but it's only when it happens to you do you think about seriously."

"How do you take it seriously other than thinking about it more?"

"I still send her family cards on her birthday to let them know her life had meaning. I go on fundraising walks every year for awareness programs. Small things, but things I wouldn't have done otherwise."

"Makes sense. And I guess you're writing about it."

"Not so much recently. I've been stalled. It's funny, after I read your book, a part of me thought I should do a female response to your book, like a rap artist, but another part of me thought, I should make art proactively instead of as a reaction to someone else,'" Lakhi said.

"All art is a reaction to something else. It's just a question of whether the thing you're reacting is important enough to react to. Obviously my book is not, though I was pretty proud of it."

"Why don't you think it's important enough?"

"The sales numbers made that clear. And the only review ripped on it. You'd think you get used to bad reviews, but you never do, because most of the time the journalist is just trying to make a name for himself."

"I wouldn't think about it. You did something awesome. I definitely identified with a lot of what you wrote. And now I know why you call me 'Lakhi'."

"Why's that?"

"Because you don't think 'Alaknanda' is cool enough."

She began adjusting her nose-ring.

"It's cool, I like it. I just like nicknames. Where did you grow up again?"

"New Jersey. Edison. The American capital of Indians."

"Oh, so you're hard core Indian inside."

"Oh, yeah. Indian Sunday school, movies on Friday, cultural programs on Saturday. Dance lessons every weekend."

She described slapping her feet with the jingle-jangle of ankle bells while performing bharatnatyam for the Indian community in a high school auditorium.

"We proved that white flight has nothing to do with being Democrat or Republican," she continued.

"What, all the white families moved out?"

"Or sent their kids to different schools."

Ravi had grown up with a simplistic understanding that racism was bad and chafed at perceived slights over his race. At university, this obvious conclusion about race had fragmented into discussions about the legacy of racism, policy approaches to racism, representation of race in the media, reverse-racism, the effect of academic analysis of racism on policy. Every topic became sliced so thin that it seemed the whole point of analysis was to justify someone's career as an academic. Ravi circled back to the simplistic view that racism was bad, but that the simplest way to overcome his role as an outsider in a white world was some unique combination of charm, assimilation and self-righteousness. Maybe it wasn't so simple. Maybe adaptation wasn't enough.

"That doesn't mean we didn't try to be American. I was even a cheerleader for a couple of years," Lakhi continued.

"That explains…"

He paused.

"Explains what?"

"No…"

"Come on, say it."

"Why you look good in a bikini."

She smiled.

"You don't have to hold back on compliments."

"I didn't want to get accused of objectifying you. You're what, like 25?" he asked.

"26. Why?"

"Just curious."

"And you?"

"I'm a bit older than you."

"How much older are you? You don't look that much older."

"Eight years."
"That's not a big deal."

"For Indians it is."

"Maybe my friends' parents. Mine are actually pretty chill."

"You know, I've never dated an Indian girl."

He smushed a French fry into the ketchup as she shifted in the booth, putting her legs up on the cushioned seat and placing her arm on the backrest. Her boots dripped onto the vinyl next to him.

"So, are you afraid?" she asked.

"No. I mean, maybe subconsciously I associate all Indian women with my Mum."

"That's pretty Freudian. What don't you like about your Mum?"

"It's not that I don't like her. I love my Mum. But I couldn't live with my Mum. Too many judgments, expectations and conspiracy theories."

"So you assume all Indian girls are that way?"

"Maybe sub-consciously I decided it's not worth the risk."

"Am I judgmental and full of expectations and conspiracy theories?"

He returned her stare to see what type of answer she was expecting.

"Not that I can tell. What do you think about the moon-landing?"

"Hah."

She took a French fry and eyed it before taking a bite.

"Do you like to dance?" she asked.

"I like to watch people dance."

"You're in a band! How can you not like dancing?"

"If I've had a few, I like it. I'm just not good at it."

"Have you heard of Basement Bhangra?" she asked. "They have it tonight at SOBs."

"Haven't heard of it. Is that an invitation?" Ravi asked.

"Yeah. Unless you consider it too controlling."

He left his credit card on the bill and excused himself to the bathroom. After a hypnotically satisfying gusher, he washed his hands and exited the bathroom. He recovered his card, and they left to summon a taxi outside. He remembered writing a song the prior week with a killer chorus—*there's nothing I can't do, there's nothing I can't say, there's nothing I can lose, there's nothing in my way*—set over an electro beat with a clipped distorted guitar, which lifted his mood. He still needed to complete the phrasing of the verses, but he had the beginning part—*You give me strength, strength when I'm feeling down, you give me strength, the strength that I need to go on*—inspired by a vision of watching his family from a window.

Every taxi that passed had an illuminated sign indicating it was taken, so they descended into the subway station across the street to take the L train to the 1 train, which would drop them within a block of SOBs. He swiped his MetroCard for both of them. On the platform, she warned him away from standing too close to the yellow line. A bearded black man was playing a blues guitar riff Ravi had seen him play in other stations on a beat-up Fender. Ravi tossed a ten dollar bill into his case, one dollar for every time he had meant to tip him. He saw Lakhi wrinkling her eyebrows as she appeared to be contemplating him.

"Ravi Anjani. You're not who you pretend to be."

"You thought I was intelligent and charming, and you're discovering what a profligate I am?"

"See? I wouldn't have thought you even knew the word 'profligate'."

"Just because I know how to be one doesn't mean I know what it means."

They boarded the train and sat next to each other. He viewed their upside-down reflection in the subway window, his lips and nose resting on the Namaste clasp of his hands, a symmetry of composition lacking only a centered hair part, and her face peering up as if seeing a deity, in this case Dr. Zizmor in his ad for skin treatment. They looked like they could be a couple. The train braked into Sixth Avenue, and he swayed into her, apologizing but also tempted to keep his face close to hers. They disembarked and went up the steps with a tuna-packed crowd of others. The tunnel to the 1 train was long enough to host a seated Chinese man playing the zheng, a woman selling used shoes and DVDs and a man playing the saxophone, all in front of billboards advertising the latest musicals and safe sex.

"Have you ever busked in the subway?" she asked.

"Nah. Maybe I should get Ian to do it with me."

"I'd come and watch."

They disembarked at Houston, just a few blocks from the club. Ravi noticed the inked visage of Andre the Giant on the base of a street lamp. He had seen the same stamp on scaffolding, posters and other empty canvases around the city but had never understood what it meant. He asked Lakhi about it, but she didn't know, either.

After clearing the bouncer, they checked-in their coats in the basement. She was wearing an outfit that was edgy but casual—jeans with plastic buttons lining the outside of one leg and a blue wrap blouse. The dancing wouldn't start for another hour, after nine, and the crowds wouldn't arrive for two. They ordered drinks and sat at the bar to the backdrop of Indian lounge music, a mélange of sitar melodies, female vocal improvisations and movie dialogue samples set over stuttering drum machines and electro-bass.

"So what's next? Do you want to stay in television?" Ravi asked.

"Not really. I learned a lot, but honestly, you were the most sincere person at the show."

"Really? I thought there were some good people. Renee. John, meaning Wang. Aasif."

"Yeah, they're fine. I mean, more like, people at my level don't want to be friends because they're too busy trying to curry favor with the people above them. And the people above my level all act like they're doing you a favor in talking to you. It's a bunch of hierarchal bullshit, pardon my language."

"That's entertainment."

"I know, but what I said about my college roommate, until you experience it yourself, you don't really believe it. Anyway, I'm done with entertainment for a while. I've applied to be a paralegal. A lot of my friends are doing it. How about you? What's next?"

"My agent is talking to MTV about a sitcom based on my *Guide*."

"Really? When's that happening?"

"Don't know, I just found out about it. If your paralegal thing doesn't work out and my show does, you can come work on it. And if my show doesn't work out and your paralegal thing does, you need to convince them to hire me," he said.

"Deal," she said, holding out her hand for a shake. "Though not if it's just holding a camera and getting coffee. I'd want to write for the show."

"Fair enough."

He shook her hand and held on to it for an extra moment. The club had started filling out. The opening thump of bhangra attracted a handful of people to start dancing, and she stood up, pulling him out to the floor. He looked down at her as they circled around each other.

"See? You know how to dance," Lakhi said.

He had promised himself he wouldn't pursue her. Was it the two Scotches that were leading him back down a path of irresponsibility? Or had he felt a dormant identity within him awaken, something unpretentious and vaguely Indian, that would actually him reform his life? What if she was in the process of changing her life just like he was, and by helping him out figure out his identity, things would get better for her?

Ravi hadn't danced to bhangra in ages, but it felt comfortable and evocative. They both twisted their hands like the upright arm was changing a light bulb and the hanging arm was flushing a toilet, but she graced them with subtle flourishes with her shoulders and hips, while flirtatiously crinkling her eyes. Ravi felt the tractor beam of sex, and occasionally placed his hand on her hip, which she allowed for just a moment before swirling away. A spectrum of scents engulfed them on the dance floor, from heavy musk cologne to a pungent fenugreek to a subtle rose perfume.

After three songs, they cooled down with a drink at the bar before bumping back through the crowd to jerk their shoulders up and down in unison with others and point to the ceiling with both hands. The beat could work with some of the new songs Ravi was working on, which could be both innovative and marketable.

A bump from behind spun Ravi into a couple in front of him, who told him to watch it. He apologized and turned around to pass on the message, but the amoeba-like motion of bodies made it impossible to identify who had pushed him. Lakhi asked what happened before they resumed bouncing to the beat. A moment later a stronger thrust from behind sent Ravi to the floor. He looked up at a tall Indian boy with thin black glasses flanked by another Indian and a white guy.

"Ajit!" Lakhi screamed. "Don't be an asshole!"

"This is your boyfriend?" Ravi asked as he dusted off his pants.

"*Was* her boyfriend," Ajit said, his voice shaking.

The crowd stopped to watch. Ravi felt a rush of blood to his brain and anger to his fists, just like when he had popped that journalist in the face. He saw Ajit's face almost in slow motion, and debated in micro-seconds whether to give a head butt or knee his groin before shoving him into his friends. But an unexpected glimpse of the future arrived in his brain like Indiana Jones on a swinging rope, showing him Lakhi's mortified face and a judge sentencing him to actual prison time. So instead he grabbed Ajit's collar and said, "We're here to dance. If you'd like to meet up later, make an appointment," with enough of a saliva-misted puff of air to make clear he would back it up. He turned back around to face Lakhi, who seemed upset.

"Do you still want to dance?" he asked.

"Not really. Do you mind if we leave?"

Ravi cleared the wet locks of hair from his forehead with the back of his left wrist and in a continuous motion whipped his hand to snap the index finger against the middle finger.

"As you wish," he said.

He grabbed her hand and pulled her through the crowd into the crisp freeze outside.

"*Princess Bride?*" she asked.

"I thought you didn't watch popular movies."

"That one is brilliant."

He led them to the stairs down to the 1 train, where at least it would be warm. She leaned into his body and looked up at him.

"I'm sorry about what just happened. We only dated a few months. I thought I would give a 'traditional' Indian a try, but he was a condescending prick. He's been trying to get back together. I didn't know he would be there."

"It's fine."

Ajit was actually a decent-looking chap, which further validated Ravi's interest in Lakhi.

Over twenty minutes, three express trains rattled through the middle track, teasing them as they waited for the local train. Eventually one rumbled in, and they took it to Christopher Street, walking to his apartment from there. He felt like he had passed an emotional pop quiz. He wouldn't mind finishing the evening on his sofa exploring other sides to her Indian identity as a reward for figuring out a few new sides of his own, even if it meant satisfying karma a different way to get twenty nine thousand dollars.

Excerpt from
Ravi's Guide to Being a Cool Indian

Adventure

Indians are always analyzing things. What stocks should I buy? What colleges are best? Who has the nicest house? Did I get fired because I'm incompetent or because I'm Indian? Can reading this Guide make me cooler?

It explains a large degree of our success, the ability to identify a problem and correct it. But an adventure by definition requires you to suspend your analysis and go forward in the absence of perfect information or guarantees you'll get what you want. Principle #1: An adventure requires you to act on an impulse before thinking about it.

Buzzthief was performing at a concert in Delhi as part of a larger bill that included AR Rahman and some other well-known Indian musicians. Half-way through our set, the audience wasn't paying attention to us and had even started throwing samosas at Ian. I grabbed the mike from Ian and recited a cliché Bollywood line—"Bakwas bandh karo. Me teri jaan, teri pariwar, teri sare khandan ke tukde…tukde kaardunga." Stop the nonsense, or I'll tear up your life, your family, everything you own, piece by piece.

Suddenly, everyone became silent and stared at me. I grabbed an acoustic guitar from the side stage and returned to the mike. I sang the dramatic opening line to "Me Hoon Don" from the Amitabh movie Don*. The crowd kept watching me, so I continued despite the fact that I couldn't remember half the lyrics, couldn't properly pronounce the other half and couldn't sing on key if my life depended on it. At the chorus, the whole audience started singing along and drowning me out. They demanded I sing another one, so I guessed the chords to "Yeh Dosti" from the movie* Sholay *and bumbled my way through. When I finished, we returned to playing our set, though now the audience started dancing along. I recited Bollywood dialogue in between songs to entertain them.*

If I can sing in front of thousands of people in a language I don't really know, there's no excuse for you for not asking out every man or woman you find attractive. Shaving your head to see how it feels. Jumping a fence just to see what's on the other side. Taking your car up to 90. Principle #2: The only time you feel truly alive is when there's a chance your life might not be the same afterwards.

Chapter 13
Jag in a Jaguar
Manhattan, New York

Vineeta

Despite sub-freezing temperatures, Vineeta was sweating in Ian's fur aviator hat and a parka. The two of them paced the sidewalk with entwined arms in front of Ravi's twelve-story building. She felt secure in this hunched cocoon of Ian's muscular frame.

Ravi's building was in the heart of the Meat-Packing District, though it now mainly housed clubs, fashion boutiques, cafes and apartments. She fell for the possibility it was Ravi every time the doors slid open, duped by a woman with a walker, a man with a baby stroller, a couple arguing about some annoying thing the wife always allegedly did and a woman on a cell phone.

She had invited Ravi to join them to go Christmas shopping at the Woodbury Commons outlet. It would allow Ian to tell Ravi he was ready to re-form the band. She had tried hard not to influence Ian's decision. He had independently concluded that the slickly produced songs he had been asked to sing for his solo album were inane–*You make me feel like a raindrop in a storm, first I'm falling, then I'm calling for you to keep me warm.* When he had complained, the studio musicians invited him to demonstrate some creative vocal genius. He searched for melodies by grunting "yeah" until he ran out of ways to pronounce it and scoured his mental dictionary for a meaningful word, unearthing such SAT gems as feckless, duende, perambulatory, none of which conveyed anything emotionally real.

This was Ravi's genius, some primal connection to his emotional self which frothed over in his every gesture, like a B-grade rock version of Mozart.

Ravi finally made his appearance in a leather jacket, giving each of them a hug.

"Thanks for showing," Vineeta said.

"No problem," Ravi said, without an acknowledgement of her sarcasm. "So, I finally know why I didn't see the two of you much for the past few months."

She fidgeted with her back pocket.

"Well, we didn't want to say anything in case it didn't work out. Are you okay with it?"

"Didn't see it coming, but I guess you could be compatible. At least you don't have to hide it."

"You didn't answer my question," she said.

"You're both adults. My opinion doesn't matter."

"It kind of does," Ian said, his breath condensing into rising wisps.

Ravi took out his cigarette lighter and started flicking it open and close before putting it back.

"Look, you're my best friend, you're my sister, so in a lot of ways, it will be amazing. You're both good people, so I can see it working out. It's a bit weird, too, but we'll figure it out. At least you don't have to hide it anymore."

"And we appreciate what you did on that front," Ian said.

It was true. Vineeta didn't have to hide Ian. Unfortunately, now she had to find a way to hide his mom. She was that special American blend of diligent, vulgar Christian who sometimes voted Democratic, sometimes voted Republican and sometimes preferred watching the Price is Right to voting. Apparently the main advice she had given Ian when the band went on tour was to not go through the drive-through too many times, or he'd end up with a side order of herpes.

Ian beeped open the blue Jaguar he had illegally parked on the street. It had a particular shade of cobalt blue which gave Vineeta an almost erotic thrill, perhaps some nostalgic connection to the dome head of R2-D2 or to nights drinking Skyy Vodka with cranberry juice.

"Whoa. Are your royalties more than mine?" Ravi asked.

"No, it's Jessica's, I need to return it. She has some of my computer files on her computer, and she's refusing to send them to me. So I'm refusing to give her car back," Ian said.

If it hadn't been Ian's prior year tax return on her computer, Vineeta would have told him it wasn't worth fighting over.

"That seems like a particularly stupid deal for her, but it's good to see you standing up for yourself. How about I take it for a spin?" Ravi asked.

"Well, I don't know…the insurance and all that," Ian countered.

"If it covers you, it should cover me."

"I don't know, man."

"Okay, just let me sit in it for a minute."

Ravi walked around to open the door to the driver's seat when a large man charged towards them from down the block shouting, "You, stop! Stop!"

Vineeta's first instinct was to run, but Ravi jumped into the car while shouting, "Oh, shit! Let's go!", and slamming the door.

She and Ian quickly obeyed.

"What's going on?" Ian asked while pulling the seatbelt before closing his door.

"Just close the door!"

"Well can't you…"

"GIVE ME THE KEYS!"

Ian handed over the keys as Ravi lurched the car forward. The large man looked like a threatening version of Curly from *The Three Stooges*. He banged his fist on side and gave chase as Ravi pulled forward on Washington. She fumbled with her belt buckle as Ravi took a left on Gansevoort past the entrance of the Hi-Line Park, right on 10th Avenue, and finally onto the West Side Highway heading North.

"I think we lost him," Ian said.

"What was that about?" Vineeta asked, her heart suddenly beating fast.

Ravi licked his teeth nervously.

"Not sure. I just saw the man charging at us, I thought we should get going."

Vineeta suddenly remembered their conversation in London about money and Ravi's strange behavior thereafter.

"It has something to do with why you need money, isn't it?" Vineeta asked.

"It's possible he's a creditor coming to inquire on the status of payment."

"You seriously owe money to a bookie?" Ian asked.

"I owe money to lots of people. I don't discriminate," Ravi said.

"Why didn't you just ask Dad for money?" Vineeta asked.

"That was the plan, but it would have added too much stress after your revelation."

"Why didn't you tell me first?" Vineeta asked.

"It's not my proudest accomplishment."

Ravi turned on the radio.

"Do you mind finding something soothing?" Ravi asked.

"No, turn that off," Vineeta instructed Ian. "I'll give you the money."

"No, I'm close to getting a deal that could resolve the issue," Ravi said.

"When?"

He hesitated.

"This week."

"So, then explain that to him."

"I think we're past the point of explanations. As soon as I get paid, I'll pay him. You know, I never noticed all the interesting things along the highway. Is that a museum?" Ravi asked, pointing to an Alps-inspired frosted cascade of glass.

She ignored his question. Ravi wove in and out of three lanes of traffic as they passed the Chelsea Pier driving range, the Hustler strip club and a bowling alley. He looked in the rear view mirror and remarked, "Slight problem."

She and Ian turned to see the thug from earlier on a motorcycle.

"Just pull over. I'll tell him that I'll give the money," she said.

Ravi sped up into the fourth lane as the highway widened.

"You're not getting involved in this," he said.

"I won't be getting involved. I'll just pay off your loan."

"You have a spare twenty-nine thousand dollars?"

"Whoa," Ian said.

"You lost that much money? Forget it. Yes. I'll get the money, I have a 401k," Vineeta said.

She could see Ravi considering the offer, tapping a finger on the steering wheel. He pursed his lips and began taking deep, steady breaths. He suddenly swerved from the far left across all four lanes to a symphony of honks to reach the 57th street exit.

"Oh, God! What are you doing?"

"We shoot through midtown, cut up 6th Avenue and go into the park," Ravi said.

"Please don't drive like a maniac. It's not open on weekends," Vineeta said.

"It is for us."

"Just pull over!" she shouted.

"I'll drive more carefully. Sorry about that," Ravi said.

He sped down 57th past awnings and construction sites for five hundred luxury apartments and waited at 9th Avenue. At least the stoplights would control Ravi's worst impulses. Vineeta turned around to see the motorcycle overtaking the cars behind them by driving in the wrong lane at the same time Ravi observed it in his rear-view mirror with a defecatory curse. Ravi accelerated through the red light and a small gap between a swarm of speeding cars, followed by scurrying pedestrians who cursed them with wild gesticulations.

"Let me out of the car!" Vineeta shouted.

"Look, I'll get us out of this."

Vineeta knocked her knees with anxiety, eyeing the side mirror at every light for evidence of a crazy man chasing them. Ravi made a triumphant turn onto Sixth Avenue, chockful of buses, taxis, trucks, SUVs and vans.

"Can you knock some sense into him?" Vineeta pleaded with Ian.

"This is stupid, man, just pull over," Ian said.

When the light changed, Ravi illegally zoomed forward past 59th into Central Park Drive, pausing for a group of tourists before trailing a horse carriage driver to the main loop heading north. Bicyclists and runners shouted a variety of epithets, though he intently watched the rear view mirror.

"We have company."

Vineeta turned around hoping for the police. No luck.

"Why don't you talk to him? He can't do anything to you here with all these people," she suggested.

"Why not? It's New York."

"How did he find you?"

"He knows where I live, but I usually leave the building from the back. Unfortunately he somehow manages to install a tracker on my phones."

They followed the southern end of the park under the branches of beech trees behind bicyclists before heading back north on the east side of the loop slowly driving alongside the horse carriages that entered at Fifth Avenue. More choice insults inspired Ravi to roll down his window.

"Pregnant lady in the back!" he shouted.

Pedestrians moved to the side while the carriage drivers who spotted the lie continued haranguing them. Ravi sped past 72nd street as the crowds dwindled. The man chasing them sped up as they whizzed through the park at sixty miles an hour. Ravi swerved to avoid a family with a stroller crossing the street.

"If not for the fact that there's a crazy man chasing us, this is kind of exciting, you have to admit," Ravi said. "What else is going on with you?"

His hands were gripping the steering wheel tightly and his face had tensed up considerably. She could tell he was trying his hardest to pretend this wasn't a big deal.

"Seriously? You want to chit-chat while we're being chased by your bookie?" Ian asked.

"Why not? It will act as stress relief."

Vineeta tried to figure out what Ian was thinking as he looked back at her.

"Okay, then. I'm ready to get the band back together," Ian said.

"You're really going to raise that now?" Vineeta asked.

They glided on a straight patch of road.

"Really? What happened with the solo album?" Ravi asked.

"The first session was terrible. I knew it and the label knew it. So they suggested I take a break to polish up my voice, but a few weeks later I heard the same songs I had been recording on the radio performed by another singer. I'm cool with us touring and making an album together, instead."

Vineeta turned to observe the thug screech to a halt before an irate bicyclist.

"You know, when you said you were ready to move on, I told my agent she needed to find me something else. I just found out last weekend that MTV wants to develop a sitcom based on my *Guide*. I'm supposed to meet the writers next week. If I get the gig, I won't have much time to do anything else. And I obviously need the money," Ravi said, navigating the downhill curves near the city pool with aplomb.

"Oh," Ian said.

"You know, it's probably better to have a longer discussion about it under less stressful circumstances," Vineeta said.

"Good idea," Ravi said.

She could see Ian felt hurt. Maybe she should change the topic. She was sure Ravi would find a way to make time for the band when he had time to focus on it.

"What about the…" Ian began.

"If we're all going to die, I'd like to know one thing," Vineeta said.

"Shoot," Ravi said.

It sounded good when she said it, but was there one thing she really needed to know if they were going to die? There was. But would she want to ask the question with the greater likelihood being that they would live?

"Well?"

"Did you know about Dad's affairs?" she asked.

"Do you specifically know something happened, or you're just speculating?" he asked, looking back at her.

She hesitated, but now she had opened Pandora's box. She laid out what she knew about the professor their father had kissed.

"Now that you mention it, I know which professor you're talking about. I guess I probably noticed that she happened to be around his office once in a while. I didn't know anything specific, but I'm not surprised. Dad's surprisingly smooth around women. He gets a little more enthused and wittier. So it sounds like he got tempted, and stuff happened."

"Why doesn't that bother you?"

He shrugged his shoulders. When they reached 110th Street, he exited the park and continued north on Adam Clayton Powell Boulevard past a series of six-story red and white block apartments.

"It's not my issue to be bothered by. We're not responsible for Mum and Dad's relationship, just like they're not responsible for you and Ian. It's amazing that any two people can manage to stick together for so long."

"It meant our family was a lie. It meant that everything they were teaching us was a lie."

"Maybe your perception of them as one morally authoritative unit was the lie."

She had gone this far, she might as well go the distance.

"Then what about Shushruth?"

"What about him?"

"Did you ever think it was strange he looks just like you?"

"So what, you're saying Dad and…that's crazy."

"I heard Dad talking to Pankaj's mom in London," Vineeta continued.

"And they said that?"

"Not directly, but it was obvious that was what they were talking about. Think about it—we were living in London. You were around five years old. It was probably easier for Pankaj's mom to give Shushruth to her older sister knowing he wasn't her husband's child. It would explain why Pankaj's family moved farther away."

Ravi turned left onto 115th and right onto Frederick Douglass Boulevard. She didn't see any signs of the crazy man behind them. Ravi slowly ran a hand through his hair and back down his neck before lightly slapping his cheeks.

"I think we lost our friend. Look, what you're saying is crazy. I can see it. It could be. I mean, I guess we're lucky it didn't blow the whole family up way back when. But now that we're here, it's kind of cool in a way. Shushruth's a great guy. We grew up just like we were brothers. Maybe that's why you're always telling me to embrace suffering. It all works out in some way."

"You spin everything into something positive. Dad cheating on Mum was not a good thing," Vineeta said.

"I'm not saying it was. I'm just saying it's not for us to judge. Mum and Dad are people who make choices just like us. Mum could have left him, but she didn't. And if she's made peace with it, then we can, too. Now they've given you the chance to make whatever choices you want to."

"You mean they've given you the chance to do whatever you want," Vineeta said.

"You have everything I have."

"You're a boy. You're Mum's favorite, so she forgives everything you do."

"And when you didn't go to med school, they forgave you. And you're dating…well, Ian… and they've made peace with it. You just tested different lines than me. Look, our parents aren't perfect, but they did a pretty good job. In the end, we own who we are and the choices we make."

At 125th Street he pulled over.

"What are you doing?" she asked.

"I've endangered enough of your day. I'll get out, you guys drive to the mall and I'll link back up with you later."

Vineeta locked eyes with Ian.

"You should…" he began.

"Join us," she finished.

He unbuckled, stepped out and peered back into the car.

"I appreciate the sentiment, but wherever I go, trouble seems to follow. I'm sorry for this little excursion. Sorry about the band, the previous requests for money, the *Guide* and anything else I've messed up. Have a nice day at the mall. I think Pankaj lives around here. Maybe I'll drop in to see how he's doing."

With that, he began jogging down the block heading east.

Ian entered the driver's side of the car, so Vineeta moved into the passenger seat. He asked her if she was okay. She reclined the seat as far as it would go and closed her eyes, trying to calm her heart down. Ravi was teaching her to own her choices, but had also saved her from disaster the week before. Now that he was owning his choices, what could she do to save him?

Excerpt from
Ravi's Guide to Being a Cool Indian

Sports

Google *"greatest Indian athletes of all time"* and what do you get? *Vishwanathan Anand, a chess player, a list of men who play cricket, a game that is somehow lazier, longer and more boring than baseball, and a list of the people who have won India its nine Olympic gold medals. Not in one year, mind you, but ever. The closest the average Indian ever comes to athletic greatness is by wearing a Roger Federer cap and rooting for a Swiss man playing tennis, presumably because a lot of Bollywood movies are filmed in Switzerland and you can't get seriously injured playing tennis. Is it the diet? The poverty? The inability to bribe someone to do the work?*

Principle #1: Choose a sport where you don't actually need to be athletic.

Growing up in England, we understood this principle, gathering at the brick schoolhouse to play cricket, chalking wickets on the wall.

"Karan and me will be captains," I announced.

Karan had green eyes, fair skin and a swagger, which made the adults monitor him as a prospective mate for their daughters. The parents didn't realize that boys like Karan flash a nice smile before ducking into the alley for a smoke and joke about how retarded they are.

I took Shushruth as my final selection and Karan ended up with Pankaj, who had negotiated the right to bat first for his team in exchange for letting us use his bat. The game stuttered through good and bad plays, groans and exhortations.

"Just try to punch the ball on the ground to the left," I advised Shushruth for his turn at bat.

He swung hard and lined the ball up the street, bounding back and forth for three runs before they retrieved the ball.

"That was good, though risky," I said in my defense.

Shushruth scored a respectable nine. The game bumbled through two complete innings until I came up to bat a third time down by eight with the end of the morning service approaching.

Normally I would have said "Graham Gooch comes to bat" because I rooted for the English cricket team like the rest of my chums while Dad rooted for India, but India had just won the World Cup. In the tournament, Kapil Dev scored a world record 126 runs in a single at bat against Zimbabwe, and helped India beat England with one of the greatest catches of all time, sprinting twenty yards and cupping the ball with both hands with his back to the batter. I knew how to move with the wind.

"Kapil Dev comes up to bat and predicts a sixer."

I pointed my bat far over everyone's' heads, and the fielders backed up even further into the street. Then I punched the ball to Karan's left and scored a quick three runs as the fielders scurried in to recover from my deception. The next bowl, I drilled the ball over their heads for another four runs. Six more runs later, I popped out and declared the inning over so that Karan's team could bat without an argument that the game was a draw.

"Hurry up! Hurry up!"

Karan ordered his team to run back while picking up the bat and staring at me with determination.

"You're not up. Pankaj is supposed to bat," I pointed out.

Karan started to argue, but knew I was right and placed the bat in Pankaj's trembling hands. Everyone knew the game was effectively ours. Pankaj was the least athletic child in England. Pankaj protruded his rear end and held the bat slanted across the wickets instead of upright, I think because his wrists were too weak to hold the bat properly. I felt some pity and bowled a spinner without much pace so he could at least get his bat on the ball. He swung wildly, almost falling down with the force of his swing, and smacked the ball over our heads towards someone's backyard.

"Go, go!" I shouted at our fielders.

Pankaj chugged back and forth between the wickets three times before the strenuous wheezing began, the bat actually helping his running equilibrium. As he circled into his fifth round, I feared the humiliation of being beaten by a Pankaj shot while I was bowling. One of our fielders finally threw the ball towards me. It rolled to my feet, and I picked it up and fired it at the chalked wickets while Pankaj futilely ran towards the other set for the prospective tying run.

"Yeah!!!" our team shouted, giving each other high fives.

Karan ran up to Pankaj. I postponed the celebration to listen.

"Why'd you keep going? I told you to stop!"

"You can't even run, fatso," one of the other boys said.

The rest of the team crowded in a semi-circle around Pankaj.

"Yeah, anyone else would have scored ten runs on that. He must eat all the prasad every week," another shrinky-dink added, describing the sweetened wheat and raisin dessert served at every religious gathering.

In what should have been Pankaj's finest moment in cricket, his flushed face began twitching and priming his tear ducts.

"He hit the ball farther than you did," I shouted over.

"So, if he can't even score any runs, what difference does it make?" the shrinky-dink retorted.

He was younger than Pankaj and called himself Bobby. His real name was Piyush, which admittedly needed revision, though changing it to Bobby just previewed a severe self-loathing and insecurity which ultimately caused him to convert to Catholicism, marry an Irish girl and move to Birmingham to work as a barrister. I walked over and bumped my stomach into Bobby's chest.

"It means he's better than you at cricket, right?"

"No," he whispered with ruddied cheeks.

"What was that, P.U.?" I asked, holding my nose.

"Nothing."

"Okay, then shut up."

I turned around and put my arm around Pankaj's shoulders.

"Let's go. Who's got the ball?"

One of my teammates retrieved the ball from near the curb and tossed it back to me. Shushruth sidled up next to me as we walked back into the hall.

Principle #2: Life is a sport with winners and losers, so make sure you join the right team to lift you up when you need it.

Chapter 14
Catharsis
Manhattan, New York

Pankaj

Pankaj assumed it was a food delivery man ringing the wrong apartment, but the intercom buzz was at least some distraction from the inert weekend routine of browsing the internet at home and going out to browse the internet at Starbucks. He approached his entry door only to find Ravi in the video screen waiting outside, nervously looking back and forth behind him.

"Hey. Wasn't expecting you," Pankaj said.

"Okay. Are you going to let me in? It's kind of cold."

"Okay."

Pankaj had ignored his Mum's directive to contact Ravi, as well as Ravi's voicemail and text contacting him. He had taken control of the relationship. In a few months, give or take a few years, he would develop a group of friends without Ravi's help. At least he was in New York, where he could network and explore, finally free from years of living at home in Ealing. Perhaps the Indian girls who had grown up in America would be impressed by his European upbringing or position, though none of them had made eye contact with him at the recent gathering of the Network of Indian Professionals he had attended.

As long as it was Ravi groveling to him, he could live with a reunion. He tried to plan out his first few sentences.

"Yeah, the move went fine," then be silent, or, "I'm good. You?", or "Did you need something?"

He quickly threw stray clothes and papers in a closet and straightened the furniture. He logged off his work website to make it look like he hadn't been working. He loved analyzing data and scouring news stories for a little edge that would give him a sense of how the market would open and trade on Monday, but also recognized the addictive quality of this endeavor in an age of infinite information. It left him with only one thing to talk about when he met other people.

He scanned his living room. He would sit on his sofa and let Ravi sit in the chair, though the sun was directly shining on the sofa. He pulled the shade down a bit. A knock on the door. Pankaj intentionally paused before opening the door, where Ravi seemed to be jogging in place. Ravi stepped forward and raised his hand for a high five or shoulder hug, but Pankaj stood still.

"Yo," Ravi offered.

"Yo."

"Yo-Yo Ma," Ravi said. "Now you're supposed to say, 'Yo mama.'"

"I'm not saying 'Yo'…it."

Ravi stepped in, pulled the door behind him and looked through the floor-to-ceiling windows to a view of the apartments across the street.

"Nice place you've got. I like it. Your neighbors can watch you dance in your underwear. Gives you the audience you've never had. How long you been here, like two months?"

"Since the beginning of October."

"Which is two months. Just in time for it to be cold and dark and depressing."

"I'm used to it from London."

"True. I had dropped you a line, then my parents were asking if I ever heard back, so I figured I'd see how you're doing in person."

"Doing fine. I got your message."

Ravi walked in and plopped himself into the sofa.

"I'd prefer if you don't wear your shoes in the apartment," Pankaj said.

"Yeah, okay. So why'd you choose Harlem?"

Ravi unlaced his shoes, theatrically lined them up and looked at Pankaj for approval.

"The broker recommended it. Said it was hot and twenty percent cheaper than the other good neighborhoods."

"That's true, in a way. It's 20% cheaper, but 50% less gentrified. You'll need to take a thirty minute train to see people dressed like you. Someone like you belongs on the Upper East Side, maybe the Upper West Side. Me, I like the Village, though I've thought about shifting to Brooklyn. Doesn't your firm give you, what is a called, an expat package, corporate housing, all that?"

"The corporate housing was full up, so I got an allowance."

"Then what do you care how much it cost?"

"I got to pocket the difference."

"Nice. So what made you want to move here? It's not like you know anyone here, except me, and I'm clearly not on your guest list."

Pankaj noticed some footsteps outside and Ravi glancing at his front door.

"It wasn't a social move. Some of us have careers to worry about."

"What can you do here that you can't do in London?"

Why was Ravi suddenly talking softer? Pankaj reflexively lowered his voice, too.

"I'll be trading Latin American currencies."

"Is that better than trading currencies in London?"

"It's not better. It gives me a chance to learn another market, which will help me down the road. You need experience managing risk to get promoted. And I'll get to know more senior people."

At least that was how Pankaj's boss at National United pitched the transfer to him after he had been passed over for Managing Director. Questions from a couple of colleagues about how he felt about moving to New York so that his boss's friend could take over Pankaj's position in London suggested additional considerations.

There was a knock on the door.

"Please don't answer that," Ravi whispered.

"Why not?"

Ravi silently shushed Pankaj with a finger.

The knocks turned into a stronger banging as Pankaj looked at Ravi for a facial explanation. The banging gave way to muffled shouting in some Eastern European accent.

"Open up! If you're there, we talk."

Ravi repeated his shushing. More banging, more shouting.

After two minutes, the footsteps retreated. Ravi crawled lightly to where Pankaj was sitting and motioned for him to crawl into Pankaj's bedroom. Pankaj followed on his hands and knees, feeling ridiculous. He tried to remember whether there was anything sensitive lying about in his room—dirty underwear, dirty magazine, or just plain old dirt—but he didn't think so. He lightly closed the door behind him, leaning up against his bed across from Ravi, who was leaning against the far wall.

"Sorry about that. We should keep it down for a little while," Ravi said.

"What the fuck kind of trouble are you in?" Pankaj asked, unsure of whether to be concerned or angry.

"Let's just say, a little bit bigger than I should have gotten myself in."

"Why do you keep dragging me into your messes? Leave me alone!"

"I didn't mean to. He kind of surprised me at my building."

Ravi explained the car chase with Ian and the serendipity of being close to Pankaj's apartment.

"That's not lucky for me! Should we be calling the police?" Pankaj huffed as quietly as he could, which took away from the satisfaction of his anger.

He imagined his first brush with fame being a newspaper article chronicling his demise—"He was a London banker who had recently relocated to the city. Colleagues described him as 'hard-working, but a loner'". Or what if Ravi was involved with drugs and Pankaj somehow got implicated? He could get fired and lose everything he had worked for.

"And that will accomplish what exactly? They'll protect us today, but we'd get…surprised tomorrow," Ravi said.

"*You'll* get surprised tomorrow, not me."

"Dalinc isn't the assassin type. He's a more break-your-bones type."

"Oh, that's better. How long are we going to be stuck here?" Pankaj asked.

"Hard to say. It could already be fine now, but I think give it about an hour."

"How much do you owe the man?"

"Twenty-nine thousand."

"And you don't have that much?"

"It's kind of a long story. Which involves you, funnily enough. How about we have a drink, and I'll give you the whole bit," Ravi suggested.

Pankaj thought about it. A drink would calm his nerves.

"I usually drink scotch…" Pankaj started.

Pankaj only kept a $200 bottle of Glenlivet 21 at home. Did he want to waste it on Ravi?

"Actually, I have beer..." Pankaj said.

"Nah, scotch is good."

Pankaj had promised himself never to let Ravi make a fool of him again, yet here he was crawling on his knees out of his own room to quietly serve Ravi an expensive glass of scotch. He approached his liquor cabinet and stood up to pour a couple of snifters. The bottle clinked against one of the glasses and he froze. He heard some movement in the hall, and the door-banging resumed.

"Open up!"

The muffled voice from before. Pankaj wasn't sure what to do, so he stood still. After a moment, Ravi emerged from the room.

"I heard you, keep it down," Ravi said forcefully, walking to face the door.

Ravi peered into the peephole, but Pankaj knew that the dim lighting of the hallway made it hard to see anyone clearly. Pankaj's heart was beating fast, though he was also curious what was about to happen.

"Open the door," the man said.

"It's not my door to open. Your credit card didn't work?" Ravi asked.

Pankaj pulled out his phone. Should he call the police? Did he have any weapons in the house if this man managed to get in?

"What was that?" the man asked.

"Last time you used your credit card to break in," Ravi said.

"Don't always work. Fucking latch too far inside."

"How'd you get in the building?"

"Followed delivery man."

Pankaj had thought about getting a bolt lock installed, but had figured the odds of someone breaking into his building and randomly picking his apartment out of the sixty apartments in the building was low. He had also thought about getting the front door sanded and polished into an industrial metal finish like his boss had done in his apartment, but figured no one would be looking at the front door for any extended period of time.

"I know you want your money. And I'm close to getting it, but I need two more weeks," Ravi shouted at the door.

"You said last weekend, I gave you extra week. Already has been three months."

"And if I was asking for three more months, you'd have every right to be skeptical. But I'm only asking for two weeks because I actually have the money lined up."

"Boss getting pissed off. He gonna break my fucking fingers if I don't break yours."

Ravi looked at his hands, which caused Pankaj to reflexively look at his own hands.

"I get it. I promise, this will be the last extension. We can even agree on a time to meet. Two weeks from today at 3 p.m., come to my building. I'll have the money."

There was a brief silence.

"Thirty thousand. You got to pay more."

Ravi creased his eyebrows staring at the doorknob.

"Okay, thirty thousand, two weeks from today."

"If you move away, I come back here. Next time, no talking, just breaking. You got?"

"Yeah, I got."

The footsteps in the hallway seemed to confirm the man's departure.

"What the fuck?" Pankaj exclaimed. "He's going to come back here?"

He picked up the bottle of Scotch and slammed it back down, unsure of what he should be doing.

"No, because I'm going to meet him like I said. I could use that drink now," Ravi said, requisitioning the sofa.

"I don't want to die because you're a fucking a moron," Pankaj said.

He poured out two glasses. He wasn't going to ask Ravi how he preferred his Scotch, instead delivering the glass clean and taking the opposite chair. "How hard is it to save thirty thousand dollars?"

"That's a matter of perspective. If you sit at home wanking, probably not very. I thought I could make it back in Blackpool, but that didn't go as planned."

"Yeah, you think? Anyway, I get it. You bring a criminal to my apartment, but you're Mister Cool, I'm Mister Loser," Pankaj said, shaking his head in disgust.

"I wasn't thinking of you. I was more referring to my lifestyle. Considering the situation, it's pretty clear who the loser is."

At first, Pankaj had started to get angry again, but now realized he should be reveling in the schadenfreude of Ravi trying to rationalize the tatters of Ravi's life. He could even rub it in by digging deeper into the different angles of Ravi's decline.

"Why wouldn't you just ask your dad for a loan?" he asked.

"I kind of did, but I couldn't exactly tell him what it was for, so he wasn't as generous as I was hoping."

"What about your job? I would have thought you got paid quite well. At least that's what all of us assumed," Pankaj said, hoping for another injection of pure, unadulterated schadenfreude.

"The show is being canceled."

"Really?" Pankaj asked, feeling a tingle in his veins. "And the *Guide*?"

"Sold 897 copies."

"I guess that does suck. You'll get something else, you always do," he offered.

Validation. Life was a marathon. Ravi may have won the first few races, but Pankaj was about to win the one that counted.

"MTV said it wants to make a sitcom based on the *Guide*. That's why I'll be able to pay him back in two weeks."

Pankaj had expected to enjoy the schadenfreude for more than ten seconds. Now the tables had turned. He was being tripped at the finish line.

"You're not serious," he said.

"I'm never serious. But according to my agent, they are."

"Well, fuck. So I get to be the butt of your jokes on television."

Pankaj imagined his mum and dad watching an episode of him getting his pants yanked down in gym class. Or trying to ask girls out by asking if they went on dates.

"I didn't think about it that way. I promise—I will leave you out of it. I mean, as much as I can. I can give you a different name or something. They can cast someone who has hair and a hipper taste in clothing," Ravi said.

"You're an asshole."

"I didn't mean it that way. I just mean—look, I'll check with you before you're in any episode. I don't know why you're all that worked up. Nobody watches MTV anyway."

"Somebody's watching or they wouldn't make the show."

"Okay, a few people will watch it, then it goes into the dust bin of history. I could use the money, but after that, who cares?"

"I care."

"Alright, you're right, let me think about it. There's always a solution."

Pankaj eyed Ravi grumpily.

"You're still an asshole. You came here to escape a loan shark. You didn't come to see me," Pankaj said, cashing in on the guilt trip in a tone suggesting that he didn't actually care, though inside he kind of did.

"I did leave you messages that you didn't respond to. Today is fate bringing us together."

"Why would it do that?"

Ravi pursed his eyebrows and seemed to fidget a bit, before rubbing his hands together.

"You seem to think that I was trying to steal your girl in London. But I wasn't hitting on her, I was trying to get her to like you. I mean she did dance with you."

"So what, you're saying that you made her dance with me?" Pankaj said, turning back in an accusatory pose.

Ravi seemed to hesitate for just a moment.

"No, not at all. Just that I had been talking you up. Did you get her number, by the way?"

"Yes, but it didn't work…out."

More accurately, the number didn't work. *You have reached an unassigned number.* He didn't need to give Ravi something else to make fun of.

"You're better off, she wasn't very nice. But this is about you and me. You stopped talking to me to prove a point, and it's proven. I don't want you upset."

Pankaj had been pushing for a sincere apology, but now that he seemed to have the closest thing to an apology that Ravi was capable of, he wasn't sure what to do with it. Did he want to resurrect his friendship with Ravi?

"It's not just about London or Blackpool. You've treated me like a loser since we were kids. And the last couple of years, it's like I'm not even there."

Pankaj was surprised at the depth of his own resentment, and ashamed that he was putting his vulnerability on open display. Maybe he should go back to cheap scotch that just knocked him out quickly.

"Wow, you're going that far back? I didn't think I did. I treated you like everyone else."

"See, there's where we're different. I treated you like my brother," Pankaj said.

"I didn't mean it that way. You are my brother. I just meant that…I like to joke around, right? And… I read a great quote-'If you get pissed off by every rub, how will your mirror get polished?' Some Persian poet. Probably didn't say 'pissed off', but the point's the same. You're too sensitive."

"I'm too sensitive? Really? About being interrogated at a casino because you tried to cheat? Or about being made to look like an idiot in your book? Or dealing with some lunatic who shows up at my apartment to kill you? Or because you danced with the girl you knew I was interested in at the wedding? That's getting pissed on, not pissed off," Pankaj spat out, standing up to pace the edges of his Turkish area rug as his anger returned.

"You're right, I've messed up a lot of things. But if you don't give me a chance to make things right, how can I fix things?"

"Maybe I don't want them fixed."

They looked at each other in silence for a long minute.

"You're an adult, you have that right. But I really view you as my brother. And if you gave me the chance, I think we'll both gain more from this relationship than we'd lose," Ravi said.

Was Pankaj too sensitive? It was true that Ravi and Shushruth would get far less bothered about other people's comments than Pankaj would. It did often feel that the world was out to get him, from his parents to his employer to his friends. His rational brain would certainly conclude from that pattern that maybe he was the problem and that somehow he over-reacted to little slights where others let things go. Maybe that's even why he hadn't been promoted.

But Ravi did also go overboard, sometimes for the good, sometimes for the bad. Pankaj wanted to stay non-committal about the relationship. He needed time to think about it. He could just change the subject.

"Whatever happened with the girl whose number I gave you?"

"Yeah, I met her, in Madrid. It was nice, but she was already engaged. Anyway, I've moved on. Trying to clean up the karmic mess I made by letting her go."

"You think your life is a mess?" Pankaj asked.

This was a concession he hadn't heard before, some self-awareness that suggested Ravi was actually capable of change. Ravi squinted at him and appeared lost in thought, his legs swaying like butterfly wings. Pankaj wasn't sure if he should say something more or wait for Ravi to break the silence. Ravi started biting his thumb fingernail. The seconds passed uncomfortably, as if Ravi was examining the core of his soul.

"I mean, it's not that much of a mess," Pankaj said to fill the silence.

Ravi slowly started nodding, glancing around the room before looking back at Pankaj.

"I didn't make Managing Director, if it makes you feel better. That's why I got transferred here," Pankaj said.

It hurt to acknowledge the truth, but he had wanted to discuss it with someone for months. His parents didn't understand the promotion track, so he didn't let them know he had been passed over. Ravi looked at him with serious intensity.

"Sorry to hear that. I know it's something you really wanted. Did they tell you why?"

Pankaj felt his arm pits getting wet and intertwined his fingers.

"Something about learning more about the markets. But the guy they replaced me with is good friends with my boss in London. He's getting promoted despite the fact that he calls me every other day on what to do."

"So don't."

"Don't what?"

"Tell him what to do."

Pankaj reflected for a moment.

"How? He's the boss' friend."

"What's he asking about?"

"Market intel, what trades to put on."

"So here's a better idea. Give him fake intel. If he lost a lot of money, that would be the end," Ravi observed.

"I couldn't do that."

"Because you're applying for sainthood? You don't win these battles in a courtroom."

Pankaj reflected for a moment.

"He would tell them it was my idea. Everything is on a recorded line."

"Unless you called him on his cell phone."

"He would still blame me."

"You're not telling him what to do. You're telling him you heard a rumor…" Ravi said.

A thought flashed in Pankaj's mind. Suddenly it seemed possible. His pulse started racing in excitement, and he started talking before he even knew what he was going to say.

"That a big fund is loading up on a position, so he should load up, too! He'll be too stupid to realize the currency is about to tank because of something else happening in the news."

"And then you take the right side of the trade, and make the money he's losing."

"I can't trade the same currencies, and it would be too obvious," Pankaj said. "But I could take a position in a correlated currency."

There was usually one moment every month when there was suddenly a big shift in one of the currencies, where the right amount of intel and intuition allowed a good trader to make a lot of money. Or make another trader lose a lot of money. Pankaj's head spun as he tried to work through all ancillary considerations that could muck up Ravi's idea. And he immediately thought of one. He slowed his breathing and looked at the floor in defeat.

"It doesn't help my cause. Maybe it stops him from getting promoted. But it doesn't get me promoted," Pankaj said. "He'll tell my boss I was the reason for his loss."

"Once he's cocked up the whole thing, the higher ups will get involved and see who made money and who lost money.Who do you think they're going to call to clean it up?"

There was a logic to it. Not fool-proof, but reasonable. Maybe there was a way he could set it up so they did call him. This was next-level Machiavellian stuff. Pankaj had never appreciated that there might actually be some strategy behind Ravi's actions.

"With this kind of thinking, how did you get yourself in such a mess?" Pankaj asked.

"It's possible I go too far sometimes," Ravi said.

If Ravi could take a hard look at himself, Pankaj could certain do the same.

Pankaj could tell Ravi was already thinking about something else. Ravi sucked in his cheeks and puckered his lips, releasing them with a space-age suctioning sound, as if he had reached some decision.

"I have a question. Did you see the last Batman movie?" Ravi asked.

"*Batman Begins*?"

"Whatever it's called. The Batman guy…"

"Bruce Wayne?"

"Him, he's up at some monastery at the top of a mountain in Tibet or something because his life is a mess. I was thinking that would be cool way to re-set. Vineeta has been telling me for years to go to a Buddhist retreat. Apparently even Bowie is a Buddhist. Now Tibet would be a little tough to get to, and we don't speak Tibetan. But Vineeta says they have really cheap retreats in the Catskills. What if the two of us do a weekend retreat? It will be a bit of a re-set. We can catch up, maybe they teach us some techniques to get things on the right path."

"Not my thing," Pankaj said, retrieving the scotch bottle from the kitchen to re-fill their glasses.

"It's not my thing, either, but that's the point. Our thing isn't going exactly the way we want it to. I mean, you could have read my *Guide* and got enlightened for free, but maybe this will help you get going the right way."

"I couldn't sit and meditate for hours."

"And you think I could? We'll do our best."

"I don't think so."

"It's only two days. We could go next weekend."

"I've got work to do."

"All you've done for the past few years is work. Maybe it's time to work on your personal life."

"By taking advice from a bunch of baldies with ponytails?"

"Who cares about the instructors? Have you ever been to a yoga class? There's like 25 women in tights doing all these poses," Ravi offered, half-heartedly pulling his leg up. "That's the thing you never understood. It doesn't matter if the Backstreet Boys are good or not if the girls like them. And it doesn't matter if the baldy enlightens you if the girls think he does."

"How are you going to pay for it?"

"It's actually quite reasonably priced, a few hundred bucks each. And I still have my backup credit card."

Pankaj felt the limbic struggle between his scotch-infused amygdala telling him to give in to this emotional nostalgia of friendship with Ravi and his hippocampus telling him from experience it wouldn't end well. Pankaj's hypothalamus envisioned the girls in tights and pressed the response buzzer before his frontal lobe could properly weigh each possibility and squash the idea.

"I'll think about it."

And as he thought about it over additional drinks while enjoying the thought of getting his career back on track thanks to Ravi's idea, it seemed right. Not to mention that the last time he was with Ravi, he had seen a naked woman. Hanging with Ravi was like trading foreign exchange, you could lose big or win big. As they started planning for the following weekend, he knew he would hate himself in the morning, but the excitement of possibility felt good now.

Excerpt from
Ravi's Guide to Being a Cool Indian

Literature

If you read books by Indian-American authors, you'd think we're the most repressed and depressed people on the globe. One book takes two pages to describe the inside and outside of a mango, which is meant to symbolize the main character's struggle to live between two cultures. Another advertises its "pathos", which seems to mean people sitting around thinking without any humor, suspense or profound observations. The plots drag through racist name callings, racist beatings, cultural clash divorces and deaths of people too weak to fight back against a racist system, as if the tragedies of real life are inadequate for poignancy. Occasionally objects transform into other objects, like water into diamonds, to make things seem more important.

It's not that these voices aren't vital to advancing the Indian cause. They help put me to sleep when I haven't been drinking. And from a social progress standpoint, they are like the annoying neighbors who smell because they don't wear anti-perspirant because the plastic containers are bad for the environment. You need people who care that much about a cause, you just don't like them. The books bring attention to the truly oppressed, but they also spread the notion that the only way to fight oppression is by whingeing. Principle #1: If you're going to write the great Indian novel, make it about someone who's winning, not whingeing, because the fact is, we have the highest average household income of any ancestry in America, and it's not even close.

You can open your book with this golden nugget from when I was seven or eight, back when shorts almost reached your crotch and tube socks reached your knees. I was sitting on the stairs between Bob's Fish and Rasheed's Barbershop waiting for a haircut in Ealing steering one of those electronic racing games. Three punks with leather jackets, crewcuts and metal piercings came up to me and took turns speaking.

"Wot's that game you got, Paki?"

"No, he's Haji, like that servant in that one comic strip."

"Why don't you be a peaceful Gandhi and hand it over."

The third one motioned for the game. I told him to go fuck himself, and the shortest one asked me if I thought was smart. I was, because I jumped off the stairs and started running. The short one started chasing me while his friends shouted for him to teach me some manners. I curved through parked cars across the street and could tell I could outrun him, but stopped next to a white Peugeot, crouched down and waited. He tripped on the curb while navigating through a van and a car, and I ploughed into him with my shoulder, landing on his chest. He started wheezing and turning red like he couldn't breathe. My game had splintered on the sidewalk, so I tumbled off him, grabbed as many pieces of the game I could before his friends arrived and ran home.

If I had told my Mum, she would have instructed me not to go to the barbershop alone, but you can't hide from people who try to intimidate you. We can all pretend to be civilized and whine about discrimination on some Oprah discussion panel, but they'd have tried to beat me if I was Indian or not, right? People always take out their insecurities on some group they perceive as weaker or inferior or more prosperous. Even Indians and Chinese oppress their own kind if it lines their pockets. Principle #2: If you're going to succeed, you can't get angry at people for being people or complain about the odds of success, though you can punch someone when they deserve it.

At least in the UK and America, institutionalized racism doesn't stop you from starting a Subway or Motel 6 or even a rock band and earning your way to respectability and power. If an American showed up with nothing in Beijing or Mumbai, they wouldn't be allowed to bribe their way to the top. If they wrote a novel describing the skin of a white peach, no one would buy it. Now, after centuries of enslaving and oppressing other races, no one is going to feel sorry for poor Americans trying to immigrate to Asia, but you get my point.

Mango novels are the epitome of the immigrant paradox—the authors both want the right to complain about their unique circumstances, while reveling in their unique identity (and even make their career based on it). I would rather save my sympathy for the deaths of real people and people who adapt, succeed and gloat, but I suppose as long as mango novels help Indians whinge their way to the top, I can live with it, because however you slice the mango, success is the best revenge.

Chapter 15
Buddhist Retreat
Catskills, New York

Vineeta

Vineeta observed the people waiting on the median as cars whooshed down Houston in both directions. She in turn was waiting on the curb in front of her SoHo apartment for Ravi to pick her up to attend a monastic retreat upstate. Ian had flown home to support his mom through a surgery for a hernia and couldn't join. She had invited herself along to the retreat because she still had some nagging anxiety that her life wasn't quite…aligned. She had a pretty good guess why.

She was on healthy speaking terms with her parents thanks to Ravi's intervention. Her job at the UN was good. At times it was inspiring, funding projects around the world for water wells, schools and health clinics, and at times mundane, drafting resolutions that were never adopted. Her relationship with Ian was working. After she got past the joy of realizing her childhood crush, she began to appreciate how he was the right mix of steady and understated, like Hans, and unpredictable and quirky. And Ravi said that he had lined up the money to pay off his bookie, loan shark, or whatever he was called.

All was good except for Ravi's revelation about the source of funds for paying of his loan—an advance for a sitcom based on his book. She thought she had gotten over the fact that he had mocked their family in print, but began envisioning scenes of her back in college, wearing droopy sweaters and sweatpants, studying on the weekends and going on secret dates with nerdy men. She imagined their parents depicted as stereotypical immigrants, with silly accents and a preoccupation with grades and marriage. And she feared the social impact of comedically playing to a Westerner's understanding of minority experience while ignoring the darker sides of being a minority in America . The latter had taken added importance now that she was dating Ian, whose family had experienced things that were far more oppressive than the occasional epithet.

The blue Jaguar pulled over to the curb in front of her. Ravi motioned her in from the driver's seat. He popped the trunk for her carry-on bag before she fell into the leather bucket seat.

"Ian lent you the car?"

"It appears that way."

If Vineeta hadn't known that Ravi rarely combed his hair, she would have thought that his bedhead had been perfectly styled to make it appear he didn't care what it looked like. He lurched the car forward toward the FDR.

"By the way, I know I told you Pankaj is coming, but there's also an ex-colleague of mine who wanted to join, so we'll pick her up on the Upper West Side and then get Pankaj in Harlem," Ravi said.

"Is she like…a 'her' that you're interested in?"

"It's possible that things could progress that way."

"You could have mentioned it before."

"You're right, but she kind of decided last minute."

"Maybe that's a sign you're meant to be together."

Vineeta had been hoping to have some alone time with Ravi to discuss the *Guide*, get some assurances about Ian and straighten out her alignment, but yet again, he had managed to surprise her by bringing along a companion who, unlike Pankaj, would probably monopolize his time. They exited the highway. She sulked by picking at her nail polish as they worked their way through the East Side traffic lights. Bike couriers darted past, while customers in sunglasses and wool coats lined up on the sidewalk for bagels and coffee at a popular pastry shop. Eventually Ravi coasted through the sub-level transverse of Central Park and up Central Park West. He pulled to the curb across from the Roosevelt statue in front of the Natural History Museum. A short Indian girl approached the car and threw in a duffel bag into the trunk before opening the rear door. Ravi had dated models and women with angled faces that proved geometric theorems, so Vineeta was surprised to find that the girl's features were rounded and asymmetrical, highlighted with a nose-ring. Vineeta turned around and extended her hand.

"Hey, I'm Vineeta, Ravi's sister."

The girl introduced herself as Alaknanda, Lucky for short, and said how excited she was for the trip. She had a cute mannerism sprinkled with deliberate blinks and head tilting, but it seemed affected. Still, she spoke warmly with an intense focus when Vineeta was speaking. Vineeta was curious whether Ravi's first experience with an Indian girl would be any different than his prior girlfriends.

Vineeta felt like she was intruding on a date and was relieved to pick up Pankaj a few minutes later, who loaded a full-blown suitcase into the trunk. Pankaj ducked into the car, and she immediately smelled one of those overpowering adolescent scents—Axe or Drakkar or something. She asked him how he was settled, and after providing details, he apologized for not being in touch. He continued the small talk by asking Lucky how she knew Ravi. When Ravi turned the radio on, it smoothed over the initial awkwardness. They drove over the GW bridge and whizzed up Palisades Parkway under a gray sky and past bare trees. The side conversations became more natural and pleasant, until they began their ascent in the Catskill mountains.

"Your family must be excited about Ravi's show," Lucky said.

"I guess we'll find out," Vineeta said over her shoulder.

"Oh."

Vineeta turned around to clarify.

"I mean, of course we're happy for Ravi, but it's premised on his *Guide*, which ruffled a few feathers," Vineeta said.

"I didn't know," Lucky said.

"It's all good, we've been talking it out," Ravi said, glancing back.

Vineeta noticed Pankaj biting his nails behind Ravi. Was she saying too much with someone she just met?

"Look, it was a funny piece, but I think by mocking the way we grew up, he was suggesting Indians should accept Western culture as the frame of reference."

There, she kept it from being personal. His show was not just mocking her, but all Indians.

"But we moved to a Western culture and the audience is Western, so maybe that's the right frame of reference," Lucky said.

"I'm not sure 'right' is the right word," Vineeta replied. "If not for the colonial dominance of the West, maybe Eastern culture would have become the world's frame of reference."

Her neck hurt from straining to look at Lucky while she was talking.

"I don't think anyone's arguing colonialism wasn't problematic, but that doesn't mean his show needs to be viewed through a political lens. Most people get that racism is bad, and can also find it funny when you don't understand what you're supposed to do in a new culture," Lucky said.

Vineeta debated responding. Was this good intellectual rapport or an impolite aggression for her first interaction with Ravi's girlfriend, or whatever she was? For that matter, shouldn't Lucky be the one trying to win over Vineeta?

"Right, but how much adaptation does society have a right to require? It's one thing to joke about being frugal, it's another when a governor calls you 'macaca' or a cop assaults you because you didn't understand what he was asking you to do and doesn't get prosecuted. In some ways watching his show is like being a wealthy Indian who votes for a candidate who prioritizes lower taxes over a candidate who prioritizes justice. It ignores the big issue in exchange for a selfish benefit."

"Those are interesting points, but I kind of liked that it didn't take a stereotypical terrorist or overt prejudice angle. I thought his book walked a fine line between being insightful and light and joyful," Lucky said.

"But it matters, right? Because if you're making a show about immigrants and covering the difficulty of assimilating, you're implicitly saying it's a good thing they're here. Then you have to answer how much assimilation is required. Should they be allowed in if they're orthodox? Should they be required to speak English?"

Ravi interjected.

"All good points. But it is a guide to being cool. I thought I was winning the Indian race to be cool, but it turned out I was scaling the Poconos while Kal Penn and Jhumpa Lahiri were ascending Everest. Anyway, the book was supposed to explore that for all the trouble it was growing up here, it also made us unique. It certainly gave me a purpose, a reason to fight to be recognized instead of failing my way through school and stocking t-shirts at Selfridges. Some girls even found it exotic. The show isn't a political statement."

"Why not?" Vineeta asked.

Ravi began drum-rolling his fingers on the steering wheel while preparing an answer, but Lucky interjected.

"I think just by being represented on television, that helps push political change without asking for it."

"If you trust in slow change, you get no change. If you push for radical change, you get slow change," Vineeta said.

Vineeta noticed Pankaj looking on grimly.

"What do you think?"

"Ravi already knows what I think."

"I promised him he wouldn't be a character on the show," Ravi said.

"What about me?" Vineeta asked.

"Honestly, the script was so bad it would be best if none of us were in the show. Lucky, how did it go? She has an incredible memory," Ravi said.

Lakhi pursed her lips and looked up in preparation, before staring forward and lowering her voice an octave.

"Dad: Ravi! I've been looking for you all afternoon.

She switched to a British accent and gesticulated loosely for Ravi's lines.

Ravi: In the garage refrigerator? Next time check my room first.

Dad: Your mother wants to talk to you. There's a girl she wants you to meet.

Ravi: Do we have to meet? Couldn't we just sleep together and go about our own way?"

"Impressive imitation of Ravi. But the dialogue is shit," Pankaj said, who appeared to look at the Lucky girl for affirmation.

Ravi continued, "It's funny, I was thinking a talk show would be even better. We'd bring in celebrities with an immigrant story and riff on a topic from my book. Like bring in a famous Jewish person, and they riff about Jews supposedly being cheap, and then I joke that Gujaratis being known as "Gujjus", which sounds like "good Jews", and also being known as being cheap. Then we compete with each other over the ways that our families were cheap."

"See, that's just reinforcing the stereotype," Vineeta said.

"No, it's mocking the stereotypes. I could see Conan doing a segment like that," Ravi said.

"Great analogy, a white man responsible for creating Apu the convenience store owner mocking ethnic stereotypes," Pankaj said.

"Well, whatever. You do what you do. I came on this trip to clear my head, not confuse it more," Vineeta said.

She stared out the window as Ravi swung the car through bends in the pine-tree forest. As she constructed new arguments why *Ravi's Guide* was a problem—it was disrespectful to their parents, it glorified a superficial lifestyle, it ridiculed Indian culture, it didn't factor in racism against other races—she tripped over a slight inconsistency in her thinking. She had been disrespectful to her parents, lying to and borrowing money from her father and loudly bristling at her mom's viewpoints. She had partaken in the superficial lifestyle Ravi's career had offered her access to. Maybe she was even guilty of being a superficial Indian, never seriously considering any of the Indian men she had been set up with.

She was a bit Western here, a bit Indian there, a bit Hindu here, and a bit Buddhist there. Had she just assimilated where it was convenient? Maybe that's what Shiva and Buddha were getting at. Destroying her illusions and embracing suffering meant owning up to whom she was, the good, the bad and the ugly. It wasn't her father's affairs, or Shiva, or her mother's criticisms or *Ravi's Guide* that had made her life difficult. It was her own lack of accountability, exemplified by the fact that she was annoyed at Ravi for inviting Lucky, annoyed at Pankaj's cologne, annoyed at Lucky's viewpoints, right before attending a Zen retreat which preached the importance of not getting annoyed.

She was critical of Ravi for not thinking through the consequences of his actions on other people, but she had been no better in dealing with their parents. If anything, while she claimed to be practicing Buddhism, Ravi had unknowingly been practicing it—he never seemed flustered by the things that got in his way. He accepted them, worked through them and moved on. He had helped her out with their parents. He had somehow managed to patch things up with Pankaj and gotten him to attend the retreat.

Fixing her alignment wasn't simply premised on Ravi not doing his show. Of course, she would need to talk to him to make sure he didn't repeat the mistakes of his *Guide*. But she also needed to find contentment within herself regardless of what others in her life were doing. It meant recognizing the mostly positive impact her parents and Ravi had on her life instead of being resentful of the things that had made it more difficult. What had Ravi said in Ann Arbor? She owned her own choices. Now that she had almost gotten her life in order with a job and boyfriend she liked, her parents' commentary shouldn't matter as much. In fact, she should be recognizing them for all they had done for her, an affirmative gesture of gratitude which would re-align their relationship for the future. Too bad she didn't have Ravi's skill for the grandiose.

They arrived in the middle of the woods for the 5pm orientation at the Zen Buddhist Meditation Center just as the sky blackened to night, following other groups into a converted barn, with a red brick exterior and grids of windows.

Ravi

Ravi peered up at the supports of the gambrel roof and then at the people. No shaven heads, orange robes or even one Asian running the place. First the West stole Asia's resources, now it was stealing its culture. A short white balding man with flared eyebrows and a goatee introduced himself as Bergman Roshi and explained the central tenet of Buddhism as freeing oneself from desire.

"So it's like the opposite of alcohol," Ravi whispered, though no one laughed.

Roshi pontificated about the noble truths of Buddhism and the pathways to achieving them. They would apparently being doing a lot of sitting around and thinking, called zazen. In addition, each group would be assigned one meal in which they helped prepare the food or help clean up. Ravi raised his hand.

"So would you say Buddhism is more a philosophy than a religion?" Ravi asked.

"I know you have a lot of questions, but I would ask everyone to hold on to them, I think most of them will get answered in due course."

After the orientation, the crowd dispersed and each of them took their luggage to their respective rooms. Ravi and Lakhi settled into a drafty wood cabin with an ineffectual space heater and two twin beds. Ravi had claimed on the application that Lakhi was his wife in order to share the room. Still, the rules for the retreat included abstaining from "intimate behavior, including in private rooms, in order to focus all energies on achieving a higher meditative state." She unpacked her clothes into a rickety dresser while Ravi propped himself up on one of the bedrests with a pillow.

"It's funny, my sister always lectures me about embracing suffering as a fact of life, which is apparently a Buddhist thing. Like, instead of avoiding it, you have to experience and witness it, and separate the physical self that is suffering from the inner being that is at peace. Then you transcend your suffering and accept the things you can't change. Yet suddenly now she wants me to fight racism. If people accept the things they think they can't change, nothing changes."

"Do you think the two philosophies are mutually exclusive? Like, why can't you be Buddhist but still fighting for change? It's just saying not to allow your inner self to get corroded as you are fighting for things that are slow to change."

"But the people who are willing to fight usually fight because they are upset, not because they have inner peace. I mean, I guess there was MLK and Gandhi. But let's face it, I'm not them."

"You're far sexier."

"I'll take that."

Ravi had never really made the connection, but in some ways he was already Buddhist. He had always accepted being slighted over his race as a part of life. He noticed on the elevator that most white people only greeted him when he was with someone white, despite living in the most liberal bastion in America. But it hadn't bothered him because he had given them the benefit of the doubt, attributing it more to tribalism than racism. People could be sincere and caring, and still instinctually cluster with the people they identified with most, sometimes along economic lines, sometimes along political lines, sometimes along cultural lines, sometimes along racial lines. Certainly Indians themselves were clustering with each other. Ravi liked hanging out most with people who grew up like him—Ian, Pankaj, Shushruth, all outsiders in America. There were a few white friends who he would include in this category, too, but they were outsiders for some reason, too—gays, Jews, eccentrics.

But now as he reflected on those academics in college studying the nuances of racism that he had dismissed, and Lakhi's observation about white liberals sending their kids to schools across town to avoid being the minority in Edison, and Vineeta's observations about actual violence against Indians, and the psychological wounds Pankaj had clearly suffered in growing up in London, maybe there was more to the topic of racism than he had always assumed.

Lakhi turned around and suddenly stared at him. She had a funny way of protruding her lower lip when she was worried about something.

"Do you think your sister hates me?" Lakhi asked.

"What, because you disagreed with her? We disagree all the time."

"But you're her brother."

"She doesn't hate you. You'll get to know each other better over the weekend."

Ravi hadn't thought his relationship with Lakhi was yet at the stage where he would need to worry about whether his family would like her, but it was an interesting question. Vineeta should like her—Lakhi was articulate, engaging, confident, a good listener. But those were just words off a dating site. The instinctual reaction people had to one another was much harder to peg, especially when they weren't hoping to see the other person naked.

They left the cabin to meet the others for dinner. Ravi went to retrieve Pankaj, while Lakhi went to retrieve Vineeta. He walked to a nearby cabin and knocked.

"Ready to go?" he said after Pankaj opened the door in a Hugo Boss sweater.

"It's fine. Though those alleged attractive women you mentioned aren't here."

While that judgment was true for Ravi, he was pretty sure it wasn't true for Pankaj. Heidi Klum could be at the retreat, and Pankaj would insult her looks just to shield himself from rejection.

"I don't know about that. Give it a chance."

As Pankaj went to put on his jacket, Ravi spotted the gigantic toiletry bag Pankaj had hung on the inside of the bathroom door.

"For all the shit you bring, you should look like Brad Pitt," Ravi said.

"For all the shit you say, one would think you are Brad Pitt," Pankaj said.

"Touché. By the way, I'd appreciate if you didn't mention the little incident from last weekend to anyone. The money's lined up. My agent managed to negotiate an advance."

Would Dalinc really have broken his bones if Dalinc had made it into Pankaj's apartment? He had taken subconscious comfort that Dalinc wouldn't want to discourage other celebrities from gambling by injuring him, but he wasn't sure he was still famous enough for anyone to notice.

"Congrats I suppose," Pankaj said.

They headed to the cafeteria, where Lakhi and Vineeta were already sitting at a long table discussing dance classes in the city, which was a positive turn from the car ride. The four of them went to the buffet island to fill up their plates and returned to a broader conversation about classes each of them had taken in the city. Facing each other, it was much easier to keep the conversation light, as Pankaj seemed excited at being able to talk to a girl he wasn't related to, Vineeta avoided further political commentary and Ravi joked about the karate-style robes some attendees were wearing.

Each of them retreated to their cabins. As Lakhi finished her bathroom ritual, Ravi wondered whether he should push the twin beds together or whether Lakhi would want to respect the rules of the retreat. He waited for her to emerge, and when she did, she headed straight under the covers before he could propose otherwise.

After brushing his teeth, he settled into his bed and stared at the golden wood ceiling. Coupled with the smooth polyester border of his pearled flannel blanket, he felt like he had been transported to the 1970s. Too bad Vinod uncle wasn't around to appreciate the place. He started a game of solitaire on his phone but an image of 70s sitcoms flashed through his brain—*Sanford and Son*, *All in the Family*, *The Jeffersons*, *Three's Company*. Which of these was his sitcom like? Why did he suddenly have an unsettled feeling when he thought about his sitcom? It should have made him feel happy—it both solved his money problems and gave him a new challenge and career. He turned to Lakhi, who was reading a novel.

"Do you think I should do the show?"

She folded her book down on the bed.

"Why do you ask?"

"You heard Vineeta in the car. Instead of finding it funny, everyone I mentioned in the book was ticked off. It's not like I can change the entire set of characters."

"That's probably for you to figure out with your family. Maybe you should talk to all of them about it, first."

"I could, but it's not like they can consent to not being offended in the future. Not to mention that Vineeta seemed to be implying the book itself was racist."

"I didn't think she was saying that. I thought she was more making the point that white males have controlled everything for centuries. Power, money, voting, resources, culture. So any opposition to that will seem extreme, meaning, maybe you may perceive her viewpoints as extreme only because you accepted the white male perspective as the starting point."

"She's right, I did accept that as the starting point," Ravi said.

"So part of the battle is getting people to recognize that. But the other part is getting people to agree about whether and how society should adjust for that. Some people argue that even though most people aren't racist, the existing system perpetuates racist outcomes and should be changed. Others think any attempt to address the legacy of racism is itself racist. Though most of them happen to be white males who benefited from this history. But then the white males are able to point out that the people who want to address the legacy of racism often avoid talking about personal responsibility because they don't want to sound racist."

Up to now, Ravi had quickly dismissed people who didn't agree with him. He always viewed his shows, books and music as a platform for his own viewpoints. But Vineeta, Lakhi and Pankaj had been making points he hadn't considered.

"Maybe that's what the show could be about, this kind of dialogue. Exploring the nuances on each side. Like the next evolution of *All in the Family* and *Everybody Hates Chris,*" Ravi said.

"I like it, if you can make it happen."

"If I can make it happen without ticking my family off."

The next morning began with zazen, where Ravi lined up in a row facing another row trying to sit cross-legged on a cushion trying to concentrate on existence. Bergman Roshi led the room through breathing exercises where participants inhaled deeply and counted off slow exhalations. Ravi fidgeted while thinking about whether it was possible to really explore tribalism in a sitcom premised on double entendres on a network known for *The Grind*. Without offending Pankaj, Vineeta and the rest of his family. While turning down Ian's request to re-form the band. At least it would keep his limbs intact. He briefly entered the black red nothingness of his brain for a few moments of true zazen before latching back on to his list of anxieties. When zazen was finally finished, the monk handed out a liturgy encouraging everyone to become one with nature, let the universe's energy pulse through them, abandon the pursuit of things which don't exist and find the solution within themselves. They broke for a lunch of salad, rice and vegetables with tofu in the cafeteria.

"So Pankaj, how did you like the zazen?" Vineeta asked at the table.

"You know, it was surprisingly relaxing. I admit I was skeptical of this whole thing, but as he led us through the breathing and visualization exercises, I felt a release of chemicals in my brain. I liked what he said about focusing without focusing on something. Do you meditate every day?"

"Not every day, maybe three times a week? It really helps me detach and de-stress. Ian likes it, too."

Ravi hadn't felt any rush of chemicals. Was Pankaj pulling Vineeta's leg or was he being sincere?

After lunch, they were each directed to help clear and wash the dishes. Upon finishing, Ravi left for a one-on-one session with Bergman Roshi. The monk invited him into his office and directed him to sit down in front of a desk with statuettes of the Buddha—a gold one posed under a tree, a jade one posed under an umbrella, and a wooden one with an offering tray. Roshi asked a few background questions before asking what he hoped to achieve by attending the retreat.

"Clearly not getting…" he started, catching himself before adding "laid", a tic from years of juvenile bantering with the band. "I'm not really sure. But I had this question about the liturgy we read—if the solution is within ourselves, then why do we need the retreat?"

The monk had looked uptight to this point, with his impassive demeanor, pink head and white beard, but now smiled.

"You don't need the retreat, you can practice these same things at home. We just teach you the methods for finding the solution, but you ultimately must find it on your own."

"What if I like pursuing things which you might say don't exist?"

"Things exist, we see them around us. The characteristics we attribute to these things are what don't exist. So when you desire something, you are craving something imagined."

"We live in our imagination, that's all we have," Ravi said.

"Buddhism helps you learn how to live outside your imagination, to detach from your likes and dislikes."

The monk waved his hands, as if there were some force circulating in the room that Ravi could latch onto.

"Sounds a bit circular, right? Cause it's your imagination that's imagining to be outside itself."

"It's as circular as asserting your own existence. If you have faith in your existence, you can have faith in objective perception."

"But I like subjective living."

"So that's a good start. If you like subjective living, why are you here?"

"Well, life had gotten confused for a little while. Some of the people I'm close to didn't seem to be happy with me."

"Like who?"

"Well, my ex-girlfriend Pilar. I mean she likes me, but she prefers her fiancé. My sister. My cousin Pankaj, though I think that's worked out. A…business associate named Dalinc. Good guy, a little high strung. Not sure about my parents, but they're used to me. I don't know if I should count…"

"That's okay, I understand. A large number of people. What things did you do that caused them to be upset?"

The monk leaned forward on his desk. Ravi now noticed a large silver bowl on a shelf behind him, as well as a monk certification scroll on the wall.

"That depends. But they're all a little unhappy about a book I wrote. Kind of a memoir thing. Except for Dalinc, he wasn't in the book, really a different issue."

"And why did you write the book?"

Why exactly did he write the *Guide*? The money was decent. His agent stressed expanding his brand. He thought it would be entertaining. A part of him thought of it as his formal statement about life and cultural assimilation. Ravi had thrived because he had adapted to American culture. It was the core principle of his *Guide*, in fact, the core principle of evolution. In the process of adapting, though, what had he lost? What had his family lost? Like Vineeta and Pankaj, he had lost some sense of self. His parents had lost a chance to relate to their children. And he had lost his sense of duty to his friends and family. But all that was too much to discuss with a Jewish man who wanted to be Asian, when Ravi was an Asian man who had spent his whole life proving he was American.

Ravi rocked his bottom back and forth on the seat cushion.

"Just for fun," he said.

"Fun is nice, but it's temporary. If you release your ego, you will find something deeper, more fulfilling. Peace. Tranquility. Love. It's possible to renounce selfish desire and place other people's welfare ahead of your own. It's possible to achieve a transcendental satisfaction which no longer requires acceptance by others. You know what you may find helpful? Here is a short biography of Siddhartha, who became Gautama Buddha."

Roshi retrieved a book from his bookshelf and extended it to Ravi, who took it and left the office as dusk began to set. The others weren't in their rooms, so he situated by the fireplace in the converted barn watching orange specks float off the crackling logs like flies. He began reading the book and seeing parallels between his life and Siddhartha. Maybe he was re-living Siddhartha's life. Siddhartha was an Indian prince who relinquished all the benefits of a celebrity to meditate in the forest to discover fulfillment, which is where Ravi found himself now. It had never occurred to Ravi that to reach fulfillment he should be suppressing desire rather than embracing it, especially when Pankaj had demonstrated the slippery slope from suppression to repression.

A light rain had started outside, plinking off pools of water into stars and bubbles. After a little while, Vineeta entered the barn and plopped herself into the sofa across from his, removing her shoes and pulling her feet up on the cushions.

"Where are the others?" he asked.

"Just came back from a walk with Lakhi. She had an appointment with Roshi which probably saved us from getting wet. Pankaj went to his room."

Ravi fashioned a fake cigarette out of a work schedule someone had left behind on the coffee table.

"Yeah, that's good. I was just reading this book the monk gave me. Do you believe in reincarnation?" Ravi asked, leaning back into his sofa with his fake cigarette pinched between his fingers.

"I know it's not scientific, but I've always believed in it, because I can't imagine not being in existence," Vineeta said.

"What if it was scientific, like if your DNA is identical to someone else's from history and you're predisposed to a certain actions, like when they find two separated twins and it turns out they're both lawyers who've been divorced twice and like to watch 'Dr. Who'," Ravi said.

"But that wouldn't be you. Reincarnation isn't about duplication, just preservation of the soul," Vineeta said.

"But what if the soul was identical? It would just mean the soul had no memory of the prior soul."

"So what if it were? It wouldn't mean anything to your current life. It would just mean humans are meaningless clones," Vineeta said.

"Unless you knew you were a clone of someone important. If you knew you were identical, then it would be a barometer of sorts. You could tell if you were outperforming or underperforming. And if you had a clone of someone like Einstein, you could train that person to solve big problems. Or if you had a clone of this Siddhartha fellow, you could see how that person handled present day problems," Ravi said.

"So that's who you think you're a clone of?" Vineeta asked with a sharp head bob.

"What makes you think I was thinking about myself?" Ravi asked.

"Do you ever think of anyone else?" Vineeta asked.

"Aaah, never mind. When do you see Roshi?" Ravi asked, nibbling on his fake cigarette.

"Tomorrow morning."

"But you've done this before, so what is left to talk about?"

"I actually wanted to talk about some things with him, but changed my mind."

"What, like Ian?"

"No, like…it doesn't matter. Things with Ian are fine."

"That's good," Ravi said.

"He mentioned your conversation about the band. I think it's good for him to try something new. He signed up with a couple of consulting companies that assign you to projects in your field of expertise. Maybe they can find him something that gets him back into political science."

"Oh right, that was his degree in college, right?"

She nodded and started picking at a toenail before looking up.

"I'm sorry if that initial conversation with Lakhi was a bit…tense. I like her. She's different than the other friends you've had," Vineeta said.

"How?"

"She's obviously really sharp. She's pretty confident. We'll get used to each other."

"I wasn't worried."

"You never are."

Ravi crumpled his fake cigarette and tossed it on the coffee table.

"I was thinking about what you said about the sitcom. I need the money, so I've got to do it. But if I ever got the chance, I'd make a talk show you'd like. I'd interview guests and explore their hobbies with an Indian twist. Cooking chana masala with Zadie Smith. Discussing *Midnight's Children* with Tony Blair. Flying an Air India jet to Bombay with John Travolta. Riding a motorcycle from Bombay to Delhi with Ewan McGregor. Taking Kanye West to Khujaraho, where they have an erotic sculpture temple, since he's both religious and likes strip clubs. Then we could discuss what it means to be an Indian immigrant."

"Sounds like a fun idea, but you don't have to tailor things to my tastes. It's just…dating Ian kind of doubles down on race and cultural identity issues. So maybe that's been on my mind."

"I kind of liked the idea. I could explore the line between racism and tribalism. Talk about…"

"You know who your first guests would have to be if you did the talk show?" Vineeta interrupted.

Johnny Depp? Keith Richards? No, she must have been thinking about someone Indian.

"Amitabh Bachchan?"

"No offense, but I don't think you have that kind of pull," she scoffed.

"I was just trying to think who you were thinking of."

Pankaj suddenly appeared to their left, approaching the coffee table while balancing paper bowls full of pretzels and chips and apple juice boxes. He crouched down and released them with relief.

"Did you raid some kid's birthday party?" Ravi said.

He'd have to ask Vineeta later who she had in mind.

"I'm really hungry and thirsty, but dinner doesn't start for another half an hour. Do you want one?" Pankaj said, extending a juice box towards each of them.

Ravi thought of a good one-liner, but it was the first time in a long while that Pankaj wasn't self-consciously being a banker.

"No thanks. How was your session with Roshi-san?" Ravi asked.

"Good, he's surprisingly articulate. Gave me some good ideas."

Pankaj looked calm, maybe even happy. Apparently all he had needed to loosen up was a weekend with other people. Lakhi appeared shortly thereafter, and they went to dinner together.

That night Ravi slept serenely, dreaming about going on tour with Siddhartha through the forests. He was his interpreter, except that Siddhartha never spoke and Ravi delivered his thoughts to a gathering of disciples by playing a silent guitar. Ravi became so engrossed in translating more accurately that he didn't realize that months had passed, the trees had lost their leaves and everyone had stranded him.

When Ravi awoke from the dream around five a.m., the wind was whipping the trees violently in the blackness. He slipped out of bed, put on a flannel shirt, jacket and pants and went outside, crunching pine needles as he walked towards the expanse of the garden. The moon gave just enough light to see the silhouettes of shapes, as if he was living in an abstraction of reality. He felt aware of time and dimension and waved his hand slowly in front of his face. In this moment, he was free from judgment, both his own and others. Aware of his small place in the universe. He didn't need to be the second coming of Siddhartha, he was the first coming of him, alone in a forest with people just like him.

He should have felt content. He had mended fences with Vineeta and Pankaj, started dating a woman who had helped ground him, was back on good terms with Ian, somehow lined up a new job that paid well and was on the verge of paying off Dalinc. He thought by sprinkling a little Buddhist enlightenment in the mix, he would be feeling fulfilled. Yet if existence was built on the lies people told themselves like Roshi had posited, then Buddhism was the concession that Buddhists weren't very good at creative lying. Ravi liked engaging, screwing up, learning, absorbing, coping, adjusting. Desire and adventure fueled him, even if it set other people on fire. While others needed Buddhism to douse that fire, he just needed to figure out how to put his desire to its most useful use. The problem was that the sitcom didn't appear to be his most useful use. Was the talk show he had posited to Vineeta a more meaningful project? What was the purpose of either show, anyway? To enlighten him or to enlighten others? To find a clearer vision of what it meant to be a cool Indian?

He returned to a strand of thought from his session with Roshi. He had approached life from a singular perspective of adaptation, which was preferable to Vineeta's approach of confusion, Pankaj's approach of persecution and Ian's approach of detachment. If they weren't so busy assimilating, would they have approached life differently? With a new emphasis on adventure, or ambition, or compassion, or sincerity, or fulfillment, or connection? Or was assimilation just a different pathway to the same destination?

He started recalling different incidents in his life which might help him with the answer—the incident on the steps of Rasheed's barbershop. Negotiations with the record label. Trips with his family. Even if he could catalogue every memory he could recall, how many days of his life could he reconstruct and what pattern would they demonstrate? Reflected through the warped mirrors of memory, was his life even authentic, or just a fiction extrapolated from pictures, other's recollections and vague recollections? If he had enjoyed the journey, did any of that matter? What if he didn't?

As he crossed a short bridge over a small pond onto a pagoda style worshipping platform, an image flashed into his mind of the first time the band had played to a venue of 10,000 screaming fans. The night zipped by so quickly on adrenalin and later vodka that Ravi couldn't say that he enjoyed it even though every moment had been ineffable—the sound check on a stage half the size of a football field, the hour backstage joking with the boys while the opening act played, the actual performance, the cell phones swaying like an electronic wheat stalks in appreciation, the after-party, the party after the after-party. Events like these no longer connected to specific feelings, more a general nostalgia, whereas when his mum and sister recounted things, they talked about the people they were with and seemed to be re-experiencing the joy or heartache of the moment. Was his lack of emotion a male/female difference, or had he been so caught up in his ego and ambition that he hadn't processed events emotionally, or had the pace of the band's career just prevented him from doing so?

He blew out clouds of vapor, reminding him of his lyric from "Glitter in the Road"—*I see my life as a wisp of smoke, interesting twists that only I can note, then disappearing like it never existed at all.*

His head swirled from trying to make sense of his life. From trying to figure out the purpose going forward.

The last few months had been different. He had been emotionally upset over Pankaj's estrangement. Over Ian's decision. Over Pilar's diagnosis. Over the Thanksgiving brouhaha. So he was capable of emotion, at least when people he cared about were involved. Maybe he just needed to focus on generating positive emotions with his loved ones rather than living a series of silly anecdotes that led to them having negative ones. He wanted his parents to be proud of him, to see that he was capable of taking responsibility of his finances and of acknowledging the sacrifices they had made in immigrating to America. He wanted Vineeta and Pankaj to forgive him for disrespecting them and perceive him as a classy ambassador for Indian-Americans. He wanted to re-structure his friendship with Ian so that they continued to be in each other's lives with an unspoken level of trust and understanding. He wanted to be something more than a two hit songwriting wonder, sitcomesque racial philosopher or MTV t.v. host with a large gambling debt.

He had made some progress on all of these fronts, but unlike releasing an album, he wasn't eligible for a Best Comeback Grammy to let him know how he was faring. He wished there was one simple action to satisfy everyone, move forward with a clean slate, keep emotionally centered, be a catalyst of progress beyond himself and still retain the essence of who he was. He knelt onto the worshipping platform and lay his arms forward into a prostrate praying posture, cleared his mind of all of these thoughts, and for the first time that weekend, floated in a dream-like mental state. He might have confused it for sleep, except for the euphoric glow he felt five minutes later suggesting a release of chemicals like Pankaj had described earlier that day. He didn't know yet where he was going or how he was going to get there, but at least he was ready for the ride.

Excerpt from
Ravi's Guide to Being a Cool Indian

Religion

I know better than to suggest one religion is cooler than another. Hari Om. Insha'Allah. Amen. Every religion has something particularly appealing. Buddhism delivers Nirvana (not just the band), Islam boasts virgins in the after-life, Christianity has the Eucharist wine and Hinduism tells of superheroes with blue skin, multiple arms and cranial rivers.

I once said that I was vegetarian in an interview and justified it with some Buddhist mumbo jumbo about compassion. After that, even the girls Ian was hitting on began looking at me like I knew the meaning of life. I had to stop wearing my wooden bead necklace. Too much responsibility. But if people were willing to think I'm a spiritual leader, what does that say about where people are willing to place their faith? It's annoying when some cricket player hits a great shot and points to the sky, as if God has nothing better to do than make sure a ball travels a few feet farther. Principle #1: you create your own destiny.

My view on the matter may have been formed one fateful day in London many years ago. Mum and my aunts dragged Pankaj, Shushruth, Vineeta and me to the Hindu temple, as they did every week during our childhood. Dad never came, saying things like, "Today I have to work so that we can feed you, which is what God wants most."

The Shiva-Vishnu temple we attended in Ealing faced another temple across the street, where South Indians worshipped the same Gods using different names (i.e. Venkateswar-Balaji). The two sects had built separate temples because their spiritual leaders in India gave conflicting advice about the most auspicious directional entrance to the temple. We typically arrived late to the converted lecture room, settling behind a few hundred people in the lotus position on the floor in front of the four-armed idol of Vishnu in the center, his four-armed wife Lakshmi to his right, and a shivalingam to the left. Streams of incense smoke meandered to the ceiling and filled the room with a mystical scent. A bearded priest with a string necklace, orange robe and wiry white hairs sprouting between droopy weathered pecs droned incantations none of us understood while intermittently tossing rose petals or oil on a small fire. Then he stopped to deliver wisdom with the cadence of a beat poet and head motion of a ballad singer.

"In this life, there are……...three things, we must all wish for……The first is to love all people……..The second....is to love ourselves……...and the most important.....is to love God. Because God is in all of us……...the three things are really one."

I made Pankaj and Shushruth sit in front of me so that I could maneuver a gray stick figure away from falling hammers on Pankaj's portable Nintendo Game & Watch. Every time I set a new high score, I pointed to the priest in emulation of a cricket batsman. He looked at me perplexed. Once in a while Mum would look back and tell me to be quiet if she heard me talking or shifting too vigorously in and out of the lotus position. Vineeta echoed Mum's expression through her Coke bottle glasses to emphasize my immaturity.

"I once knew a woman………she told me about her son, who had become, very sick….She asked me to ask God to heal her son…."

Tears infected Mum's eyes. Vineeta sombrely pursed her lips. My aunts shook their heads in sympathy. What struck me as absurd even at that age was how Shushruth's mom fervently thanked Shiva for providing her with Shushruth through her sister, while never faulting him for making her infertile in the first place.

My Hinduism knowledge mainly consisted of the entertaining mythology I had learned from Amar Chitra Katha comic books—the avatars of Vishnu, the adventures of the Pandavas, the life of Krishna. The larger concepts of karma, reincarnation and nirvana sounded magical, but didn't comport with the reality of maintaining the lotus position for two hours in a crowded room with a spectrum of the kind and the malicious, the generous and the greedy, all of whom controlled their own choices.

I was furiously avoiding falling hammers on the Nintendo when I was just one hundred points from the high score. I decided to challenge Vishnu—"if you're there, stop me from getting the high score"—which he didn't. The rest of the sermon, I kept offering him new challenges—"make the priest shut up right…..now". "Make Pankaj fart." When none of those things happened, I decided that something wasn't true simply because an old piece of paper said so. If I was going to put faith in someone that made no sense, it might as well be me.

I don't judge the others for going to the temple. Though most religions make Star Wars look like a documentary, they all get the basic notions of human behavior correct. Principle #2: while I encourage you to eschew cumbersome headgear if coolness matters to you more than piety, it's okay to visit the mosque, temple or church once in a while to pick up some tips on how to behave and form a community. Just don't go overboard and start consulting astrologers about the most auspicious time to become cool.

Chapter 16
Ravi's apartment
Manhattan, New York

Pankaj

After months of using taxis, Pankaj decided to brave the subway system. He waited for the A/C train, but on the third B/D train in a row, he capitulated and boarded, crammed in with people from nations he could only guess—Jamaicans, Guyanese, Puerto Ricans, Chinese, Vietnamese. Then he made the mistake of disembarking at 14th street instead of West 4th, lost in a subterranean maze of people.

"*Om Mani Padme Hum, Om Mani Padme Hum*," Pankaj chanted to himself to literally *praise the jewel in the lotus*, but metaphorically *transform his body, speech and mind into that of the Buddha* so that he wouldn't get frustrated.

Since returning from the retreat the prior weekend, the chanting and meditation had replaced checking the markets every hour, while the Noble Truths—everything is impermanent, he shouldn't cling to unsatisfactory things, there is no such thing as self—had helped him stop worrying about how he would be perceived on the subway or while walking the streets. He liked that Buddhism gave him control over himself by detaching himself from his emotions. It was also consistent with his upbringing, a syncretic religion that shared many of the tenets of Hinduism.

He picked a random exit, climbed the stairs and tried to surmise which way was southwest without using up the data limits on his phone. An indirect forty minute walk later, past chain stores and ice cream shops, large restaurants and red brick churches, run-down knick-knack stores and tarot card readers, townhouses and warehouses, he finally made it to Ravi's building with pink ears and a mucus-stained set of leather gloves. He paused to check in with the doorman after going through the revolving doors, but the doorman was retrieving a package so he continued to the elevator to Ravi's floor.

They had agreed to meet for a drink earlier in the week, though Pankaj planned to surprise Ravi by taking him for dinner at Ocho Cinco in appreciation of the retreat, which had jolted Pankaj from a lingering sense of anxiety. He also needed some advice for his coffee date the next day with a girl he had met after meditating at a Buddhist Center in the city.

He had been rolling up his mat when she had introduced herself. At first he had wondered whether she was going to try to pitch him on expensive personal training sessions or to recruit him into some cult. Instead, she had simply noted that she hadn't seen him meditating there before and noticed how intently entranced he had seemed, like he had been meditating for years. She had been hoping he could give her some guidance on how to focus better. He wouldn't have noticed her on his own, but who was he to turn down a request from a girl with a nice smile wearing tights to go for coffee? She had looked at him in a way he had never seen other than in ads and movies. He needed tips on how to cultivate the relationship. The fact that she was from the Caribbean might require some finessing with his parents in the future, but he figured that maybe Ravi would have some ideas about that, too.

He walked down the hall and heard voices in Ravi's apartment. Maybe Ian was joining? He knocked and heard the voices stop. After a pause, Ravi's muffled voice rang out.

"Who is it?"

"Pankaj."

Were they whispering something about him? No, he wasn't going to be drawn in by negative thoughts. There were lots of reasons they might be whispering. Ravi cracked the door open.

"Yo," Pankaj said.

"Yo."

"Yo-Yo Ma," Pankaj said.

There, he could show that he had a sense of humor.

"Yo Mama. Um, what's up? What are you doing here?"

Ravi's face looked tense. Pankaj had never seen him so humorless.

"Remember, we had agreed to meet for a drink?"

Pankaj had considered confirming earlier in the day, but hadn't wanted to seem needy.

"Is this…not a good time?" Pankaj continued.

"That's…one way of putting it."

Why had Ravi hardly opened the door? Pankaj felt his blood rising. He couldn't remember the chant, but told himself to calm down.

"Dude, we made plans."

Ravi seemed to be indicating something with his eyes and a head tilt. Suddenly Pankaj remembered. This was Ravi's re-payment day. But he also vaguely recalled that the meeting time was three, and it was already after five. Beyond which, Ravi was going to repay the man.

"If you're going to make obvious, just let him in," an Eastern European voice from the apartment said.

Ravi rolled his eyes.

"Fuck."

Ravi opened the door further, and Pankaj saw a tall, stocky man with a buzz cut, black t-shirt and a tan Members Only jacket standing by the far wall in front of a poster of the guitarist from The Clash smashing his guitar. Pankaj debated whether to step in or run away, but felt awkward leaving Ravi in whatever situation he was in. He stepped in, and Ravi closed the door.

"Who are you? You are friend?" the man asked Pankaj.

"Is this the guy…" Pankaj said.

Ravi nodded.

"Not exactly a friend," Pankaj said.

"Family?" the man asked.

Pankaj looked at Ravi, unsure if he should answer.

"You two are together?" the man asked.

"What?" Pankaj asked while Ravi guffawed.

"I don't know. He doesn't like to talk about women, you say you aren't friend or family. You're like banker?"

"Why do you say that?"

The man waved his hand up and down.

"Shirt, pants, shoes."

The man suddenly fixated on Pankaj's hand and waved Pankaj over.

"Let me see watch."

Pankaj walked over and held out his hand for Dalinc to see. The man moved Pankaj's wrist back and forth with his meaty hands as if trying to determine if it was authentic. Pankaj worried that his watch might end up becoming a part of the discussion, but felt a dissettling dissonance between this thought and the chants he had repeated to himself all week—everything is impermanent, he shouldn't cling to unsatisfactory things. The problem was that the watch was satisfying—a sapphire blue chronometer with precision sub-dials and a self-winding mechanism—even if he knew it shouldn't be.

"Bru-get. This is expensive one?

"It cost a little."

The man nodded his head in respect and let go of Pankaj's hand. He relaxed, relieved that his watch was out of the limelight.

"This is Dalinc," Ravi said.

"Nice to meet. You have water?" Dalinc asked, turning to Ravi.

"Like, to drink?"

"What else, to take shower?"

"Flat or sparkling?"

"I try sparkling."

"There's a faucet and glasses in one of those cabinets," Ravi said. "I can blow in it if you want bubbles."

"You fucking…" Dalinc said, waving the back of his hand as if to slap Ravi.

Dalinc walked around the kitchen counter and rummaged through a few of the wall cabinets before taking a glass and getting some water. Pankaj looked at Ravi to ask questions using facial expressions—what the hell is happening, and what the hell are we going to do about it? Ravi was biting his lip and looking through Pankaj.

"This guy, he don't have even water. I look in fridge, only batteries. How you even afford to live here?" Dalinc said.

"I probably won't for much longer," Ravi said, turning toward Dalinc.

"Well, today you don't pay, I break fingers," Dalinc said, returning to the living room.

Ravi looked at his hands and wiggled his fingers.

"Normally a right-handed person would say the left hand, but I need that one for fingering the guitar. So maybe the pinkie on the right hand? Or this being the first one, maybe the pinkie toe on my left foot?"

Dalinc looked at his phone.

"Once I'm done, it won't be pinkie anymore."

Didn't Ravi have the money? Pankaj started intensely perspiring. What was happening?

At the Buddhist retreat, Roshi had made Pankaj realize he needed to evaluate relationships with greater detachment. When Ravi wasn't ditching him at casinos and mocking him in guides, Ravi was entertaining and generous. They had shared so many experiences together that they would always be a part of each other's lives. Pankaj had loved Ravi like a brother, and with a little more work, could feel the same way again. Roshi had recommended that rather than going through cycles of camaraderie and silence with Ravi, he needed to maintain the right distance at which they interacted. He needed to focus on the ways in which Ravi could make his life better and capitalize on those things, like career and dating advice, while firmly declining to get drawn into things that would agitate him. Roshi had suggested that at their next meeting, which was today, Pankaj try to start the relationship fresh, without any of the emotional baggage of the past.

As with all things Ravi, leveraging Ravi's skills with women and calibrating the distance of their relationship sounded simple in theory. In practice, Pankaj had fallen into the middle of a loan dispute with overtones of physical mayhem. Maybe Roshi was wrong. Maybe Ravi was beyond redemption. Could Pankaj get out of the apartment before the thug detained him? But if something happened to Ravi, the cops would easily be able to figure out from the elevator cameras that Pankaj had been there. What would his family think then?

Dalinc walked over and showed a picture to Ravi. Pankaj scooted next to him to observe a group of fingers bent at a right angle.

"Shit…" Ravi said. "You didn't really do that, did you?"

Ravi's face contorted as if understanding for the first time that this thug might actually break his hands.

"I thought you said you were getting the money," Pankaj said softly.

Had Ravi been lying the whole time? Or was he in deeper trouble than he had let on? Was this whole thing drug related?

"I was. But then I changed my mind," Ravi said without looking up from the phone.

Dalinc jerked his head towards Ravi.

"What kind of stupid this is? You don't have money?"

"Well, I was about to get it, but if I did, it would have left a lot of people unhappy, and I'm trying…"

"You could have got money?" Dalinc asked aggressively, nodding his head with emphasis. "You said today you pay me."

Dalinc waved one hand in disbelief.

"Why would you change your mind?" Pankaj asked.

Ravi walked over to his sofa and sat down. In the windows behind, Pankaj could see the downtown high-rises. Ravi held his face in both hands before slowly combing his fingers back through his hair, staring at the floor and looking back up for his sentence.

"The show…didn't feel right."

"Are you sure you have the luxury to decide what's right and wrong?" Pankaj asked.

"It's probably the only luxury I haven't taken very often."

Ravi looked at Pankaj and moved his eyes just a few degrees into a detached acceptance. Ravi's penitence was a whole another level of crazy. While Pankaj was glad he wouldn't be the butt of Ravi's jokes, if their positions had been reversed, Pankaj would have taken the show, especially with a loan shark threatening to maim him.

"Is this for me? Because I'll be fine," Pankaj said.

Ravi's brows furrowed as he gathered his thoughts.

"It's been easy making art for myself. At some point I figured out how to make it for other people. But the real challenge is making it so that the people you care about the most like it." Ravi turned toward Dalinc. "Before you do whatever you do to me, can you just let him go? He has nothing to do with this."

Yes, that's right. This wasn't Pankaj's problem, and he would happily leave without looking like a coward by suggesting it himself.

"I don't have time for feely-touchy stuff," Dalinc said.

In a magical transition from the verbal to the physical, Dalinc seemed to finish his sentence while simultaneously placing his glass on the coffee table, grabbing Pankaj and hammerlocking his arm behind his back. Pankaj cries through the man's meaty hand and weighed biting the man's fingers vs. the consequence of upsetting him further. A painful yank to his shoulder cleared away this debate, and he kicked his legs as the hulk leaned back to lift him into the air.

"Jesus, stop! I'm the one who owes you money!" Ravi shouted, jumping up from the sofa.

"Yes, but he's the one who actually has. And he's getting on nerves."

Pankaj felt his panicked eyes observing Ravi rush over to yank on Dalinc's arm.

"Let him go! Fuck up my arm if you have to."

"Okay, your choice."

Dalinc released Pankaj and leapt toward Ravi.

Ravi

Ravi closed his eyes tight and internalized the pain that Pankaj had externalized while Pankaj massaged his arm. Was that a muscle or tendon ripping? The pain was more effective in clearing his mind of thought than meditation. He could feel Dalinc's heat and belly on his back. He opened his eyes and saw Pankaj on the verge of tears. If Dalinc had been on time, at least Pankaj would never have known about all this. What was Dalinc's endgame? He didn't seem concerned that Pankaj would run out or shout for help, though in New York no one was likely to help anyway. Unlike Londoners, they all assumed if you were getting clocked, you probably deserved to be clocked.

A second yank made Ravi grimace and close his eyes again.

"Aaaaahhhh," Ravi moaned.

"Feel like calling papa?" Dalinc asked.

Ravi shook his head.

"You better come up with idea. Right now, your arm okay in three days. If I pull a little more," Dalinc said, tightening the arm lock a few more millimeters, "maybe it takes two months. And if you wait another minute to find out how far I can pull …"

Dalinc clicked his tongue and whistled, looking back at Pankaj.

As wasp-sting pulses fired through the nerves of his arm, Ravi's stopped wondering whether he was an idiot for passing on the sitcom. His mind dissolved into visions of the prior week. He had called his agent and said he didn't want to do the sitcom unless he had complete artistic control. She had argued with him for over an hour, clearly exasperated. She had called him back a day later to see if he had simply been having a fit of "artistic temperament". When he had held steadfast, she had called the network, which had promptly nixed the idea and after he had refused to relent, his advance.

The pain subsided slightly. He had made the right decision. How could he fulfill his duty—that's the word he had always avoided, an actual obligation to be fulfilled rather than simply exercising an option to do something nice—to his family if he sold them out by making a caricature version of them? By making a sitcom that suggested it was Indians' duty to conform to America without also suggesting that it was America's duty to blend its heritage with the people entering?

His agent had, to her credit, acknowledged some admiration at Ravi's newfound integrity, though her tone also had suggested some skepticism about whether it would last. She had asked if he was dating someone, clearly implying that he was under the unfortunate influence of some Svengali. He had mentioned Lakhi, though he had made clear that Lakhi was advocating for him to do the show. When he had asked his agent to pursue his talk show idea, she had seemed dismissive, but to his surprise, had called back on Friday with the teaser that PBS was interested. Which was interesting, but not interesting enough that Dalinc would care unless it included a re-payment.

Ravi considered asking Vineeta or his father for money, but if someone else bailed him out yet again, when would he ever become the man he wanted to be? He needed to fix this mess to remind himself not to get into another one in the future, and to stop involving other people in his drama. He looked over at his guitars. The Taylor acoustic on which he had written "Hey Love". The Fender Jaguar electric on which he had written "Shake Shake Shake". The Les Paul replica he had used to record "Blow Out the Moon". This Siddhartha complex was going to strip him down to his core.

"The guitars," he offered.

"What I do with guitars?" Dalinc asked.

"They're worth a few thousand."

"Too little and too heavy. I'm not EBay."

He had been expecting the guitars to buy him a few more weeks. Now what? He had reached a point in the cycle of pain where he had accepted that his arm may never be of use again. Having accepted this truth, he just needed to remember that the pain itself was only temporary. Hallucinatory thoughts seemed to address his need for money—he could start working for Dalinc. He could sell all his things on EBay and move back in with his parents. He could do a David Blaine type special where they filmed how long Ravi could handle this excruciating arm lock.

He saw Pankaj looking desperately at his watch. Was he timing Ravi's tolerance for pain? Did he have somewhere to be?

Pankaj looked at Dalinc sadly.

"Take the watch. It's yours," Pankaj said.

His hand trembled as he unstrapped the watch and held it out to Dalinc. Dalinc loosened his grip ever so slightly, which allowed a surge of blood into Ravi's arm and a sharp tingling sensation. If Dalinc reached out for the watch, it would at least give Ravi some temporary relief.

"How much worth?"

"Thirty thousand. It's the Marine edition. You can look it up."

Dalinc released Ravi's left arm.

"Awwwwwhh," Ravi moaned, leaning over, breathing out and massaging his shoulder. He tested the arm. It functioned, though it hurt to lift it up more than a few degrees. Blood slowly returned to his brain so that he could think again. Dalinc began looking the watch up on his phone. Ravi looked at Pankaj from his crouch.

"Don't give him the watch. This is my problem," Ravi said.

"What fucking idiot you are. He wants to give, you take," Dalinc said without looking up from his phone. "I want to take, he gives. It's like *Fiddler on the Roof.* He is matchmaker. You know this song, 'If I were a Rich Man'?"

"Yeah, I know it," Ravi said, trying to figure out if Dalinc was going to make a crack about Pankaj being the rich man, Dalinc becoming the rich man or Ravi not being the rich man.

"Good song," he said, swiping on his phone.

Ravi looked at Pankaj again.

"Why are you doing this?"

Pankaj's eyes shifted a few times before he looked back at Ravi.

"You'd do it for me. Probably after you caused me to get in debt in the first place, but that's a different conversation. Anyway, I bought it to show it off to my colleagues, and they just made fun of me for getting the rubber strap instead of the fifty thousand dollar titanium one. You can do all the right things, and getting a promotion still comes down to who's the bosses' best friend. Which is why Buddhism makes so much sense. Everything is impermanent. We shouldn't cling to unsatisfactory things. There's no such thing as self. So it was meant to be."

Pankaj was standing a little more erect. Ravi looked at him in appreciation and resignation. He would pay Pankaj back. He had just proven he could be responsible when he set his mind to it.

Dalinc's head bobbed up and down in satisfaction as he looked up. He strapped the watch to his wrist and admired it. Ravi caressed his arm and tested it again. Still hard to lift up. He probably had a torn rotator cuff.

"You okay?" he asked Pankaj.

"Not too bad. I didn't get it as badly as you did."

Dalinc waved his arms out as if they were the best of friends greeting each other for the first time.

"Pleasure meeting. If watch is fake, you will regret."

"It's definitely real," Pankaj said.

Dalinc headed to the door, before suddenly turning around. He was looking past Ravi and started walking in his direction. He brushed by Ravi. By the time Ravi realized Dalinc was reaching for his Fender, it was too late to object.

"Maybe my son wants to play guitar someday."

Dalinc returned to the door, allowing the guitar to swing and bang against it.

"Now hopefully I still have time to catch football match. You've heard of Nikola Kalinic? He's best player for Hajduk Split. My friends like Dinamo Zagreb, where I grew up, but father come from Split, so I watch them as kid."

"Don't really watch football," Ravi said.

"Well, don't matter. Anyways, hopefully we never see each other again. I like you. Stop gambling."

"Agreed. Give my best to your wife and son," Ravi said.

Dalinc nodded and left. Ravi followed Pankaj to the sofa, where they looked at each other for a few moments. Pankaj started shaking, and Ravi couldn't tell whether he was laughing or crying until he saw the tears and snot. He got up to get a paper towel for Pankaj from the kitchen. Pankaj cleaned his face and calmed down.

"That was scary. He could have…" Pankaj said.

"Yeah. I'm sorry. I tried to warn you."

"And he nearly broke your arm and you…gave regards to his family?" Pankaj asked.

"He's a nice guy when he's not threatening to kill you," Ravi said, still in disbelief as to what had just happened.

Pankaj chuckled through his tears.

"And you're an entertaining guy when you're not humiliating and endangering people. Figures you like hanging out together."

"Look, what you just did was…" Ravi said.

Ravi genuflected before Pankaj, kissing his feet like Shushruth had done with the housekeeper. It was an inspired gesture that he intended sincerely.

"Don't, man. I don't need that," Pankaj said standing up to move away. Ravi leaned his head in Pankaj's direction.

"I know I'm a shitty cousin. Thanks for being there. I'll pay you back," he said.

"Whenever, we'll figure it out," Pankaj said.

"As soon as I get paid for my next show, we can start a payment schedule."

Pankaj looked back at Ravi blankly.

"Are you speaking theoretically, or you actually have a show lined up?"

"Kind of in between."

"Fuck…." Pankaj said, massaging his wrist where his watch used to be.

Ravi saw Pankaj's lips moving as if he was chanting some four word phrase.

"It's a good thing, right? It means I'll be able to pay you back so you can get a new watch. The one with the titanium band. But for now, it's just a possibility anyway, it may not happen. And if it does, it will probably be sandwiched between *Sesame Street* and *Wall Street Week*, so who knows whether anyone will watch it."

Pankaj began biting his thumbnail

"I'm not worried just about the money."

"Oh, right. Well, it's not about you or anyone in the family. It's a talk show."

Ravi jumped back onto the sofa and explained the idea he had had at the retreat about examining cultural assimilation via dialogues with celebrities, and about using Buzzthief as the talk show house band, which might give the band new life.

"I'm sure it'll be good, but I can't believe you turned down a chance to pay back that maniac and save your life for a chance to be on a public television station," Pankaj said.

"Honestly, I can't believe it either, but I wanted to do something more meaningful the next go-around. Besides, when I get money, it doesn't tend to hang around very long. It's like all those presidents start fighting with each other in my wallet and some of them have to go. So the less I make, the less I will lose."

Pankaj sat back on the sofa.

"So now what? We're supposed to go to dinner, no?" Pankaj asked.

"I think the time has come for me to watch my budget," Ravi said.

"It's on me. I've been wanting to try this restaurant called Ocho Cinco."

"I've taken enough of your kindness for the day."

"Well it's not entirely free. I need some advice."

"About what?"

Pankaj explained that he had met a girl the prior week and wasn't sure how to talk to her in a manner that might mess things up before they started. Ravi grabbed his jacket from the closet and ushered them out of the apartment to the elevator bank while rambling out some advice.

"I'm sure you know you should pay for her. But if she doesn't offer to pay by the third date, call it off. Smile a lot and ask her questions. Don't say anything that you actually believe. Whatever she says, just agree with her."

"I don't want to pretend to be someone I'm not."

They boarded the empty elevator. Ravi tried to press the button with his left hand before switching to his right.

"Therein lies your problem. When they sold you that watch, did they say it tells time as well as a 5 dollar watch from Kmart, looks exactly like the knock-off version you can get for 50, and has a name no one outside of people on Wall Street have heard of? Or did they say it was an exclusive piece of art that you would pass down to your children? You've got to market yourself. She's pretending to be an enlightened and sophisticated New Yorker, you're pretending to be a chill British yogi. Once each of you has had a chance to take off the wrapper, you can worry about whether you plan on using the product forever."

The digital counter of the elevator ticked down as Pankaj looked down at his shoes and stepped one foot onto the other.

"And how exactly do you get to the part where you take off the wrapper?" he asked sheepishly.

Ravi knew Pankaj was hopeless, but he had never been sure if Pankaj had ever kissed a girl or not before until now.

"If she's willing to come to your apartment, she wants it as much as you do. You just can't be overeager. Have a glass of wine, sit next to her on the couch, and at some point when there's a moment of silence, she'll look at you straight in the eyes. That means you should lean forward, etcetera etcetera. Just make sure you've taken precautions for in case the moment progresses".

The elevator gently glided to a stop and released them into the lobby.

"And when do you usually tell your parents you're dating someone?" Pankaj asked.

"You're not really dating until it's been at least a couple of months, and you haven't even gone on one date."

"Right, I get that, but on the off-chance we're still dating in a few months… she's from Caribbean, and I don't know what I'd tell my parents."

"Well, thanks to Vineeta, you have precedence to refer to. And given that she's from the Caribbean, there's a good chance she's got some Indian blood. We were slaves down there just like the blacks. So you can just tell your parents she's part Indian," Ravi said.

"She doesn't look Indian."

"And you don't look like Brad Pitt, so tell them you're even."

"What's with you and Brad Pitt?"

"I suppose nothing. He's rich and famous, and I…I'm just Ravi Anjani. But I kind of like it that way."

They waited to hail a cab in front of the building. Somehow, some way, Ravi had become who he was always supposed to be.

Part III
Just Desserts
May 2008

Excerpt from
Ravi's Guide to Being a Cool Indian

Final Thoughts

You may be thinking, but Ravi, didn't your last album flop? Are you really still cool? Why should I listen to you? The great John Lennon is known for giving peace a chance, only needing love and imagining a brotherhood of man, yet abandoned his first wife and son so he could diddle women across the globe. The messenger may be flawed, but the message remains.

Life is a negotiation for who you want to be and who society wants you to be. Sometimes you win, sometimes society wins, and sometimes you realize you didn't want to be the person you thought you did. I have imparted the wisdom for you to find a better you, to navigate the shores upon which your parents landed in search of a more prosperous future. It is your duty to fulfill the destiny they were seeking by speaking in hipper lingo, wearing more stylish clothes and helping to define the culture, all while retaining the essential familial values of being Indian. Go forth and be cool, and don't forget to invite me to your next party.

Chapter 17
The Premiere
Manhattan, New York

Ravi

Ravi headed from his apartment to the Corner Bistro near 8th Avenue. If a visitor asked what was so special about the West Village, Ravi couldn't have pointed to a specific landmark or feature. Tall, medium and short buildings sat side by side in brick, concrete or glass, some covered in green scaffolding every few blocks for building repairs, a few covered in graffiti on the side of an exposed wall. Bikes that weren't worth stealing were locked up in front of caged basketball courts. Parked cars obscured the trees, and trees obscured the sky.

But he would tell the visitor to walk through the Village on a spring weekend to see the pedestrians in a motley array of clothing—gray suits, rainbow clown suits, Bergdorf Goodman summer dresses, black trash bags, slim fit cuffed jeans, oversized jeans with exposed underwear. The Village was a carnivalesque college town, a wild music video, a surreal dream. Clothing, age and mental fitness didn't matter here. Everyone was unified by a single pursuit—getting to their next destination fast, as evidenced by the, cars, taxis and buses jockeying for pole position to be the first to the next red light. What was the next destination? Usually one of the restaurants, cafes or bars catering to every ethnicity and socio-economic group.

Ravi waltzed into the Bistro in a cream linen jacket Lakhi had bought him for his birthday when they were puttering around SoHo a few weekends before. It was his first luxury in months, along with this night out. With Lakhi's help in drafting a budget and actually adhering to it—meals at home, movies at home, basically everything at home—he had already paid off his credit cards and a quarter of Pankaj's loan with his modest income from the talk show. He spotted his cousins at the counter.

"Gents," he said, embracing Shushruth and in turn Pankaj with a bro-hug.

Shushruth had flown in for the taping of the premiere and was staying with Pankaj. His hair was short and slickly parted, as if his wife had tried to give him a hip look but had just made him look like an elementary school-boy. Pankaj was now sporting a mini pony-tail. Ravi had suggested they catch up on their own, before meeting Lakhi, Vineeta and Ian for dinner. Ravi ordered their preferred drinks at the counter before they organized into a triangle.

"It means a lot to me that you flew out," Ravi said.

"How could I miss it? This is a big deal," Shushruth said.

Ravi hadn't invited anyone to his Cool Kid's premiere. Why did this show feel more important? Maybe because he actually cared what his family thought about it. Was there anything in the first episode that would offend them? The second and third? He hoped he got the hang of not offending people so that he didn't have to think about it so much.

"So what's new? How's married life?"

"Falguni is pregnant," Shushruth said, beaming with pride.

So much for Ravi's wedding present. Keep it to himself. What was the word for it? Anodyne. Be Anodyne, like a new superhero.

"Congrats! That's awesome. When's the due date?"

"It's only been two months, so we're not telling everyone, but I thought you should know. Maybe don't mention it to your parents or it'll get back to my parents and then to Falguni, and she'll get upset."

Ravi nodded. Pankaj gave Ravi a look suggesting that she got upset a lot.

"There's no question the world could use another Shushruth. Cheers," Ravi said, raising his glass for the others clink. "And you, how did your date go?"

He looked over at Pankaj, who had stopped dating the woman from the yoga studio. Or more accurately, had been rescued from the relationship by Ravi. After three months, she had managed to move in with Pankaj, initially seeding his apartment with her clothes and toiletries on weekend stayovers and subsequently announcing she had given up her lease on her apartment. At first Pankaj had felt flattered until it had gradually dawned on him that she had an active social life that didn't include him. After a series of fights in which she had avoided detailing who she was socializing with, he had reached out to Ravi for advice. Ravi had made him change his locks and leave all of her things in two discount suitcases with the doorman for her to pick up.

Recently he had squired Pankaj to an event organized by the Network of Indian Professionals, working the room until they had found a woman open to meeting Pankaj for a date.

Pankaj shrugged his shoulders.

"We met for a coffee, but I'm not sure it'll go anywhere."

"Well, there are plenty of fish in the sea," Ravi offered.

Anodyne. He was Anodyne.

"Yes, you're a very eligible bachelor. You know, I forgot! You made Managing Director. We have to have a special toast," Shushruth said.

"To the honorable yogi investment banker, Pankaj Shah," Ravi said, again raising his glass for them to clink.

The three musketeers, armed with beers instead of swords. Their arms formed a pyramid, each one necessary to keep the whole thing from falling apart.

"You know, I wanted this promotion a long time, but it wasn't until Buddhism showed me that it wasn't that important that I was able to act the way I needed to get it. Kind of ironic. So to the extent there's something you really want, you should give the meditation another try, though the satisfaction of getting it won't be what you think," Pankaj said.

"That's good advice, I should definitely start meditating," Shushruth said.

Pankaj had annoyingly started making pronouncements like a wise sage, but it wasn't like Buddhism had taught him how to manipulate the firm into giving him a promotion or how to extricate himself from a bad relationship. But Ravi wasn't going to say so. Anodyne. Be Anodyne.

"Agreed, we could all use more spirituality in our lives," Ravi said.

After they spend half an hour catching up on the details of their lives, Ravi noted they should leave for their seven o'clock dinner reservation. Lakhi had convinced him that showing up where and when the time was right could actually be the same place and time he had agreed to. They walked five blocks to Crispo on 14th, where Vineeta, Ian and Lakhi were waiting behind a floral wrought iron gate to receive a series of cheek kisses and handshakes and shoulder hugs. They entered through the cabana door extension into a brick room aglow with warm yellow lights and arranged with wooden café tables. A server led them to their table, where Pankaj funded a bottle of cab and an appetizer order of gorgonzola stuffed green olives, stuffed zucchini flowers, bufala mozzarella and beef steak tomato caprese and burrata with figs.

"So Ravi was telling me you started at a law firm?" Pankaj asked Lakhi.

With the make-up and dress she had worn tonight, she didn't look like the same woman Ravi had started dating. She had also grown her hair out at his request, which made her look more feminine.

"I took a paralegal job. For a long time I thought I wanted to be a writer, but I think writing jobs have specific requirements that can be quite different from what you want to write, and trying to get the things you want to write published requires a lot of time and effort without paying any bills."

Ravi was thankful that she had left off that Ravi's show could only afford a single writer, and he couldn't afford to hire someone with no experience. He had chosen an Indian writer who had worked on *The Daily Show* and some episodes of *The Office*. Lakhi had said she understood, and also had thought it would complicate their relationship if they worked together. So she had accepted a friend's invitation to apply for a position at the law firm where her friend was a paralegal.

"That's a good position, I have friends who are doing that," Vineeta said. "If you're ever interested in a position at the UN, let me know."

"Thanks, I might take you up on that at some point."

"How's your consulting thing going?" Ravi asked Ian.

He and Lakhi met up with Vineeta and Ian once or twice a month. Sometimes they hung out with Ravi's other friends or with Lakhi's friends or nobody else at all. Friendship was a zero sum game. One minute with one person meant one less minute with another. So he wasn't always up to date on Vineeta and Ian's latest happenings. He felt awkward asking either one about the state of their relationship because it felt like he was betraying the one he hadn't asked the question. The way Vineeta held Ian's arm whenever he saw them suggested things were going the right way.

"I like it. It was hard to get assignments at first because it had been so long, but once the first employer told the agency I was good, I started getting more offers. I'm doing research for a think tank now. It can be a little tedious, but it pays the bills," Ian said.

"That's the theme of the night. To paying the bills!" Ravi said, lifting his still empty wine glass for everyone to clink.

They broke off into a few side conversations as the waitress arrived with the wine and baskets of bread.

"How are you feeling about tomorrow?" Vineeta asked him, seated directly to his right. "Ian says the rehearsals went well."

The original bassist and drummer had declined joining the reunion, so Ravi had hired session musicians, including a keyboard player.

"The new guys are better musicians than I am. It took them one rehearsal to nail all our hits. We needed another session to get down show cues and little fill-ins, but they're pros."

"Well, it should be good. It will be good. I'm proud of you. I know it wasn't easy choosing this over the sitcom," Vineeta said, splitting a stuffed olive with her teeth.

Ravi kind of wished he had done the sitcom. Being a clown came more naturally to him than interviewing first and second generation immigrants to glean greater truths about assimilation and humanity. But maybe he was just fearful of failing.

They spent the rest of the evening in restrained chats about real estate, vacations and the weather. In the old days, Ravi would have closed down the bar and told wild stories from his days on tour. Now as each of them had started pairing off and defining who they wanted to be, Ravi felt less of a need to amuse everyone by testing their limits. He knew it was a step forward, committing to ideals that were greater than himself—love, justice, friendship, real estate. In New York, always real estate. But inside these new walls, in which he became Anodyne and no longer ribbed the others about their foibles, also meant that something had been lost.

They split up after dinner. Ravi and Lakhi walked home in a side-hug against a strong easterly wind. They compared notes on conversations from the evening. She was his new confidante, the one he could drop his façade and discuss foibles as much as he wanted without worrying about being judged.

In the morning, Ravi sensed Lakhi turning over on the other side of the bed. From the Queen Murphy bed, he could see everything in their tiny five hundred square foot studio apartment—the kitchen, sofa, television and Mondrian reproduction on the wall facing them. It cost three thousand a month, but by moving in together, they were able to split the rent.

He stepped out of bed, feeling just the right level of energy for the taping of the show's premiere. Some mornings he felt tired, others so energetic that it was hard to focus on a single task because it felt like he was making inadequate progress for the level of energy he possessed. Today he was laser-focused after months of designing the talk show set, hiring a writer, developing themes and format, and booking guests. He would go to the studio for a make-up pat down, rehearse with the band, practice his monologue, tell his writer which questions he wanted to use, welcome his family to the set and tape the show.

After a quick shower and shave, he fingered through a stack of t-shirts in the closet. *Legend* or *The Queen is Dead*? *Queen II* or *Unforgettable Fire* or *Songs in the Key of Life*? He wasn't sure if he should go with the group he liked best or was most mainstream or reflected Buzzthief's sound. Ian had already chosen *Aladdin Sane*, the one that would have satisfied all of these conditions. He yanked out an arm-thrusting silhouette of Freddie Mercury, the original Indian rock God. Cool, ingenious, flamboyant, excessive. Take away the genius and he and Ravi weren't all that different.

People celebrated Mercury's excess because of his genius. People resented Ravi's excess because he wasn't one, and now he had to go back to being a mortal. Mercury had abandoned his name, Farrokh Bulsara, and never had the chance to take it back. Instead of returning to life as a mortal, he had burnt out with his excess.

Perfect.

Ravi layered on a blue linen sports jacket, indigo jeans and Converse shoes while Lakhi showered. He mentally ran through some of the one-liners his writer had written him. As he prepared coffee and toasted a couple of bagels, Lakhi began dolling herself up in traditional Indian clothing, the charade he had asked her to continue until his mum had fully accepted that they were living together. His mum was happy that Lakhi was Indian, even if she was Punjabi. Ravi told Lakhi to talk a lot about cooking and Indian movies with his mum, which had worked pretty well the previous day when they had met his parents for lunch.

He ate his bagel standing up and announced, "I think I'm ready. I'm going to go to the studio to prep."

"Are you excited?" she said while adding a necklace at the dresser mirror.

Excitement was for when you were confident in what you were doing. Ravi had no idea what he was doing with his show. Would people really want to listen to a discussion about being Indian? Maybe the sitcom would have been less insightful but more effective. But he had never backed away from ambition and risk. If he was going to fail, better to fail trying to be innovative.

"More focused."

"Well, enjoy it, you're going to be awesome."

She came over for a waist hug and face stare. He wasn't sure whether to interpret her wide-open eyes as pride or connection or joy. They kissed before he went down to hail a taxi to the PBS studio on West 33rd.

He greeted the crewmembers who were setting things up and checked the tuning of his guitar. The instruments were set off to the side in front of a blue curtain. Ian wandered in.

"Well, this is it," Ravi said across the stage.

"Yeah. You excited?"

"It's weird, at one point we played before ten thousand fans, now we're doing this. It's like we're starting all over again. But that can be exciting, I suppose," Ravi said.

"I bet more than 10,000 people watch the show. It'll actually be a bigger audience."

"Yeah, but they're not tuning in just for the band. Maybe it'll help sales of the back catalogue and we can go on tour once we'd taped the full season."

"If we think of it, like, I don't know, maybe a permanent side gig, then we can never be disappointed. We still have some fans, which is better than starting out."

Ravi hoped the band would become popular again, but also knew that for now, his main focus should be on being an effective talk show host while Ian's main focus should be on the consulting gigs.

"That's a good way to think about it. It was a little hard to let go at first, you know, because we created it," Ravi said.

"It will always be there. The hits we had are still good songs."

"Good doesn't make it immortal. How many composers does anyone remember from Mozart's time? Probably only Mozart. So outside of the Beatles, the Stones and maybe Stevie Wonder, the rest probably don't even make it to the clearance bin in a hundred years."

"We're in good company, then. Bowie, The Smiths, U2, Prince. Well, maybe not them, but Men at Work, Terence Trent D'Arby, Frankie Goes to Hollywood."

"Frankie Goes to Hollywood?"

"'Relax' is pretty good."

"We had, like, three hits."

"Okay, Counting Crows then. I'll take that. We touched someone's life. Someone's listening to one of our songs right now," Ian said.

"Well, I'm glad I took the ride with you," Ravi said, lifting his hand for a fist bump.

"Same," Ian said.

The other band members arrived to prep their equipment. When they were ready, the band rehearsed two songs, pausing to discuss tempo, stage movements and dynamics. They discussed when they would add musical flourishes throughout the show. A sound engineer adjusted their volumes until Ravi was summoned to the front desk.

Vineeta and his parents had just been adorned with necklace guest passes. He could see his mum beaming with pride over this pass which was completely unnecessary because no one was trying to sneak in to see his show. He finished hugging them when Shushruth and Pankaj arrived. Shushruth rushed forward to touch Ravi's parents' feet as a show of respect, while they touched his head to bless him with long life and prosperity. Pankaj bowed slightly instead of reaching all the way down to their feet to accept a tap on the shoulder.

Ravi ushered all of them into the front row of the taping studio. Most of the audience seating was still empty. Bharti turned around to the two females behind her.

"This is my son."

When they only nodded politely, she continued.

"This is his show. My son," she said, pointing to Ravi.

He nodded, though he knew that they were bored tourists or housewives who had been recruited off the street.

"Oh, you must be proud," one of the women played along.

Bharti beamed with pride and turned back around.

"Anyone want *thepla*?" she asked, pulling out a Ziplocked stack of pungent flat breads from her purse.

"Mum, don't open that! There's no food allowed in here. And everyone will smell it," Vineeta said.

"Just one, what's wrong? Pankaj, you take one?"

"No auntie, we just had breakfast, I'm fine."

Ravi took one and folded it up into his hand, though everyone else declined. Bharti returned the edible stink bomb to her purse.

A stagehand tapped Ravi on the shoulder to tell him that Lakhi had arrived in the lobby with a cohort of fifteen mostly-Indian friends.

"I've got to greet some more people. This is George, he's going to take care of you from here on out," Ravi told his family, motioning to the stagehand. "The make-up artist in the back can touch you up with powder so the lights don't reflect off your face."

Ravi left to meet Lakhi, thanking her friends for coming before leading them to their seats. Some of his and Ian's friends and industry associates were also coming, though they were more likely to show right before the deadline so that he could only chat with them after the show.

He retreated to his changing room to go over his monologue and study the writer's notes about the interview. He tapped his foot nervously while swiveling in his chair. He heard the audience outside starting cheering, and after a pause, cheering even more loudly. The show director was coaching them to cheer enthusiastically every time the applause sign came on.

Ravi had done numerous interviews for *Cool Kids*, but that was months ago. Not to mention that he had always viewed that job as slapstick, an opportunity to ridicule his guests rather than explore serious topics and be funny without being offensive. Now his heart was beating loudly as he tried to do something different and become someone new, all while inaugurating his show with non-celebrity guests.

An assistant summoned him once everything was ready. From behind the curtain, he spotted some of his friends chatting with each other or lost in thought. The stagehands had somehow managed to complete the audience with tourists plucked from the street. The show's director motioned to the stagehands to shut the lights off and leave the studio in blackness. Ravi waited behind a curtain as Buzzthief started building orchestral notes and a tabla beat into a crescendo with funky thumps. He strapped on his guitar for his moment to shine.

A spotlight dramatically revealed Ravi slamming out a sitar-like improvisation as two Bharatnatyam dancers slinked around him and Ian began yelping "whoo hoos". As previously instructed by the show's director, the crowd stood up and clapped. He walked up behind Ian, who started singing a refrain Ravi had composed for the show—*You're in the right place, at the right time, pull a chair up, pour a glass of wine, listen closely, pay attention, for enlightening conversation*. His heart slowed back down as he played, almost in time with every other beat of the song.

They closed the intro with a count-off, and Ravi left his guitar on a stand before assuming the mike. The beaming lights triggered a drop of perspiration, but he had been instructed not to wipe his face given all the make-up. He pretended he could see the audience, but the intense spotlights made it hard to even recognize his family with the glare.

"Thanks for watching, I'm Ravi Anjani, former host of *Cool Kids* and guitarist for the band Buzzthief, which conveniently is the house band. The only way we could convince PBS to greenlight the show, two for the price of one. I'll bring them back later this show. This week, we've lined up some amazing guests, including the acclaimed author Zadie Smith, the actor Kal Penn, and the virtuoso rapper will.i.am from the Black Eyed Peas."

Some coached applause.

"Why did anyone of them to agree to come on the show? Because I promised to give them some of my mom's theplas. Any Gujjus in the house?"

A few assorted cheers for his Gujarati heritage. Ravi took the thepla out of his pocket, held it up for display and started eating it, which was a terrible idea because it started sticking inside his already dry mouth. Maybe he should have previewed this improvisation with his writer before filming. He started coughing, and the audience laughed as if he had intended to do that.

"Ssssspicy!" he said, playing along.

As he continued coughing, he gestured to his staff for a glass of water to clear his throat. The editors would have to edit that segment.

"You're wondering, Ravi, why would I want to watch your show when I can watch Jon Stewart, who's way funnier and more insightful? Because Jon Stewart probably doesn't have the gumption...I'd have used a different word, but I'm not allowed...to have his parents on his show as his first guests. Not to mention that we'll be looking to get different perspectives on race and assimilation."

Ravi hadn't wanted to use a teleprompter and now had forgotten the punchline to the Jon Stewart joke. He could tell the beginning had been awkward, but he remembered that Conan O'Brien's first few weeks had been awkward and terrible, also. If there was time later, he could ask the crew to re-tape his monologue.

"Tonight I've got the best guests I could possibly ask for. The most important Indians I know. While I spent my whole life trying to be a cool Indian, my sister recently asked me a good question: what kind of Indian were our parents trying to be? I thought we could all benefit from hearing the answer. Without further ado, my parents, Bharti and Jeevan Anjani," Ravi said, waving his hand towards them as he walked over to the blue and red armchairs grouped around a coffee table.

Ravi was apprehensive about Vineeta's suggestion at the retreat; his dad was droll and his mum unpredictable. On top of which his head writer told him not to coach his parents on what to say or it wouldn't be spontaneous and entertaining. He was only allowed to give them a few of his questions beforehand.

The band played a horn and cymbal crescendo. The backdrop to the seating was the Manhattan skyline at dusk, buildings lit up under an orange-red sky.

"They may not approve of my career, but it doesn't mean they don't like to be on television. So Mum, Dad, this is not too shabby, right?"

"It's a nice studio," his dad said.

"Very nice," his mum said, wobbling her head in approval.

His mum was dressed in a sari with her finest gold jewelry. The makeup artist had blended concealer over the hair dye that had been visible on her forehead. His father was wearing an oversized sports jacket and tapping his foot nervously. Ravi would have to align the chairs and table differently in the future to de-emphasize guests' legs and the pant tent that had formed over his father's crotch. He sat down and took a sip of water from his mug, which read "Failed Rock Star".

"I wanted you as my first guests because the goal of this show is to get different perspectives about assimilation. Over the course of the season, we'll see your generation, my generation, celebrities, regular people like yourselves, even some people who aren't Indian. Maybe we'll find some interesting patterns, and definitely I think we'll learn what we could have done better and what America could have done better. So with that boring scholarly preamble out of the way, maybe you can tell us why you came to America?"

"I went to London for my PhD and got a teaching job at the University of Michigan," his dad said.

"But why leave India, which invented math, for a country which invented Snuggies?"

"Well, also planes, televisions, cars," his dad said.

"And InstaPot," his mum added sincerely.

The crowd lightly chuckled.

"At the time, India was a very closed society, so America offered more opportunities. Now it's different, even there you can do well. But America worked out for us. And obviously we wanted you to have opportunities, which you've had," his dad said.

"Did it bother you that we—meaning Vineeta and me—grew up more Western than you expected?"

"We're proud of both. We are very modern. We never get in your way," his mum said.

He had heard versions of these lines before, whenever his mum wanted her friends to know she was proud and supportive of her kids, regardless of whether she actually was. Though was it possible that it was true? That her daily complaints about them being too Westernized didn't reflect her macro view? Maybe most people were giving off a false impression of themselves instead of the person they truly wished to be.

"If Vineeta wanted to dress like that," his mum said, gesturing to Ravi's assistant Shireen, who was wearing a skin-tight mirrored dress, "Even then I don't stop. Even when Vineeta start dating bla ..."

"Vineeta is my sister, ladies and gentleman. Please take a bow," Ravi interrupted, pointing to Vineeta, who stood up and waved to the camera nervously.

She didn't look as pissed off as he would have expected.

"And she's dating my best friend and leader of the band, Ian Wallace. An incredible singer, human being and dart board player who Mum has always viewed as a son."

The band added some musical pomp while he shook his head at his mum to stop talking. His dad started instead.

"Obviously, at times you might make choices that we aren't used to. But ultimately, we get used to it. Maybe we take a bit longer than you would like, but…" his father said.

"Our love for you is always first," his mum said.

"I always thought you loved chocolate a bit more, and possibly Amitabh Bachchan, but glad that's been clarified. Years worth of therapy I could have avoided," Ravi said, mugging for the camera, desperately trying to escape the rabbit holes his mum was digging.

A few people chuckled, presumably the Indian ones given the crescendo at the mention of the Big B. Should he divert the interview into a different direction? Or had he defeated the whole purpose of the show by not challenging his mum?

A stagehand waved a card indicating it was time for a sponsor break.

"We are going to be right back to this fascinating discussion after a quick word from our sponsor. Don't leave, or I'll make you listen to my last album," Ravi said to the camera before filming paused.

The stage manager told the audience they had ten minutes to stretch their legs or use the restroom, after which taping would resume. Ravi stood up and confirmed his parents were doing alright when Vineeta grabbed his elbow and pulled him aside.

"That was great, you're doing really well."

"You think so? The beginning was a mess."

"Look, it's your first show. It wasn't perfect, but that made it endearing in a way."

"At least I got Mum off of talking about you and Ian."

"You know, I didn't mind it. Ian and I spoke about it. He knows, in fact, he helped me understand that assimilation means changing your view on everything you were taught. About skin tight dresses and black people and a woman's role in life. And Mum has done a really good job making it work, even if she doesn't always use the right words, which isn't her fault, either, because she was never taught how to use words. But that's something you are strangely good at, when you want to be."

"So you're saying I should have let her speak."

"That's why we…well, you, it's your show…invited them as guests, no?"

He began to process her suggestion when the stage manager interrupted to go over some filming details. The stagehand interrupted shortly thereafter to indicate taping was about to resume. Ravi returned to his seat. The whole experience was whizzing by.

"Welcome back to the show, we're with my parents, Bharti and Jeevan Anjani, immigrants extraordinaire, trying to learn something about what it's like to move somewhere without knowing anything about the culture. Now did you feel you were treated well by Americans when you first arrived?"

"America good to us. We got good house, kids go to good school, look, you're on t.v.," Bharti said. "When we come here, everyone helping us, people are nice."

She smiled with the purest projection of happiness and goodwill he had ever seen from her. Back on script.

"Do you think you were more content than we were because you had accepted who you were—Indians in a bubble in America? Whereas maybe for us, meaning Vineeta and me, we were trying to be American and to change what it means to be American?"

His dad was supposed to answer this one, but of course it was his mum who started talking.

"When God first make the people, he puts them in oven and they come out uncooked. Then he puts them in and they come out burnt. Then he puts them in and they are just right. That is the Indians. The uncooked ones are…"

He had heard her repeat her friend's theory that Indians were perfectly baked and superior to uncooked white people and burnt Blacks many times, and prepared a pivot with vanilla, chocolate and chocolate chip cookies, all good, depending on which you liked. But if he didn't let her speak, why had he invited her?

"…the whites, the burnt ones are the blacks," she finished.

"I know you told us that while you were growing up, but I never thought you looked down on white people or black people."

"I don't look down on anyone. All people good."

"But your analogy does say that, right?"

"You know, kids making fun of you when growing up, I didn't want you to think you were less good. So I had to show you why we are just as good. I don't mean to hurt anyone else."

Everything his mum said made perfect logical sense within the world she had created to deal with the world she had encountered. But that was true of every person in the world. Ravi's head started clouding over from trying to dig out some greater truth from this observation.

"I guess that makes sense. You worried that getting called names would hurt our self-esteem, so you tried to build it back up with an equal counter-point. Did people call you names?" he continued.

"You know, sometimes people are looking at you funny or being mean, but I just ignore them," his mum said.

"People will call you fat, stupid, ugly, brown, whatever, because people feel better by tearing other people down," his dad said.

"In my case, I think you left off arrogant, juvenile and untalented, but go on," Ravi said.

"Where we left, there was a caste system. People would beat their servants if they made a mistake. After partition, people would kill their neighbors if they were Muslim. Whoever is angry will find a reason to attack. We never thought we were in danger," his dad continued.

"I read about these people who hit and shoot just because Indian, but this not happen to us," his mum said.

Ravi couldn't think of a snappy response, so went with the next question on a flashcard a crewmember was holding up.

"Did you feel you faced any additional challenges because you were Indian?" Ravi asked.

"Maybe, but it's relative. As I said, there were challenges in India. I think the challenges here were fewer. It's much less corrupt," his dad said.

His notes suggested that his dad would complain about the university hierarchy, but now his dad was acting as if the system was and rules were fine as they were.

"Depends which politician you're bribing. Did Giuliani ever get back to us on our offer?" Ravi asked, pretending to look offstage for an answer.

That one-liner fell flat. Was it his delivery or was it just too random and unfunny? He'd tell his writer to avoid jokes like that in the future.

"You once told me that if we moved here, I needed to fit in."

"It is human nature. If someone comes here from Russia, will you learn Russian to help them? Will you change the way you live? No, so then we have to change. And over time by us being here, they will also have to change," his dad said.

"We even have Indian temple close to us," his mum said. "I always believe God take care of everything."

"They say God works in mysterious ways—especially if you consider centuries of stealing, slaving and oppressing people to be mysterious," Ravi said.

That wasn't so Anodyne. The audience "ooohed" at that one, but Ravi wasn't sure if it was a "yeah, good one" ooh or "that was a low blow" ooh.

"No, really, think about it. How many people here are Indian?"

A decent amount of yelling.

"So you know. The Brits become one of the world's leading economies on the back of Indian labor, and what was their comeuppance? Bad teeth and bland food. Not a bad trade. They let us immigrate as recompense and what happens? We become doctors that fix their teeth and open restaurants so they can anoint curry as their national dish. Forget this God fellow, the Brits are always one step ahead. But I digress. We're here in America, where we have been thriving. The only thing we have to worry about is thinking every time we pass someone, 'I hope he notices my accent is just like theirs,'" Ravi said.

Ravi wasn't sure where that diatribe came from. He hadn't planned it, but it felt good. He wasn't meant to be uniformly Anodyne.

"But he may be thinking, 'I hope he notices my fancy jeans.' In a society, we all have insecurities that come from the rules of the society," his dad said.

"Like when you wear spandex with no shorts. Don't recommend it."

Ravi felt a bit looser, like he was himself again. There was a fine line between anodyne and offensive. He might still trip it once in a while, but at least he was aware there was one. He continued.

"But I guess we should be asking if those are the right rules. If we wait for change, it might take forever to come, but if we push for the change, it will come more quickly," Ravi said, reciting Vineeta's observation.

"Some people are scared of change. Educated people are the most scared, because they have the most to lose. So when you speak loudly, they will speak louder. They will take over the government, the courts, they will start think tanks to publish papers about why their group is succeeding on merit. I know, because I've been asked to write some of them. It is very hard to change anything other than yourself," his dad said. "That's why immigrants are successful. We are forced to change and re-examine our assumptions. The people who stay where they are at already think they know everything."

Ravi had an epiphany, linking back to something Pilar had once told him while she was reading the US Constitution.

"You know, I always thought it was on people to be self-reliant, probably because that's what you taught us. But now I'm thinking that the reason we have to hold America to a higher standard than the countries we came from is that America was founded on liberty and justice for all. That's what people mean by American exceptionalism-being truthful with itself and changing itself for the better while India and places like Russia and China go back to their old ways. And maybe that's why we're here talking, to make Americans be truthful with themselves about how they treat people of different races and sizes and genders. It's not just the same being Indian as it is being black, or overweight, or a woman. And so we have to have a different conversation about each of these things and pull back the veil of education, politics and religion that hide people's underlying prejudices. It's not enough for us to change, others have to change, too. And if we start believing it's possible, it will become possible. We can have a black president. We can have gay marriage. Because we've already had an Indian rock star."

The audience whooped and started clapping. Ravi waited for the applause to die down.

"You know I was referring to Freddie Mercury, right?" Ravi said, pulling on his shirt.

His father was slightly nodding.

"That is a very interesting analysis," his dad said. "I think America still has plenty of opportunity for people of all types, but some don't know how to access it."

Ravi remembered lessons from his sociology class in college.

"But if studies show that black-sounding names get a worse response than white sounding names with the same credentials, then the opportunities aren't the same. If blacks get the death penalty at a much higher rate than whites who committed the same crimes, the system is rigged. If there are hardly any women CEOs, it's not just because they are staying home to have babies. And you can assume that whatever's happening to them is happening in some fashion to Indians."

Was Ravi becoming like a whingeing mango novelist? Vineeta had pointed out to him that whichever group complained the loudest was usually the group that defined what society ultimately transitions to. So while lots of people wouldn't like what Ravi was doing with his show, including Ravi himself just a few months before, maybe they needed him to do what he was doing.

"Indians have the highest per capita income of any group in this country other than Jewish people," his father said to cheers in the audience.

His dad looked at the audience and gave an unexpected smile.

"I can just say for myself, America has been good to us."

"But even better for our friends. They invest in stock market, lots of money making. Your father is teaching the business, but others are making the business," his mum said.

Ravi laughed. He sensed his flippancy and effort to be more thoughtful converging into compassionate flippancy.

"And you're minding everyone's business. But I think it's fair to consider, just because it's been good to us and to our friends, doesn't mean it's been good to everyone else. Given the historical persecution of Jews for their success, maybe we should take that as a warning and not a point of celebration."

A few more claps. His dad tilted his head with a bemused smile before nodding slightly.

"Sometimes when you try to fix a problem, you make it worse. There are laws which create bad incentives and make the other side resentful. You need people to talk about that side of things. Persecution goes both ways. You're right, we should definitely have this conversation about opportunity in America for those who have been persecuted. But we should also not try to silence people who disagree with the way we think it should be done or who don't express themselves precisely. I have one colleague, he is being suspended for one or two sentences taken out of context."

A stagehand was pointing to the big clock which indicated he had twenty seconds to wrap up the interview.

"As someone who has said more than a sentence or two that could be misconstrued, I have to wholeheartedly agree with you."

A final few chuckles. Ravi turned to the camera.

"See, if you want to see how to work out decades' worth of issues with your parents in ten minutes, this is the show for you. I want to thank my parents for being good sports and coming on the show. Mum, Dad, I love you, that was a good start to a dialogue we will be continuing with the finest minds in the world later this week— Zadie Smith, will.i.am, Kal Penn. Before we take a break, my friend Shireen is going to introduce you to a microfinance charity that is doing amazing things around the world."

Shireen initiated a short video segment. The show was going to promote a different charity each episode. When the segment ended, Shireen solicited money from viewers and the in-person audience, which had each been given ten dollars each before the show to "contribute". Ravi used the interlude to tell his parents how good they had been, to get a refresh of face powder, and to relax for a moment.

He had done it. The audience had genuinely laughed at points, and he had touched upon some serious issues. He wasn't sure if he had gone too far with his Brit rant, but the editors could sanitize things as necessary. He took to the stage to close the show.

"Ladies and gentleman, you may remember a band called Buzzthief which had a few hits a few years ago. Tonight, for the first time in five years, Buzzthief is back together to show why they weren't the greatest band you ever heard, but could occasionally make you dance and know why you're alive. On drums, there's the inimitable Ed Chung. On bass, the thumper from Mars, Brett Anton. On keys, the agile Abdul Adel. On vocals, the sexy crooner from America, Ian Wallace. And on guitar…"

Ravi started wailing on his guitar.

"Here's our first new song in five years, dedicated to my family and friends, including the ones who couldn't be here tonight, called 'You Give Me Strength'".

Years before, Ravi was proud to have written a song. Then he learned to write simple but catchy choruses, which led to Buzzthief's first hits. As he learned more he experimented with unusual chord changes, drum fills, multi-tracked guitars and odd tempos. This led to the technically interesting songs on Buzzthief's next two albums, both flops. Now he had circled back to the simplicity of the hits, with subtlety layered into the playing. The process mirrored his evolution as a person. He used to appreciate people and the world at face value. Then he began to view everyone, everything and every issue as a setup for an ironic joke, exemplified by his *Guide*. And now he was beginning to see that it was much more fulfilling to cultivate straightforward relationships and appreciate their subtleties than to crack glib jokes.

Near the end of the song, Ravi stopped playing and removed his guitar while the drummer maintained a military beat and Ian chanted the chorus over a funky bass line. The crowd began clapping in time with the beat and stood up at the stage manager's direction. Ravi approached Shushruth, Pankaj, Vineeta and pulled them up on stage with his parents. He hugged his parents and extended his arms around them before facing the camera.

"I've spent the past year trying to figure out who I was, and I finally know. I'm a cool Indian who happened to grow up in London and America, and everything I've achieved is because my family was always there for me. So if you're watching this, call your parents and brothers and sisters thank them. Your dad who washed your bum or your mum who started cooking the second you mentioned you were hungry. Your sister who scrapbooked all your press clippings. Your uncles, aunts and cousins who let you stay in their homes and steal their toys. It's easy to think you should be able to act like yourself around your family while you act on good behavior around others, but I've realized it makes more sense to treat them better than how you treat others. So tell your Mum her new sweater looks good, because she thinks it does. Tell your Dad he's insightful, because he thinks he is. Tell them they're cool, because Ravi said so."

Ravi felt his eyes glossing up, almost on the verge of tears, though he hoped the audience would think that the bright lights just made it look that way.

Review of
Ravi's Guide to Being a Cool Indian II

"Visualizing Mediocrity"
<u>Music Scene</u> – *June 1, 2008*
By James Ewert

The talk show version of <u>*Ravi's Guide to Being a Cool Indian*</u> is proof that in this age of media saturation, no work is too mediocre for adaptation into another format. Monday night, we had our first glimpse of washed up musician Ravi Anjani attempt to educate us about racial issues, as if we need another pampered celebrity who made his fortune on the backs of the UK and American system to criticize the system that made him who he is...

Chapter 18
Just Desserts
Manhattan, New York

Ravi

"Fuck this, right."

Ravi crumpled the paper and threw it on the floor. A dry, burnt aftertaste of coffee manifested his annoyance while sitting at their dining room table. The media may have been saturated, but James Ewert was the fat and Ravi was the…he didn't know, but as long as he had made a couple of people smile or think, he was happy. Viewership had been steadily increasing over the first month, and prominent guests were getting easier to book. Buzzthief was recording a companion piece to their first album, with riffs, emotion and contemporary bass and drums.

Who was James Ewert to judge him? The man clearly hadn't read his *Guide* or grown up as a minority in the UK, yet deemed himself the arbiter of who was allowed to raise issues about race. Though Ravi judged other people unfairly, too. If everyone stopped judging and instead re-examined their assumptions—wait, he sounded like his dad. Eliminate bad assumptions and communicate better.

He picked Ewert's article back up. He could handle being judged. It wasn't the judgment that bothered him. It was being boxed and shipped away when his life was premised on re-invention. He would mock Ewert's article on his next show. No. He would invite Ewert as a guest and debate him. Create a line of communication.

"What's the matter?" Lakhi asked from the kitchen, newly furnished with pots and a knife set.

"Nothing. It's all good."

He finished the article, picked up his new Taylor and practiced the Tarrega piece he had been learning. The key to life was to fill it up with enough good things so he didn't have time to focus on the bad. He couldn't solve everything. There was no final justice, just desserts, beginning or end, just another year of living with himself. He would do his best to evolve and move on.

258

Acknowledgements

This novel was re-written multiple times over fifteen years (with a big gap somewhere in the middle). I fortunately liked the characters enough that I never got bored of it. I read an apt quote in a July 12, 2022 NY Times Magazine profile of Akhil Sharma: "A novel is a prose narrative of some length that has something wrong with it." The difficulty is determining whether your work has so much wrong with it that no one will finish reading it. Workshops help, but after a certain point, it's hard to tell whether you've met the threshold, especially with feedback from industry types along the lines of "I love the premise, your characters are well drawn, the dialogue and narrative tension are fantastic, but the pacing was a little off." So, you're saying my book is like a lot of prize-winning novels I've read?

With that in mind, a special thanks to Nawaaz Ahmed, Ted O'Connell, John Didday and Annie Dreshfield for reading the entire manuscript of this novel at various points of its evolution and helping me both understand the many ways my novel was not a prize-winning novel, and the ways I could try to fix them. Hopefully there is now enough right with this novel that a reader can forgive its faults.

Again from the NY Times Magazine article: "there is always something problematic about [a novel] that the novelist must push through if he or she is going to achieve not perfection but an uneasy truce with formal forces that cannot be vanquished. And so novelists revise novels, endlessly, necessarily, on the way to completing them, which is to say by accepting their problems and moving on."

I've formed my truce, and now I move on.

Made in the USA
Monee, IL
26 December 2022

19455357R00156